Bittersweet House

Liz Barzda

AuthorHouse™
1663 Liberty Drive
Bloomington, IN 47403
www.authorhouse.com
Phone: 1-800-839-8640

© 2011 Liz Barzda. All rights reserved.

No part of this book may be reproduced, stored in a retrieval system, or transmitted by any means without the written permission of the author.

First published by AuthorHouse   2/18/2011

ISBN: 978-1-4567-1394-2 (sc)
ISBN: 978-1-4567-1395-9 (e)
ISBN: 978-1-4567-1396-6 (hc)

Library of Congress Control Number: 2010919036

Printed in the United States of America

Any people depicted in stock imagery provided by Thinkstock are models, and such images are being used for illustrative purposes only. Certain stock imagery © Thinkstock.

This book is printed on acid-free paper.

Because of the dynamic nature of the Internet, any Web addresses or links contained in this book may have changed since publication and may no longer be valid. The views expressed in this work are solely those of the author and do not necessarily reflect the views of the publisher, and the publisher hereby disclaims any responsibility for them.

ACKNOWLEDGMENTS

I want to thank my dear friends of the National League of American Pen Women, Fairfield County Branch for putting up with my questions and offering suggestions when I mentally wrestle with the pages of *Bittersweet House.*

Also, many thanks to the staff of the Case Memorial Library of Orange for supporting me with their reference materials; and kudos to my buddy Leanne Pazzi for untangling my computer problems with knowledge and humor. And a special thank you to Diane Crehan, artist extraordinary and warm human being.

Chapter 1

The damn noise overwhelmed her ears. Half-dazed, Linda Cooper groped in the dark, knocking the phone off the night stand. She snapped on the light, retrieved it and managed an angry "Hello."

"I must speak to Chris," said an urgent female voice.

"Who is this?"

"Please, this is an emergency. I *must* speak to Chris Cooper."

"It's three o'clock in the morning. Are you crazy? Who are you? What do you want with Christopher?"

"Tell him it's Betti. His son, our son, is desperately ill. Chris *must come*."

"He doesn't know any Betti and he doesn't have a son. You must have the wrong Chris Cooper." Linda hung up.

The phone rang an instant later. Christopher sprang from his side of the bed and snatched it. "I'm here," he said, breathing rapidly. "What's wrong?" He appeared dazed as he spoke, his face drained of color. "Yes, I understand. You're at Boston's General Hospital. Betti, don't worry. I'm on my way. I'll be there in three hours."

Linda wrenched the phone from him and heard ... "the doctor said his situation is grave. Chris, I can't bear it. He has a 104 degree temperature. I'll just die if anything happens to our baby. Chris, please hurry."

Linda dropped the phone, feeling like a dangling puppet jerked about on strings. She watched in disbelief as Christopher began to dress.

"What's going on? Christopher, speak to me. Who is this woman?"

"I can't deal with this now. We'll talk when I return." Grim-faced, he appeared barely aware of his wife's presence as he dressed quickly and throw clothes in an overnight bag.

She tugged on his shirt. "Christopher, look at me! Tell me what's going on."

He ignored her.

Linda trailed him down the stairs, through the family room and kitchen, to the garage. "If you have a heart, if you've ever loved me, you wouldn't leave me like this."

Christopher faced her. "This is an emergency. Talk will have to wait."

In blind fury, she screamed, "Answer my questions!" She began slapping him with all the force she could muster. "*You bastard*! No, that's wrong. Your son is the bastard. That woman said 'our son', and you expect me not to ask questions? I can't believe this... it's not really happening."

Christopher grabbed her wrists to quiet her, looked at her with disdain, then rushed out. Her eyes focused on his profile, his dark wavy hair, and his broad shoulders. She watched the car zoom out of the garage and disappear into the moonless July night.

#

Will the dawn never come?

Linda had no idea how long she sat staring through the kitchen bay window seeing nothing. Yet, scenes of some woman, Christopher, and their baby played over and over again in her mind's eye.

With all the concentration she could gather, she backtracked to the good times with her husband; their honeymoon in Bermuda, the start of his consulting business, her promotion to anchor at WSEA TV, the purchase of their Seacliff twelve-room Flemish country house on Connecticut's Gold Coast. Surpassing all these eventful moments was the great sex, the humor and the joy of living they shared. But that was yesterday. Her life was like a house built on stilts in a fast-approaching monsoon. Her predicament was impossible, insolvable.

She remembered when she couldn't get enough of him. She'd wrap her arms around him and kiss him longingly. The taste of him, his graceful, yet masculine walk, his baritone voice that thrilled her; such sweet moments lingered in her mind.

The late nights when he'd arrive home dog-tired from a business trip, Linda would gaze at the strong profile, the muscular arms above the blanket and whisper, "God, you're handsome."

Does his mistress, this Betti, have a mole near *her cutesy* lips? *Is she very young with a knock-out figure? Does she give him more than I did? Maybe she gives him kinky sex? What kind of woman is she?* "If I had a gun, I'd shoot her," Linda screamed at the mirror. "No. I'd shoot him first."

She had no conception of how she got from the powder room to the kitchen. Without a notion of what to do, Linda sat at the breakfast room table with her head in her hands. The irony of it all--that her husband should have another family stashed away in Boston. He repeatedly told her that their careers were important; children could wait. She could hear him now with his clipped Boston accent proclaiming that, *a baby now would bog down their careers.* The wait turned into seventeen years.

The subterfuge of it all brought uncontrollable sobs. She covered her eyes and prayed. "God, what's happening to us? Tell me it's all a mistake. Please Lord, tell me it's all a dream, that I'll wake up tomorrow and all will be as before. If you send me a sign that all this madness will disappear, I promise to be a better Christian." It's no good, she lamented. You don't bargain with the Lord.

The rosy glow of dawn did little to soften her somber mood. She needed coffee. The simple physical act of brewing it was a welcome diversion. Although tasteless to her, the hot liquid provided a slight semblance of reality.

The clock read 7:10; too early to call anyone. She knew her former college roommate and best friend, Zita Parker, arrived at her business, Parker Advertising, before nine, even on Saturdays. Although Linda needed to lighten her grief by revealing her unbearable situation, she had second thoughts about spilling her guts to anyone. In the past she was noncommittal of Zita's once free-swinging lifestyle and bitter divorce.

"Good for you, Zita. I'm with you," Linda said aloud between choking sobs. "Love them and leave them and you won't get hurt." Zita insists men think with their penises. It may be an old cliché, but a truism that endures.

Linda trudged up the stairs and into the shower. The hot spray stung, but she let it beat down on her. She felt the need to be punished. Obviously, she was guilty of something--smothering him with love, or not loving him enough; otherwise Christopher wouldn't have built a double life. *What is all the psycho-babble that if you give your man enough love, he won't stray. Bullshit!*

She absentmindedly toweled herself dry, put on her terry cloth robe and slippers, and brushed her hair. She headed downstairs wondering how

Liz Barzda

many men out there were leading double lives? How many women naïve as she hadn't a clue to their spouse's infidelity?

Despite still feeling groggy, Linda remembered her 10 AM weekly Saturday manicure, blow dry, and massage at La Petit Spa. She hadn't the strength to show up, listen to the prattle of attendants, and pretend all was well.

She visualized Katherine Horvath, owner of the Spa, and friend, greeting her upon arriving and flooding her with attention. It was just too painful.

A call to La Petit Spa postponed her appointment till 10 o'clock Tuesday. She then phoned WSEA-TV and told her boss to get a replacement to anchor the news as she had flu symptoms. "I hope to be back by Tuesday."

The public didn't care that her world was crumbling. The station expected her to be bright and beautiful. The news had to be reviewed and delivered at 6 and 11 PM.

She had three days to pull herself together.

#

Christopher floored his BMW; eighty-miles per hour seemed like crawling, he pushed it up to ninety. Rest areas, service stations, trees and shrubs along the Mass. Turnpike seemed to meld into the background. Nothing registered but the image of his son. The need to see Sean was overwhelming. He visualized him lying motionless in the hospital, Betti by his bedside drained with fighting off hysterics. Has his temperature gone down? Was he lying in the little bed perspiring all over? His darling boy had to make it. Boston General Hospital was one of the finest in the nation; surely, the doctors could bring down his temperature. They must save him. Betti didn't give him any details, she was so distraught. And Linda screamed like a banshee. But he couldn't worry about Linda now. Sean was his first priority. The 3-hour drive seemed like a buggy ride in a slow-action movie. He felt like a trapeze artist hanging on to the horizontal bar by one hand.

God wouldn't let anything happen to his son. If he were a praying man, he'd pray now. The 23 Psalm came to mind. Surprised that he remembered, he said the words to himself. His Episcopalian upbringing obviously had more of an impact than he realized. He hadn't gone to church since Christmas Eve; even then he went only to please Linda because she enjoyed watching the children perform the Christmas Pageant.

4

Bittersweet House

Surely God would hear his petition and forgive him for being a lapsed churchgoer. Aloud he pleaded," Please Lord, cure Sean. Don't let him suffer. He's so small, so helpless."

Chapter 2

Throughout the weekend, Linda roamed the house in despair. Christopher hadn't returned and didn't call. The quietude heightened her sense of aloneness. Monday morning brought a brewing storm, with wind and dark clouds. The day matched her mood, one of conflicting emotion: hatred for her husband, doubt and confusion, intermingled with pleasant memories of the past. She trudged down the stairs to the kitchen, replaying in her mind their early years of torrid sex. Intercourse on the billiard table, up against the dressing room wall, on the staircase, anywhere--anytime--their lust demanded release. Their shared sexual appetites topped the list of their common career interests, followed by sailing, theater and partying with friends.

As the years slipped by, they eased into less torrid, less satisfying weekly lovemaking, sometimes every other week. Linda declared overwork as the culprit. Christopher blamed it on business trips and jet lag. Work dominated their routine. Although Christopher's travel schedule increased since his consulting business took off, Linda accepted it as the price paid to be his own boss and to be financially successful. Hardly a "stand by your man" kind of woman who baked cookies, Linda would, out of love, ready a drink, coffee, or a meal for her husband to enjoy after a strenuous trip.

She missed him dreadfully every time he went off on those three-week business trips. Why couldn't he call often--certainly more than once a week? She stupidly accepted his "I was too busy" excuse without question.

Now she must try, really try, not to think of him, the son-of-a-bitch. She would ignore her senses and not admit to listening for the sound of his baritone voice, the taste of his skin, and the smell of his cologne.

On his last business trip, supposedly to England to update Great Britain Communications' telecommunication system, Christopher had told her he needed to work weekends to complete the GBC proposal. How often had he mentioned changes in the client's needs that threw off his schedule and delayed his return home?

He informed her that weekends were spent working overtime in various foreign locations. *Liar*! Linda now realized many of those weekends must have been spent in Boston. *What was he doing right now? Kissing Betti and their baby?* Surely she'd go crazy if she didn't stop all this hypothesizing.

Can I forgive the cheat? Should he just pay support for the baby and we go on as before? I doubt it. What if he should die? That would solve all the problems.

"God, forgive me," she cried aloud. "How can I think such horrible thoughts?"

Last night she stood in front of the dressing room's full-length mirror in bra and panties. In deep thought, she wrapped strands of her hair around an ear, and appraised her body. Her reflection revealed a 5'-9" frame, long legs, and trim waist. Christopher called her his "sexy blonde goddess." She hadn't changed much since their wedding. Working out kept her figure toned. *What had gone wrong? How did I falter? I had nothing to do with this catastrophe. He was the fornicator and the deceiver.*

Linda forced herself to down bits of toast with tea. The morning dragged. She retreated to the study and stared at WSEA-TV's talking heads without comprehending their message. It was her station, but Linda felt far removed from the workaday world. Eventually she fell asleep on the sofa. She awoke stiff and listless. The threatening dark clouds disappeared, replaced by a blue sky. Sunshine streamed through the windows, but did little to brighten her mood.

She turned off all office equipment. All she wanted was to sink into emptiness, to isolate herself from the world. Thoughts of selecting candidates for her weekly Chronicle Connecticut program went nowhere. Her mind was blank.

At least she could sort through the mail stacked on the foyer's table. Leafing quickly through the bills and brochures, her eyes lingered on a thick envelope, the most intriguing piece in the pile. It appeared to be an invitation. She slit the flap and read:

Choices Magazine Celebratory Banquet

Honoring

Author Mary Trapp Toddman, Guest Speaker

Saturday, August 28, 2005 8 PM
Regency Grand Hotel
Seacliff, Connecticut
$150
RSVP by July 1, 2011
(203) 555-3825

Linda laughed. How perverse to receive this now. As if she had a *choice* in life. She laid down the invitation. It seemed so absurd. Zita, Margaret and Katherine would probably attend, but she couldn't think that far ahead.

The doorbell chimed, nudging her from her reverie. Through the etched glass foyer panels she glimpsed the figures of her sister, Sandra, and her five-year-old niece, Tiffany.

"What a nice surprise," Linda said, feigning enthusiasm as she bent down to kiss Tiffany's cheek and stroke her blonde curls. She hugged Sandra.

"Hi, Sis. How's TV's golden girl?" Sandra asked without waiting for a reply. "Your phone seems to be out of order, so I thought I'd better check it out. What are you doing home on a Monday?"

Linda managed a slight smile. "Felt as if I were coming down with something, so decided to stay home and kill it."

"Hate to say it, Sis, but you look like you've been out on an all-nighter. And where's that infectious grin you turn on for your TV fans?"

"I had a sleepless night, but I'll be okay." Despite the jab, Linda took every opportunity to compliment her sister. "You look great, Sandy. New haircut? Suits you. You know I always envied your naturally-wavy hair," she said, leading them through the central hall into the breakfast room.

"Thanks. Kevin likes it, too."

"I have your favorite, Sandy--Hawaiian Kona coffee." Linda bent down and rumpled Tiffany's hair. "And for you, sweet one, I have sticky buns."

Linda put on a pot of coffee and oven-warmed the Hot Cross buns.

"I came to tell you Mom called me last night really worried because she couldn't reach you," Sandra revealed between coffee sips. "She and Dad are coming to Connecticut in a couple of weeks."

"I disconnected the phone because I needed to sleep."

"Mom said she wants more than phone calls, she wants to visit in person. Complained that she hasn't seen us since Easter. They know I don't have room to put them up. I suspect your schedule is as busy as ever. Luckily, they have the good grace to go to a hotel."

Bittersweet House

"My schedule *is* crazy," Linda agreed, trying to appear rational. *With all that's going on now, I don't need folks prying into my marriage.* "Ron is on vacation so I'll have to do the 11 o'clock news as well as the six spot when I get back. Obviously, the station has someone filling in for me. I've put in a lot of extra hours; they owe me comp time. So I'll be able to spend some time with the folks." She poured milk for Tiffany and offered her a warm bun. Putting on a happy face in an attempt to lighten her mood, she patted her niece's cheek. "When Grandma and Grandpa come, I'll plan a nice day and we'll all be together. Would you like that, dear?"

"Mommy, wouldn't that be super?" Tiffany said, licking gooey fingers. Bun in hand, she slipped off the chair and skipped from the room.

Reaching for the coffee pot, Sandra uttered, "God, it's muggy out, but it's wonderfully cool in here. I wish we could afford central air. Maybe some day. Did I tell you Kevin is up for promotion? He deserves it--engineering schools three nights a week and a boss pushing him to work overtime. I sure hope it doesn't mean he'll be traveling. I couldn't handle too much of that." Sandra looked around. "Christopher not home?"

Linda said nothing.

Sandra sipped her coffee, put the cup down and fixed her eyes on Linda. "He's gone a lot, isn't he?"

"I hear from him regularly. He'll probably call tonight."

Sandra raised an eyebrow.

"Mommy, Mommy, the doll with the red dress is on the floor with a broken head," Tiffany bawled as she ran into the breakfast room. Tears streaked her cheeks.

"My hand hurts."

Sandra examined her child's hand, and then kissed it. "It's okay, baby. There aren't any cuts. What happened?"

"The doll fell out of my hand and broke," she gasped.

Linda bent down to her niece. "You know Mommy and I told you not to play with that china figurine. It isn't a toy!" Then she rose and faced her sister. "Why don't you watch your child? That figurine cost $200."

Sandra encircled the child in her arms, and faced Linda. "You didn't check to see if Tiffany cut herself. You shouldn't have frightened her. I'll pay for the stupid figurine if you're so worried."

Linda paled. "I'm sorry. I don't feel well. I'm not myself. She bent down to the child, attempting to kiss away the tears. "Darling, Auntie Linda didn't mean it. You know I love you."

Sandra pulled her daughter away. "You don't know how to deal with children. How could you? You're childless. All you know is that damn career of yours," she said, rushing her daughter through the foyer and out the front door, slamming it shut.

Linda stood motionless, then burst into tears. *How could I have hurt them? I'm striking out at my family because of him. I know, I'll call Sandra and apologize. I'll buy Tiffany a doll to soothe her.*

Accustomed to being the peacemaker, Linda had no compunction about making amends. Yes, her sister often ticked her off. She could be willful and irresponsible, but Linda loved her. She could see her now as a six-year-old pedaling her new two-wheeler, chestnut hair blowing in the wind, as big sister held the seat and guided her.

She remembered Sandra at ten, in a generous mood, insisting on pressing three of Linda's blouses for fifty cents each to buy their mother a Christmas gift. There were difficult times when Sandra ran charge cards to the max. Instructing her about budgeting was like taking a gambler to a casino for lunch and suggesting he not play the slots.

Linda knew that slipping her sister money at holidays, birthdays, and other times to get her out of monetary jams was counterproductive. Repeatedly, Sandra would say, "Thanks for the generous birthday gift, Sis." Or, "I'm a kinda short this month and I really appreciate you helping me out to buy Kevin and Tiffany Christmas presents." I promise to do better, to stay away from the malls." Linda doubted Sandra's resolve, but despite her weakness, she'd do most anything to protect her.

Yes, Sandra was irresponsible at times, envious other times, but it was immaterial. Sandra needed her. And Linda couldn't deny the truth-- need worked both ways.

#

Livid at her sister's stupid reaction to a broken figurine, Sandra zoomed her Ford Focus from Linda's driveway. She headed cross town to the Stop and Shop.

This was the first time Linda had ever reprimanded Tiffany. *What's bugging big sister? Could it be Christopher? He's certainly gone a lot. Or was it Linda's job?*

"Tiffany, stop banging my seat back there. You're distracting me."

Tiffany ignored the reprimand and gave the seat a light kick. "Mommy, are you mad at Auntie Linda?"

"No, I'm not mad at her. Sisters sometimes don't agree with each other, that's all."

"You sounded mad, Mommy. Do you love Auntie Linda?"

"Sure. Let's not talk about it anymore."

"Mommy, can we go to McDonald's?"

"We'll see, maybe after we do the grocery shopping."

Sandra drove quickly through Seacliff's Gold Coast, onto I-95, then for groceries at Stop and Shop, and finally home to Faircliff, a section she referred to as the working man's Seacliff. She promised herself that someday her little family, too, would live in the tony part of town.

Her thoughts kept focusing on Linda. As beautiful as her sister was, she wasn't perfect, Sandra told herself; then willed the debilitating thoughts from her mind. After all, she had Tiffany and Kevin. Her sister was childless.

Despite Sandra's opinion that life's scales unfairly favored Linda; she loved her sister and acknowledged her generosity.

Why shouldn't Linda be generous? She had the means; a fat TV salary, Christopher's lucrative consulting business, and that gorgeous house facing the sea. Sandra's house was a Cape Cod with an unfinished second floor. Her sister had the latest in clothes, like form-fitting designer's jeans that conformed to the body like a banana skin. Hers came from Sears, hardly couture.

It further bugged her that their parents were partial to Linda, the honor student who worked during school vacations and went on to graduate school for a master's degree in communications. Sandra tried college for a year, didn't like it, and then dropped out.

She admitted that, at forty-two, Linda was still a good looking woman, appearing ten years younger. How many times had she heard that the camera loves Linda's face?

But at least, physically, Sandra thought she didn't measure up too badly. She had a petite figure with well-shaped, full breasts, while Linda, to Sandra's eyes, seemed rather small-breasted for her five foot-nine inch frame.

Sandra told herself she wasn't really competing with her sister; it's just that Linda had everything. Well, not quite everything. This morning she noticed crows' feet around her eyes. Quite apparent without makeup, but not so on camera. That TV cosmetic artist certainly knew her business.

Another plus in Sandra's life was a husband who didn't wander. Sandra appreciated that Kevin was dependable, but hardly a man of passion.

Liz Barzda

He'd happily take care of Tiffany when he wasn't working overtime. Next month, Tiffany would be in kindergarten, meaning more free time for Mommy.

Sandra couldn't help that she loved clothes and shopping. Those overdue credit card bills and dunning letters were just too depressing. Why was there never enough money?

Chapter 3

On Tuesday morning, it took all Linda's resolve to empty her mind of Christopher and to face the world.

She opened La Petit Spa's glossy purple door, walked slowly through the marble foyer into the reception room. Her footsteps were silent on the plush Aubusson carpet, but surely everyone could hear the thumping of her heart. How does one function with a shattered heart, she wondered? She bit her lip. *I'll get through it because I must.*

"Linda, surprised to see you. We couldn't reach you for your Saturday appointment," the receptionist said.

"Sorry Darlene, I wasn't feeling well. Can Geraldine take me now?"

The receptionist checked her appointment book

As Linda waited, the spa's owner, Katherine Horvath, entered the room. Her eyes roamed over Linda's tank top and shorts. "Hi. I was a bit worried when you didn't show for your Saturday appointment. Are you okay?"

"I'm all right, Kat. Really. I had a sleepless night. Perhaps my ulcer's acting up.

"Thought your ulcer was healed."

"It is, but eating spicy food doesn't help." Better to blame her appearance on a faulty diet than be interrogated.

"Hate to be so blunt, Linda, but you look like hell. Never seen you like this. Really, dear, gray is not your color. Your horoscope says Leos should wear sunrise hues." Katherine chuckled, "You know the stars are never wrong."

Linda ignored her comments. "Can Geraldine squeeze me in?"

"I'll see to it," Katherine said as she continued to scrutinize her friend.

Liz Barzda

"Could it be TV sweeps week and contract renewal time? Don't sweat it," Katherine said as she draped her arm around Linda's shoulder. "You're the most popular on-camera talent at WSEA." Then, with a smile, added, "They'll renew."

Linda refrained from answer, but a frown crossed her face. *If only sweeps week was my biggest concern.* She followed her friend's swift steps to the pink massage room whose light rosy hue was supposed to complement the complexion. Her eyes scanned the room without focusing. She didn't feel rosy; she felt like shit. Despite her stupor, she couldn't help notice how Katherine's shoulder-length sable-hued hair fell into waves, how the buff-colored silk suit hugged her curvaceous body. A few days ago, Linda would have complimented her on her perfectly groomed appearance. Now clothes seemed unimportant, just something to cover your nakedness.

Katherine handed Linda an apple-green sheet. "Here, wrap up and don't sweat the small stuff. Remember, your fans love you."

Yes, but my husband doesn't, Linda thought.

"By the way," Katherine added, "did you receive the Choices Banquet invitation? I'm sure Margaret and Zita got theirs. We could go together. Sounds like a great evening. What do you say?"

"Sure, why not?" Linda responded without enthusiasm as she removed her dress. *Choices. What a ridiculous word. Did I have a choice in Christopher's secret life?* Linda slipped off her bra and panties. She sensed Katherine's eyes appraising her body.

Katherine, quick to note Linda's detachment said, "We'll get some color back into those gorgeous high-boned cheeks."

"I'm sorry I haven't asked how things are with you, Kat. It's just that I don't feel my usual self."

"You're forgiven," Katherine said with a sympathetic look. "But getting to the important subject--me," she chuckled, "I'm just fine, except for the bank leaning on me. Remember my telling you that the spa's renovation and addition cost much more than I expected? I've been a little slow in making payments, and the interest keeps accumulating. Damn heartless bank. I'll figure out something," She grimaced, and then put on her spa-owner's smile. "Geraldine will be here in a second for your massage."

"Let's skip the manicure and blow dry today. I'm just not up to it."

"Of course, I understand."

Linda watched her leave. For the first time, she envied Katherine Horvath. She and Katherine, buddies for fifteen years, met at the old Princess Beauty Salon where Katherine worked as receptionist, part-time

Bittersweet House

bookkeeper, and fill-in hairdresser. Linda empathized with her through her difficult years at building a business, plus the strain of keeping it liquid. Although Linda understood Katherine's search for love, she regarded her friend's bed-hopping not only stupid, but dangerous. Never one to criticize, Linda held her tongue. She hoped Katherine's new relationship with Scott would be permanent, but doubted it. Finding lasting love was a crap shoot.

Linda lay on the massage table and struggled to rein in disturbing images of friends and lovers--especially lovers. If she couldn't stop the tape in her head from repeating, "Christopher has a mistress, Christopher has a baby," she'd have a nervous breakdown.

She closed her eyes to banish picture of the baby and of the woman unknown faces. But she couldn't stop the rhythm of the words, over and over: *Christopher has a mistress, Christopher has a baby.*

She likened her marriage to a sinkhole and her career to a roll of the dice.

"How's my favorite client?" the large-boned masseuse with henna dyed hair boomed as she swept into the room. "We missed you Saturday."

"Sorry, Geraldine. I wasn't up to it."

"Oh dear, not feeling like a cinema queen today, I see," Geraldine said as she inspected Linda's face while reaching for the almond oil. "Never you mind. I guarantee to ease those tensions. Don't I always? Now, want to tell me what's causing knots in your neck and wrinkles in your forehead?"

"I'm not in a revealing mood," Linda snapped, then apologized. "Sorry, Geraldine, I've got a wicked headache."

"You're forgiven. Guess it's none of my business." The masseuse lathered Linda's body with oil. "This will rejuvenate you." Her practiced hands worked her client's body, rubbing, stroking and kneading.

Fear and doubt began to fade. Christopher, his mistress, and their child receded from her mind. Television ratings and performance evaporated. Worry about a possible dewy-skinned anchor replacement half her age diminished. She drifted off. There was her mother as a young woman with an infant in her arms. But Linda wasn't the baby. Then the faces changed. Linda was holding the baby, but it slipped from her arms. She screamed as the infant hit the floor.

"Are you all right?" Geraldine worried. "You cried out."

Perspiration dripped from Linda's face. She couldn't breathe. She raised up to get some air.

"Just a nightmare." But she wasn't okay. The dream baby who fell from

15

Liz Barzda

her arms haunted her. The dream never let up, repeating itself night after night. But she couldn't see the baby's face. Was it hurt? Could it be the infant she longed for, the one Christopher repeatedly assured her that they would eventually have? She, like a fool, had believed him.

Face it Linda, you'll never have a child. She dressed in a daze; told Geraldine to bill her, and was about to exit the reception area when Katherine stopped her. "You've come back to life," she joked, then added in a softer tone, "Don't forget to call me about the Choices Banquet. Let's do lunch with Margaret and Zita. It's been ages since we've been together to just talk. I miss it."

"Sure, why not?" Linda replied with indifference. She gazed at her friend with envy. How lucky to be such a free spirit, to have a lover instead of a husband, to call the shots and screw the world.

#

Alone in her private office, Katherine took a deep breath and ran her hands down the knee-length, black linen dress as though smoothing out the wrinkles of her life. .

Her life did have wrinkles, but she would straighten them out. Money and love; that's what it's all about. Love never got her anywhere, but money did. Money took precedence in her book; love was secondary. If her lover Scott asked his father for a low interest loan as he'd promised, her money worries would be over. She'd press Scott; he with the big laugh and forgotten promises.

Love? Katherine doubted her lover would ever commit to a monogamous relationship. Although they were a couple, he was probably cheating on her. But there were ways to keep him in line, she assured herself.

Dismissing Scott from her mind, she thought of Linda. She had never seen her friend look so beaten. Katherine's deep brown eyes stared into space. *Something was terribly wrong.*

Rather than spend time stewing, she'd ring Margaret Dolan. Surely Margaret would know what to do. Aptly dubbed "Mother Superior" for her wisdom and compassion, she, Linda and Zita, like novitiates, often turned to Mother Superior for succor.

Katherine skipped quickly through the social amenities and honed in on the subjects of matter to her.

"How's business, Margaret?"

Bittersweet House

"Luckily, the real estate market's still strong and we're selling, "Margaret answered happily. "And yours?"

Katherine sighed as she scribbled boxes and circles on her note pad. "Clients are coming in, but moneys are going out too fast. The bank won't extend my loan. Scott promised a low-interest loan for me from his father. I 'm hoping he'll come through."

"I'm sure he will."

"And if he doesn't, there are other avenues, like borrowing from the Mafia," Katherine quipped with false giggles while filling her doodle boxes with dollar signs.

"Kat, that's not funny. You're playing with fire. And you know the Mafia's deserved reputation. My brother-in-law, Michael, has one word for them-- deadly."

"I was joking."

"It didn't sound like it to me."

"Don't worry about me. Everything will right itself. I really wanted to ask you about Linda. She was in the Spa for her weekly massage and she looked like a tank ran her down. I've never seen her look so bad. It wasn't the Linda we know," she said. "Have you any idea what's wrong? Do you think it's Sandra? Linda doesn't say much; but I hear her sister's often financially irresponsible and Linda helps her out. Maybe it's Christopher; seems he's away more on business than he is at home."

"I can't picture Linda not looking her best," Margaret replied. "Hope it's nothing serious, but I haven't a clue. I ran into her at Nordstrom's last week. Seemed fine then."

"Do you think you might be able to find out what the problem is? She may need help."

"We have to be careful to not put our noses where they don't belong. It may be nothing."

"I don't think it's nothing. She looks deeply disturbed."

"Hmm. I think it's time Zita and I pay her a visit."

Let me know what happens."

"I'll call you," Margaret promised. "Love you."

#

Katherine sat at her desk replaying the conversation in her mind. Margaret was a dear, and the best real estate broker in the area. Zita, dependable as a blue chip stock, still neither women was a risk taker like herself.

17

Liz Barzda

Nevertheless, with their combined talents, Katherine felt that whatever kind of predicament Linda is facing and too stubborn or foolish to ask for help, surely her good friends can bale her out. She'd phone Zita later and make a date to visit Linda.

That filed away, her mind centered on business; the endeavor, next to love, she enjoyed more than anything. Being your own boss became a close second. Self-assertive when necessary, she had the stuff required to succeed. Although it still rankled when a local accused her of speaking over anyone who had the floor at the building and zoning meetings. "Rubbish," Katherine shot back. "Those who never relinquish the mike at town meetings are there to hear themselves talk. I'm here to see that zoning laws are properly enforced--and to defend my rights. I haven't the time to listen to their nonsense."

Katherine admitted to being strong-willed, but aggressive, never. She recalled the years of labor it took to create La Peite Spa. In high school, she cleaned the neighborhood beauty parlor every day after class. Saturdays were spent shampooing heads one after another.

After working her way through community college for an associate degree in business administration, a course in a beauty culture school, and years spent in what amounted to apprenticeship in various beauty parlors, she finally arrived in plush spas where she learned the European methods of skin care.

Her savvy use of public relations drew well-heeled clients to La Petite Spa; its beautiful surroundings and impeccable service kept them returning. She courted print and TV reporters by giving them a substantial discount for beauty services. The business ran smoothly; it was just the nasty problem with the Metro bank. She'd do almost anything to hold on to the Spa. If Scott didn't come through with the loan, there was the *other* way.

Chapter 4

Comfortable in her air-conditioned Cadillac DeVille, Margaret glanced in her overhead mirror to check her makeup. A reflection of a fairly wrinkle-free face, gray hair with blonde streaks and hazel eyes brought on a grin. "Not bad for a fifty-two-year old babe," Margaret said aloud, revealing her right cheek dimple. She maintained that talking to herself when alone assured the correct response.

As she drove through Seacliff's shoreline area past the proposed Forest Park development and approached the city's commercial area, Margaret mentally reviewed the agenda she planned to discuss with Zita Parker.

First, a rundown of the Forest Park and Seacliff Villas brochure schedules and costs, then Linda's dreadful appearance at the Spa. She looked as though a train had run over her. Zita assuredly would know if Linda were having a problem; they'd been best friends since college.

It was ten o'clock as she swung her car into Parker Advertising Agency's parking lot, right on the button... so much business to cover. Imagine Kat pretending to joke about a Mafia loan! Margaret shook her head. *Inconceivable. Could she actually be contemplating such a stupid move?*

Margaret dashed to the agency office to escape the stifling heat. "Sally, I'll go right in. Ms. Parker's expecting me,"

"Would you like coffee?" the secretary asked with a toothy smile.

"Great idea. That'll rev me up."

She entered Zita's office without knocking and sank into a deeply upholstered chair. "It's so damn hot out there, not fit for your worse enemy, but this room is like an oasis." Her spirits always revised when she took in the room's robin's eye blue and silver walls and its trickling wall fountain. "It's so cool and comfortable here; I'm refreshed every time I visit. Now

I'm ready to lock horns?" Margaret joked while taking in the trim figure behind the steel and chrome desk. Zita looked terrific in a well-cut beige cotton suit highlighting her strawberry blonde hair. *Smart look. And smart gal.*

Margaret admired Zita's business zeal. In high school, she worked part-time selling advertising space for a weekly newspaper, then TV advertising space during her college summer vacations. After college, Zita established her one-woman agency that eventually led to the ownership of a full-service advertising group. She had the business background to properly service her clients. Soft, dove-gray eyes and wistful-sounding voice added to her sympathetic persona, but concealed the steel will she had developed.

"Hi, Margaret. Good to see you. How've you been?"

"Busy as sailor in a leaky ship."

"How's that handsome husband of yours?"

"Jack's fine. He's a sweetheart. Went off at the crack of dawn for nine holes of golf at the club without waking me," Margaret said, slipping off her shoes and revealing scarlet toenails. "Ah," she sighed, "That feels better." She crossed her still shapely but slightly plump legs.

"Hope you don't mind, but I think better in bare feet."

"Whatever makes you happy."

"Let's talk basics before business--how's your love life, Zita? Anything new?"

Zita beamed. "Sure is. I've been seeing Peter Romano. Fun without frustration. No serious entanglement and I intend to keep it that way."

"Good thinking. Let's hope he brings you better luck than David did," Margaret said with a sympathetic look.

Sally knocked, and then entered with a tray of coffee and Danish. She laid the tray on the credenza, poured the coffee, and closed the door quietly as she left.

Margaret bit into the Danish, with obvious pleasure. Zita pushed her plate away and sipped her coffee.

"Take a look at these," Zita said as she passed the Seacliff Villas sketches over to her friend and client.

Margaret slipped on her reading glasses and perused the work closely.

"Notice the artist's excellent positioning of the houses, offering the best sea-front view." Zita said of the multi-million dollar complex. "The project should make you a bundle."

"Nice," Margaret replied, not wanting to appear over enthusiastic.

"And now for Forest Park." Zita unfolded renderings of a dozen three-quarter million dollar homes on one-acre rolling hill lots. "Though the lots aren't as desirable as Seacliff Villas, they're appealing and should sell fast."

Margaret bobbed her head in agreement as she studied the sketches. "These look great. I wouldn't change a thing. I spoke with Joe Arcara and worked out the building schedule. He's ready to begin digging next month. Ann Marie is project manager."

"Terrific. Who'd have guessed tough Joe would let his daughter take over the job?" Zita asked, twirling her pen in thought. "Arcara and Daughter. Can you believe it? Looks as if women may yet make it in a man's world. And why not? Ann Marie has business smarts, knows construction, and works well with men. She deserves it."

"It'll be great to have her aboard. When can I expect the finished brochures?"

"You'll have two glossy brochures in a month."

"By the way," Margaret inserted, "I wanted to clue you in on Linda. Kat told me she came to the Spa yesterday in lieu of her Saturday usual and looked like a best friend just died. I can't picture Linda down in the mouth; she's usually so upbeat. What do you think could have happened?"

"Haven't a clue, Margaret. Had a quick lunch with her at the coffee shop near the studio last Tuesday. Seemed okay then. Maybe I'll surprise her and drop in. Think I'll swing by her place as I have a little time."

"Good idea. Perhaps you can find out what's up."

Margaret wrinkled her nose. "There's a rumor Kat's having money problems. Seems she expanded and renovated beyond her business potential. She's so impulsive. Heard talk she's actually thinking about a Mafia loan. Can you imagine such stupidity?"

"The thought of her in cement shoes has crossed my mind," Margaret said ruefully.

Zita shook her head. "I thought she had more sense."

Margaret sighed. "Doesn't look like it. I'll talk to my brother-in-law Michael. He's with Seacliff's Undercover Drug Unit and can give me some advice."

"Can't hurt."

"Almost forgot. Just one more thing--on a happier note. Are you going to the Choices Banquet? Did you receive an invitation?"

"Yes, on both counts."

"We can make up a table with Linda and Kat and spent the night toasting ourselves." Margaret let out a laugh, "To the Barren Babes. We're aptly named. Don't you agree?" Zita attempted to match Margaret's frivolous tone, "Better than calling ourselves the 'Fruitless Foursome'." Margaret rose. "Why not the Fabulous Foursome?" she said with a chuckle, added her favorite catch phrase "Love you," and left.

Zita watched her depart and marveled at Margaret's supposedly humorous disregard of being childless. She could never laugh about being barren. But wouldn't it be a plus if she had Margaret's optimistic nature, her sense of humor?

#

Zita reviewed all Margaret had said. She'd have to lean on her staff to finish those brochures in a month but it was doable.

Kat was another story. Zita knew her friend was impulsive, but believed her business had more potential and eventually would be on solid ground. Perhaps Kat's lover, Scott Bowman, would come through with a loan. So much for assumptions. He was a putz. Everyone knew he cheated on her.

And what was happening to Linda? She couldn't fathom her coolheaded best friend out of whack. Perhaps Margaret could sort it out.

Her mind refocused on Margaret. What a lucky woman--an adoring husband, a rock-solid marriage, and a thriving real estate business. And smart to boot. It was understandable that the three of us sought her advice. But life was never perfect. Not even Margaret's.

Zita knew Margaret and Jack yearned for children, but supposedly couldn't conceive. Nevertheless, they were a happy couple. You just can't fake that, Zita knew from experience.

Scenes with her ex-husband David flashed across her mind. Their discussions of a family, their fights, months of painful invitro-fertilization treatments, infidelity and finally their acrimonious divorce. She buried her fear of running Parker Advertising Agency alone when David walked out. Determination kept her grounded.

Small in stature, only 5' 2", Zita created the illusion of height and strength by carrying herself well and projecting a stance of competency. Her hand swept across her forehead as if to obliterate the hateful memories. Enough of yesterday's failings. Time to pursue a potential client and get out the promised brochures. She buzzed Sally. "Please bring in the Heritage Real Estate file."

Bittersweet House

#

After checking out American designers' autumn creations at Nordstrom's and lunching in a crowded Seacliff mall restaurant, Margaret headed back to her office. As her car traveled on to the Merritt Parkway into the center of the city, she thought of Linda's and Kat's difficulties. Their problems gave her pause to reflect on her life with Jack.

No one had to tell her how fortunate she was to possess one of the few long-standing marriages in her set. So what if they didn't have children? There were other compensations--their work and her nephew Gregory O'Neil, whom they both adored.

Their careers were fulfilling; his as Seacliff Hospital's CEO and hers as sole owner of Heritage Real Estate. Best of all, they never bored each other.

Like many marriages, they had weathered some bad times. She recalled how devastated Jack was when he learned his sperm weren't plentiful enough to produce a child. She opted for adoption, but Jack was adamant about having a child of his own flesh and blood. That was more than a decade ago. They got over it.

At times Margaret felt almost guilty about their love-filled marriage, as if it would dissolve if she became too complacent, or too happy. She buried the anxiety deep within her, refusing to dwell on it, or even mention it. One just didn't talk about it when friends (like Kat) had obvious romantic problems. She knew Jack adored her. He told her repeatedly that she was all the woman he ever desired. "I love your dimpled cheeks, all three of them." That remark earned him a good poke in the ribs.

Thoughts of compatibility and sexual delights with her husband receded from her mind. The disquieting news about Linda and Katherine took hold. What in the world could be wrong with cool Linda who always appeared in command of a situation and of herself?

Could Kat be over her head in the extravagant renovation of her spa? As for her personal life, Kat admitted to jumping into too many beds too quickly in the past. She insisted it was love with Scott Bowman. Does he feel the same, Margaret wondered?

She pondered Zita's situation. She knew that Parker Advertising Agency continued on its path toward profitability and that her friend's ex-husband, David, was out of her life for good. But Peter? Like a dark horse, she didn't know if he could stay the distance. Be optimistic and hope for the best, she told herself.

Liz Barzda

Kat was a different matter. Could she actually contemplate something as destructive as playing around with the Mafia?

Chapter 5

Despite Sunday night's Valium, Linda slept fitfully entangled in twisted dreams. Her morning shower and black coffee did little to erase her lethargy. She couldn't face the crew at WSEA. *A look at her and they'd know something was amiss. People have a way of seeing through one's facade. One more day at home, then I'll bounce back.*

The muscles of her neck tightened at the thought of lying to her boss, News Director Jack Cohen. She told him that she'd probably be in on Tuesday, but that thought loomed over her like a boulder aimed at her head. She'd try for Wednesday. He had told her not to push it; come in when she felt better. She stood in the breakfast room and stared past the patio, past the back lawn, toward Long Island Sound. Fog blanketed the water, virtually obliterating the horizon. She tried to focus on the blurred view, but she couldn't decipher what was real and what was illusion. Their so-called happy marriage was an illusion, like a mirage at sea. The emotional pain was nearly too much to bear, but she mustn't wallow in it. Yet, the good times refused to stay buried.

She remembered the parties on the sun-filled patio, grilling steaks while couples swam in the pool and others ran down the beach and dove into the waves. Laughter filled the grounds. Music emanated from the sound system. There were guffaws when Linda and Christopher revealed tidbits about local personalities in television and international business. Guests contributed bizarre stories of their respective professions and businesses until the laugh level zoomed to a crescendo.

Linda recalled peaceful weekends when she and Christopher sailed their 32- foot sloop Cygnet to an island off Long Island Sound. They'd swim off the boat and picnic on the dunes as the setting sun bathed the

Liz Barzda

horizon and water in shades of burnt orange and shocking pink. The sky turned to cobalt blue with glimmering stars hovering over them as they made love in the sand, reveling in the smell and taste of their bodies.

They shared opera, ballet, and theater in New York with friends, followed by a late night supper in the Four Seasons or a new trendy restaurant. Occasionally on Saturday when Christopher wasn't consulting with GBC Ltd. in London, or meeting with some third-world dictator to set up a telecommunication system, they'd spend the day in Connecticut's northwest corner seeking out antiques. They'd stop at a country inn for dinner and laugh over their so-called finds. Christopher insisted he spied the owner of the area's most prestigious shop age an antique table by distressing it with a heavy chain.

Those days were filled with excitement--mostly centered on Christopher. After 17 years of marriage, he still exuded sex appeal. His faults were minor ones, like predictable nightly snoring. Although it annoyed Linda, she'd retreat to the guest room when it became unbearable; Christopher refused to do anything about it. And he was a procrastinator, always leaving the details of house maintenance and repairs to her. Nevertheless, she loved the sight of his six-foot, two-inch muscular body, his gray-green eyes that appeared to deepen as he made love, and the sound of his rich baritone voice. They were a universe in themselves. How could he love someone else? And even more hurtful, how could he refuse to let a baby come into their marriage, but make one with his lover?

She would not think of *that* woman, rather she'd concentrate on work. What work? If only she could remember. Something about her Connecticut Chronicle program. Linda squeezed her eyes closed. *Think. Think.* She massaged her forehead. *Now I remember, I need an interview for my upcoming Connecticut Chronicle program.* Linda booted the computer, stared at the monitor--nothing. Not a glimmer of an idea. Perhaps if she gazed at the screen long enough, her brain would conjure up a name. Some notable to be interviewed.

The door bell rang, startling her. Who the hell that? She wondered as she headed for the foyer. I don't want to see anyone. She opened the door to July's dense humidity and Margaret. "What are you doing here?"

"Trying to get out of this heat. And that's a hell of a way to welcome a friend," Margaret said with a throaty laugh that never failed to cheer. "Aren't you going to invite me in?"

"I'm sorry," Linda answered as she ushered her friend in and led the

Bittersweet House

way to the kitchen. She forced a faint smile, "It's just that I didn't expect you on a Tuesday afternoon. You're usually in your office at this time."

"So I took some time off and went out of my way a few miles to see you. Never tire of driving the shore route, but I'm tired of trying to reach you by phone, fax, or e-mail. What's up with you?" Margaret asked as she pulled the chair from the breakfast table, and then slipped off her shoes.

"Nothing. I just need some R&R," Linda replied as she reached for coffee cups. "I think it was a bug. It knocked me out. Can't you tell?" Linda asked, pointing at her wrinkled silk pajamas.

"I've seen you look better, darling. Could it be that you're hiding out, or is it because you miss that handsome man of yours?"

Linda evaded Margaret's questions. She longed to unburden herself. Shocked, hurt, embarrassed, all the negative emotions weighed on her heart. For years, the BB's shared laughter and pain; still she couldn't admit that her so-called "perfect marriage" was nothing more than charred memories. "I'm not hiding out," Linda lied, filling Margaret's coffee cup. "It's just that things are uncertain at the station. My contract's up for renewal."

Margaret reached for her friend's hand. "Really? This is your old buddy you're talking to. I know it's sweeps time, but it never discombobulated you before. Is there something else? Something I can help with?"

"No. I just need time to iron out a few minor problems." Linda withdrew her hand, looked away and managed a laugh. "Must be that upcoming forty-third birthday that's bothering me."

"Sure," Margaret said with a quizzical look, then brightened the atmosphere with a cheery, "Birthdays are wonderful, although too many of them can age anybody--except you. Have you any idea how many women are envious of your face and figure? No wonder Christopher still adores you. By the way, how is handsome? And where's he been? Haven't seen him for ages."

Linda gave Margaret a sidelong glance. "Christopher's fine. He's been busy in London trying to get a consulting contract. I expect him home this weekend." Linda rose to get her friend another cup of coffee--anything not to meet Margaret's eyes. Then she remembered. "Sorry, I haven't asked about Jack. I seem to be so absent-minded lately. How is he?"

"He's stressed out because the hospital board is fighting him on putting up a new wing or renovating a couple of the older buildings."

"That's nice," Linda responded absently.

Margaret shot her a quizzical look.

"Forgive me, Margaret. I don't know what I'm saying." Linda palmed her forehead in frustration. "Must be the bug." She rose to refill their cups.

Margaret placed her hand over her cup. "No more for me, but I'll tell you what you can do. You can get some rest and rid yourself of this funk you're in. An afternoon with Zita and Kat would do it. How about lunch the Saturday after next? You should be well then. It's been weeks since we've been together and had a good laugh."

Rather than listen to more advice, Linda nodded, "Okay, it's a date."

"Let's make it the Mediterranean," Margaret suggested. "I love their food and the ambiance. I'll call Kat and Zita. Speaking of Kat, have you heard that she's borrowed to the hilt and overextended because of the Spa's renovation? Rumor says she's begged Scott to ask his father for a low-interest loan, and if that doesn't work she'll talk to the Mafia. Can you imagine? Who in the world would she know in the Mafia?" Margaret asked as she fished around for her shoes with her toes. "Where are those damn things," she groused as she got up and headed for the foyer.

"I trust Scott's father will come through," Linda said. "But nothing is certain." She twisted a lock of hair around an ear and said in a soft voice, "You know that Kat and Scott have double-dated with Zita and her new boyfriend, Peter Romano. Peter's uncle is Joe Arcara, the contractor. Just because Joe is in construction, it's assumed he has a working relationship with Mafia characters. I don't believe he's one of them." Linda continued with a grimace, "But he does know a lot of wise guys. I imagine Kat will pump Peter for Mafia names." Linda followed Margaret to the front door. "It doesn't mean his uncle will comply. Kat needs a good scare. Playing around with the mob will cost her more than money. Someone's got to get through to her. Maybe the three of us can get her to see the light."

Margaret reached for the door handle. "Don't sweat it, sweetie. Just look after yourself. Seems like you could use a week of sleep." She smiled, then tenderly touched Linda's cheek, "Take care. Love you."

Linda closed the door and dwelled on Margaret's words. *Maybe the three of us can talk sense into Kat. Help Kat? I can't even help myself.*

Chapter 6

Zita Parker opened her living room sliders and inhaled the emanations of Long Island Sound. The sight of a distant freighter in the setting sun brought a longing to escape the demands of her business. What a hellish Wednesday! Clients expected instant results from Parker Advertising Agency's creative concepts. Breaking in new sales associates added to her frustration.

She retreated to the bathroom, wrapped a towel around her strawberry-blonde curls, filled the Jacuzzi, climbed in, closed her eyes and purred. The day's turbulence slowly ebbed away. Unpleasant images evaporated, replaced by past memories.

Zita saw herself as a high school student working part-time in an advertising department of a weekly newspaper, studying with her roomy and best friend Linda Cooper at the University of Connecticut, and then selling ad space for a mid-sized daily. After five years she worked her way up to advertising manager. It took another five years till she opened her one-woman advertising agency. Six years later, the Parker Advertising Agency boasted a staff of 12.

The scenes vanished. Like a broken record replayed, David's image kept reappearing. Zita felt her neck muscles tense at the thought of that son-of-a-bitch ex-husband. The man who promised to love, honor and cherish *until death do us part*, took a powder when her more-than-$45,000 attempt at invitro-fertilization didn't take. *Poor man, he couldn't take all that stress.* To recover, the *dog* found a bitch who promised sex without stress.

Twenty years of marriage down the toilet. Every day she cursed him a bit less because every day she felt stronger. She was well rid of him. Parker Advertising was more than holding its own. As much as Zita cursed David

Liz Barzda

for walking out on her with his blonde bimbo, at times loneliness engulfed her. But she wouldn't yield to it. Men were untrustworthy. Screw them! She vowed all her energy would be devoted to her business--until she met Peter Romano. He had accompanied his uncle, Joseph Arcara, to a meeting in Zita's office to discuss the preliminary plans of the Forest Park and the Seacliff Villas developments. Peter repeatedly pressed for a date. After a dozen tries, she finally said '*yes*,' and was glad she did.

She had fun. Furthermore, here was a man who didn't pressure her for sex on the first date. She smiled, thinking about the guy with the tough exterior who turned out to be a pussycat. Things were going well. She introduced him to Italian operas and museum openings. The poor man assured her that he loved every minute of it--anything to please her. Lazy Sundays were often spent picnicking on a grassy knoll watching jet planes leaving contrails in luminous blue summer skies. They laughed over her little faux pas, like the time her fishing line caught his and he had to disentangle it before she reeled in the 18-inch blue fish.

Zita stepped out of the tub, wrapped herself in a towel sheet, and reached for the dusting powder. Her mind still on Peter, she admitted he was a bit rough around the edges, but she didn't care. To survive in the construction business, a man had to be tough. But not when it came to her. His actions said 'I care about you'.

The dressing room phone rang, disturbing her daydream.

"Hi, Margaret. How you doing? What's up?" Zita asked.

The usual pleasantries and questions out of the way, Margaret got to the business at hand. "We're all meeting for lunch. Want to come?"

"Sure. When?"

"Saturday after next, noonish at the Mediterranean."

"Count me in."

"I told you about Linda," Margaret continued, "We could try to find out what's bothering her, or at the least cheer her up. And how about Kat? Personally, my opinion is a kick in the rear would be appropriate."

"Kat needs a good scare, "Zita said. "She's being a smart ass, playing out of her league."

"Right," Margaret concurred. "Kat is Kat."

"Unthinking at times," Zita said brushing her hair, "but she's one of us, a *Barren Babe*, no matter what. Whatever Linda's problem, she needs time to sort things out. But you never know. Just the four of us being together might help."

"You got it," Margaret said. "Talk to you soon. Love you."

Bittersweet House

Zita sensed the warmth of her friend's smile through the phone. So upbeat. God, how she loved wise, warm Margaret, a lucky woman with an enduring marriage. Zita felt a pang of regret over her broken union. True, she was fortunate to have found a man like Peter, who appeared to truly care about her. But a legal union? She'd been there, done that. What a disaster! Why would any sane person choose legal servitude instead of a free single life?

#

Clad in her blue sweats, the dictionary on the sofa by her side, Katherine Horvath worked a crossword puzzle. She filled in the empty squares with force, breaking the pencil point. Disgusted, she threw the pencil down and stared at the phone.

That rat said he'd call. Frustrated over Scott's behavior, she ranted, "I'll kill him if he doesn't get that loan from his father for me. I'll give him till ten tonight to phone." She thought of throwing a TV dinner into the microwave to get her mind off her lover and financial problems. Instead, she filled a tumbler with vodka and soda water, sipping it as she paced the living room. Finally, settling in front of the bow window, Katherine gazed at the blurred pink and gray sunset. It wasn't enough that her hefty interest payment was due at the bank in three weeks. She also had to worry about Scott her playboy lover who fancied himself an executive in his father's business.

Is that bimbo-of-a secretary, Beryl Blair, with her exaggerated English accent, sucking up to him? Is he humping her? Katherine ran her fingers through her shoulder-length sable hair and wondered what he could be doing on a Monday night. Nobody goes out on a Monday night. The phone rang. Frowning, she reached for it and snapped, "Yes."

"Wow, Kat. How about a hello?" Margaret said in her usual sunny tone.

"Sorry, Margaret, I thought it was Scott. But I'm glad it's you."

"Want to have lunch with Linda and Zita, Saturday after next?"

"Sure. Where?"

"Noonish at the Mediterranean. It's been a month since we've been together. I dropped in on Linda this morning. I hate to say it, but she looks like hell; is closed-mouth about everything. Maybe we can help her out of that black hole she's in."

"Whatever works." A disturbing thought flickered through Katherine's mind. *Could there be problems in the Cooper household?* She shook her head. *I'm just being paranoid--thinking every guy is cheating on his girl.*

"Count me in," Kat said with a happier ring to her voice.

"Great. Can't toast the *Barren Babes* without the fourth member," Margaret said, then paused. "Would you believe I'm still uncertain about our name?"

"I don't see why. It's an honest tag. Maybe not the best choice by some standards. Screw them. Just so people don't refer to us as the barren bitches."

Margaret chortled, "Suites me."

Chapter 7

True believers in the "shop till you drop" edict, Sandra Duboise, and her friend, Darlene Moore roamed the discount outlets at Seacliff's Golden Mart Mall, then zeroed in at Couture House.

"Oh God, they're so beautiful I can taste it," Sandra exclaimed as her eyes drank in Donna Karan's chiffon gowns in earth colors. She gripped Darlene arm. "I may not be a Vogue model, but I'll bet next week's grocery money I'd be a knockout in one of those."

"They're to die for," Darlene drooled. "Go in and ask if they're available in your size. But first, remove your nose from the window; you're creating streaks."

"Very funny, Darlene. Just once I'd like to buy something, anything, in an elegant shop without worrying about price. Shopping discount is a bore. Kevin would have a cow if I bought another thing." She grimaced, "He keeps reminding me that we're choking in plastic. But when his promotion comes through there'll be more money." The thought of additional money brought a full smile to her face.

"Even if you could afford it, where in your world would you wear a designer's creation?" Darlene asked.

"To the Plentfield Country Club Holly ball, the Seafair Yacht Clue New Year's Eve bash, or a dinner party at snobbish Mrs. Goodwin's on Summerfield Hill. My escort would be a CEO, a politician, or a dirty old man with big bucks who pines for my body. I would delight him with my sexual prowess," Sandra laughed. He'll think he died and flew into to a Mormon's household with a harem of teenage wives."

"In your dreams," Darlene chuckled. "I'm bushed. How about a drink at Maxi's. Do you have time? Who's baby sitting Tiffany?"

"Not to worry. Mrs. Brody is watching her. The dear woman told me to shop as long as I like." Sandra had no qualms about leaving her little girl; Mrs. Brody was so reliable. If only her husband, Kevin, would refrain from reminding her about her shopping sprees and the baby-sitting charges.

Aiming for Maxi's Restaurant, they wove in and out of the path of night shoppers, mostly teenagers and career men and women laden with bags and packages. Sandra's eyes darted from one shop to another and from one good-looking guy to another. The look was usually returned. It gave her a warm feeling. She needed attention. She deserved it. Kevin was too busy working overtime to massage her ego. She couldn't remember the last time they went to a party or enjoyed a night of dancing. Her body ached at the thought of what she was missing.

Maxi's was packed with a typical noisy Friday night crowd. The women felt welcomed in the convivial atmosphere of laughter, conversation and TV's blaring of a Yankee-Red Sox game.

"Let's sit in the cocktail lounge. It's a lot more fun checking out the customers at the bar, imagining who they are and what they do," Sandra said as she placed her new tank top on a chair.

Darlene laid her boxed sale dress on the floor between her legs. "Can't lose this. What a bargain," she enthused about the two-piece blue linen outfit. "Kat will love it. I can wear it at the Spa and dress it up for a heavy date." She knew the royal blue would deepen her gray-blue eyes. "Peter Romano should see me in this."

Sandra gave her a questioning look and flashed a smile at the tall, broad-shouldered waiter. "Sam Adams for me."

"Make mine a white Zinfindel," Darlene ordered.

"So what's doing at the Spa? If you think I'm prying, I am," Sandra admitted when the waiter left to get their drinks.

"Well, a while ago, Anne Marie Arcara was in for a facial and manicure. You know how she's always running on all eight cylinders? Seems she neglected to sign a contract requiring her signature. Her cousin, Peter Romano, brought it to the Spa. What a hunk! He's gorgeous. What do you know about him?"

"Whoa," Sandra said extending an open palm. "I hear he and Zita Parker are a twosome. I doubt Zita would appreciate you trying to horn in. What about Roland? How do you think he'd feel about your hots for his cousin? You've heard the rumors about his uncle, Joe Arcara, being in bed with the Mafia?" Sandra shrugged her shoulders, "But who knows? It may not be true. Be careful, I wouldn't want to see you end up in the

Bittersweet House

river." Sandra concluded, raising her eyebrows in mock fear as she gulped her beer.

"Not to worry. I don't intend to horn in on Zita. Peter is an unknown quality; I prefer a sure thing. Roland Arcara is crazy about me. And forget the Mafia rumors; they've been circling around his dad for years. Nothing to it."

Darlene leaned in closer, "You can't see him from where you're sitting, but there's a handsome guy at the end of the bar staring at us. I wonder who he is and what he does?" She elbowed Sandra in the side. "He's coming this way."

Sandra studied him as he swaggered toward them. His well-cut sport shirt and Armani slacks complemented his dark good looks and muscular body. She took in his build, his thick curly brown hair, brown eyes and easy smile. About 40. A real macho man. As the stranger approached, Sandra put on her "come-join-us-face." He sat, tugged at his collar, then directed his infectious smile first at Darlene, then Sandra. His eyes lingered on Sandra's breasts.

"Hi girls. Sorry, I should say women. I'm Bruce Miller. You're much too pretty to be drinking alone. How about I buy you a drink? A threesome can be real friendly."

After exchanging names, Bruce told them he was a solid citizen from Tulsa, a district manager for Temptress Products working out of his condo. He'd been a Boy Scout, went to church occasionally, wasn't a serial killer, and was divorced.

Following three beers and the "what do you do?" litany, the horoscope bit, and "What's your favorite TV program?" plus office humor, Darlene was ready to head home. She picked up her purse and package. "It's getting late and I have to work tomorrow. Are you coming, Sandra?"

"What's your hurry? It's only 11 o'clock."

"It's late for me. Kat expects me to be at the reception desk on the dot of nine. Won't your babysitter be anxious to leave?"

"Don't be a prig. Stay and have another drink. You needn't worry about Mrs. Brody. She's a dear. I told you she'll stay as long as necessary," Sandra countered with a hint of annoyance in her voice.

Darlene pressed, "I *really* think we should go."

"Don't play mother," Sandra snapped.

"I'll be glad to drive her home," Bruce said.

Darlene looked at her friend, but Sandra avoided her eyes. She was behaving like a woman prisoner on her first date after confinement,

Liz Barzda

savoring all the bull this bozo was spouting. *Good* Lord, *she's tipsy*, Darlene noticed.

"I'll be talking to you," Sandra slurred in a dismissive tone.

"Did I tell you about our new intimate apparel line? Gorgeous materials and patterns," Bruce said while putting his arm around Sandra and squeezing her shoulder. "I can get you anything you want, wholesale. You'd be a knockout in our new number called 'Midnight Magic', a black satin nightgown sans panties, but with a matching hair ribbon. Cute, eh?"

"I'll pass on the lingerie," Sandra said, "but another beer would be nice. "She held up her empty glass.

Darlene looked at her friend with resignation. She rose, said a quick goodbye and left.

Sandra couldn't remember when she had such a good time. Three beers led to a fourth, than a fifth. Bruce nibbled her ear while his hand roamed up her thigh.

"Umm," she said in a cutsey voice.

"You are adorable. I've never met anyone so sexy," he said as he squeezed her leg, sending ripples of pleasure through her body.

She could feel the dampness between her legs. It was exciting, yet confusing. Was the room spinning, or was she just imaging all this? It didn't matter. Nothing that felt this good could be bad. But was there something she had to do? Something about going home?

"Listen, lil' darling. Let's go someplace more interesting. You deserve better than a bar," Bruce said as he took her arm and helped her up from the chair.

"I think I should be going home or something like that," Sandra giggled.

"Don't you worry. I'll take you home. I wouldn't leave a lovely creature like you stranded," he reassured her as he gripped her buttock and said," You're the tastiest thing that's happened to me since my divorce."

He propelled her through the parking lot, zigzagging through rows of cars. He settled her in his car, stroked her hair long, soft hair, and began kissing her throat, her ears, and her face. His breathing raced along while his hands explored her body. "It's so good," he groaned. Sandra felt his hardness pressing against her. She mirrored his pleasure, oblivious of time and place.

"This is too good to enjoy here," her newfound friend said as he started

Bittersweet House

the car. It seemed no time at all that they left the Seafair suburbs and were parked in a Marriott Courtyard Motel back parking lot.

"What are we doing here?" Sandra asked.

"Just getting to know each other, you sweet thing," Bruce said as he encircled her waist and pulled her to him. He kissed her passionately, his tongue exploring her mouth, his lips dribbling kisses down her neck. His fingers rubbed her nipples, his hands repeatedly squeezed her breasts.

"You're a horny bastard," Sandra tittered, "but I love it."

"There's a lot more coming your way," Bruce promised as his hands massaged her thighs. He retrieved a vodka bottle from the glove compartment and took a couple of long gulps. "Have some."

Sandra pressed her lips to the bottle and drank. His breathing accelerated. "Here have another swig."

"No thanks. I probably had enough."

"Don't be silly. It'll make you feel good, so mellow."

"Okay. Why not?"

"Told you you'd like it. And I have something else you'd like." He brought her hand to his crotch, working it up, down, and around.

"Oh darling, this is so great. I want more. Let's go in where we'd be much more comfortable." He opened the door, came around her side and eased her out of the car.

"We're going to have the best fucking time you've ever had," he laughed as he helped her steady her steps. "And I mean that literally."

"Promise?" Sandra said with a giggle.

"You can bet your pretty pussy on that." They hurried to the motel lobby. He signed the register, handed the clerk a credit card, ignored checkout time and continental breakfast spiel, then guided Sandra to the room.

"That king-size bed looks inviting, lil' darlin. First, let's have a drink to whet our thirst for love." He half filled two tumblers with vodka. "Here's yours, beautiful."

Sandra watched him gulp the drink. "I think I had enough."

"Come on sweetie, just a little drink. Guaranteed it won't hurt you, just make you happy. Hey, we deserve to be happy, don't we?"

She downed her vodka and slurred, "This is sush a niffy idea."

"Told you you'd like it. And I have something else you'd like." He took her hand and placed it on his penis. "Feel how hard it is," he groaned. "Ready just for you." He kept her hand there. "Pet me," he pleaded. Sandra squeezed him and laughed, "How do you like that?"

37

Liz Barzda

"Love it," Bruce moaned, then helped her out of shorts and top and eased her bikini pink panties down to her ankles. She held onto him as she stepped out of them.

"Seems to me I shouldn't be here," she said in a tiny voice.

"Don't say that. I can hardly wait and neither can you."

He carried her to bed and slipped his hand between her legs, squeezed, then stroked her vagina. She gasped as he kissed that very secret part of her. Kevin never did that. Moaning with pleasure, she responded to him, lost in the deliciousness of it all. In a hoarse voice she whispered, "Please God, don't let it stop."

His breathing quickened as he picked up the petting pace. "You're a lovely creature. I have to taste all of you," Bruce licked her breast, stomach, thighs, and the wetness between her legs.

She cried out in relief as he entered her, probing faster, harder, deeper.

Sandra's motions mirrored his. Time and place had no meaning. Her body craved rapture and responded to his rhythm his thrust, his hunger.

Chapter 8

Through partially opened blinds, slivers of sunlight beamed into Sandra's eyes. She squinted and groaned, then raised her head. She scanned the room. Where the hell was she? Just maneuvering her legs out of bed made the room swim. Christ, her head hurt! She hobbled to a round table and glimpsed the ashtray matchbook--Courtyard by Marriott, Seacliff, Connecticut. She leaned on the table and took in the room; a clone of a thousand American motel rooms with its round table, chairs, dresser, desk, night stands and bed. Her eyes focused on the bed. "Oh God," she moaned. The disheveled sheet still held the contour of a body. It was all so fuzzy. She dug into her memory and recalled the good-looking guy she and Darlene met at the bar. What was his name?--Bruce, that was it. He sweet-talked her into the car, then kissed her face, neck and fondled her breasts. She wondered what time he left. It didn't matter. He'd gone and she had to get dressed.

The lovemaking in bed. Why couldn't she picture the details? She must have been crazy to drink so much, to let herself go. Okay, she'd been tipsy before and played around a little, nothing serious, just some harmless kissing. This episode was different, serious for a married woman.

What if he didn't wear a condom? Surely, she had asked him. It came back to her. "Don't you worry your pretty little pussy, I'll take care of it," he had said. She sat down, put her head in her hands and blubbered, "I'll die if I become pregnant, or Kevin finds out what I've done. He'll never forgive me. He might leave me and take Tiffany. Lord, no. Oh God, help me." She checked her wristwatch on the dresser--6:o'clock. Kevin would be home from the night shift around 7:30. There was time to call Linda. Good old reliable Linda. Thank God for her. Her sister wouldn't let her

Liz Barzda

down. She'd drive her home and never tell a soul about the motel incident. First would come the lecture, then Sis would forgive her. Again.

She dialed Linda's number and a sleepy voice answered after the third ring, "Hello."

"Linda, please come and get me. I'm at the Courtyard by Marriott Motel on Route 67, room 103. I'm in trouble. Please, Linda, hurry."

"What the hell are you doing at a motel at this ungodly hour?"

"Don't ask, just come."

"I hope this isn't one of your pranks."

"No, it isn't. Please, I need you." Sandra hung up the phone and let out a deep breath. How would she explain her stupid behavior to big sister who never seemed to have problems? She paced the room. Bruce got her drunk, took advantage of her. Yes, that's what she'd say. Sounds plausible.

Yet, some subconscious sense of responsibility strained to poke through. Sis seldom chastised her for minor transgressions, but this time would be different. Linda would level the big guns at her. The vocal volley would go something like this: "Sandra, bar hopping with your single friends is dumb. Suppose Kevin found out. What do you think he'd do? You're messing up your life. Promise you'll never do it again. And mean it."

So much for last night's foolishness. She'd put it out of her mind. Shit! She just remembered, that damn long green, skirt and see-through top she just couldn't live without was still on layaway. If she didn't pay up, she'd lose the deposit. Lousy timing, but big sister would come through after she'd cooled down. And how about the tank top she bought last night? Heavens knows where that ended up.

Then there's the other problem. Kevin repeatedly asked her not to charge anything until the bills were paid. She recalled him blurting, "We can't afford to buy anything now. You know it's tough on one salary. Things will get better when I get my promotion."

Linda, too, warned her about maxing out her card and offered to draw up a budget. "I really don't need it," Sandra insisted. Now, frightened and humiliated, she realized she was being unfair. Sis often shielded her extravagance and bar-hopping from their parents, as well as from Kevin.

Sandra turned on the shower full force. Perhaps the stinging water would erase last night's craziness. Crazy and dangerous, Sandra admitted. Linda was right. No more bar-hopping, except with Kevin. No more shopping sprees.

A hard scrub, especially between her legs, didn't remove the memory of his dick penetrating her repeatedly. *Admit it, you enjoyed every thrust.* With

Bittersweet House

an intense effort, Sandra tried to direct her thoughts into more responsible channels. She'd get a part-time job in September when Tiffany started kindergarten. She shut her eyes and asked God for a deal. If He would make sure Kevin never found out, and allow her life to stay intact, she'd vow never again to be a pick up.

#

Coal black clouds rolled in like vultures about to pounce on a weakened prey. That's just how Linda felt—a weakened creature without support. Distant thunder and windswept trees along the Merritt Parkway added to her feeling of despair. Rain began to fall, their drops matching her tears. She blinked several times to clear her vision and her mind. *Isn't it enough that* Christopher's *treacherous behavior with* a *mistress and baby nearly destroyed me? Now Sandra calls from a motel in near hysterics, begging me to come.* She dreaded to think what Sandra had done.

Is there anything good left in my life? Linda wondered as she raced into the city in twenty minutes. She hurried through the motel lobby, glanced at the night clerk and headed for room 103. Her only concern was to find Sandra and get her home.

Linda pounded on the door. "Sandra, it's Linda. Let me in."

The door opened and a subdued Sandra said, "Thanks for coming." She ran her fingers through her wet hair, "Please don't lecture me."

Linda shot back, "What the hell is going on here?" Her eyes roamed around the room, zeroing in on the disheveled bed. "Who was here with you? Somebody you picked up?" She grabbed Sandra's arm. "You must be crazy."

"Don't," Sandra implored. "It isn't what you think. I didn't go out looking for this. It just happened. Darlene and I were out for some fun. We had a few drinks, met a nice guy. Things got out of hand."

"What do you mean out of hand? You're talking like a high school kid. How can you be so as stupid to go to a motel with a man you don't know? He could be a serial killer. He could have AIDS! What are you exposing yourself to? And Kevin? And *Tiffany?*"

"Please stop. I know you're right. I've been beating up on myself. I just want to go home."

Linda's tone turned cold, "This is not a little thing, Sandra."

Sobbing now, her sister answered, "I know. I'm sorry."

Linda checked the room. "Want these?" she smirked, handing Sandra the pink panties that lay on the floor. "Now get dressed." They walked briskly down the hall, with Linda virtually propelling her wayward sibling out the door and into the car. She loved Sandra, but at times wanted to throttle her. Yet, she couldn't give up on her.

Linda remembered 6-year-old Sandra on a cloudless summer day pedaling her new two-wheeler, chestnut hair blowing in the wind. With a wide smile, she thanked her big sister for holding the seat and guiding her. Then gripping the handlebars, she yelled, "Let me go. I can do it myself." She fell, scraping her knees and cried. Linda picked her up, wiped her tears and told her everything was all right.

It seemed to Linda she'd never stopped rescuing Sandra.

A clap of thunder broke Linda's reverie and brought her back to the present. Halfway to Sandra's house, rain began to pelt the windshield. The weather was as bleak as her marriage and her sister's shenanigans. Linda blinked her eyes, attempting to hold back tears. But she couldn't keep from probing. "Don't you know you're playing with fire? Just suppose your pickup is HIV positive; you could be dead in a year. Did he use a condom?"

"Yes, he did," Sandra replied without with downcast eyes. "You don't have to refer to him as a pickup. He was just a sweet guy I met. We had fun over a few drinks. Things weren't supposed to have gone that far. But they did. It could happen to anyone."

"What about Kevin? Suppose he finds out?"

"Kevin doesn't have to know," Sandra said, twisting the chain on her purse. "You wouldn't tell him, would you? Please don't. You know I'm sorry."

Linda parked the car in front of the house and grabbed her sister's hand. "You know I love you, but what you're doing could be disastrous. I want your word that it will *never happen again*. Promise."

"I promise. Thanks for bailing me out. I don't mean to do these stupid things. They just seem to happen. Tell me you forgive me."

Linda released Sandra's hand, hugged her and said, "I forgive you. Remember, you're a mother and a wife. You don't want to lose your husband and home for one crazy, wild night."

"No, no, of course not," Sandra scrambled out of the car. "Now I have to face Mrs. Brody's inquiring eyes."

Linda shook her head as she watched her sister scoot down the path. *Will Sandra ever learn?*

Chapter 9

Five o'clock on Friday, Linda checked the assignment board and sighed with relief. There were no additional stories beside her name, just the usual six and 11 o'clock news spots. Her Connecticut Chronicle interview was due Thursday; sufficient time to meet the interviewee, write the story and arrange for taping.

As she approached her desk, her eyes zeroed on Christopher's picture, with a swift movement, she tossed it in the drawer. She couldn't stand looking at his smiling face.

Work was her only salvation. Despite her problems, she still loved the hum of the newsroom with its ringing phones, clicking keyboards and network shows flashing on monitors. Attaining a celebrity interview other reporters coveted, reporting the local and international news, meeting the public, and signing autographs at charity events gave her a high. She loved it all. At times she couldn't believe her good fortune at becoming anchor.

Linda switched on the overhead monitor to catch the live news and material emanating through the wire. Two local stories needed additional details.

She jumped as arms encircled her shoulders. "You startled me, Ron."

He held on to her. "I heard that you got sick because you missed me. A week covering the Governors' Conference in Colorado and you fall apart without me. You did miss me, didn't you?"

Linda disentangled his arms. "Sure, partner." She gave him a quirky smile. "Whatever you say."

"I really missed you. It's more fun working with you than catering to those publicity-hungry politicians. Tell me it's true that management had a difficult time finding a competent replacement for me."

Liz Barzda

Linda rolled her eyes. "Brad Jamieson was adequate, but couldn't compare to you."

"I figured as much. Seriously, I trust you didn't have anything contagious. Just kidding, you look kind of tense. You okay?"

"Being sick is the pits. Had an upset stomach, but I'm fine now. Sue Wong sat in for me?"

"I'm sure Sue did fine." He looked into her eyes with admiration, "But she certainly doesn't have your mellifluous voice."

"Thanks. You know how to make a gal feel good."

"How about dinner?"

"No thanks. I'll get something from the cafeteria."

"Not those cardboard sandwiches? Can I, at least, tempt you with a corn beef on rye and a beer? Guaranteed to improve the state of your health."

"Really, I need to catch up. Maybe another time."

"Sure," he said as he turned away with slumped shoulders.

Linda watched him go. He was really a nice guy and first-class anchor person. But she didn't want to think about men now, any man. She headed to the dressing room for makeup repair before the 6 o'clock news: a redo of mascara, blusher, lip gloss and a brush through her blonde hair.

She scanned her face in the mirror and noticed slight lines around her eyes. Time for a face-lift? God, she hoped not. Surely, she had more years before the camera. Some mature women, especially those anchoring the news, were visible these days. After all, 42 isn't old. Some considered it middle age. She considered it her prime.

When gray-haired women hold anchor spots, vying with men, then they'll be equals, she mused. Probably never happen. Too bad.

Despite the inequities of the business, Linda was mindful of her fans and appreciated their loyalty when they e-mailed or called the station. It was nice to know they enjoyed her work and her appearance. She especially appreciated WSEA's cameramen and newspaper reporters who referred to her as TV's Golden Girl. How long will she remain TV's Golden Girl?

As long as possible.

#

Linda returned to the office after a quick dinner in the cafe. She checked the 11 o'clock news items, and jotted down ideas for Connecticut Chronicle. Following the late news report, her shift was virtually over.

Bittersweet House

"Let's cap off the day," Ron said following his turn bidding good night to the viewing public. "I can use a drink." He dropped his program notes into the desk slot and searched her eyes for acceptance. "Hey, I'm not hitting on you, just being friendly. I don't think Christopher would mind."

Linda smiled. "I'm sure he wouldn't. Let's go." *Why not, I've nothing to come home to.*

They walked the three blocks to Ryan's Bar, its cool dark ambiance a welcome escape from the July heat. Linda headed for a corner table, preferring to be less visible; luckily those rimming the traffic pattern were taken. With effort, she smiled at media colleagues. Ron waved to his cohorts across the room and back-slapped those in his path.

The bartender made a beeline for their table. "Nice to see you folks. We've missed you." He stared at Linda with admiration. "What can I get you, beautiful? Where've you been? Watch you on the tube. You're the best thing WSEA has. Hope they know that."

"Thanks Ted. Be a pal and tell my boss," Linda said, attempting a smile. "A Coors Light would help remove the salt mines taste."

Ted glanced at Ron. "What's yours?"

"Guinness Stout and bring some nuts."

He watched Ted walk away and laughed, "The guy's mesmerized by you. I can understand that."

"Let's not blow things out of proportion."

"Just telling the truth. Here's more. I've been tracking the weekly ratings. Your show's doing great. And so is our 6 and 11 o'clock news. Contract renewal is a sure thing."

"You're always so positive, Ron."

"Why not? The ratings have been consistently high. What's to worry?"

How about a husband with a mistress and a baby? Or a 42-year old female anchor in a medium that glorifies youth? Linda forced a smile. "We've been a team for five years. I guess the public isn't clicking us off."

"Why should they? We've worked our asses off to get where we are. Remember those green years in rinky-dink TV stations? How long in the trenches, twenty years? We deserve the salaries and the perks."

Ron's words jogged her memory: the college years working gratis as a part-time intern, the first break after graduation as a gofer at a 10,000 watt radio station in the Connecticut boonies, and then the biggie -- an honest-to-goodness TV channel, admittedly, a minor one, as the weather

45

girl at Norwalk's channel 20. A tough climb to a major market, but worth the sacrifices. Linda wanted it to continue. The satisfying work and the camaraderie of her peers were paramount; however one needn't dismiss the recognition and perks that came with the job.

"Yeah, I sure do remember those great character-forming salad days. Wendy the Witch kept after me to send my video to major markets -- my first on-camera reporting job in Portland, Maine wasn't her idea of TV fame. Sorry, I promised not to talk about my ex, but she's like a wasp; the more you swat, the more determined she is to sting. Would you believe, she still thinks we should reconcile?"

Linda couldn't stifle a grin. "Try another tactic. If Wendy thought you were interested in someone else, like Sue Wong for instance, maybe she'd buzz off."

"Maybe."

Ted smiled broadly as he approached Linda and carefully set down her beer and glass. He plunked down Ron's and asked, "Anything else, sport?"

"A little privacy would be nice."

"Suit yourself."

Ron drank from the bottle. "Ah, liquid gold." His eyes locked onto Linda and his mouth spread into a grin. "You playing cupid?"

Linda filled her glass with beer, sipped a little and said, "No, but I think Sue has a yen for you. Forget I said that. Seriously, can't you feel her eyes on you?"

"Never noticed. Let's forget about my ex--and the sometime women in my life." He reached for her hand. "I'd rather talk about you."

She withdrew her hand. "I'd rather you didn't."

"Why not? It's all in the name of friendship. Christopher wouldn't mind. He knows I'm fond of you. What do you think we discussed at WSEA parties? You, of course. I've told him what a lovely human being you are, and talented as well. I pointed out that you could easily make the top New York TV market if you chose. Christopher doesn't say much, but his smile says a lot."

He doesn't say much because he's occupied with his own secrets. "Good that you mentioned Christopher. Let's keep my husband in mind. And let's change the subject."

Ron brushed back the stray strands of hair from his forehead, his habit when nervous. "I'm not fond of you, I'm crazy about you. You must know it. Maybe I shouldn't be so damn honest, but I can't help it."

Bittersweet House

"Don't, Ron. We're good friends, and I'm flattered. Our relationship has to be professional. That's the only way we can work together. Let's keep it that way." *Not that Christopher would care; he'd jump for joy for a chance to straighten out his life.*

"Okay. I'll hold my peace."

"Ron, I don't mean to be unkind; we're colleagues and nothing more."

"If you say so, Linda."

"You know I'm right. I think we'd better go."

"Right. I'll get the check."

He waved Ted over and paid the tab. They exited the bar onto steamy streets. She felt as if she couldn't breathe. Was it the humidity or the state of her marriage that was choking her? She glanced at Ron. *Forget this conversation. With* a *half-dead marriage, who needs more complications?*

Ron kept silent until they reached the parking garage. "Linda, I'm sorry I spoke out of turn. Forget everything I said. My big mouth ran away with my common sense. Colleagues, right?"

"Sure. It's forgotten."

"You got it. Let's shake on that," he said extending his hand.

She shook his hand and attempted to cover up his embarrassment. "Since when have we been so formal with each other? Look, it's been a rough day, would you like to go to my place for coffee?"

"You don't have to placate me, partner." Ron's face lit up, "Just kidding, I'd love it." He followed in his car as her Lexus hummed along the city streets onto I-95, then to Seacliff's affluent suburbs and the big country house. The empty house. A house without a man, but not tonight, Linda thought.

#

In the refreshingly cool den, Linda served coffee and chocolate liqueur. How comfy to drink and converse with a man at home. How long had it been since she and her husband sat and chatted together?

"Is Christopher off on a business trip?" Ron asked as Linda refilled their liqueur glasses.

"Yes. He'll probably call tonight and I expect him home this weekend. Why?"

"I know he travels a lot. Don't you get lonely?"

Liz Barzda

"Of course, I miss him. But it's business, so I play the dutiful wife and pretend I don't miss him. It's easier that way."

"Tell me to mind my own business if I'm getting too personal."

"I'm not offended. It's a natural question." Linda noticed his empty glass. "Would you like another or a white wine?"

"White wine would be great." She could feel his eyes on her as she sauntered across the room to refill their glasses. It was gratifying to know that a man admired her swaying hips as she walked. How odd that she could enjoy his attention when her life was in shreds.

He gave her a "Here's looking at you" toast. They laughed at his Bogart imitation. "Did I get it right?"

"Who knows," she answered between sips of wine that slid down her throat like water on velvet.

They talked of favorite movies and laughed over their early TV days. "I looked like a wide-eyed-rabbit," she admitted. "My hair resembled Frankenstein's bride. Talk about big hair! I wore a rust-colored leisure suit on my first job as a TV reporter in Mobile, Alabama. Man, I thought I was in the big-time."

At ease with one another, time sped by. Linda topped their drinks. They discussed the recently-aired Indian documentary on sex and love. Its exciting aura engulfed them. Ron moved closer to her on the sofa. "Linda, have you any idea how I've longed for you? I want to love you and to have you love me back."

"Ron, I told you we're just good friends." But even to herself her words seem to lack conviction.

"Being with you almost daily and not allowed to hold you and kiss you is like giving me a beautifully wrapped Christmas present and then tell me I'm not allowed to open it."

The buzz in her head was rather pleasant. *Have I had too much to drink? So what? I haven't felt this good in days.* She gathered Ron's hands in hers. "I didn't mean to make you unhappy."

"You can make it up to me." He pulled her to him pressing his lips on hers. He stroked her hair. His eyes met hers and pleaded for acceptance.

"Ron, this is not a good idea." It felt good to be desired, but she wouldn't, couldn't. *I know what it is to love someone, but love has its booby traps.* A dim voice in her subconscious cautioned, *Be careful, you're vulnerable.*

"I'm sorry if I got out of line. I didn't mean to upset you."

"You didn't. Don't look so chagrined. It's really okay." She gave him a weak smile and led him to the foyer.

Bittersweet House

They said their good nights. She shut the door, closed her eyes and stood there for what seemed like eons. She would *not* think of her wayward husband; rather, she'd concentrate on something uplifting like Ron's friendship and the Barren Babes. She loved being a part of the BB's and valued their support. Yet, she felt hollow. Not a sound, nor movement in the house. A feeling of dread washed over her. *Is this how loneliness feels?*

Chapter 10

Zita ran her fingers through her short curly hair as she eyeballed Parker Advertising Agency's daily agenda. She mentally prioritized the projects: at ten o'clock a review of Seacliff Shores Retirement Village and Regency Condos television tapes with the photographer and copywriter, and at four o'clock--an absolute must--a consultation with her key people to finalize million-dollar advertising campaign for Seacliff's new upscale Shoreline Mall. The campaign culminated in an "invitation only" Starlight Fashion Extravaganza fund raiser for the Cancer Fund. Zita and her staff spent weeks carrying out the plan. Tying up loose ends required immediate attention.

"Final stage time, folks," she announced at four o'clock. Seated at the conference table with her were photographer, copywriter, and sales manager.

Zita leaned back into her chair, her gray eyes roving to each staff member. "This is where we are: As you know, local celebrities, professional actors, TV anchors, radio personalities and visiting celebrities have been televised in the mall's various stores, highlighting the merchandise. The hype on television, newspapers, and retailers' web pages culminates in the Starlight Fashion Extravaganza. We're zeroing in on a store a day. To create a glamorous foreground for the merchandise, the principals have been photographed with the best lighting in these posh shops. Print, TV ads and features have already appeared. Fashion show details have been ironed out and rehearsals are going well."

Zita turned her attention to her photographer. "Ken, work your camera magic and lighting for the show."

"No problem. When I'm through with them and they see the

Bittersweet House

tapes, they'll think they've been shot by one of Hollywood's great cinematographers," he promised.

Zita cupped her hand under her chin and fixed her eyes on her copywriter. "Marilyn, only a week left. What have you come up?"

"This is how I see it," she offered. "Beauty and prestige are the ticket. They complement each other like Yin and Yang. People covet prestige and respond to beauty, but don't want to be blatant about it. My copy says it's smart to be in the know. A plethora of uniquely gorgeous clothes and home furnishings await them-- at the new Seacliff Shoreline Mall."

"Good, Marilyn. Remember to emphasize the Extravaganza." Zita nodded to her sales manager, Ted. "You're next." She considered him her alter ego as they were on the same wavelength. She conceived the campaign concept; he had the competitive personality to sell her idea.

"The local celebrities and actors are all on board. They're delighted to give their time for the Cancer Fund. Of course, free publicity helps to sweeten the pot. All details with the Mall Management have been completed."

Zita mulled everything over. "Good work, Ted. It pays to point out the free publicity." Zita looked from one to another of her staff. "That's it. Thanks for your input on the Seacliff Shores and the Regency Condos projects. I believe we've hit all bases. See you on Monday." The agenda completed, Marlyn, Kenneth and Ted filed out, chorusing "Good night" to their boss.

Zita returned to her office, sat back in her black and chrome chair, stared at the color-splashed modern painting over the credenza and sighed with satisfaction. The thought of the Seacliff Shoreline Mall's million-dollar advertising budget brought a smile to her lips. She pushed the chair back, crossed the room to the credenza and poured a glass of chilled Chardonnay. The wine slid down her throat, producing a soothing inner feeling.

She sat, placed both hands behind her head and stretched. She deserved the new Mall advertising contract and she deserved her success. It took her twenty years to build the business. It grew, as did friendships with Linda, Margaret and Katherine. But Zita and Linda had a special bond. Since they were college roomies, their loyalty and respect for each other deepened with time. They laughed together, reminisced about college love affairs, discussed business, and talked about their marriages--Linda's seemingly successful, hers a definite disaster. Zita took a deep gulp of wine and coughed. Just thinking about that swine David made her gag. She rose and

51

Liz Barzda

paced the room. Memories that should have stayed buried surfaced. She saw their first home, a four-room apartment, which David assured her was ample since they had agreed a family wasn't in the immediate future.

"Without children, we're free to travel and to concentrate on our careers," he said. When she equivocated about being childless forever, he grabbed her waist and danced her around declaring, "The world is over-populated and too many people are depleting the natural resources. Only fooling, dear. If a baby is what you really want, we'll have one--some day." Then he laughed, attempting to make light of a serious subject.

Zita acknowledged that David didn't give two hoots about over-population; his major concern was continuing a free-wheeling life style.

When her promotion on the paper came through, and David was made a loan officer in the bank, they purchased their first home. Despite the pleasures of a carefree life, Zita's yearning for a child took precedence over money and career.

David made no attempt to hide his displeasure. "Are you certain this is what you want? Can you put up with 2 o'clock feedings, dirty diapers and a crying infant?"

"Yes, it's what I want. You may not think it's what you want, but I know once the baby comes, you'll love it. You truly will. Everyone says so," Zita remembered with a lump in her throat beseeching her husband.

She recalled her joy when the doctor informed her that invitro-fertilization was a solution for some women unable to conceive. Unfortunately, not for her; the program failure shattered her dreams. Why couldn't she block out the eighteen months of painful and expensive treatments she went through?

Always the baby—conversations, plans and the cost of producing an infant was more than David could stand. He took off with a 20-year old bank clerk

Two decades of marriage down the drain. Zita vowed that her business was all that mattered. Men were for sex only. *David, rot in hell, wherever you are.*

She thought of beautiful Linda with that handsome hunk of a husband and wondered about their relationship. Christopher seemed to be continually traveling on business.

Perhaps she would learn something at Saturday's BB's luncheon. *Don't think the worst of Christopher, give him the benefit of a doubt,* Zita told herself.

Bittersweet House

#

Katherine checked the computer printout of La Petite Spa's latest balance sheet. It confirmed that she could eke out the monthly payment of $4,200 on her $500,000 loan, but the renovation and redecorating overrun costs exceeded the available cash. Katherine glanced out the window and took a deep breath. If only Scott would ask his father for a low interest loan. He said he would. She had no doubt that she could repay the debt in time. She envisioned her lover handing over a half million dollar check that would wipe away the debt and save her hide. *I'll give him one more chance to get the loan from Big Daddy.*

She couldn't lose the business, not with all the planning and sweat it took to build La Petit Spa. In her mind's eye, she saw herself as a little girl cutting out pictures of beautifully dressed women with perfect bodies.

"When I grow up, that's how I'm going to look. And I'm going to have beautiful things around me," she would proclaim to anyone within earshot.

Working for a paycheck didn't build her dream business-- Grandpa's money did. Her paternal Pennsylvania grandparents, hard-working, first-generation Hungarian-Americans, knew how to create a business. Tight-fisted Grandpa built desirable, moderately-priced houses. Intelligent Grandma invested his profits.

The only word Katherine could think of was shock, utter shock when she inherited a million dollars. An only grandchild, she was eternally grateful to this wonderful man for his generosity that helped fulfill her ambition. *I owe it to Grandpa and Grandma to succeed. That was then, and this* is *now,* Katherine thought, and she would resolve her problems any way possible.

She meandered through the Spa's reception, massage, skin care and dressing rooms, checked supplies and removed yesterday's flowers. The cleaning service would detail the entire establishment; nevertheless, she believed in a white-glove inspection. The Spa was her baby.

In her private powder room adjacent to the office, Katherine sat at her dressing table and gazed into the mirror. Her reflection dredged up memories better forgotten. Memories that refused to stay buried--like her surprise pregnancy. Scott stupidly asked how it happened. "You know how it happened. You insisted on not wearing a condom. Remember saying, 'Just this once. It'll be okay. Nothing will happen."

Scott pressed for abortion with his insidious references to a baby

Liz Barzda

controlling their lives, the loss of freedom and romance. When she ignored his lectures, he spelled it out for her. "I don't need a baby in my life. I can't handle it. If you love me, you'd understand. The procedure will be our secret. No one need know."

It was two years since the abortion, yet the terrible scene still haunted her. She thought she'd put it to rest; but like a sore that wouldn't heal, it oozed and oozed. She shook her head in an attempt to dislodge the haunting confession.

Katherine stood up and ran her hands over her stomach and down. She finally cleared her mind of the abortion, but the lack of money and Scott's horniness still bugged her. She bit her lip. *How the hell am I going to get the loan and rein in lover boy?*

Chapter 11

The black BMW zipped along at 80 per, blurring images of Connecticut's gold coast towns and cities. Trees, vegetation and rest areas receded as the car sped along the highway. In an hour, Christopher would be at home with Linda in Seacliff, but his thoughts remained in Boston with Betti and Sean.

He replayed scenes in Boston's General Hospital where he and Betti prayed for their baby as the boy struggled for life. They sat by his bedside for hours waiting for the doctor to tell them their son would recover. Finally, Dr. Skubus announced, "Sean's fever broke. His temperature dropped to near normal and he's past the crisis." Christopher pumped the doctor's hand repeatedly, as he said, "Thank you, doctor," to himself.

"Thank you, thank you," Betti said, tears streaming down her face. "And bless you."

Christopher felt euphoric over his son's recovery. He kissed Betti again and again. They clung together, overwhelmed with happiness. Never in his 48 years had he felt so complete. Infused with a sense of well being because of Betti and Sean, Linda and Seacliff seemed far off.

He'd been gone six days and hadn't once called her. Time revolved around visiting his son in the hospital and comforting the mother of his child. Still, the problem of his marriage weighed on his heart.

Conflicting thoughts of the two women brought on a throbbing headache. He pictured his wife as a swan: graceful, beautiful, aristocratic, his mistress (how he detested that word) a panda bear: warm and cuddly.

He recalled the day he literally bumped into Betti Novak, nearly knocking her off her feet as he rushed to exit the Boston office of Great Britain Exploration, Ltd.

"Shit," she yelled, as her purse and art portfolio flew out of her hands.

Christopher reached out and grabbed her around the waist before she swayed off-balance.

"Are you okay? I'm so sorry. Did I hurt you?" He bent down and retrieved her purse and portfolio. "I'm such an ass rushing out like that." He held her belongings with one hand and put his arm around her shoulder. "Here, lean on me. You look a little shaky."

"Why can't you watch where you're going?" she said brushing his arm away while attempting to steady herself.

"I'm usually not so clumsy. Honestly. Look, at least let me make amends." He searched her eyes and smiled. "A drink might make both of us feel better. There's a decent bar around the corner. It's 5 o'clock. Nobody works beyond 5. How about it?"

"I do. At five, I'm just getting my second wind. I've got a lot of work to do. I was about to run a business errand before the interruption."

"How could it hurt to have a little time out? A break would do you good."

She turned her cat's eyes on him and the corners of her mouth lifted slightly. "I suppose I could use a drink. It would be nice to sit down."

They introduced themselves and sauntered to a nearby pub. The long bar rapidly filled up with commuters and natives. Christopher claimed the last two seats and flagged down a waiter.

"What's yours?" the harried bartender growled when he finally came over.

"I'll have a Cabernet Sauvignon."

"Make mine a Merlot," Christopher said. He lifted his eyebrows when the server left. "What a bundle of joy he is."

"He'll never win the employee of the month award," Betti responded.

"It's nice to see you relax and smile. Forgive me for staring, but did anyone ever tell you that you have beautiful hazel eyes?

She smirked, "Actually, yes."

"I'm not putting you on. Your eyes really do glow."

"Thanks for the compliment. But you haven't told me where you were rushing to."

"A client. I had an appointment with the VP of our South American Division."

"Sounds important. I'm sorry if I've upset your time table."

Bittersweet House

"No problem, Betti. Do you mind if I make a call?"

Before she could respond, he removed the cell phone from his jacket pocket, punched in the numbers, and left a message that there was an emergency and he would reschedule.

"I hope I didn't damage any of your artwork," Christopher said. "It is artwork, isn't it? Obviously, you're an artist at Boston's GBE, Ltd. What kind?"

"I'm sure the drawings are fine. They haven't been stepped nor sat on. To answer your question, I'm the assistant art director. I've seen you walking through occasionally. Now I can put a name to the face. And just what is *your* position with the company?"

"I'm their telecommunications consultant."

Betti's eyes widened, "Impressive title."

Christopher took all of her in; tawny hair, like honey, eyes rimmed with dark lashes and a well-stacked figure. The kind of body any man would adore exploring. They had another drink, then managed to snag a table. He centered the conversation on her, asking about her work, hobbies, and whether she had a boyfriend.

"Not at the moment, but the situation is open to change. How about you? Married? Involved?"

"I'm married," he admitted, but didn't elaborate.

Betti regaled him with office gossip about R.B. Shelbourne, GBE Ldt.'s North American president. "Would you believe he bumped into me rounding a corner in the hall?" She gave out a light laugh. "Appears that happens to me a lot, doesn't it? Well, our esteemed president apologized profusely. To make sure I wasn't hurt, he patted my shoulders. 'Hurt anywhere?' I shook my head. 'How about here?' he asked, lightly touching my waist and hips. "I'm fine," I insisted. "Should I bring him up on sexual harassment?" Betti asked, feigning seriousness. "I'd be out of there so fast; there wouldn't be time to pick up my purse. Chances are I'd never see him again. If I do, I'll walk backwards. Oh, my God, I'm blabbing like a teenager. Tell me you're not a personal friend of Shelbourne's."

"I know him, of course, but we seldom socialize together." He reached for her hand. "Don't give it another thought. You're delightful," Christopher said, noticing that her tawny hair complimented her eyes. "And you have a lovely laugh, so genuine."

Betti looked at him intently, "Seeing as you're my protector, would you like to come up for coffee? I live in Beacon Hill, not too far from here."

Intrigued by this young woman who seemed to be at home with herself,

Liz Barzda

laughing and conversing without posturing, so different from the women in the corporate world or in Linda's TV sphere, Seacliff and home receded from his mind. They walked the cobblestoned streets to her Victorian townhouse where she made coffee and cold roast beef sandwiches. Classical music poured forth from FM radio. She talked about her job, Bean City, and all its cultural offerings. Christopher offered little of his background, other than he lived in Connecticut and his business travel often took him to Boston, New York, and abroad.

He couldn't get her out of his mind and found himself visiting whenever he could snatch a few hours or a couple of days away from business and his wife. Chris loved the attention she lavished on him. When he crossed the threshold, her eyes would shine like lighthouse beams directed solely on him. He delighted in the youthful energy Betti radiated whether cooking him a last-minute meal or caring for their son.

His mind lingered on the first time they made love. How could he ever forget it? It was like being shot with B-12 laced with 120 proof whiskey. They had twice gone out to dinner and a movie. As a special treat for her birthday, they dinned and danced at Boston's classy Ritz rooftop garden. The following day, she prepared a roast duck with fresh vegetables, followed by tea and cherry cobbler. "This is terrific," Christopher enthused, chewing on the crispy, dark duck skin. "Are you being especially nice to me just because I took you dancing?"

"You're practically salivating. If all it takes is cooking to keep you dancing with me, bring on the rations."

Christopher couldn't recall the last time Linda served a home-cooked meal. Generally they ate take-out or dined in restaurants.

"Let's forget desert. I'm stuffed," she said licking her lips, then searched his eyes. Her lips formed a smile, "I have something better than chocolate mousse in mind." They took the stairs two at a time to the third floor bedroom. He carried her to the bed, removed her dress, bra and panties and feather kissed her from her forehead to her toes. "I've been itching to do this since the first day I saw you." His breath raced like a tornado, "Make me a happy man. Tell me it was the same with you."

"Yes, yes," she cried. "I couldn't wait to feel you in me."

They'd made love--once, twice, three times--in the big brass bed, laughing over coarse jokes during foreplay, and then savoring acrobatic intercourse.

What started as a chance meeting, a flirtation, had escalated into a full-blown affair. He didn't mean for it to be so. At first he told himself

Bittersweet House

it was just a pleasant interlude. She was an antidote to those physically draining business trips and lonely hotels. The mutual attraction, based on fun, grew into something much deeper on her part. He didn't know how to end it. And then her pregnancy!

Much to his surprise, Betti's temper flared when he suggested she get an abortion. "I'll never kill my baby. Do you hear? I'll never kill my baby. I'll have this baby, with or without you."

"You're overwrought. Betti. This is an impossible situation. Let's talk it out."

"How dare you say I'm overwrought! You're talking about killing my baby--our baby," she screamed. "How could you?"

"Pull yourself together. I didn't know you had a temper. Don't let it get the best of you."

She glared at him with disgust. "You talk about temper. Yes, I have a temper," her voice rose in fury. "So what? You're pussyfooting around the real issue. Let's talk about murder, murdering our baby."

"Be reasonable, Betti. I can't handle this now. You know I'm married. Give me time to work things out."

"Don't throw your marriage status in my face. We're through. I can't bear you any longer. Get out," she shrieked and lunged at him. He stepped back and warded her off with his hands.

She covered her eyes and through choking breaths repeated, "Get out." She wouldn't look at him. Wouldn't answer his questions. He left feeling like the world's worst bastard.

On his last visit to Boston, he phoned her, but she wouldn't see him. He pleaded, "Let me help you. I bear half the responsibility here. Let me take care of your medical bills. I'll send you a monthly check for the baby."

He could picture her standing with her back to the brick kitchen wall in her townhouse, her face hard as marble. "I don't need money from a baby killer. I can pay my own way. My baby and I will survive. I want nothing to do with a man willing to suck his baby out of the mother's womb. You're history."

Christopher sent eight monthly four thousand dollar checks. None was cashed. Obviously, he was *out* of Betti's life-- permanently. Dealing with clients occupied his time, but not his mind. Guilt gnawed at him.

Betti repeatedly refused to take any more of his calls. What he figured to be the eighth month of her pregnancy, he phoned her workplace. "I'm sorry," said the receptionist, "Betti Novak is no longer employed here."

59

"Can you tell me when she left? This is her cousin, Jake. I haven't heard from her lately, and I have some important family business to tell her. I've been calling, but she now has an unlisted number. You wouldn't by any chance have it?"

"I'm sorry, sir, we can't give out personal information," the receptionist said, then disconnected.

He slammed the phone. "Fuck it all!" Even though she wouldn't speak to him, he did his duty and sent another check. No sweat. The generosity of his action assuaged his feeling of self-reproach.

He and Linda seldom discussed his 10 million dollar plus portfolio. The inherited Cooper money was his to do as he pleased. Digging into it wouldn't alter their life style. Their combined incomes assured a more than comfortable one.

His mind focused on the infant's welfare. At least the housing needn't be a problem, seeing Betti's mother left her the handsome Victorian townhouse. He would keep sending money. Perhaps one day she would relent and cash the checks. Then an unexpected phone call came. In a cold voice, Betti informed him that she didn't need his money, but decided to bank his checks for the baby. No, she wouldn't see him, but would have someone phone him when the baby was due.

The following month, Betti's cleaning woman called, "Miss Betti's in labor and I'm driving her to Boston General Hospital." Elated, Christopher swore that nothing would deter him from seeing his baby, if not at the birth, shortly after.

He remembered how nervous, yet proud, he felt inquiring about Betti and their baby. The nurse informed him that Betti Novak had an 8 lb.-3 oz. baby boy the night before. "She's in room 203. You've got to be the father. I can tell, you're beaming all over."

"Yes," Christopher admitted without hesitation.

He raced to the room and hesitated in the doorway. Betti's eyes were on her baby as he nursed at her breast. She looked up and smiled at her lover. Relieved, he placed the pink roses on her bedside table, kissed her lips and gingerly touched the baby's head. The sight of *his* baby suckling at his lover's breast filled him with joy. "Oh darling, I'm so happy you're here," Betti beamed. "I forgive you. I hope you forgive me for all the horrible things I said."

Christopher caressed her check. "We forgive each other."

"I couldn't be angry with you after I saw our beautiful child. Our baby." She reached for his hand. "He looks like you, eyes more green than blue. Would you like to hold him?" She placed the baby in his arms. Choked with unexpected emotion that seemed to well within him like a bursting dam, Christopher peered at his son, as if he were searching for his very essence. He wanted to hold him forever. "Chris, nothing seems important now just as long as we're together. I want to name him Sean after my father. Is that okay with you?"

"Sweetheart it's fine. It's a great name." Christopher placed Sean in her arms, then closed the door. He lay down by her with the baby between them, careful to leave enough breathing room.

"Don't worry," Betti said. "He's not as fragile as he looks."

"My son...he's perfect." Christopher closed his eyes and slept.

He awoke with a start. "What?"

She laughed at his bewilderment. "You dozed off for a few minutes."

He felt groggy, yet contented, still a part of him pricked at his truthfulness and loyalty. How about his wife, his home, his Seacliff life. Can he deny them? *Is there a part of him that still loves Linda?*

Chapter 12

Returning home from Boston, Christopher tried to ignore the downpour that hammered his windshield. The rain beat a tattoo and the windshield wipers swished: Betti, Linda, Betti, Linda. He gripped the wheel attempting to think of something, anything other than his problems. He'd think about Sean and his future. A baby required more than a roof over his head. He glanced in the mirror. A man with a deep furrowed brow, character lines around his mouth, and dark circles under his gray eyes, stared back at him. He looked his age.

Images of Linda kept appearing. It seemed a century ago that they were happy. As the years slipped by, sex remained lusty, but hardly explosive. Their marriage took on a predictable routine, albeit a pleasant one.

How would she greet him now? Would she scream at him and demand details of his trip to Boston? He couldn't face the barrage of questions. A tirade would undoubtedly ensue. His dashboard clock read 12:20 A.M. Surely, Linda would be in bed. Lord, he hoped so.

#

His conflicting emotions whirled around in his mind. He recalled the carefree years at Princeton, where he majored in economics, and the memorable day of the Yale-Princeton football game when he met this goddess-like creature named Linda.

"Linda, meet my buddy, Chris Cooper. He looks harmless, but don't let that handsome face fool you. He doesn't have my strength of character, nor my loyalty," Brad Pickford said in jest. His head turned from Linda to Christopher trying to gauge their reaction to one another.

Bittersweet House

Linda gave Christopher a radiant smile. "Hi. You've got my favorite masculine name. Suits you."

"I'd believe anything you say, gorgeous." Christopher stared at her sculptured face. Hair the color of spring wheat. Star sapphire eyes. She stared back.

"Hey, you two, remember me?" Brad said in a piqued voice. He brought her to the game, but even a blind man could perceive the sparks flying between them. Christopher remembered the torrid love making following their dates, how her sexy 5'9" frame fit his 6'2" hard body. The passion continued into married life, but career advancement became of equal importance. When Linda landed her first radio job and Christopher started his consulting business, they were on the path to success. It took two decades to achieve their goals: Linda as news anchor in a major TV market; he as a telecommunications consultant with a dozen clients.

As he neared Seacliff, Christopher continued his recollections--Linda complaining about his frequent absences, his insistence that they had years to become parents, and why is it they hadn't had a vacation together in years? He assuaged her fears by pointing out the necessity of meeting prospective clients on their own turf in the States, as well as London, Brussels and Paris; he pointed out that their careers were at the apex and now wasn't the time to slack off; and he assured her they would sail the Hawaiian Islands next winter.

Despite their financial and business success, Christopher knew that Linda harbored the disappointment of not having a child. In the early years, he'd repeatedly told her they needed to establish their careers before taking on family obligations. Linda concurred, but after five years she confronted him. "We've got a good foothold on our careers. I think it would be nice to have a baby. After awhile I could go back to work, resume my career. You *know* we can afford a nanny."

"Linda, we should wait. You're getting hard news stories at the station. You don't want to give that up. Out of sight and WSEA will forget all about you. And my business has finally taken off. We're just getting a good foundation in our careers. Let's not blow it. Time enough for kids."

She backed off temporarily, but Christopher knew his wife ached for a child. He vowed never to lie to himself and had no qualms in admitting he lacked fatherly tendencies. Five years stretched to twelve. Linda no longer brought up the subject, much to his relief--until now. Having a baby didn't fit into his plans.

If he weren't in such an untenable position, he'd laugh at his own

Liz Barzda

situation. Unfortunately, laughter wouldn't solve the problem of his stupidity. He drove the car into the garage thinking there must be a way to extricate himself. A son by another woman, how in God's name could he straighten out the mess?

He entered the house, passing through the laundry room, into the kitchen, where a stove light glowed. Silence. Linda was obviously asleep. God, he hoped so. He headed for the den, his haven where soft chairs, sofas and mahogany paneling created an inviting setting. But he needed more than a comfortable background to totally relax. A stiff drink would help. He half filled a tumbler with Jack Daniels then lowered his long frame into the armchair near the fireplace. He couldn't get his mind off the fast track. Thoughts of his reputation as a stand-up guy in business and in his personal life dogged him. How did he regard himself now? Was he immoral? More tired than he realized, Christopher let out a deep sigh.

The whiskey calmed him sufficiently to think beyond his character and his predicament. He rose to check the message machine and noticed the barely legible note on the desk. It read, "Sandra's in trouble. I have to go to her at Seaacliff's Marriott Courtyard."

He switched on the machine and ran through four messages for Linda and five for himself before hearing Sandra's cry, "Linda, you've got to help me! Come right away! I'm at the Marriott Courtyard. I really need you." It wouldn't be the first time Linda had rescued her sister. He was tired of Sandra and her scrapes. Linda should let her fend for herself. Count on Linda, the enabler.

Apprehensive, Christopher climbed the stair to the master bedroom. Soft light emanated from the room. He grit his teeth, pushed the ajar door open and saw her sitting up in bed with a book.

She didn't greet him, just stared.

"Aren't you going to say hello?" he asked.

She threw the book down and glared at him. "Should I kiss you and ask how everything went--*Daddy*? Isn't that what all good wives do when husbands are gone for days without even a phone call?"

"I had to go. My son was seriously ill. Surely you can understand that. And I had to attend to business."

She sprang out of bed and faced him, "Right, how is he? I hope he's recovered, truly I do. Now ask me how *I'm* doing," Linda said, her voice rising. "You can see I'm not doing well. I think about you doing business--the business of making love with your whore." She pounded on his chest. "You bastard. I'd like to kill you--kill the both of you"

He grabbed her wrists. "For Christ sake, Linda, get a hold of yourself. Can't you understand that an innocent baby almost died."

She wiggled free. "I said I'm glad he recovered. Shall we now resume our lives as though nothing happened? Or would you rather your son came to live with us? And how about what's-her-face? I know what we'll do. We'll have a ménage à trios" She turned her face from him and looked at the ceiling, speculating, "But that wouldn't be the correct number, would it? The baby would make four. Alas, what are we to do?"

He looked at her in disbelief. "You really are crazy."

"Why don't you ask me what I've become? You don't want to ask? Okay, I'll tell you. I've become a fool, a gullible fool. No, that's not quite right. Gullible, maybe? Fooldom, I've just acquired," she said with a hollow laugh that turned into a sob.

"Linda, please! We can work this out."

"Of course we can, being intelligent, with-it professional people. Isn't that right--husband?"

"I can't talk to you when you're irrational."

"Right. I'm not rational, just a stupid, betrayed wife. But what are you?" She wagged her finger at him. "You're despicable. That's what you are, Christopher."

"Things are bad enough now. Let's not play 'my character is better than yours' because then we haven't a chance at settling anything."

"Maybe I'm not with it? Having an affair these days while married is hardly eyebrow lifting. But a baby with another woman, well, that could put a bit of a damper on a legal union. Remember, how we talked about what our marriage would be? We agreed on the old-fashioned kind, you know, the kind our folks had. As the marriage vow says, 'Forsaken all others'." She sniffed her tears. "Isn't that a hoot?"

"Stop it. You're not making sense."

"Yes, I'm making sense. *You*'re making babies."

He turned his back to her.

"Don't you dare walk out on me. You've turned our lives inside out as if nothing happened, and you don't want to hear the recriminations."

Christopher scowled then faced his wife. "I'm sorry I hurt you. I know I screwed up. I can't undue what's happened. But I *do* have a responsibility to Sean. Can't you understand that?"

"Of course, you do. Just what does that entail? And don't forget Betti. Surely, you have a responsibility to her as well."

Liz Barzda

Christopher shook his head, "I can make financial arrangements for Sean. Have a heart. The scenario can play itself out."

"How about Betti? Will you make the same arrangements for her? What do you mean by 'playing itself out'? Do you mean when you're tired of humping each other, we'll be as we were? Oh, but that can't be, can it? Sean must be considered and cared for."

"You just don't get it, do you? No matter how contemptible you see me, I'm not what matters. This is about Sean, not about us, we're secondary."

"Not about us. That's fucking right." She laughed, "Is there an 'us' anymore? Probably not. We're expendable. I think what you really mean, Christopher, is that I'm expendable."

Her laughter rose to a hysterical pitch that grated on his nerves. He turned away. "I can't take anymore of this."

"Really? Just what do you plan to do?"

"What do *you* want me to do?"

"How do I know? You got into this ugly mess, now get yourself out."

"Linda, you're demented!" He turned from her and slammed the door shut.

Chapter 13

In the privacy of her office bathroom, Margaret Dolan checked her appearance in the full-length mirror. The reflection of a dimpled, slightly plump, but still handsome woman smiled back at her. Reasonably satisfied with the image, Margaret's mind focused on the luncheon date with her nephew, Gregory O'Neil.

It had been a month since she had seen Greg. She couldn't wait to surprise him with the check. Her brow wrinkled. Should she tell him about the other money? She thought today might be the last opportunity she would have to talk with him for some time. In a few weeks, he'd be off to the Yale School of Architecture. She loved him dearly. They laughed at the same jokes, discussed family, and sent each other funny cards on birthdays and holidays.

Greg O'Neil and his father, Michael, a police sergeant with Seacliff's Undercover Drug Unit, often dined with the Dolans; more so after Jennifer, Michael's wife and Margaret's sister, died of cancer three years ago.

Margaret couldn't erase the image of her sister's wasted body nor her pained expression at their last hospital meeting. Jennifer's indelible whispered words were lodged in her mind, "Maggie, I'm tired. I think Greg visited me a little while ago? He did, didn't he?"

Margaret nodded. Words wouldn't come.

Jennifer winced in pain then a look of sadness spread across her face. "I'll never see my son again. Tell him my love will always be with him. He's not your responsibility, I know, but can you do me a huge kindness? Could you and Jack look after him? He may be considered an adult, but he's still my baby." Her voice faltered, and she closed her eyes. "You will do that, won't you Maggie?"

Margaret bent closer to Jennifer, willing herself to keep the tremor out of her voice. She swallowed hard, then smiled, "Of course, Jen. You know Jack and I love Greg. We'll always be there for him."

"Remind Greg of me once in a while. You won't mind if I take a little nap?" Jennifer turned her face to the wall. "See you next time."

"Love you." Margaret let go of her hand, kissed her forehead and hurried from the room.

Jennifer died that night.

The bond between Greg and his aunt and uncle deepened after his mother's death. Margaret slipped into a natural surrogate parent. She kept Jennifer's spirit alive by sharing reminisces with Jennifer's son. She and Jack would occasionally invite Greg to accompany them to New York for a Broadway play and end up in a funky restaurant. Camping excursions with the Dolans brightened the teenager's weekends.

With an effort, Margaret cleared her mind from the past. The noonday sun beat down on her as she walked briskly through Heritage Real Estate's parking lot, her mind focused on her nephew.

She cruised out of Seacliff's Industrial Park in her Cadillac De Ville, drove to the north side of town and on to Arcara and Daughter Company's industrial yard. Greg spotted her car, walked toward it with all the spunk of an eighteen-year old.

Margaret thought him handsome, despite the fact that his face was a little too thin. But there was no denying his lustrous blue-black hair and agile, muscular body. Intelligence shone from his light blue eyes that studied people and their surroundings. He's so like my sister, Margaret remembered, the same coloring, the same smile, but not quite the extrovert Jennifer was. Lately, he seems to keep more to himself. I suppose that's to bury the hurt of losing his mother three years ago.

"Hi Maggie, how's my favorite aunt?" Greg asked with a smile.

Margaret wrinkled her nose, "You know you're not to call me Maggie. My name is Aunt Margaret. I'll forgive you today because you'll be gone in a few days and you don't have much time to enjoy my charming company. So make the most of it," she shot back with a grin as he slid into the car.

He patted her cheek. "Should I call you Dimples?"

Despite her pretense at annoyance, she laughed and her dimple deepened. "You better not," she warned.

They stopped at the Nor'easter and opted for lunch on the patio where they could enjoy the breeze off the water and watch the swishing waves. The sight and smell of Long Island Sound gave Margaret a sense of

Bittersweet House

well being. Helping her nephew in any way she could gave her a sense of purpose beyond caring for Jack and the fulfillment of work.

The patio filled up quickly and she felt lucky to have gotten the last table by the seawall facing the water.

The petite red-headed waitress rattled off the day's specials without taking her eyes off Greg, forgetting that she had already mentioned the fresh shrimp. Greg's eyes followed the waitress' swaying hips as she departed the patio.

Margaret sat there without attempting to suppress a smile, then asked, "How's your Dad, Greg?

"He's okay, but disturbed about the increase drug use among high-school kids," Greg answered with a barely noticeable sigh. "I know Seacliff High had somewhat of a problem, but now there's a program that identifies and helps probable users. It's not known that Dad initiated the program. That's the way he wants it. Most of his work is still with the Undercover Drug Unit and relating to catching the dealers and the big distributors. It's a tough haul. I think the work gets to him."

"You ought to convince him to take a couple of days off before you head for Yale, just the two of you. Spend some time together, enjoy each other."

"Good idea, Aunt Margaret. But how do you convince an old workhorse that the Unit can run without him?"

Margaret reached for his hand, "All you can do is try." She removed her hand and on a lighter note asked, "And how are you doing? Learning anything usable from the construction company?"

"I've learned to pick up materials from the company warehouse and bring them to the job site. You know what they say about starting from the bottom. One can't get any lower than a gofer. There's no place to go but up," Greg laughed. "Seriously though, I've learned a lot just by watching and listening to the carpenters and foremen. I'd like to work construction every summer."

"Arcara should take you on, being the good worker you are. You may even go beyond gofer," Margaret teased.

The waitress reappeared with their shrimp salads and iced tea on a large tray. "Is there anything else I can get you?"

Margaret piped up, "Everything's fine. Thank you"

"By the way, Auntie, do you know Ann Marie Arcara, the company's VP?" Greg asked.

"I know her," Margaret's forehead creased. "Why do you ask?"

"How do you know her?"

"Persistent little devil, aren't you?" Margaret joked. "She's a friend of Darlene Moore, you know, the receptionist who works at La Petit Spa, Kat Horvath's place." Margaret moved her drink aside and continued. "Occasionally I've bumped into Ann Marie at the spa. Why the interest?"

He bit into a large shrimp. "Sometimes her office door's open and I can see her working estimates when I'm looking for a foreman or filling a supply order."

He frowned and lowered his voice. "The laborers in the yard would like you to think they're on the inside and know the Mafia connections. I can't picture Ann Marie Arcara or her brother Roland involved in such dirt. They seem decent," Greg said, draining his soda. "True, the old man looks like he can take care of himself. Hey, you never know. What's the straight poop?"

"Those stories have been floating around for years," Margaret responded, "I wouldn't give them any credence." She sipped her ice tea. "Believe me, Joe Arcara can more than take care of himself."

Greg forked a sliced tomato and looked toward the sea. A dreamy expression crossed his face. "There's a freighter. I wonder where it's heading? Just seeing it brings out the wanderlust in me. I'd love to travel, maybe work abroad for a couple of years."

"You mean during college vacations or after you graduate?" Margaret didn't wait for Greg to answer, but continued, "Speaking of college, I have something for you." She put down the nibbled French bread, opened her purse and handed him a check. "A little going away present, for clothes- -or whatever. You know we expect big things from you." She chuckled, "Bribery often brings results."

"Little? It's much too generous," Greg exclaimed, staring at the 1 and three 0's clearly written. "And I can't accept it since I've decided to put off college for a while."

Margaret leaned back into her chair. "What do you mean put off? You've been accepted and enrolled. Put off till when? Why would you want to interrupt your education?"

"Raquel, that's my girlfriend, thinks I should live a little; you know, take a year or two off before starting college. Have some fun. She's says we should move in together." He smiled then bobbed his head. "Yeah, I think she's right. You've got to meet her, Aunt Margaret. She's gorgeous. She makes those MTV stars look like beauty contest rejects."

Bittersweet House

"Greg, you can't mean it! Why would you want to postpone college? Sometimes it's difficult to get back on track. You can still have your beautiful girlfriend without interrupting your education."

"It's only temporary. No big deal."

"Greg, please think it over. You can't disappoint your dad. More importantly, how can you put your future on hold?"

He looked at his watch. "Hey, got to get back. The foreman will be looking for me."

Negative thoughts raced through Margaret's mind. I'll bet she's a hot number. What kind of a girl would deter a young man from attending college? Whoever said, 'lust is a canker sore to the mind' hit it right. She's a factory worker, probably an oversexed teenager who believes Greg doesn't need to further his education. If that sounds prejudicial, so be it.

Margaret tried to wipe the disappointment from her face and voice. "Yes, it's time to go." She caught the waitress' eye, paid with her credit card and included a generous tip.

On the ride back to the construction yard, Greg talked mostly about his job, steering away from his new girlfriend or college.

"Thanks for everything, Aunt Margaret." He kissed her cheek. "You're the best."

"Love you," she said as he closed the car door.

Oblivious to the industrial plants and small neighbor shopping areas she passed on the way back to the office, Margaret reflected on Greg's news. Not going to Yale? She couldn't believe he could dismiss college so easily. Who was this girl Raquel? Guaranteed she'd given him imaginative sex as he'd never experienced to dissuade him from furthering his education.

What to do about it? That was the big question. Convincing her brother-in-law, Michael O'Neil, to accept money for his son's education might be superfluous as things seem to be developing. She knew her husband's kindness to Greg was partially on her account, although Jack was genuinely fond of the boy. In truth, she realized Greg was the child they never had.

Jack didn't balk when she suggested supplementing Greg's partial Yale scholarship. Not so with Greg's dad.

"Thank you very much Jack and Margaret, but I'm capable of taking care of my own," Michael O'Neil said with cold fury.

He managed the partial tuition this year, but the Dolans knew it strained his resources. He couldn't possibly manage three more years.

Margaret pondered how to help without incurring Michael's wrath.

Liz Barzda

She definitely decided not to inform Greg about the bank account she and Jack set up to carry him through school--especially with the *girlfriend* looming over the horizon to sabotage everything.

As Margaret approached her office in the new Executive Complex, she reflected how the word dysfunctional could apply to most families these days. It seems after one problem is solved, another fills the gap. Time passes so quickly, she mused. Does one get caught up in chasing success, or was all that goal achievement a substitute for children? She and Jack ached for children. The media, friends, and society reinforced the thought that if you hadn't babies you weren't whole. Thoughts of kids of her own gradually faded with the years. Still, she had much to be thankful for; Jack was the administrator of Seacliff's Baldwin Memorial Hospital, her business continued to grow, and they had friends with similar interest. True, she would never have the experience of bringing life into the world, but she remembered the hurt when new acquaintances remarked, "Oh, you don't have children," while their eyes said, Oh, you poor soul. The hell with them! Who needs people who think this way?

Friends tagged her, a workaholic. Admittedly, she relished the lifestyle her business afforded. Just as gratifying was the sense of accomplishment. Her friends, Linda, Zita and Katherine, understood her philosophy; their business acumen and ambition drew them together, as did their childfree state. Talk of children was not consciously ignored, but sometimes deferred if even one of them felt the pain, fortune, or misfortune of being childless.

Back in her conference room, Margaret switched off all personal thoughts. She'd expeditiously led her fifteen-member staff through Heritage Real Estate's weekly issues. With sales goals projected and advertising loose ends finalized, the business promised continued profits. Her advertising hype emphasized the company's expertise--Number One in the county--selling more residences than any other company.

When the staff left and her firm shut down for the night, Margaret sat in her leather chair for a breather. So good to sit and do nothing. She stared into space and tried to empty her mind. But jumbled thoughts of her life sans motherhood intruded. Maybe I don't have it all, but pretty close. Being a beloved aunt is super; suits me just fine.

Then thoughts of Greg surfaced. His father may guide him to manhood, but Jennifer entrusted Jack and Margaret to watch over him. She saw herself as his guardian angel. How would she get him back on track, away from this girl, this Raquel--whomever, whatever she is?

Chapter 14

Linda spent a restless night snared in dreams of being lost in a factory, with no clue how to get home. Images of rows of women glued to humming sewing machines who paid no attention to her enhanced the anxiety.

"Please help me, I'm lost. I don't know how to get out of here. Can you tell me how I can get home?" she pleaded. The women paid no attention, they kept on stitching.

She woke in a sweat, unable to shake the dream. Why did it haunt her? The sleeping pill made her groggy, adding to her frustration. What did the dream mean? She held that dreams had no significance in one's life. Surely they couldn't be interpreted -- that was for superstitious people, those who believed in astrology and numerology.

Or, is it? Never mind about astrology-- why couldn't she shake the repeated dream? Could it be that she was lost in her marriage with no route to a solution?

Linda rose slowly and tiptoed to the shower to not wake Christopher. Then she remembered that he spent the night in the guest room, and she didn't give a fig whether he slept or not. Inconceivable that her waking thought centered on him. Sharing the bed would have been intolerable. Long-time habits die hard. But she'd get over it.

The hot water stung her body, but felt good, like releasing impurities from her soul. Did she have any impurities that festered like a virus causing a sickness in her marriage, something she was too busy to ascertain? Hardly. Christopher tore their marriage apart. Would he try to shift the blame on her?

She had neither the time nor the inclination to delve into her subconscious and play psychiatrist early in the morning. Her inner voice

Liz Barzda

said, *"You've got to face the problem. It won't disappear. You can't go on living like cats ready to spring and destroy each other."* She shook her head as if to say I can't stand thinking about him another minute. With the twist of the shower control, cool water cascaded over her body, restoring a semblance of normalcy.

In her dressing room, Linda slipped on panties and bra, then sat in front of her dressing table mirror and talked back to herself. *"Don't bug me. My marriage dilemma is something I can't solve in a heartbeat."* Tired of examining her motives and characteristics, she checked her face. Jaw line still firm. Faint crow feet around eyes, but not particularly noticeable. Forehead still smooth. Neck slightly crinkly. Her translucent skin appeared dull. She opened her eyes widely. Where did the sparkle go? The luster of life faded with her husband's transgressions. He took away the joy of sex, of companionship, of trust.

She listened for signs of Christopher, but heard only the hum of the air conditioner. She wanted to avoid him at all costs.

She dressed in a powder blue silk blouse and gray linen skirt. The blouse would play up her turquoise-blue eyes. Linda realized she now needed more beauty aids. Her pastel blonde hair that friends and fans likened to golden threads, could now be labeled 'dirty blonde'. *"What's become of the sheen in my hair?"* she moaned. Surely, the studio hairdresser and makeup artist would work her magic. And her navy blue linen blazer in WSEA's dressing room would help bring her on-camera face back to life.

She scooted to the kitchen, downed a glass of orange juice, picked up her purse and car keys, and hurried into the garage. She stopped for coffee at Starbucks, where she ran into her co-anchor, Ron Richards.

He with coffee and muffin in hand claimed the just vacated table. "First time I've seen you here in the morning. It's only 10 o'clock. What gives? Don't tell me you're giving the station free time when you needn't be?"

Linda uncapped her coffee. "Bite your tongue. Lord & Taylor beckons me, not the station. And Christopher came home last night. I didn't want to disturb him, so I left early," she said with as much conviction as she could manage.

"Nice that he's home."

Did she detect a hint of sarcasm in his voice?

Ron leaned back in exaggerated disbelief, "Is coffee all you're having? You need nourishment to keep that smooth voice flowing."

"It's all I ever have."

Ron shrugged then leaned in closer. His lips spread into a wide grin. "Have you heard? Hank's asked me to do a series on Connecticut's forgotten widows, seniors barely scraping by." He didn't bother to hide the excitement in his voice.

Linda smiled, "Sounds like a terrific idea; you're just the guy for it." She looked away from him and mused. *Ron's renewal was not yet signed and here he is with a plum assignment. Lucky! Had time passed her by for the serious stuff? Get with reality,* Linda told herself. *Consider yourself fortunate if your contract is renewed.*

He looked at her intently in an attempt to hold her attention. "The first segment of my series will air sometime in September." In jest, he rubbed his hands together. "Man, this is going to be fun. I'll be downloading info on widows and their finances, interviewing old gals I know, and check out those in retirement or convalescent homes willing to talk. What do you think?"

"I have no doubt the series will be a success."

"Thanks," Ron said softly as if to downplay his good fortune, then changed the subject with, "Shifting to more important matters, did you get a look at the receptionist filling in for Penny? What a looker!"

"No, but I'm sure you'll tell me about her," Linda said sipping her coffee. And you'll probably tell me the new weather girl is sleeping with the boss," she quipped in feigned disbelief.

"You know about that? I thought I was the only one."

"You're too much," Linda said with a laugh. It felt good to laugh, to act silly with a friend.

"So whad'ya think? Contract renewals a done deal?" Ron asked.

"Absolutely. How could it be otherwise?" she answered with a chuckle.

Ron grinned, "I like your positive attitude. You're so upbeat."

"Thanks." She managed a smile; but trying to maintain a cheerful countenance was a stretch, and a strain.

"Surely you don't doubt yours will be renewed?" He rested his hand under his chin and just stared. "Linda, I work with you all day, five days a week and never get enough of you."

She wrapped a wisp of hair around her ear in frustration. "We agreed not to go there."

"Sorry, can't help myself. You light up any place you happen to be. You're like the sunshine in an Alaskan winter."

"Not for everyone. You haven't seen me when I'm ready to kill, like the fan who writes to ask who did my facelift. Or how about the so-called admirer who insists I can't be a bona fide journalist? According to her, I never had print experience. I could throttle her."

"Had to be a woman. I knew it. A man would never say that to you."

"Right. Women can be devils," Linda snickered. To herself she declared, *"Men don't make nasty remarks, they just trample on your heart."*

Chapter 15

In a few hours La Petite Spa would be as hectic as noonday traffic in Rome; but at 8 a.m. Katherine savored the stillness of the empty spa. To add to the expected frenzy, her newest esthetician, Mary Lucas, would arrive in half an hour, and Katherine needed to check the acids required for facial peels and acne scars.

Hiring another high-priced technician to her salon at this critical stage in her financial situation might not be a cost-effective move, but she judged it a viable popular service that should pay dividends.

She examined the seaweed, collagen and acid supplies in the double cabinet before inspecting the skin care, massage, hair dressing rooms and reception lobby. Katherine removed one of the long-stemmed yellow roses from the hand-painted vase on the desk and sniffed its scent. Still fragrant.

In her private powder room, she freshened the flowers with water then returned them to the reception area. The Spa would soon open, but she must first pin Scott down for the loan from his father--get the unpleasantness over before the clientele arrived.

He promised to call her at home last night. She had waited what seemed like an eternity--patience was not one of her virtues. How much longer must she wait? She didn't care that she begged for money and begged him to keep loving her. He did love her, didn't he?

"You're the only woman who matters in my life," he had said.

"How about the ones who don't matter?" she asked herself. Katherine knew he fooled around. Rita, her hair stylist, who had seen Scott in the spa, remarked that she loved to do him, then chuckled, "I mean his hair." Rita

Liz Barzda

had no qualms about telling Katherine she spied Scott with a knockout blonde at the Lime Rock auto races.

It hurt to know the man you loved cheated on you. Still, Katherine believed Scott loved her, but told her so only once. Her brown eyes shone at the thought of their acrobatic lovemaking. Once after the sweats and howls of intercourse, he said in an erotically soft voice, as if someone forcibly extracted words from him, "When I'm deep within you, it's as if your soul melds with mine. Sleeping with you in my arms is sheer contentment--all my problems fade away." Then, he whispered, "I love you, Kat." How sweet to hear the three words that meant more to her (almost more) than anything in her life. She replayed them over and over in her mind. Although, he never repeated the words, she sensed he loved her all along, but did he cheat on her? Probably. He certainly wouldn't be held to a commitment.

Today she'd pocket her pride to get what she wanted, an understanding with Scott and money from his father. But doubts nagged at her again; why didn't that son-of-a-bitch return her call? Nervously, she ran a hand down her black silk skirt. She punched in his number for the third time. The phone kept ringing. "Where the hell is he? His office? No way would he ever see the inside of Bowman Plastics before 9:30." She booted up her computer and sent him an e-mail. "Let's see if the bastard answers," she said aloud.

Darlene, the receptionist, knocked once, then entered Katherine's office with Mary Lucas. Together, boss and new employee reviewed health codes and customer and company requirements.

At nine o'clock the first customer arrived. Thoughts of money and Scott were put on hold.

\#

At 3 o'clock, her first opportunity for a break, she gave Scott's number another try.

"Scott Bowman's office," announced a British female voice.

"This is Katherine Horvath, I'd like to speak with Scott."

"I'm sorry, Mr. Bowman is unavailable. May I take a message?"

Katherine frowned. "No. It's personal. Do you know when he *will* be available?"

"I believe he'll be in conference the rest of the day."

Katherine felt the rush of anger. No way would Scott be in conference

Bittersweet House

all day. He'd find a way to wiggle out of it. Where was he now; either gambling at one of the Indian casinos, or filling the head of a pretty female employee with sweet talk before knocking her up.

"How may I help you?" the voice asked.

"Please ask him to call Kat."

She's covering up for him. I know they're in cahoots. He never told me she was a Brit. Her mind raced from Scott to this secretary who fronted for him. What does she look like? Has he been humping her?

"Did you say Kat?"

"Yes, I said Kat. Are you his secretary?"

"Yes, I'm Mr. Bowman's secretary."

"And your name?"

"Beryl Blair."

Katherine could swear she heard a giggle from the other end.

"And your number please?"

Katherine's temple began to throb. "He has my number."

"I'll pass on the message."

Katherine detected a smirk in the responses. Yes, definitely a smirk in that pronounced British tone. Annoyed, she hung up. *I'll bet she takes elocution lessons to retain that British accent.*

She checked the work schedule and noted that La Petite Spa's Friday appointments were back-to-back and would continue until 8 p.m. Katherine felt hunger pangs in the early evening. She needed nourishment now. Black coffee and half an English muffin for breakfast, and a small yogurt for lunch didn't satisfy. She opted for a sandwich and a breath of fresh air.

She informed her secretary, Jean, that she was off for a bite to eat and would be back in an hour. She emphasized, "If Scott calls before I've returned, be sure you take a message."

The hell with worry about plugging up her arteries. She stopped at the nearest fast-food and ordered a cheeseburger and French fries. She could hear Scott's warning, "Those calories will make you look like a stuffed sausage." Well, he could go to hell.

Katherine drove onto I-95 and toward Bowman Plastics in Crestwood, Seacliff's old industrial part of town.. She parked a few rows away from the visitor's section, far enough not to be recognized, but close enough to see who exited the main entrance.

The grilled burger's aroma permeated the car. She took a hefty bite and kept watching. After sitting in the car for 15 minutes, she saw Scott exit the building laughing with an attractive woman with red hair who

Liz Barzda

echoed his laughter. He once mentioned his secretary, but not her name nor her good looks. She could be Beryl Blair. He wouldn't waste his time on a woman who wasn't a looker. Katherine stared as they walked to his car. Burger juice dripped down her chin. If she confronted him about sleeping with this woman he'd probably invent a cock-and- bull story that would do justice to a prize-winning novelist.

She'd been true to Scott, even flipped off some hunks that came on to her. She wouldn't be lied to, nor made a fool of. Her impatience and too-passionate nature simmered, like a dormant volcano about to erupt.

Chapter 16

Zita rubbed her temples as if erasing the frenzied day. She read her e-mail, deleted junk messages, shut down the computer then checked her voice mail.

TGIF and thank heaven she had Peter to look forward to. What a godsend! She felt so comfortable with him. No pretense about him. So his grammar isn't perfect and his laughter is a bit too loud; but underneath that tough exterior she sensed a sensitive, compassionate man. What would her friends think of him? She knew Margaret, Linda, and Kat to be fair-minded. How could they resist a muscled specimen with curly, coal black hair, an easy smile and those green-speckled brown eyes that seemed to search the core of you? She certainly couldn't. Still, one couldn't anticipate how they might react.

After the divorce, it took Zita time to regain faith in herself. David had shattered her belief in her attractiveness and strength as a woman. The boundless energy she once exhibited slowly returned, as did her straightforwardness and known loyalty to friends and business acquaintances. Pleased that she had regained most of her strengths, Zita was still mindful of the need to have her ego bolstered often, and her habit of telling it like it is before thinking about the consequences. *Not to worry.* She'd *work on it.* She left the office at 6 o'clock and beelined to a gourmet market for French bread, salad, greens, barbecued chicken, and ice cream with chocolate sauce. She picked up a bottle of French Chardonnay at her favorite spirits shop. *Voila! An almost home-cooked meal.*

Peter was expected for dinner at 7:30. She foraged for the best place mats, lit candles in the dining and living rooms, and chose soft background music for a romantic mood. He wouldn't forget this night. She'd satiate him

Liz Barzda

with passionate sex, then envelope him with tenderness. *God, I feel sexy. It's in the air. The place is oozing with it,* Zita admitted with pleasure.

She mascaraed her eyelashes, ran a comb through her strawberry blond hair and made a moue to the mirrored image. *"Not too bad for a 42-year old broad. Peter thinks I'm the best thing since Princess Diana."*

He arrived right on the button, greeted her with a lingering kiss then held her at arms length. His eyes roamed from her shining hair to her glowing face and on to the white gauze top revealed her straining nipples itching to pop through.

He let out a low whistle, "Wow, you're something else. Would I get burned if I touched?"

Zita's smiled. "Maybe later." She reached for his hand and led him to the sofa.

"You're beautiful." He ogled her as if glued to her face and form. "You know, don't you?"

"Thanks. Now, what would you like to drink? I have whiskey and wine. Or would you rather have a beer?"

"Beer's okay. You've got a really nice place. How long have you been here?"

"A couple of years. I sold the house in Shorehills Estates when David decided on screwing an airhead blonde would be more fun than marriage. I decided on this condo. Love it."

Peter waved his hand around. "Did you do all this?"

"Decorating is my hobby," she said with pride as her eyes scanned the living and dining rooms done in varying hues of rose and beige.

She retreated to the kitchen; returned with a couple of beers, glasses, and a carafe of Chardonnay on a tray. "So, how did your week go?"

"It was a tough one. We're behind schedule on the Reynolds Computer addition. Some of the foundation forms need to be reset. It's a headache. Management is getting panicky."

Zita patted his cheek. "I'm sure you'll get the job done."

"Thanks." He took a gulp of beer, grabbed her wrist and pulled her to him. "It's really terrific to have someone like you believe in me."

"Can't drink my wine if you're holding on to me." He reluctantly let go.

"My uncle Joe says he believes in me, too; but let me tell you, he's a pusher. Keeps telling me what a great foreman I am while piling more jobs on me. Me and my cousin Roland like to kid the old man and call him the 'slave driver'."

Bittersweet House

Zita sipped her wine. "Peter, don't think about work, now. We've both had stomach-churning days. Let's just relax and enjoy each other."

Besides food and drink, her mind jumped to more sensuous matters, like love making-- an added treat after desert. With a half-hearted stab at conversation, she asked, "Do you and your cousin work closely or see each other?"

"I don't see Roland much. He's the company comptroller. We're like in different parts of the business, but we go to lunch sometimes; that's if I can get an hour off without a looming emergency." He took another swig of beer. "Enough about me. How's your advertising campaign for the new mall coming?"

Zita laughed, "The retailers are falling over themselves to sign with us for TV commercials. They have enough marketing sense to know that featuring local celebrities draw; still, they're emphatic about being featured on camera themselves. They insist that they're the ones capable of presenting and selling their own merchandise. Right. Like they know what they're talking about. I hate to say it, but some of them have faces that need air brushing. Badly. God forgive me. No getting away from it: everyone wants his 15 minutes of fame. But despite putting up with these retail divas, the campaign is working out wonderfully well."

She carried the carafe and a beer to the dining table, disappeared into the kitchen, and returned with the salads. She invited him to sit. "This looks terrific," he grinned, digging into the greens. "It's nice to have a home-cooked meal. Eating out every day is the pits."

"Peter, this is hardly home cooked," Zita said sheepishly. "Take-out is more like it. But thanks for the compliment."

"So what else is going on in your life besides work? He put his fork down and gazed at her. "My mind is full of you. I'm constantly wondering where you are and what you're doing."

"Let's not get possessive," Zita replied with little conviction. She didn't feel smothered by him, rather felt protected, cared for. Still, how well did she really know this man? Is permanence in his vocabulary? She mustn't think far in advance. She traveled that road, and what did it get her? Nothing but heartache.

Over chicken and desert, Peter brought up the latest movies and baseball games. Zita offered a few comments as she sipped her second glass of wine. She suggested coffee in the living room. They never touched it. Fully relaxed after a satisfying meal, Peter caressed her face. "You know,

Liz Barzda

you're something special." He gently kissed her eyelids and hair. "I've been with a lot of women in my 45 years, but never one like you."

"And so are you." Zita studied him, a slow smile inching up from the corners of her mouth. *If my friends knew I've dated Peter for a month and we haven't slept together, they'd howl in disbelief.* She circled her arms around his neck and drew him to her. *That's about to change now.*

He lifted her from the sofa, carried her to the bedroom, gently laid her on the bed, and removed her top. He buried his hands in her silken hair. His lips brushed her eyes, ears, and throat. His tongue explored her mouth and breasts. She chuckled, "What do we have here? Down, boy."

Peter's breath came fast and heavy. "Never say down. It's up and at 'em."

"Not so fast." She slipped her panties down onto an ankle and twirled her foot around and around. "Watch this. I can repeat that 50 times without loosing my panties." She let out a giggle. "Cute, eh? Bet you thought I couldn't do it."

"You're driving me crazy." He seized her foot, kissed it, then parted her legs and stroked her vagina faster and faster.

She wrapped her legs around his waist as he sucked her nipples. He lifted her buttocks and rained kisses down her hips and thighs. Streaks of fire shot through her as he tasted the secret fold of her body. Her breathing accelerated, matching his. He withdrew his mouth from her wetness, stroked her hair as if to slow her down and prolong the pleasure, than to built up to the height of ecstasy. She moaned and clutched his penis.

She lifted her hips, palmed his penis as if to guide him into her, then let go and tried to push him off. "Want to be mad with desire? More foreplay will do it."

"What do you mean more will make me mad with desire? I'm burning for you now."

"This game is called 'how long can you hold it.' Guaranteed to drive you crazy with lust. If I grab and pet your penis till the count of 50, you win--that's if you don't come first."

"That's a game? It's not, it's torture. You're so hot, I can feel it. Your pussy is like a raging fire. I'm the fireman whose eruption can put out the fire. I'll have you calling for 'more, more.' It's lousy to be a tease."

She lightly brushed her fingers against his bulging penis. "Didn't anyone ever tell you that patience is a virtue? You know anything worth doing is worth waiting for. It makes loving so much more exciting." Her words were meant to heighten their lovemaking, but she couldn't and wouldn't wait any longer. Wild with desire, Zita longed for his thrust and begged, "Oh, Peter, now, now." He entered her hard, pulled out and slowly entered her again. And again. Their bodies rocked together. Exquisite pleasure filled her being and brought on intense spasms. Zita screamed, "Promise me it'll always be like this." He burst out with, "Zita, I love you. God, I wanted to do that the first time I saw you." The union of their bodies convulsed in ecstasy, sweat, and moans. "I tried to hold off for a while, to taste every inch of you, but I couldn't. I'm sorry I came so soon. But we have to do it over and over again until I get it right."

Zita placed his head on her breast and moaned. "Practice makes perfect. Take a nap now then we'll play more games. We'll screw and screw until our timing becomes perfect."

Peter laughed, gathered her in his arms and sighed with pleasure.

Zita watched him for a bit till her eyes closed. When she awoke, he was peering at her with wonderment.

"Do you know you're like the goddess of love; playful, gentle, and lustful rolled into one? Isn't it time for another game?" He held her close. "You don't know what you're dealing with, lady. I can go on fucking you day and night. But only you. I mean it."

"Thanks, darling. You're the best game player I've ever had." Zita frowned, "but why the woeful expression?"

"This is more than a game of sex with me, Zita. I love you. I don't mean just for now or this season, but for keeps."

She leaned against the headboard. "I can't say I'm surprised, Peter. I'm sure you can sense my feelings for you. Actually, I do love you, but you know I've been hurt. I promised myself no man would ever hurt me again."

"I'll always love you. I'm not like your ex. Zita, I'd never hurt you. I'll seal that oath with my blood if you want me to."

"Nothing as dramatic as that. Just give me time, Peter. Let's seal our love with wine." She padded naked to the kitchen and returned with a bottle and two glasses.

"To our love in this crazy world," Zita offered.

"To my commitment to you," Peter responded.

They clicked glasses and drank.

Peter put his arm around her shoulder. They sat in bed without speaking. Zita, enraptured by his commitment, felt happiness infusing her.

They dozed off and on. "Isn't it wonderful that we both have a whole Sunday off?" Zita enthused.

"It's a rarity, for sure. What do you say we go fishing? Haven't done that in ages."

"Maybe. Or we can go kayaking on Lake Zoar. Kat said she and Scott tried and it's loads of fun. What do you think?"

"Sure. I'm willing to try anything."

"About Kat, I hear she's still considering the crazy idea of going to the Mafia for money if her boyfriend, Scott, doesn't convince his father to give her a low-interest loan."

"Why wouldn't her boyfriend ask his father for the loan?" Peter looked at Zita quizzically, "He really cares for her, doesn't he?"

"I'm sure he does, even though everyone knows he plays around. I don't think Scott wants to lose her. If it came down to an ultimatum, I think he'd mend his ways. I have a feeling he's tasting all the female goodies he can till then."

"For your friend's sake, I hope you're right. As far as the money goes, if she thinks she's going to get a loan at the going bank rate from the mob, she's crazy. That's big trouble. But don't worry; I know how to fix that."

Zita's forehead creased, "What do you mean 'you know how to fix that? You're not going to do anything crazy or unlawful?"

"Of course not. I wouldn't do anything without your say so."

"Promise," Zita urged.

"You have my word on it. Whatever I do would be within the law, maybe quirky, but legal." A grin crossed Peter's face. "It's creative problem solving. All your friend needs is a good scare. That would set her thinking straight."

"Maybe so."

He gathered her in his arms and held her. Neither spoke. The warmth of contentment spread throughout her body. All the horrors David inflicted upon her receded into the bleak past.

Chapter 17

Christopher held a circus-theme wrapped package under one arm and quickly unlocked the shiny black door.

What a relief to be out of Boston's dragon's-breath heat and into the cool air- conditioned foyer of Betti's Beacon Hill house. He took the stairs two at a time anticipating Betti and Sean waiting for him on the second floor landing.

But Betti stood alone, looking like a summer daisy in white shorts and a yellow chemise top. She held out her arms to him, breathing rapidly, eyes twinkling in expectation, lips blossoming into a full smile. He put his briefcase and package down, swept her into his arms and planted kisses on her face, neck, and arms.

"How I missed you. You look so good. And you smell sweet, like honeysuckle after rain," Christopher said. He ran his hands through her tawny hair, kissed her eyelids, and explored the curves of her body.

"I've missed you dreadfully; it's been three weeks," she lamented as she led him into the second floor living room. "All I could think of is when you'd be coming. Sean recognizes your picture and repeats 'Daddy, Daddy.' Isn't that the most marvelous thing?" Betti said as she clung to him. "Where is he?"

"Taking his nap."

She gazed into her lover's eyes and drank in the sight of him. "I told him Daddy was coming, but he drifted off, just couldn't keep his eyes open."

He aimed for an easy chair, settling her on his lap. "Sorry I couldn't get here sooner. The plane was delayed. I sat in the airport for an hour. And I feel sweaty; probably smell like a bull elephant." Extricating himself from

Liz Barzda

Betti's arms, Christopher rose and stared open-mouthed at Sean's portrait on the wall above the mahogany end table. "When did you do that?"

"I just finished it," Betti answered, smiling in anticipation of a compliment. "Thought I'd try pastels. Do you like it?"

"Amazing. It's just like one of my baby pictures."

She turned her head, and in a sad voice countered, "I wouldn't know, never saw your baby pictures."

"All babies look alike." He regretted the remark as soon as it left his lips. The trite phrase wasn't meant to hurt, but to deter conversation from prohibited areas. "I have to have a peek at Sean," he said avoiding her intent look. He ran up to the third-floor nursery, with Betti trailing behind. He passed the master bedroom and noticed the room had been redecorated in pink, rose, and green print--so like Betti, upbeat and colorful.

Whenever he entered the nursery, Christopher felt a glow, like sunshine, radiating from his child. The nursery rhyme figures Betti had painted behind Sean's crib appeared to dance on the yellow wall. The afternoon sun sneaked through the blinds and turned his child's tawny hair to gold. Christopher marveled at skin smooth as pink silk, and little hands curled tightly ready to punch the tiger in his dreams.

"I wouldn't disturb him for anything. But a quick shower and then loving you to pieces."

He relished the sting of the water's force as his thoughts ping-ponged from Boston to Connecticut. Perhaps it would wash away the problem tearing him apart. If someone had told him years ago that he would be leading a double life, he'd have split his side laughing. A double life--like the melodramatic black and white movies of the '30's shown late at night. If it isn't a double life, What is it? A mess! That's what it is, Christopher confessed.

He couldn't deflect thoughts from Sean, Betti, and Linda. He had wounded his wife. He saw no way out. He'd put everything on hold. But he couldn't obliterate the past, nor the present. Scenes he'd rather keep buried kept surfacing.

Like the first time he set eyes on Linda at the UConn-Yale football game. He likened her to a Teutonic goddess with those turquoise-blue eyes, pastel blonde hair, and statuesque body.

"I've got to see you after the game. Let me take you to dinner," he had insisted.

When his fraternity brother objected to Christopher horning in on his

Bittersweet House

date he said,"Don't go ape, ol' buddy, then turned his attention back to Linda and whispered, "I'll call you."

"Linda, don't pay attention to him. He's a dirty young man catting around for beautiful younger things like you," her date said, jesting to hide his disappointment.

Years later Linda admitted to Christopher that she would have followed him anywhere that day. "I took one look at you and said to myself, 'He's for me. He's gorgeous. I'd love to pet him.'"

Christopher recalled the winter night in his bachelor pad in front of the fire when he asked her to marry him. They had discussed their career dreams and promised each other a vacation in some romantic spot, after five years of work dedication. When the five-year plan was up, he suggested a passionate getaway. "If you can't get away now, move in with me. If that's not your thing, there's another option--marry me. I want to sleep with you every night. I want to make love to you, over and over again, and not worry that one of us has to leave."

He could still hear her laugh. "That's rather an underhanded marriage proposal. But you knew I'd say yes. Didn't you?"

"Yes, because we love each other like crazy. Not only do I love every inch of you, I want to be with you all the time. Being with you is a perpetual high."

He remembered how he chased success in the satellite telecommunications industries, with an eye to eventually having his own consulting business. Not only for himself, but for Linda.

He toweled off forcefully, as if the physical action would rub away his worries. With a twinge of guilt, he recalled talking up advantages of a child-free marriage. He pointed out the difficulty of bringing a baby into the world: "Just too much pain; what with drugs, AIDS, using up all our natural resource and kidnappings." Christopher didn't dwell on his priorities--money and career advancement. "Let's hold off about having a baby for a few more years." He saw himself espousing in a pompous manner, "The world is over-populated. We needn't add to that burden. We've got time to have a family, darling. It's hardly a sin to want the two of us to have more good times." How her eyes had shone when she spoke of their guaranteed successful future. "I see myself as a TV anchor, and I see your consulting business booming. Children will come later."

In retrospect, he realized Linda's total commitment to marriage. Christopher had no doubt, that if her career threatened their marriage, Linda would opt for the stability of a lifetime together.

Liz Barzda

Deep in his private world, Christopher was unaware of Betti standing by the bedroom door.

"Umm, you look so good," she said, watching him as he combed his black, wavy hair. "And you smell good, too. I missed you." She walked toward him, wrapped her arms around his neck, nuzzled his face, removed the towel from his waist, then pressed her body against his. He groaned with desire as he drew her to the bed. He removed her top. She flung her shorts and panties to the floor. His fingers gently outlined her body. His hands cupped her breasts, massaged her thighs. The wetness between her legs screamed for his thrusts. A baby's cry emanated from the intercom.

"Bad timing," Christopher said panting. He rolled onto his back. "Can't we ignore him just for a few minutes? I want to make love to you and never stop, till...till we're incapacitated from fucking."

"Darling, I know how you feel." She brushed the perspiration from her forehead and reluctantly drew away from him. "I want you desperately but I've got to check Sean."

"Cutting off lovemaking just as a man's is about to insert his dick into a heavenly velvet muff can make a man go blind, you know," Christopher guffawed.

"I'll see that that doesn't happen." Betti tittered, "Anything to save your sight."

They entered the nursery and saw Sean asleep on his back, his arms spread out. "All's well. He probably had a bad dream," Betti said. Christopher stared at his son with awe, amazed at the absolute love he felt. Seeing Sean sleeping peacefully filled him with a sense of fulfillment he didn't believe possible.

"Isn't he the most beautiful child you've ever seen? I never dreamed I would ever have a child this wonderful," Christopher said unabashedly as he gently swept a curl off Sean's forehead.

Betti chuckled, "Remember me? I had a little to do with it."

The scene would have been foreign to him ten years ago--even last year.

"You must be hungry. Did you eat on the plane?" Betti's words brought him back to the present. "You'll need energy for an all-nighter." She grinned, "I'd better feed you. Would a sandwich, salad, and milk do the trick?" He watched her with admiration as she placed the food before him.

Betti sat opposite her lover and stared into his slate gray eyes. "You

Bittersweet House

have that faraway look, or is that blank stare focused on business? How did you make out with England Telecommunications?"

"Things look promising, but I won't know till I hear from their SOB chairman. He's cautious and won't commit till they crunch the numbers a dozen times. He wants a near-guarantee that my new world-wide system will improve their bottom line."

In a positive tone Betti said, "I know you're stressed out chasing prospective clients around the world, but I also know you'll land ET, Ltd." She hesitated a minute, and added, "Do you ever think of us on those business trips?"

"I think of you and Sean all the time: while working in my office at home, at a function or social gathering with people who mean nothing to me, and even on the golf course. I wonder what you two are doing at different times of the day. Is Sean hurling his mashed potatoes on the floor? Are you two making bubbles in his bath? Are you taking him to the park playground to see the children?" Then Christopher remembered, "I have something for Sean. I can't wait to give it to him."

"Please, no more stuffed animals. His room is turning into a jungle."

"Seriously, Betti, is everything all right? Is there anything you or Sean need?"

"We're fine. Your check arrives promptly the first of every month. Money isn't what's missing."

A cry bellowed, the kitchen intercom interrupted her words, words Christopher felt were heading into irresolvable territory.

"Come," Betti said as she sprang and reached for his hand. They quickly climbed the stairs. "We should have gone to bed when we had a chance. We'll make love all night. I promise," Betti said heading for Sean.

"Hi, sleepyhead. Look who's here. It's Daddy." She picked up her son and covered his face with kisses. Sean broke out into a wide grin.

"Daddy," Sean said as Christopher embraced him, kissed him repeatedly, then swung him around and around. The child's laughter tingled in his ear.

"Daddy has something for his boy. I'll go get it and be right back."

"Let me have him. He's probably wet." She set him on the floor, reached into the chest of drawers for fresh training pants.

Christopher came back in a flash and Sean grasped the package his father held out. They tore at the ribbon and paper. The little boy's eyes widen as he inspected the colorful musical zoo. His father pressed the driver's head to produce music and animal sounds. Sean got the idea and mimicked his father's actions. "Look, Mommy," Sean said and clapped his hands.

"It's wonderful, darling," Betti said. She beamed at her son as she attempted to get his pants on.

"I want play," he cried.

"In a minute."

Sean yelled, "Let me, let me."

"Look at that! He's brilliant," Christopher declared as his boy maneuvered strong, little legs into fresh pants. "And how he's grown since I've last seen him."

"How much will he have grown before you see him again?"

"Please, don't," Christopher whispered. "We were having such a good time." He avoided her eyes and crouched down to face Sean. "Do you want to play with your new toy, or would you like to try the swings at the playground, sport?"

Before Sean could answer, Betti piped up, "How about if we go to see the swan boats again? Remember when Mommy and Daddy took you to the park for a ride in the big swan? Wasn't that fun?"

"Swan boat. Ride the swan boat. Let's go Daddy," Sean said, tugging at Christopher. "Can I take my zoo train with me, Daddy?"

"Sorry, Sean, we can't make it today. We'll go another time."

"Why Daddy?"

"Because there's so little time." He turned to Betti. "I must be in New York on Monday. I have a mountain of work to prepare before pitching my client."

Betti stared at him. Seeing the disappointment in her face, Christopher added, "I just remembered the swan boats operate till 5. We can squeeze it in. There's time."

"Yes, squeeze us in," Betti snapped as she grabbed her son and ran down the stairs.

"Mommy, Daddy, boat ride now," Sean cried.

Guilt enveloped Christopher. He wouldn't disappoint his son, no matter what. They could make the Gardens before closing time. A little stroking and pleading for forgiveness would bring Betti around.

Chapter 18

It had been months since the revelation of Christopher's mistress and baby, still Linda's nightmare persisted. Short periods of sleep intermingled with tossing and turning. Bereft of peace and energy, she wondered if the hell would ever end. She had to have it out with her husband, come to a decision. Try to make some sense of her life. But how? She couldn't wipe out his other life and revert to the way things were.

Linda showered and dressed quickly. She trudged down to the first floor feeling as if stampeding steers had trampled over her. Things couldn't go on like this. Yet she had no idea what to do. The aroma of fresh coffee drew her to the breakfast room and the inevitable confrontation.

Christopher had his back to her, feeding bread into the toaster. Such a mundane thing. She pictured him doing the same in Betti's kitchen. *More so of late, I'd wager, breakfasting in two households.* She stared at his broad muscular back that once conjured sexual desire. Now she wanted to *claw* at him for destroying their lives. "Would you like toast?" he asked without turning.

"Don't trouble yourself. I'll do it." Through the French doors, she viewed a flimsy sun struggling through a gray sky. Just like my life, she thought wearily.

He slid bread into the toaster, "No trouble."

She noticed the table set for two and how calmly he met her eyes as he poured the coffee. She knew him to be determined and self-reliant in business, but this was different. Could he really be so composed?

"You okay?" he asked.

"What do you think, Christopher?"

Liz Barzda

"Let's try to be civil today. We can't continue to hurt each other like this."

"If nothing else I'm civil, Christopher. Haven't I always been civil to you, my sister, my parents, my friends? Did I miss anyone?"

"Linda, I'm sorry. I know I've hurt you dreadfully; but believe me, it wasn't intentional."

She felt her cheeks flush with anger. "Isn't this when you say,' But darling I didn't plan it, it just happened'? Please spare me the dramatics."

He reached for her hand. "Let's at least talk about what we're going to do."

She jerked her hand free.

"I know you don't believe me, but I do care about you."

She pushed her coffee aside and glared at him, "Did you say those words to what's-her-name when you were humping her?"

"Linda, stop it!"

"No, I won't stop it. Tell me about your romance. Did she chase you and beg you to fuck her?"

"It isn't the end of the world because I have a son. I know my responsibility to him. My trust fund will take care of Sean's financial needs."

"Don't patronize me. I don't give a damn what you do with your trust fund. Don't you realize I'll never feel the same about you? You've lied to me. How many years have you lied to me?"

"Linda, listen to me. We can go on as before. I'll keep sending Sean money every month. Our lives needn't change."

"Our lives changed when your seed took hold in her uterus. Everything is different now. How often will you be gone visiting Sean and what's-her name? Isn't it wild, the man who didn't want a family now has a son? Your baby will be looking for his daddy. And will you be wondering what he's doing every day?" It was the first time she spoke the boy's name. It felt strange.

"I suppose you've never done anything you regret, never had a misstep," he shouted.

She slapped him. "How dare you? Are you saying I might have had an affair? Never. I *never* had an affair. I wanted a marriage like my folks had. You know, till death do us part." She shook her head. "Isn't that a hoot, Christopher? You married the one woman who still believes marriage is a sacred covenant. Shades of Dr. Laura."

He rubbed his cheek; then grasped her shoulders. "Stop this nonsense."

Bittersweet House

She pulled free of him. Unable to hold in her emotions any longer, Linda began to sob.

He gathered her in his arms. "I care about you. I truly do."

It felt so good to be held--but not by him. She couldn't stifle the hate in her heart. She wanted him to suffer as she had. Revenge would consume her until she hated even herself. She broke free and wiped her tears. "I'm going out."

"When will you be back? We can't go on this way. How can we resolve this?"

She turned away from him. "You figure it out."

#

The August humidity took Linda's breath away, forcing her to quicken her steps to the Mediterranean's entrance. She vowed to be upbeat for her friends, to banish the thought of her husband, his mistress, and their progeny. She scanned the restaurant's cool dining room and noticed BB's at a corner table.

"We're one up on you." Zita held up her wine glass in salute and smiled approvingly at Linda in her classic white linen dress.

"You're looking so great. It's almost illegal. Leo's look good in anything they drape on their bodies," Katherine said.

"Thanks. How are Seacliff's women of substance?" Linda asked with a forced smile, glancing from Zita to Margaret to Katherine.

"Hungry," Katherine grinned. "It's schmoozing time. We're here to spread love--to those who deserve it." She narrowed her eyes, "and to diss our enemies."

"I'll drink to that," Margaret said, lifting her glass. She filled Linda's wine glass and handed her a menu.

"What do you suggest?" Linda inquired of the waitress.

Margaret piped up, "We're going with the lobster salad and Chardonnay, per our wine expert's suggestion."

Zita bowed her head to her friends. "Thank you fans."

"Make mine the same," Linda said to the staring waitress.

"Aren't you the anchor on WSEA? You do a terrific job," the server gushed.

"Thanks," Linda said, turning away so as not to prolong the conversation.

After the waitress departed and inquiries regarding the health of spouses and lovers out of the way, Linda said, "I want to hear everything. It's been too long, but first a toast to us. Here's to Barren Babes. Lovers come and go, but friendships, like Switzerland's banking system, endure forever."

"Amen to that," said Zita. "Somewhere in the Bible it says, 'a faithful friend is the medicine of life.'" She raised her right eyebrow and chuckled, "Men may hurt us, but our friends ease the pain."

Katherine added, "Here's something I want you, dear friends, to remember: Money, can't buy love," and with a laugh added, "but it can put you in a strong bargaining position."

"Here's a truism," Margaret offered, "Business is like sex. When it's good, it's very, very good; when it's not so good, it's still good."

"I'll drink to that," the BB's said in unison.

"Darlings, we have everything," Katherine interjected. She sounded like an old-time movie queen. "Linda informs the citizenry via the boob tube, Margaret houses them, Zita's words get them to spend money, and I make them beautiful. Ain't life grand?"

"Couldn't be better," Linda said with as much conviction as she could muster. She turned to Zita, "What's up with Parker Advertising?"

Zita broke into a broad grin, "We're submitting what I think is a super advertising proposal for the new Shoreline Mall. But you never know. The competition's keen. Still, I have a winning feeling about it."

Katherine said, "Terrific. Now, let's get to the good stuff. When are we going to meet Peter?"

"You will," Zita responded without elaborating.

Linda sensed Zita's reluctance to say more.

"Isn't he Joseph Arcara's nephew?" Katherine asked. "I'll bet Scott knows him. Scott meets so many people through his business. He even knows the wise guys in construction."

Linda noticed Katherine and Margaret forking bits of lobster while ignoring Katherine's comments. *Hope to heaven Kat's given up the crazy idea of Mafia aid for her spa*, Linda mused.

"Kat, did Darlene tell you I was in late last night for a massage and haircut?" Zita queried with lifted eyebrow. "I hadn't seen your completed renovation. It's beautiful."

"Didn't it turn out well? My clients just love the new look. Damn, there goes that phone again," Katherine complained, digging into her purse. She listened, then, "Yes, I did call but that was yesterday, you schmuck. Dinner tonight? Why not. Pick me up at 7. And Scott, don't be late."

Bittersweet House

Linda noted the last minute date and wondered how long Kat would put up with Scott.

"We've got a lot to celebrate--friendship, and good business," Margaret said. She held up her wine glass, took a sip, "Especially good business."

Linda smiled at Margaret, realizing that if she could reveal her pain to anyone, it would be to the more compassionate Margaret. But she couldn't. Instead, she asked, "So Margaret, where are you foraging for gold now?"

Margaret smiled, "You're the first to know. Heritage Real Estate will have an exclusive to sell the million-dollar-plus homes going up at Oceanside."

"Super," Linda enthused.

"Congratulations," Zita said.

"Money goes to money," Katherine declared.

Margaret wrinkled her nose and broke into a grin, "Thank you all."

Katherine leaned forward. "Just to get off the crass subject of money, I have to tell you about one of my clients who invited me to a party at her home. You won't believe it. Her five year-old kid insisted on staying up after 10. This over-aged Madonna-wannabe mama let her daughter tap dance on the coffee table. Have you ever?"

"Not to be coarse, but is she by any chance related to your friend who cleaned the toilet bowl with her husband's toothbrush because he cheated on her?" Zita asked with a straight face.

The foursome burst out in laughter.

"Not to be indelicate," Margaret said, "but I can't let this go by. Jack told me his secretary put insect powder in her husband's underwear because she suspected him of two-timing her."

Laughter erupted again.

"Almost forgot," Linda added. "Here's the latest bulletin on Jan Ritter. You heard that her husband, Elliott traded her in for a teenage model? Well, Jan got her revenge. Awarded, 3 million in the divorce settlement, she gave a half million to the Catholic Church knowing how much Elliott loathed the Church."

"There's a round left from this second bottle," Margaret said with glee. "Let's kill it." She poured for all. "Here's to us, the BB's. We may be barren; but we prefer to think of ourselves as beautiful, brainy, bold and benevolent.

"Hear, hear," they all responded.

#

Liz Barzda

On her drive home, Linda felt the support and joy of the Barren Babes still surrounding her, as if they were omnipresent. She rethought their conversation and laughed again at their silliness. But her friends were going on with their lives while she felt suspended in time and place. She wanted to hang on to the fun and support garnered by these reliable women, but they went about their business and she was alone.

In an attempt to shake the blues, Linda drove to the Seacliff Mall and wandered into Lord & Taylor. She checked out the perfume and jewelry counters, inspected the new shoe lines, sportswear, and dress departments for a preview of fall fashions.

After an hour, her interest began to flag. There was no more avoiding it. It was time to go home. Her route took her past St. John's Episcopal Church where she and Christopher were married. She stopped and entered the cool edifice. The pews were half filled at the 5 o'clock service. Do these people come to church on Saturday so they can sleep late Sunday and have the rest of the day for good times? If this were Christmas or Easter, St. John's would be full. Not a regular churchgoer, Linda felt she had no right to criticize others. She hadn't been to service since Thanksgiving. And yet, the church beckoned her, as if it would infuse her with the spirit of love and banish hatred from her heart

The Lesson and the Gospel had obviously been read and the Lord's Prayer recited as the priest was into his homily. "....we are told to forgive. We are not promised that it's going to be easy. After all, God's forgiveness of us was anything but easy. It cost him the sacrifice of his beloved Son on the cross, thus the cost of forgiveness is high. We, when in the course of our lives are called upon to forgive those who wronged us, may expect at some time to also pay a high price. "The price might mean personal pain and sacrifice. It might mean giving up things we have a right to. It might mean welcoming people back into our lives that we'd just as soon shut out forever.

"God recognizes that for humans, forgiveness can be a long drawn-out process. A period of time may be necessary to work things through and to pray over the pain we are feeling. Ask God to give us the Grace to be able to forgive as He has forgiven us."

After the Bread and Cup were prepared, Linda joined communicants at the altar.

The priest delivered the Sacrament. "The Body of Christ, the bread of heaven."

Bittersweet House

"The Blood of Christ, the cup of salvation."

She took the wafer and wine, lifted her eyes to the Cross, and prayed, God *banish hate from my heart. Help me to do right. Open my heart to love and forgiveness. Amen.*

As she descended the stone church steps, Linda added to her prayer, *Forgive us our trespasses as we forgive those who trespass against us. Please, Lord, let me know true forgiveness. Show me the way.*

Chapter 19

Zita bit her lip and pressed the bell. She waited. Where the hell is Linda? Impatient, she stabbed the bell three times. Finally, the door opened. "Zita! What brings you here?" Linda asked, obviously surprised.

"I know we talked at lunch a few hours ago and I should have called," Zita blurted, "but I just had to talk to you, one on one."

Linda closed the front door and led Zita into the den. "How about a drink, or a cup of tea? You look like you could use a drink."

"Is it that obvious? I don't know how many times I've been up and down the shore road from Seacliff to Greenwich. I can't seem to clear my head, to make sense of my feelings. I'll take a drink."

"Have a seat. Relax." Linda said as she aimed for the bar and held up a wine bottle. "Try this. I think you'll like it." She handed Zita a full glass. "It's Henry of Pelham Chardonnay."

"Thanks." Zita took a hefty swallow. "It's good." She laid the glass on the end table and frowned. "I tried to be upbeat at lunch." She ran her fingers through her wavy strawberry-blonde hair that sprang back into place. "But if I don't get to tell somebody I think I'll burst. I could talk to Margaret or Kat--but I'd rather cry on your shoulder. We've been through so many crises together. This is different."

"You seemed okay at lunch--bubbly, conversational. What happened between then and now?"

"It's difficult, but I'll try," Zita answered as she sank into a wing chair and clasped her hands together. She swallowed hard, picked up her glass and took another gulp, then settled back and pressed her eyes shut for a moment. The strained expression eased. "I can't believe how lucky I am to find a guy as sweet as Peter. You remember how bitter I was when David

100

Bittersweet House

left me for his cutie? I've pushed it to the back of my mind and almost forgotten it. Peter talks about our future together, but to be honest, that scares me. I don't know whether we can have a future together."

"Why not? What's the problem?"

"He wants to marry me."

Linda grinned, "You call that a problem?"

"There's more." Zita paused and let out a heavy sigh. "He wants children."

Linda raised an eyebrow. "Oh?"

"I'd move in with him tomorrow if it were just the two of us, but Peter says kids need structure, a home with a mother and a father. Little does he know."

"Perhaps you'll have them. It's still possible at 42."

"Possible in some cases, not mine." Tears welled in her eyes. "You know what I went through with in-vitro fertilization and exploratory operations: the drugs, the money, the miscarriages, the pain. That shit David only pretended grief--no baby meant more freedom for him, less responsibility. I'm certain he did a tap dance when my doctor told him I couldn't have children."

Linda walked over to Zita and took her hands. "If Peter loves you, he'll take you as you are. Don't torture yourself. You might get pregnant again. Miracles have been known to happen."

"Not for me. After four miscarriages, a tubal pregnancy, exploratory surgery and four in-vitro's, I've had it. I want to obliterate all of it, get it out of my mind forever," Zita, said rocking back and forth. "Sorry. Here I am burdening my best friend with past history."

Linda smiled, "You know the old cliché, 'What are friends for?'

Zita pressed on. "David and I had to meet with a psychiatrist to see if we were both stable enough to go through with in-vitro. I felt his questions weren't pertinent. Nothing on child-rearing; rather, questions on our marriage, what our life was like, our social life. I don't have much faith in psychiatrists. Their questions are theoretical at best and have little to do with real life. That period in my life was an emotional roller coaster. It takes six months every time you go through in-vitro. Never again."

Zita dug into her bag for a tissue and wiped her eyes. "That's the end of the sad story, Linda. It's all behind me, but I'm frightened. I don't want to think of this baby business at all, but Peter loves children. Did I tell you he's three years younger than I? I don't know what to do. Should I tell him

Liz Barzda

I probably can't have kids? Is it fair to leave him a glimmer of hope when I don't believe it myself?"

"Well, if you say 'probably,' that's not lying. You can't predict the future. Stranger things have happened. How about adoption?"

"I've thought about it, but he talks about a family of his own. I'm afraid he'll reject me, Linda. I can't lose him. Isn't it odd that I almost passed him by because he isn't polished and would rather watch baseball than ballet? Now I can't live without him. And besides, he's handsome," she laughed. "Man, what a body!"

"You almost missed a good bet. A polished veneer doesn't mean the wood underneath is necessarily strong. But Peter sounds solid."

"I feel empty. Do you really believe he could still love me if he knew?"

"He loves you just as you are. Take my word on it," Linda declared. She kissed Zita's cheek.

Linda's comforting words helped Zita regain her composure. She smiled. "He'd better, or I'll stick pins in a voodoo doll and twist them as I chant his name." She gave Linda a bear hug.

"When am I going to meet Peter? He does exist, doesn't he?" Linda said playfully.

Zita's face brightened, "You'll meet him soon, I promise." She turned serious again. "Linda, I love him. He truly cares for me. *Me.* He's real, nothing artificial about him. When we go out, he'll ask what movie I'd like to see and where I'd like to eat. On the weekends, he likes to go hiking or fishing; so we do the outdoor things. He's considerate and kind to everyone, even though he's in a rough business. When a man treats you that well, you can't help loving him. Every day I love and appreciate him more."

"If he's what you believe him to be, go for it! Why are you unsure of a future with him?"

"He wants to take care of me. Can you imagine?" Zita said shaking her head. "And I *do* want to be cared for, to have a strong man protect me. Women are supposed to stand on their own two feet, but when a loving man helps to support you, you feel as if you could walk a tightrope."

A contemplative expression crossed Linda's face. "If truth be told, the majority of us want it all."

"Maybe it can be done," Zita said with a shrug, "if you get the right guy. Look at you. You've managed to hold it all together--a husband, home, a career."

Linda rose, turned her back on her best friend and stared out the window. "You don't have to be like me, Zita. You have your own life. Seems to me it's going in the right direction."

"We're supposed to be able to carve out a life without a man. But the hell with the feminists! I want Peter's love and protection. Never in my wildest dreams did I think a man could be central to my life again. I have my own business, and I'm doing well. After that putz David left me, I proved I could make it on my own. But now I don't want to. Not anymore."

Linda turned and faced Zita. "So don't. Enjoy the fact that Peter loves you."

"Peter isn't perfect, of course, and certainly not articulate. He's not a college graduate, but he's intelligent, a hard worker, and he says his uncle plans to bring him along in the construction business. Eventually he'll be able to buy in."

"Thanks for listening, Linda, and lightening my mood."

Zita looked around the cherry-paneled room. It's masculine feel always brought Christopher to mind. "Is Christopher home? I'd like to say hi. I haven't seen him in some time, since Margaret's birthday bash for Jack."

"He's out doing some errands, but I'll tell him you asked about him," Linda said as she accompanied her friend to the foyer.

"Tell him I asked about him only because I'm dreaming of his body."

"I'm sure," Linda said with a laugh.

Zita kissed Linda's cheek. "Thanks for listening. You're special. If I could, I'd fashion my life after yours."

#

On her drive home, Zita rehashed her conversation with Linda. Her demeanor appeared as supportive as always, yet Zita sensed her best friend's detachment. Linda said nothing about what she and Christopher were up to. And why hasn't anyone seen him?

Back in her condo, Zita promised herself that negative thoughts would not sabotage the evening with Peter. This night belonged to them. She wanted it to be festive, beautiful, loving, all the elements that added up to a celebration of their engagement.

She would tell him that she couldn't have children. But not now. She dabbed Calvin Klein Obsession perfume behind her ears, wrists, and

Liz Barzda

her bare, tanned inner thighs. She slipped on a short black silk dress, careful that no residue of makeup touched the fabric, and strapped on high heeled sandals that showed off her shapely legs. Half-carat diamond earrings completed the overall easy- but-elegant look. She wanted Peter to be bowled over, to tell her how gorgeous she looked. She wanted him to eat her up. She slid Celine Dion's "Power of Love" CD into the player to heighten her romantic mood. They planned to dine and dance at the Hilton. She pictured Peter looking at her with love and lust in his eyes. Zita closed her eyes and danced over to her dresser. She pulled out a black evening bag, did a happy twirl-around and danced back to the mirror for a last look at a woman who was about to be engaged. She couldn't wait to answer his proposal. "Yes, yes, yes." Almost seven o'clock. Peter would be here any moment.

She watched her reflection, zeroed in on her mouth and said, "Peter, I'm so lucky to have you, you gorgeous man. I'll marry you and keep jumping your bones until you beg for mercy, all 5 feet 2 inches of me." Zita threw back her head and laughed at her own zaniness.

The phone rang. She let it continue for four more rings, debating whether to answer it or not. She certainly didn't want anyone to hold her up. If it were important, they'd call back. Rather than have a ringing phone spoil her mood, she picked it up and with an irritated tone said, "Hello."

"Hi Zita, it's David. I'm coming up to see you--for old time's sake."

Chapter 20

The setting sun stretched red, yellow, and orange colors across Long Island Sound like party streamers. Margaret stared out the Cadillac's open window, breathed in the sea air and intertwined her fingers behind her neck. "Don't you just love it? If I could, I'd swallow everything my eyes could see. It's so beautiful." As they drove along the Seacliff Shore, she kicked off her sandals, leaned into Jack and brushed the hair from his forehead. He turned and smiled at her, uttering not a word, but his eyes conveyed love. "I never tire of looking at the water, nor of you. Jack, we're so fortunate to have love, work, family and friends. Sometimes I worry that it won't last, that something will happen to screw it all up."

"You worry too much," he mocked.

"I suppose you're right." A frown crossed her brow. "It was a hell of a week, what with pushing Joe Arcara to keep on schedule for the Forest Park development dig. He's making noises about being behind on his Jenkins factory addition, but I'll keep reminding him that my clients are eager to see their homes go up."

Jack kept his hands on the wheel, turned to his wife and pecked her dimpled cheek. "Don't get all uptight about it. Joe may not be on schedule, but he'll catch up and deliver the goods. He's worth waiting for. With Arcara you needn't worry about shoddy workmanship or inferior building materials."

"You're right, but I have to be on top of everything. Keep reminding him. Luckily, Seacliff Villas are on schedule. Joe knows they're top priority. He's already begun digging." Margaret placed her hand on Jack's shoulder, "Okay, now it's your turn to unload."

"What's to complain about? Should I worry that the hospital board is fighting me on the new hospital addition? Should I worry about borrowing money or having a fund-raising campaign to make the addition feasible?"

"Yes," they said in unison.

"Perhaps a big donor will come along and finance it all--highly unlikely," Jack laughed. Margaret looked at him with pride. "You're a terrific president. I know you'll convince the board to build that addition. It's desperately needed."

They continued riding, savoring the breeze and the breaking waves. A frolicking couple caught Margaret's attention. "It's Greg!" she exclaimed. She watched her nephew chase a pretty young woman in a hot pink and yellow bikini. "I wonder who the girl is? Stop the car."

From the shoulder, the Dolans watched as Greg pulled the girl toward him, wrapped his arms around her and laughed. As they approached they heard the girl warn, "Hey, not so tight, you're choking me."

Greg loosened his grip on her as he saw them approach.

"Aunt Margaret! Uncle Jack!" Surprised to see you here." He bent down and kissed his aunt. "What's up? Giving up smelling the roses for the smell of the sea?"

"Something like that," Margaret said, and quickly glanced at the olive-skinned, dark-eyed beauty. Jack shook hands with Greg and cast an admiring look at his companion.

"Aunt Margaret and Uncle Jack, this is Raquel Lopez."

"Pleased to meet you." Raquel said.

"Nice to meet you, Raquel," Margaret said as she took in the girl's sensuous mouth, flowing black hair and sexy-looking body.

"Raquel and I met at Arcara & Daughter. A lucky day for me. We've become really good friends. Isn't she beautiful?"

"Greg, I think we're more than good friends," Raquel challenged. "Wouldn't you say?"

He ignored her question and addressed his aunt and uncle. "Roll up your pants, Uncle Jack, and walk in the water with us. It's warm. Come on, Aunt Margaret, you're already barefoot."

Margaret looked from Greg to Raquel. "We don't mean to intrude."

"You're not intruding," Greg insisted. "Are they, Raquel?" He didn't wait for her reply, rather pulled his aunt toward him.

"No thanks, it's tempting, but I think I'll pass," Margaret said drawing away. "You go ahead, Jack. I'd like to sit on the sand and talk with Raquel."

Bittersweet House

"Sure, you two get to know each other," Greg said. He kissed Raquel. "Say nice things about me."

"Greg has mentioned you and his Uncle Jack often," Raquel said as she sat down on the blanket and trailed her fingers along the sand.

"His uncle and I are very fond of Greg. Perhaps you already guessed." Margaret sat and wrapped her arms around her bent knees. "How long have you known him?"

"We met in June when Greg started at Arcara. I work in the cage where gofers and expediters come for tools and supplies needed by the construction crews. We've been together every weekend. It's been great."

"You two haven't known each other very long. It's lovely that you get along so well. Unfortunately, summers are short and he'll be leaving for Yale in a few weeks."

"Margaret, ours is more than a summer romance," Raquel snapped. It wasn't lost on Margaret that the young woman addressed her by her first name. "Greg and I are close; very close. He suggested living together and putting off college for a while."

Margaret did her best to hide surprise and anger. She put a smile on her face and said, "That's strange. For years Greg talked about attending Yale and becoming an architect. I can't imagine he'd give all that up."

"It's what he wants. It's what we both want," Raquel said. "We love each other. The future will take care of itself."

Margaret looked at the young woman whose overt sexuality could derail her nephew's promising future. "Raquel, would you mind if I asked you how old you are?"

"Not at all, I'm eighteen. An adult."

"So is Greg. Ever since grade school, he focused on becoming an architect. He'd sketch buildings and think how he'd use new products to give his buildings a distinct appearance. He intends for his work to be easily recognizable--like his signature. I can't imagine he'd give it all up so easily."

"I don't know about that. I just know he wants to be with me. Anyway, he's smart and he can keep working at Arcara's. Maybe someday he'll be a foreman."

Her words were like a blow. Margaret took a moment to collect her thoughts before replying. "There's nothing wrong with being a foreman, but Greg has a special talent, and I wouldn't like to see it sidetracked."

"Greg knows what he wants. What he wants is me. And I feel the same about him. So it's really our business. Don't you agree?"

Liz Barzda

"No, I don't. Let me be candid with you, Raquel. You're only looking at the situation as it is now. That's what young people do. I'm looking at it from all sides, to the future. I know what his mother would have wanted for him. I know he's capable of it. I also know that his life will be enriched with a fine university education. I want to see him live his dream. If you truly love him, you'd want the same for him."

"He doesn't need a degree to be happy." Raquel tossed her head, dismissing Margaret's wisdom. "He has me." Margaret framed a response in her mind, but before she could utter it, Raquel added, "And we're going to live together. Maybe my mother will let us fix up the basement. Greg will continue in construction. Everything will be cool."

Momentarily, taken aback by Raquel's news, Margaret was grateful for the fellows return. "Hey, my two favorite women," Greg beamed. "Hope you got to know each other. Uncle Jack and I talked mostly about the Boston Red Sox, but we did briefly mention both of you," he said, wrapping his arms around Raquel.

"It was nice to talk with you, Raquel," Margaret said, then smiled. "I feel I know you quite well."

Raquel smiled back. "Likewise."

She turned to her nephew and kissed his cheek, "Love you."

#

Margaret and Jack rode home in silence. The sun had set, and shades of gray blanketed the sky, mirroring Margaret's mood. "What's wrong?" he asked. "I sensed tension between you and Raquel. "Don't you like her?"

Margaret sucked in her breath then exhaled. "No, I don't like her. How can I like a young woman who's shattering Greg's future? She's dissuading him from attending Yale, and thinks it's just grand for him to continue working construction?"

"Are you serious?"

"I wouldn't joke about this. Imagine what Jennifer would think if she were alive. My sister would be heartbroken!" Margaret reached for a tissue and wiped tears from her cheeks. "Jack, she mustn't spoil his life."

Chapter 21

"When will you be home?" Kevin asked as he watched Sandra deftly apply lipstick with a brush.

"Don't worry, I won't charge a slew of things, just a blouse. Darlene and I will check out the sale at Whitney's. I'll be home before Tiffany gets back. Did you see how excited she was when Linda picked her up for lunch and a visit to the zoo?"

"I guess all kids love a one-on-one visit with a favorite aunt." As an afterthought, he added, "Tell Darlene to be careful. Thunderstorms are predicted."

The doorbell rang. "That must be Darlene," Sandra said as she scooted to the bedroom, snatched up her purse and headed for the door, Kevin a step behind. "There's ham if you want a sandwich. I'll fix dinner when I get home. We can go to the movies tonight if you'd like. I'm sure I can get Mrs. Brody to babysit Tiffany." She pecked Kevin on the cheek. "The Sunday mall crowd takes the fun out of shopping." She laughed, a soft, bell sound, which he adored. "But we'll press on. See you later, hon," then she darted out the door.

His eyes followed her as she hopped into Darlene's car. He waited until they were half a block away, then dashed into the garage, started the car, and sped down the street in a flash.

He caught up with them on the thruway, careful to keep four vehicles behind

Darlene, wove in and out of traffic passing cars at 75 mph. *I'll bet they think it's all a blast; speeding, shopping, and probably drinking.* How many times had he brought Sandra home from a party after she draped her arms around some guy's neck and kissed him, too slushed to know what she was doing? *She could spend Sunday afternoon with me, but she'd rather go carousing with Darlene.* He didn't give a shit about the heavy rain battering his windshield. He had to find out what Sandra was up to. As if he didn't know. He winced at the embarrassing memories. Last night at work, he overheard two of his co-workers in the john ridiculing his wife.

"Hey Shorty," Frank said to his buddy, with a raucous laugh. "Did I tell you I saw Kevin's wife last week going into the Marriott late at night with a young dude?"

"No kidding? Are you sure it was her? What the hell were you doing there at that time? Trying to lay some chick?"

"You got it. She said no go and I told her she was missing a good time. But I know that was Sandra I saw. I'd know that body anywhere. Can you imagine her stepping out on Kevin? He must be a real klutz. Man, if I had a chick like that, I'd give her enough dick so she'd never stray. Probably wouldn't be able to walk out of the house."

"Yeah, sure. You're all talk. No way could you satisfy her, you with your miniature minnow." Shorty howled.

"Want to compare?" Frank shot back, then continued, "But what I should have done was wait around till she came out, then ask her if she wanted to party with a real man."

"Knock it off, Frank. Kevin's a good guy. What's the point of making fun of him? Maybe the guy's hurting."

"You might be right. But if I were Kevin, I'd keep an eye on her."

Kevin kept perfectly still in the last stall until he heard them leave. He replayed that scene in his mind over and over. It was probably a pattern with Sandra; meeting men at motels, kissing them, probably fucking them while he was at work. And where was Tiffany when all this was going on? Probably with the baby-sitter. Good, reliable Mrs. Brody. The rain blurred his vision. He white-knuckled the steering wheel, straining to see between the swishing wipers. He was losing sight of them. He pressed hard on the gas pedal. The speedometer registered 75, then 80. He passed the car in front of him, then the next.

As he was about to pass the third car, it darted out to move ahead. Kevin turned sharply left to avoid a collision, but his car went out of control on the rain-slicked pavement, hit the median barrier, bounced off, spun to the right, crossed the lanes, went off the road and, with a horrendous crash, struck a tree, winding up in a mass of glass shards and twisted metal.

Bittersweet House

Traffic screeched to a halt, windows rolled down. People craned their necks to view the mangled car.

"Sandra!" Darlene gasped as she looked through her rear view mirror, "I can't see too well with all this damn rain, but I think there's a bad accident behind us. Looks like a lot of vehicles. Remember, I spotted a car that looked like Kevin's three cars back weaving in and out of traffic. It couldn't be Kevin, could it?"

Sandra palmed her mouth to stifle a cry. "Dear God, I thought you were joking. You really think it's Kevin's? It can't be!

"Get the phone out of my bag and dial 911," Darlene ordered. With trembling hands, Sandra punched in the number. She managed to relate the accident location to the dispatcher.

Darlene sped to the next exit, down the ramp and reluctantly slowed down at the four-way stop. "Can't you go any faster?" Sandra cried.

After three red lights and another four-way stop, they finally were back on the thruway and sped to the accident site. They arrived before a police cruiser, fire truck and ambulance. The police had opened the passenger car door. An officer noted the air bag didn't inflate. Another checked the blood-stained victim for life. When the paramedics arrived, one of them released the victim's seat belt, careful to avoid numerous pieces of glass strewn about.

Sandra pushed her way past the police officers to reach the victim. "I think it's my husband. Let me see him!"

She gasped at the sight of his bloody face. "Oh, Kevin. My God, he's all cut up. He's going to be all right, isn't he? Tell me he'll be all right." She held her head in her hands and wailed. "He's getting all wet."

"There's a pulse, ma'am," the paramedic said. "He's alive, but we have to get him to St. Mary's Hospital right away. Do you want the police to drive you there?" the young paramedic asked solicitously as he and his partner carefully moved Kevin into the ambulance.

"I'll drive her," Darlene said. She steered Sandra away, helped her into the car and secured her seat belt.

"Oh Lord, what have I done?" She looked at her friend as if in a daze. "Darlene, why was he following us?"

"Sandra, I don't know."

They reached the hospital and followed the ambulance to the emergency entrance. Two nurses grabbed the stretcher and propelled it into an emergency cubical. Orderlies ran out and transferred Kevin onto a gurney.

Liz Barzda

Sandra and Darlene ran after hospital personnel. "I'm sorry, but you can't come in," one of nurses declared at the emergency entrance.

"I'm his wife. I have a right to know what's happening."

"The doctor has to do an initial assessment to determine his injuries. He'll let you know his condition as soon as he finishes the examination," the nurse assured her, then disappeared through the double doors.

After office personnel took insurance and Kevin's health history, Darlene led Sandra toward the lounge. "They'll call us when they know something."

"How long do you think it'll be? They will save him, won't they? Tell me they'll save him."

"I don't know, Sandra," Darlene responded as she brushed wet hair away from her friend's face. "We have to wait and hope for the best."

Darlene held Sandra's hands as they waited. "We've been here over an hour," Sandra moaned. She rose, walked to the examination room doors, came back, sat and bit her lip. "They must know something by now."

"I know this is eating you up. There's nothing we can do but wait and hope for the best," Darlene said.

Sandra jumped up when she noticed a nurse cross the room. "Were you in the emergency room when they brought my husband in? His name is Kevin Dubois. He's all right, isn't he? He's got to be all right."

"Your husband is in the operating room. We'll let you know his condition as soon as we can."

"Can't you tell me anything? I'll go crazy if I just keep sitting here without any information."

"I'm sorry. We're doing our best," the nurse responded, then turned and left.

"Please, God, let Kevin live and I'll never ask for anything again." Sandra turned to her friend. "Do you ever pray, Darlene? I used to pray as a kid, but haven't for a long time. Oh God, I'm so sorry now, so sorry for those selfish prayers, thinking only of myself."

"How about some coffee?" Darlene asked. Anything to momentarily distract Sandra from the terrible accident.

"No. I can't swallow anything." Sandra answered and began biting her nails. Darlene brought coffee anyway. Sandra shook her head. Her eyes never left the doors, watching for the doctor.

"I'm to blame for this," she said between sobs. "He wouldn't have followed and driven like a crazy man if he didn't suspect me of cheating. I never cheated on him-- except that one time. That was because I had too

Bittersweet House

much to drink and this creep took advantage of me at a motel. I know I've been crazy Darlene, partying and all that crap, but I love him. I love him."

She looked at Darlene with eyes that pleaded for understanding. "You believe me, don't you? Promise you won't tell anyone about the hotel incident. Only Linda knows. She came for me at the motel when that rat took off while I slept. But it didn't mean anything." She covered her eyes and groaned, "Stupid me."

"Stop torturing yourself," Darlene soothed. *Kevin will make it.*

"But it's my fault. The accident, everything. How can I live with it?"

After what seemed like an eternity, the doctor emerged from the operating room. His face mask hung below a haggard, expressionless face. "Mrs. Dubois, we did our best. I'm sorry. He didn't make it."

Sandra screamed, "I'm sorry. I'm sorry. God, forgive me."

Chapter 22

On Monday, La Petite Spa's receptionist, Darlene Moore, greeted and checked customers eager to partake of the latest in skin care, massage, and hair styling. They waited for their technicians in a spacious reception area where crewel-embroidered French chairs and rose-colored Queen Ann wing chairs on an Aubusson rug produced an elegant ambiance. Coffee and tea, served in Royal Albert bone china, and soft classical music added to the elegant atmosphere. Katherine walked down the crystal-lit mauve hall containing rooms for facial, Swedish massage, body scrub, foot, and hand treatments. All were occupied. Her clientele appreciated the renovation and passed the word to friends. Business was booming. Through one of the partially opened doors, Katherine heard Mary, her new esthetician, exclaim the benefits of the Swedish massage to wealthy Mrs. Vinton. "This treatment will relax, revitalize and renew your body, stimulate circulation, relieve tension and flush the lymphatic system." Katherine smiled at Mary's pronouncements, thinking the old Mrs.V. needed to overhaul her testy personality more than her body. She passed the foot therapy room and sniffed the light scent of peppermint and foot cream oil that wafted through the air.

"First the salt bath, then the massage, followed by a pedicure. Your feet will feel brand new," a therapist promised. From the body scrub room, "Umm, this is divine," came the sleepy voice Katherine knew to be Buffy Baxter, Seacliff's society maven, who adored the overhead Vichy shower and the aloe vera gel exfoliation. The addition of the fountain, courtyard and chef proved a boon to business. Clients loved the added luxury features. Despite the surge in income, Katherine still worried about

Bittersweet House

finances. She visualized the bank squeezing her like a lemon until her body would be nothing but pulp.

Scott just had to come through!

Katherine's stomach knotted. Why hadn't he approached his father about the loan? Couldn't he see she was on tenterhooks? His old man was rich. All he had to do was ask. Scott's father surely wouldn't refuse his only son.

As disturbed as she was about Scott's procrastination, it was nothing to what she felt about his infidelity. Her fists clenched at the thought of him with Beryl, that Limey with a sham Mayfair accent.

She thought back to the scene of Beryl and Scott laughing together as they headed for his car. Where were they going? Probably to his condo where he'd screw her.

She checked her watch; five o'clock. Scott was to pick her up at seven. Many of the Spa's clients would be powdered, buffed, sprayed, polished, and out the door by seven. Others, corporate-types, would be serviced by the evening crew who worked from five to midnight. Katherine figured she could wind up her supervisory duties by six, barely sufficient time to get home, shower, and dress.

But first she'd call Scott to remind him of their date. It wouldn't be the first time he'd forgotten. She grabbed her phone and punched in his number. No answer. "Shit, he's not home," she spat. Just for the hell of it, she tried Beryl's number. If he's with his secretary, it'll be the last time they'll ever be together, she vowed.

"Hello," said a sexy female voice. "Who's calling, please?" She heard whispering in the background, then, "Scott, I can't hear when you're talking." Katherine stabbed the disconnect button, then threw the phone against the wall. Plastic shards skittered across the floor.

She kicked the phone fragments around and around. *Fuck you, Scott Bowman. I'll get you for this. How can you swear you love me, only me, then treat me like some stupid bimbo? You won't get away with it. And that goes for your little whore, too.*"

There was a light rap on the door. Darlene poked her head into the room. "I'd like to leave at seven, if it's okay, got a heavy date with Roland."

"That SOB better show up," Katherine threatened under her breath.

Darlene raised her eyebrows. "Are you talking about Scott? I don't know where he is now, but I saw him at the casino on Friday."

Liz Barzda

"What are you talking about? You saw him at the casino? What casino?"

"At Foxwoods. Roland took me there on my day off. We had a great time," Darlene's face lit up. "Played the slots and won $25."

"How nice," Katherine said through tight lips. "Are you sure it was Scott? Who was he with?"

"Of course I'm sure. He was with an attractive gal with reddish hair. She had an English accident. Could've been his secretary. Heard him call her Beryl. They must have made a bundle playing blackjack. She clapped and carried on like she won a million."

"Thanks for that tidbit, Darlene. Good night."

"Darlene shrugged her shoulders. "Good night. See you tomorrow."

#

Katherine sat behind her desk and toyed with the idea of a drink, then thought better of it. She needed a clear head more than she needed booze. Scott was like a disease; still she didn't want to lose him. She loved his infectious laugh, the way his eyes lit up when she removed her bra and panties. And when they made love, his hard athletic body went from tenderness to passion, obliterating all problems in the afterglow.

She recalled his tenderness at her mother's heart attack and sudden death. "You have *me*," he had answered when she railed against the world, striking out at the inequity of it all.

"My father deserted my mother and my little brother when I was 12. She had a hell of a life working two jobs and trying to make ends meet." Katherine confided, "Any wonder why I sometimes seem bitter?"

He held her tight. "Don't, Kat. You've had it rough growing up, but look what you've accomplished. You're smart, you have friends, and you've built a thriving business. Besides, you're cute. He covered her face with kisses. "I'm proud of you."

She remembered thinking, yes, he's proud of me, so damn proud that he still hasn't approached his father for the loan. He knows I need the money to finish redecorating. But the hell with him. No matter what, I'll get the money, with or without his help.

Her frown faded, replaced by a smile as she recalled the deliriously joyful moment when she learned her grandfather left her a million dollars. Scott was genuinely happy for her, showering her with roses and champagne. "You deserve it, baby. There's no stopping you now."

Bittersweet House

She admitted that Scott's joy in her good fortune meant more to her than inheriting the money. That kind of shared happiness can't be faked, and she loved him for it. But then came the pregnancy. Her mood went from bliss to betrayal. *God, I don't want to think about it!*

Scott said we needed to untangle our lives. Marriage had to be put on hold. Certainly we would marry in the future. But a baby? Out of the question.

She told herself that Scott actually didn't push her into having an abortion, but he turned on the pressure in subtle ways. He said a baby would complicate matters and deter me from my business goal. "Neither one of us is parent-oriented, he had said. "We're career people. I, like a fool, agreed with him." Katherine suddenly had a pounding headache. She pushed her chair back and slowly walked to her private bathroom for aspirin. She gulped the pills down with water. But the memories wouldn't subside. Like a movie, all the scenes had to be played out.

She splashed cool water on her face and ran her fingers through her long hair. Her mind relentlessly pursued the subject she couldn't block out--the abortion. It was two years ago, but it remained vivid. She saw herself alone, climbing the steps to the gynecological center where she knew they would suck out the life that was growing inside of her. She wanted to die.

She lied to her friends. She told them she'd be attending a three-day beauty and spa symposium in New York. After the surgery, she remembered how alone she felt, like the last living creature on earth.

Katherine gripped the sink. At times, she would forget about the abortion. Still the terrible episode hinged itself to the back of her mind, reminding her that something horrible lurked there, and she couldn't rid herself of it. Time passed, but the thought and feel of the surgical vacuum that sucked out the lining of her uterus, and the cramps that followed, never left her.

Lately, another thought hounded her. What if she wanted a baby, after all? What if she could have had her business and a baby? What if she could have guided an infant into a lovely, accomplished, caring human being? What if Scott had married her and they had had their baby? Katherine grimaced. That happening was as likely as ridding the world of poverty.

She returned to her office, sat at the desk and continued to review the past. Scott claimed he knew her better than she knew herself. Perhaps he was right and she wasn't mother material. He once asked her if she could devote eighteen years of her life to a child. She changed the subject. Proof

Liz Barzda

enough that she truly didn't want a baby? Better to have taken a chance at motherhood than to kill a human being, she thought. Too bad abortion was an option.

Scott never offered to accompany her to the center; but after the abortion he took her to Newport for the weekend--two blissful days of R&R and solicitous attention. The subject of marriage never entered the conversation. Would it ever? Katherine had no reservations about blaming Scott for the post-abortion infection in her birth canal that resulted in pelvic inflammatory disease. Surely she could try to forget, but easier said than done. Both born under the sign of Scorpio, a sign of extremes, Katherine knew that a wronged Scorpio can be a worse-than-vicious adversary. She could picture them spewing their venomous sting at each other. She grabbed the phone and dialed the number for Bowman Plastics. She might get lucky and reach the old man. According to Scott, he's a workaholic; probably works every Saturday.

"Bowman Plastics," said a male voice.

"Eric Bowman, please."

"Sorry, this is security. Mr. Bowman's secretary isn't in and there's no one in the office."

"I'd like you to try. This is important. Mr. Bowman is probably working. Please ring him."

"Just a moment."

"Sorry, Mr. Bowman isn't taking any calls."

"Just tell him it's about Scott."

Moments later, "This is Eric Bowman. What's this about?"

"Just thought you should know that Scott was seen gambling during working hours at Mohegan Sun Casino on Monday."

"Who is this? I don't I know you, and I don't know why you're telling me this. Don't ever call here again."

Chapter 23

In a state of unease, Linda checked the guest room, then the other rooms. Christopher wasn't home. He was out probably having breakfast. Good, she preferred not to see him.

What a blessing to have the house to herself. She put on coffee, sat at the breakfast table and stared out the window at the darkening gray sky. How her life had changed! It seems so long ago that she awakened with a feeling of physical and emotional gratification after a night of lovemaking. She assumed everything would continue in that pattern--going about daily activities and planning the future. Linda never imaged something would blindside her and rip away her rosy dreams.

She put a slice of bread into the toaster and poured a mug of coffee. She didn't particularly want either of them. She seemed brain-dead, unable to plan ahead or make decisions, a mechanical thing without feelings. Since she couldn't rise above the catastrophe or forgive her husband, she'd do nothing. Occasionally, a thought of saving her marriage would peek through her anger, but Linda would squash it like boot on a cockroach. Let Christopher solve the problem of his mistress and son. She nibbled toast and watched the dark clouds swirl in the sky. The ringing phone startled her. She picked it up "Hi, Linda. It's Art."

"What a surprise!" Her agent rarely called her at home. "What's up?"

"Couldn't resist. Just had to tell you. Got good news!"

"I could use some."

"Your contract's been renewed for two years. They know they'd be crazy to let you go with *your* ratings."

"Can't say I'm not relieved."

"Sweetie, you're in the market at the best time. The TV titans are finally acknowledging the graying of America." He added hastily, "Not that you have gray hair, but you're at the right place at the right time. What a boom time for all women on the air!"

"About time. It took the industry long enough."

"You can still run circles around all those young girls. Your name is known. You're respected. That translates to high marketability. This calls for a celebration. By the way, how's Christopher?"

"He's fine. Busy traveling. As a matter of fact, he'll be off to Europe on Monday. Right now he's holed up in the den making plans. He'll be at it all day." She had no qualms about lying. Not now.

"If his day is so busy, I'm sure he wouldn't mind if I whisk you off to the countryside. Let's spend some time together discussing WSEA and Connecticut Chronicle."

"Today?"

"Yes. Right now. We can make a day of it. There's a lot to talk about."

"But it's such rotten weather. Forget I said that. What do you have in mind?"

"We could hop up to Hartford for the Wadsworth Athenaeum, drive down to Marlborough and lunch at the Tavern and wind up at Mohegan Sun Casino."

"You're in luck, dear boy. I've put in a lot of overtime the last few days so the station owes me comp time. Sure, I'd love to go, but only if you won't subject me to bingo."

"I promise."

"Marvelous. Pick me up in an hour."

#

Rain beat on the BMW as it zipped along the Merritt Parkway toward Hartford. Linda and Art discussed the direction TV was taking, the new reporter sleeping with the news director, and the effect of the Internet on their business. Her personal problems receded, replaced by media conversation they both reveled in.

How perverse it all seems that she and her agent would spend a day of cultural and dining delights, pleasures that she and Christopher once relished. Was it almost two years that they spent such a day? "So tell me," Linda inquired, "have you heard whether Ron Richard's contract has been renewed? I know I'm not supposed to ask, but he's a friend as well as my co-anchor. We're a good team. I'd love for the arrangement to continue."

"'Cause you're my favorite client, I'll tell you. Ron's agent couldn't get a TV interview for Miss America the day after her crowning. Somehow he managed to get Richard's contract renewed."

Linda smiled at Art's appraisal of his rival's talents, but she was pleased her co-anchor would maintain his position. Rain continued all the way to the museum. They traipsed through the Athenaeum's outstanding Hudson River School landscapes and the European Impressionist masterpieces, housed in the interconnected Wadsworth building. "These paintings nourish the artistic soul. Don't you think so?"

"At this point, I don't know. We've been traipsing through the museum for two hours. Please, can't we forego viewing the Colonial furniture? I don't care if this is the country's oldest continuously operated public art museum. Give a sixty-year-old a break," he pleaded. "Maybe we're absorbing culture, but I'm ready to absorb food. He patted his paunch. "How about nourishing the body?"

They drove to Marlborough for lunch at the historic Marlborough Tavern. The hostess ushered them into the intimate Madison Room where a portrait of the fourth president hung over the fireplace. The low ceiling and dark paneled walls gave the room a cozy feeling despite the gloomy weather.

The waitress handed them each a menu quoting Samuel Johnson, "There's nothing which has yet been contrived by man which so much happiness is produced as by a good tavern or inn."

"A man who knows of what he speaks," Art declared.

Linda noted the printed material attesting to the fact that James Madison and Andrew Jackson supped at the Tavern. "Doesn't it evoke your sense of history to dine in the President Madison room?" she asked.

"Not as much as the chicken piccata, the French Chardonnay, and the kiwi apple tart," he quipped while perusing the menu and wine list.

Before dessert was served, Linda inspected a framed picture of Dolly Madison with a background of writing. "Art, the notation reads that Dolly Madison was the woman who introduced ice cream to Washington society."

"She sounds like my kind of woman." A look of contentment crossed his face. "That was a great meal. What do you say we top it off with some excitement? How about we run down to Uncasville and separate the Mohegan's from some of their money? We might get lucky."

Liz Barzda

"Why not? They have a hell of a lot more than we have." Driving rain continued as they headed southeast to the Mohegan Sun Casino. They ignored the weather and sang along with the love-gone-wrong tapes of Patsy Kline and Willie Nelson.

She wasn't a gambler, but the Mohegan setting and the hum and buzz of the gaming machines with quarters spewing out of the one-armed bandits sent a current of excitement through her.

The Casino's décor with its sculptured panels depicting Indian scenes, huge boulders, treed pillars, shields and lampshades representing hunting scenes gave it the appearance of seasonal Indian lodges. Cascading waterfalls added excitement to the surroundings.

Art zoomed to the blackjack table, where, without a doubt, he quickly reached his $100 limit and then complained that the cards wouldn't cooperate.

Linda opted for the slot machines. It gave her a high to pull the one-armed bandit, see three lemons emerge, hear quarters clang as the machine spewed out the payoff.

After a little while, she saw Art trotting toward her. "I've got to talk to you." He grabbed her arm and steered her to a corner table in the Cove Bar. He leaned forward and whispered. "I was in the john, and guess who came in? Len Bertarian, Seacliff's chief administrator, and Ed Kaminsky, the city's financial director.

"How could you tell who it was from your stall?"

"I had seen them at a baccarat table. They can afford to be high-rollers, the bandits! And I know their voices. Heard them often enough around town, spewing their propaganda. I was in the last stall, they were at the urinal close to the entrance, and I overheard them talking like crazy.

"Bertarian was probably sweating bullets. He told Kaminsky he heard a rumor that somebody planned to blow the whistle on him, the mayor, and four other city officials because of misappropriated funds to finance more than a million dollar insurance policies for them. Bertarian guessed the disgruntled city employee contacted the FBI."

Linda smelled a big story. "That's dynamite information-- if it's true. Who is this guy? Does the informer have any proof? How do you know he's on the level?"

"Come on Linda, you've been around the block a couple of times. The whistle blower, no doubt, works in City Hall and knows where the bodies are buried. The guy is trying to protect himself and his buddies. Bertarian and Kaminsky are worried. They don't want to lose those cushy jobs.

122

Bittersweet House

Linda felt a surge of excitement. "Did they say anything else?"

"Yes. I heard Bertarian say, 'Listen Ed, this is serious. I don't know who the snitch is, but apparently he wants to distance himself from the rest of us. Seems the shit's going to hit the fan any day now. That SOB went to the Feds. And he'll probably contact the media. Linda, this could be a terrific story. It's Pulitzer stuff, great for your career. Or at least another notch in your belt."

Linda bobbed her head. "You're right. It's too good to pass up. I'll do this story even if I have to do it on my own time." She chuckled, "That new notch on my belt is a sure thing."

#

The rain had stopped; night emerged with a slivered moon and endless stars. The Seacliff neighborhood was quiet and peaceful when Art dropped Linda at her front door.

She breathed in the clean smell of wet grass. With a lighter heart, she put the key in the lock while rehashing the evening. The thought of breaking a big story gave her a thrill.

As she passed the living room, Christopher intercepted her. "Where have you been?"

"I was out."

"I wish you had left a note or told someone where you'd be."

"It's none of your business. When was the last time *you* left a note?"

"Don't be stupid!" he shouted. "This is important. Darlene has been calling here for the past four hours. She needs to talk to you."

"Don't raise your voice to me. What did she want?"

"Kevin was in a horrible accident."

"Dear God! What happened?"

"He's dead."

Chapter 24

The bereaved gathered in St. John's Episcopal Church for Kevin Dubois' funeral. Attendance swelled with family, friends and co-workers who came to mourn a man barely in his prime. Rows of chairs were hastily assembled in the narthex to accommodate the overflow. It was the church where Kevin was baptized, where he and Sandra eyed each other at Bible study, where they were married and where Tiffany was baptized. A large photograph of Kevin stood on an easel banked by floral. Sandra's blanket of yellow roses cascaded over the mahogany casket.

Sandra entered the church supported by her parents, Wendell and Dorcas Beattie of Camden, Maine. Sandra looked worn; her black dress accentuated her pallid face. She seemed distant, removed from the surroundings. Her parents held her hands as they led her to the front pew, where Kevin's parents, Marie and Claude Dubois were seated with Linda and Christopher.

The Dubois clan of aunts, uncles, and cousins sat behind Kevin's parents. Kevin and Sandra's many friends were present. Her best friend, Darlene Moore, gasped when she saw Sandra. Darlene leaned closer to a mutual acquaintance and lowered her voice, "She looks ghastly. I had no idea. Her family said she couldn't see anyone."

Gregory O'Neil, Kevin's cousins and co-workers acted as pallbearers. Because of Tiffany's deep emotional attachment to her father, the family decided she should not attend the memorial service. Mrs. Brody, the baby sitter, planned for Tiffany to join her and her granddaughter for an outing at the zoo and lunch. Friends, members of Kevin's bowling team, and classmates from his engineering classes filled two pews. Some whispered about Sandra's reputation, others questioned Kevin's need to follow his wife.

Linda spotted Scott Bowman seated at the extreme left. She wondered why he didn't arrive with Kat. Why wasn't he sitting next to her?

Christopher postponed a business trip to London to attend his brother-in-law's funeral. He informed Linda that he had to forego the reception to prepare for the trip. They agreed to be civil to each other during this tragic time. In church, Linda attempted to leave space between herself and Christopher, edging closer to her father--anything other than touching her husband. She emotionally removed him from her psyche, but tolerated his presence so no hint of their marital discord would add to the family's sorrow. Her thoughts reverted to Kevin's untimely death and her sister's depressed state. Someone was mouthing words that seemed to come from afar. She finally grasped that Rev. John Hutchins was speaking.

In a mellifluous voice, the stately priest began the burial service. In the eulogy, Hugo Bassert, Kevin's close friend, co-worker, and best man at his wedding, spoke of Kevin's devotion to wife and daughter and his dedication to his work. With a sincerity that elicited sobs from the congregation, Hugo, elaborated on Kevin's personality, his ever-present smile that radiated good will. The church's soloist sang "Amazing Grace," and the congregation recited the "23rd Psalm."

Kevin's mother, Marie, sobbed into her handkerchief as the soloist rendered her son's favorite hymn, "Just a Closer Walk with Thee." Kevin's father, Claude, sat with his hands on a Bible, lips tight, staring straight ahead. Sandra, sandwiched between her parents, kept her eyes on the cross as the Rev. John Hutchins recited prayers.

"Dust thou art, and unto dust shall thou return," Rev. Hutchins chanted. The organ sounded resurrection music and the attendees began to exit. Linda's parents aided Sandra as she walked the long aisle to where Rev. Hutchins waited. "I pray the Lord will ease your pain," he said as he kissed Sandra's cheek. She made no sign of recognition, just stared at him.

He offered his sympathy to the suffering parents. He held Marie's hands and spoke from the heart. "Kevin was a fine man. Because of him this church is a better place. His lessons were sprinkled with love, and the children responded in kind."

He shook Claude's hand. "I know this is little comfort to you and his mother, but I want you to know that your son was much loved. He won't be forgotten because the love he spread endures."

"Thank you," Claude said and turned away.

Liz Barzda

Linda watched them with sadness. They were stoic people who kept their own counsel. They never inquired where Sandra was when their son met his death. Did they blame her? Did they suspect Sandra's first priority was having fun and not her husband? Linda prayed the Dubois's wouldn't harbor resentment, and that God would help them through the worst period of their lives. Linda attempted to block out the unfairness of Kevin's early death, yet couldn't completely erase the resentment she felt about Sandra's part in the tragedy. *If she hadn't been scooting around looking for a good time, Kevin would be alive today.* No, I mustn't think that. Kevin's gone. My sister is with us, but seems out of it. She'll need help.. Rev. Hutchins reached for Sandra's hands. "I'm so sorry, my dear. I know how much Kevin loved you. He told me that your love meant more to him than anything in the world. I trust that thought will help carry you through this terrible time." Sandra looked at the priest without recognition or understanding.

He turned to Dorcas Beattie, "Your son-in-law was a wonderful Sunday School teacher and a fine man. We shall miss him. I pray God will grant both families peace."

"Thank you, Rev. Hutchins," Dorcas said as she and her husband guided Sandra ahead. Sorrow permeated the site as prayers were said over Kevin Dubois. Sandra placed a yellow rose on her husband's coffin. The mourners slowly drifted away, most headed back to the church for the funeral reception.

"Are you all right, Mother?" Linda asked. Her beautiful mother seemed to have aged the last two days. Her blue eyes were misty, and the fine wrinkles in her face had deepened. "I think it best that we take Sandra home. She needs to rest."

"You go to the reception. I'll help your mother," her father offered. He looked calm, but she knew he called on all his inner strength not to break down. The mourners assembled in the undercroft, where the Episcopal Church Women had prepared a luncheon. Lace-covered tables were laden with tea sandwiches and salads. Silver coffee and tea sets, and various desserts sat on long tables. Several small tables dotted the large room. Linda acknowledged "let us know what we can do to help" offers. The buffet line moved slowly as family and friends seated themselves to celebrate Kevin's life with food and remembrances. As she walked to her table, she overheard a gossiper declare, "His wife ran around. I guess the very good really do die young." The din rose, heightened by laughter, as

Bittersweet House

the luncheon progressed. Congregants and friends expressed their sorrow to Kevin's parents before they departed.

Marie hugged Linda and shook Christopher's hand. "Claude and I thank you both for arranging the reception. I'm afraid we weren't up to it."

Linda hugged Sandra's in-laws. "That's the least we could do for Kevin." With slumped shoulders, the Dubois's walked slowly to their car with no mention of Sandra.

The undercroft emptied. Church women washed dishes and utensils, removed soiled tablecloths, and stacked tables and chairs. Only one table with four guests remained: Linda, Catherine, Zita, and Margaret.

Linda sighed deeply. The funeral was over, but the pain of losing Kevin was difficult to bear. She looked from Margaret to Zita and Kat, grateful for their presence. She focused on Kat's face and the tears that poured from her brown eyes.

"I'm sorry to be blubbering, but when someone as young as Kevin dies, it makes you stop and think of what's important in life." Katherine took a deep breath, but the tears kept flowing. "It makes you want to do the right thing, to ask God for forgiveness."

"What terrible thing have you done to ask God to forgive you?" asked Linda.

"I did a wicked thing, and perhaps God will never forgive me." She knew she shouldn't unburden herself, but she couldn't stop. "I had someone call Scott's father to tell him that his son was gambling at Mohegan Sun on Monday when he should have been working." She wiped her eyes and tried to compose herself. "Scott won't take my calls. I noticed him when he came in, but he wouldn't even acknowledge my presence. Oh God, I should die."

Margaret gently touched her hand. "You did a terrible thing, Kat, but God will forgive you if you're truly repentant. We're human, and we make mistakes. Not one of us here is without sin."

Katherine searched for a tissue in her purse and dabbed at her eyes. "Not you, Margaret. I'll bet you have nothing to reproach yourself about."

"I'm not blameless." Margaret hesitated for a moment, as if summoning courage. "I love my nephew Greg as if he were my own son. I'd do anything for him. When Jennifer was dying of cancer, she asked me to look after him. I intend to carry out her wish. I'll make it my business to see that he enrolls in Yale and is not diverted from his education by the tramp he's involved with. She insists he doesn't need to attend Yale; that he wants to

Liz Barzda

marry her, and he'll continue working in construction. She believes his family is wealthy and can set them up in style. Believe me, I'll see that it doesn't happen."

Margaret laughed, "And all of you thought of me as compassionate. Let me tell you, I'm a tiger when one of my loved ones is threatened. I'll use whatever resources I have to protect my nephew."

"Understandable," Linda said. The others nodded in agreement.

"But whatever you do isn't as evil as what I did," Katherine moaned.

"It's just a matter of degree, my dear," Margaret countered. "Who's to say which is worse, or how much blame should be administered?"

Katherine homed in on Zita. "I doubt that you have any regrets; not with a new boyfriend and a going business." Zita lowered her eyes. "I've done a few things that prick my conscience. I took advantage of David's knowledge of forthcoming real estate sales. It wasn't ethical, but I closed my eyes for financial gain. And the other day, when Peter hit David because he was threatening to take my business away, I could have called the police before he was beaten to a pulp, but I chose not to. I figured he had it coming. When Peter said he'd send a couple of wise guys just to scare David, I thought that was justified. In fact, Peter and I laughed about it. I wanted to hurt David, to get my revenge. I was devastated when he left me. So count me in as one who needs forgiveness."

Katherine sighed again and turned to Linda. "Don't tell us that you have any regrets, Golden Girl of WSEA-TV," Katherine said attempting a smile. "And your marriage. Solid. You're a lucky woman."

"Oh, yes, I'm so lucky," Linda mocked. She looked away from her friends. "What is it they say about the wife being the last to know? Count me among them. My husband has a mistress and a 2-1/2 year-old son. How ironic! The man who didn't want children is now a daddy." Her voice quivered. "Did you hear me? A mistress and a son." Until now, she didn't believe she'd ever confess this to a soul, not even her mother. But here she was spilling her guts. She couldn't stop, and she no longer cared what people thought.

"If it weren't an emergency call from his mistress screaming that their son was violently ill, I'd still be the dupe, just a stupid wife in the dark. Couldn't even share it with you, my best friends. I was too proud. Maybe I didn't pay attention to the warning signals. Were there any warning signals? I don't know. She nervously wrapped a strand of hair around her ear." Her eyes took in each one of her friends. "I couldn't admit to you that Christopher and I aren't the perfect couple. You jokingly called me

128

'Miss Generous Heart' because of my penchant for helping anyone out of a jam. That's me, Linda Cooper to the rescue. I can't even rescue myself. I'm a fraud."

Katherine's mouth dropped. Zita's eyebrows shot up. Margaret gasped.

'Shocked?" Linda asked. "So was I. My world fell apart. I wanted to kill him. He destroyed our life. Worse, he took away my belief in marriage. I may never trust a man again. I look at men now and wonder if they're cheating on their wives or girlfriends. What dirty little secrets are they hiding?" Tears filled her eyes. "Who would believe it of Christopher, that handsome pillar of society?"

Zita reached for her hand. "I'm so sorry, Linda."

Katherine shook her head. "I can't believe this of Christopher. How can you bear to live with him? What will you do?"

"Do? I've done it all-- screamed at him, slapped him, prayed that disaster would befall him."

"Is there any way out of this morass and still remain sane?" Margaret asked.

"I don't see how. Should the four of us live together as a family? Maybe," she hissed, "he could alternate spending time with me, then with her and the baby. I'm tired of it all. Let him get us out of this hell." Unable to stifle the sobs, she covered her eyes and cried.

Margaret gathered Linda into her arms. "Is there something we can do?"

"No. I'm sorry to dump everything on you, but I can't help it. This is the first time I've told anyone about my so-called idyllic marriage. I'm glad it's out. Keeping it in was suffocating me."

Zita said, "We've been friends since college, more than 20 years. You know I'm here for you, as are Kat and Margaret."

"Men are bastards," Katherine declared. "Maybe Zita can get one of Peter's wiseguy acquaintances to rough Christopher up a bit?"

"Peter and I have already gone that route. Not a good plan," Zita quipped.

"Right," they said in unison and chuckled in spite of themselves.

"It's a wonder we can find a little humor in our foibles. Laughter is good, even in adversity," Margaret proclaimed. "This is a horrible time, especially for you, Linda."

"Friendships like ours often endure longer than marriages. Let's be thankful for what we do have. Maybe prayer will help. Shall we join hands

Liz Barzda

and seek guidance?" They held hands and prayed for Kevin's soul, asking God to grant him eternal peace.

Margaret added, "Lord, we beseech You to banish greed and hate from our hearts, to live Your commandments, and to learn to truly love our fellow man. And we thank you for each other."

"Do you have to say man? Can't you say human beings?" Katherine asked in total seriousness.

Margaret smiled, and continued. "Lord, this is a difficult road for us to travel. Forgive us our weaknesses, for we repent and seek to do Thy will. Grant eternal peace to our friend, Kevin, in Jesus' name. Amen."

Chapter 25

Zita opened the door and gasped at the sight of her lover and ex-husband standing side by side. "How dare you show up here," she shrieked as her eyes bore in on David Parker. "What do you want?"

He faced her and chortled, "What, no 'hello?' after all we've been to each other? Don't bother with introductions. Your friend and I have exchanged names. I think you mean to invite me in, even though you haven't mentioned it. He brushed passed Zita into the living room and positioned himself in front of the fireplace.

Peter followed him into the room, said nothing, but kept his eye on David.

"Get out, David!" Zita commanded. Her eyes flashed from him to the poker. She lunged toward David, lost her footing and stumbled.

"Don't you lay a hand on her." Peter's voice took on a threatening tone. "You can walk out of here on your legs, or crawl out on your knees."

"What were you going to do Zita, beat me to death with the poker? No need to get hysterical. I came to offer you a business deal. Good of me, don't you think boyfriend? I assume this is your boyfriend, right dear?"

She looked to the phone. "I'm calling 911."

"I'll give you just one minute to leave," Peter said.

"Zita, put down the phone," David ordered, then turned to Peter. "You're a dumb ass if you think you can threaten me. You'd be smart to hear me out. I'll bet she didn't tell you much about me. I'm the guy who helped her build the business and who put up with her shit for years."

Although she loathed him, Zita was curious as to why she should hear him out. She slowly cradled the phone. "Peter, I know you're not afraid of him, neither am I. He had little to do with the agency." She glared at David. "I'll give you exactly five minutes before calling 911."

Peter watched David's every move.

"I won't leave till I'm ready. I was with you for twenty years, that's *two decades,* Zita, and the business still bears my name--Parker Advertising Agency. I intend to be compensated for it. Do you hear me? I want my share!" Peter balled his fist and took a step towards David. "Keep out of this," David said. "It has nothing to do with you. You don't know our history. You know nothing of the life we shared, what we meant to each other."

"Stop it! I don't want to hear any of this," Zita cried, covering her ears.

David frowned. "You're going to hear it all." He pointed his finger at Peter. "You may as well get in on it. But before we get down to business, I was curious as to how you refer to your boyfriend. Do you call him Stud? Or is his handle Choice Stud or Stud Choice?" Peter lunged at him, but David sidestepped the move. "Did Zita tell you that I used my expertise as a bank mortgage officer to locate the best building and site for our advertising agency? I'll bet she didn't. Inside information acted upon to benefit a broker is frowned upon by the Real Estate Board. But we didn't tell them, did we, hon? And how do you think your rich Gold Coast clients would react to this choice bit of information--never mind the media," David proclaimed with a grin on his face.

Peter continued to eye him. David kept up the harangue. "You've forgotten the money spent on your in-vitro fertilization procedures. I helped pay for all those. You wanted a baby and all the trappings that go with it. I didn't. Well, it's time you did something for me."

"Are you crazy? You agreed to the divorce settlement. I owe you nothing."

"You thought a divorce and a $125,000 kiss-off would get rid of me. Well, darling, that's not nearly enough. It's very simple. You have a chance to make amends, to give me my due-- half the worth of the building and the business."

She stared at him in disbelief. "You don't stand a chance. All our agreements were legally recorded. You agreed to the divorce terms. You couldn't wait to get your hands on the money. You signed off on all rights to the business in lieu of quick cash. I'll bet you blew it all in no time, and now you think you can extort more money from me. You're brain dead

Bittersweet House

if you believe I'd surrender half of property to you. You'll get nothing! Zilch."

"Zita, I can throw him out now. I think his five minutes are up."

Feigned pain crossed David's face. "Wait. Boyfriend, you have to hear this. You have no idea what we once meant to each other. Happy years, weren't they, Zita? Remember how I was there for you when you planned the office?"

Zita couldn't believe his memory was so warped. "No," she shot back. "But I do remember how you loved the life style the agency afforded us, and that you dumped me for Jessica, a bank clerk barely out of her teens. You didn't even leave a note, you coward."

Zita felt her eyes misting over. During the dark days of divorce, she often wondered how many times he had he taken his little tart to out-of-state seminars? She was well rid of him, didn't want to see him, nor hear of him--ever.

David repeatedly informed her that the business was her baby; he had no time to devote to an endeavor that might not be successful. Might even bomb big time. His banking career took precedence over her work. "Let's cut to the chase," David said impatiently. "Here's the problem, Jessica likes to play the ponies. Things got out of hand-- like $50,000 worth. Unfortunately, she borrowed from some unsavory characters. Now they're leaning on me, big time. But you can fix it. Just write me a check and I'll say good bye. That's the lesser of the two evils. That or you'll end up divvying up the business and the building."

"You heard the lady," Peter said. "Not a penny. Leave now while you can."

"Fuck you. Keep out of this, whatever your name is." David turned to Zita and snickered, "I thought you had better taste than to go for brawn over brains."

Peter lunged at David, missed, chased him around the sofa, cut him off. Then hit him full in the face. David screamed as he fell. Blood poured from his nose. "I'll get you for this," he blustered as Peter grabbed an arm and jerked him off the floor. David wriggled out of Peter's grasp and scurried to the other side of the room. He held one hand over his bloodied nose, and with the other hand, dug into a pocket for a handkerchief. "I'll sue you for everything you have, Zita. Do you hear me? I mean everything-- your building, your business."

He looked at Peter with loathing while he pressed the handkerchief over his nose. Then eyeing his torn blood-stained shirt, "I'll have you arrested. Then I'll sue you. You're finished. Both of you."

Zita shook her head. "You brought all this on yourself. I'm sorry for you, David. I really am."

"Shut up, you bitch!"

"That's enough." Peter grabbed him and shoved him to the door. "I'd have that nose attended to, if I were you. Hope it won't disarrange your profile." He ejected David into the hall, slammed the door and locked it, and took Zita into a protective embrace.

Zita clung to him. "He'll put in a complaint and have you arrested."

"I doubt it. Guys like him are windbags. He's lucky to get away with just a bloody nose."

Zita sighed. "He had it coming. And yet I feel slightly guilty. His nose is probably broken."

He kissed the top of her head while embracing her tightly. "I don't want you to worry. I've met a lot of guys like him; gutless, full of themselves and all hot air."

"Don't dismiss him so easily. His back must be against the wall for him to come up here and threaten me." She took Peter's hand and led him to the sofa. "I'm afraid of what he might do next. I wouldn't put it past him to have you arrested and sue both of us." She sat quietly for a few moments, then put her head on his shoulder. "I'm not as sweet as you think I am. I really wanted to kill him. I think I'm capable of it, and it scares me." *If Peter knew how willful I am he probably wouldn't want me? Better not to know the answer.*

"Believe me, you're not the only one who thinks they're capable of murder when cornered and threatened. Self-preservation is probably our strongest emotion. Try to get him out of your mind."

Zita snuggled in Peter's protective arms. She felt safe with him. It pleased her that he understood her primitive reaction to David's threats. "Look," he said holding her close. "It's too early to call it a night. Let's go out, have some fun, and forget that loser. A little palm-greasing might salvage our dinner date at the Hilton. We might even get in some dancing."

"I really don't feel like celebrating."

He took her face in his hands, looked into her eyes. "I don't ever want to see you unhappy. I'll always be here to protect you from that asshole, or from anyone else who tries to hurt you."

He kissed her tenderly. "You're beautiful. I can never get enough of you. But I won't be greedy; I'll let the rest of the world have the pleasure

Bittersweet House

of looking at you. Come on, get your purse. We're going to salvage this night and have a wonderful time."

"I can't resist you. You know that, don't you?" Lines creased her forehead. "You don't think he'll come up here and trash my place, do you?"

"Move in with me where you'll always be safe." "I don't know, Peter. I can't think that far ahead."

"Just to be sure your ex won't hassle you, I'll ask my Uncle Joe to send a couple of big wise guys to pay him a visit. All they'll have to do is go to his apartment, ring the bell, and stand there. David will get the message and crap in his Calvin Klein jeans."

Chapter 26

Scott checked his watch, 3:55, just enough time for the 4 o'clock appointment with his father. The old man hated tardiness by anyone, especially his son.

What is it now, Scott wondered? His father was continually on his back, hounding him because he balked at working ten hour days, including Saturdays. The company was doing okay. No reason for the old man to be in a snit. Saturdays meant little to the owner of Bowman Plastics. He reveled in the business he had developed, and nurtured its growth to nearly 800 employees. Some of the key people didn't share his total dedication to the job, but it was of little significance. The old man espoused the credo that managers who aspired to higher positions must be committed. Scott decided to gauge his father's mood before bringing up Kat's request for a low interest loan. He'd talk up her ability to pay, mentioning that her business shows signs of profitability, but the high interest loan for renovating and redecorating was choking her. If his father would accommodate her with a low-interest loan, it would mean the world to her.

The offices were virtually empty, including the outer office where Theresa, the president's secretary, guarded the inner sanctum. No one barged in on the president of Bowman Plastics, not even his own son.

Scott knocked. And waited.

"Come in," said a raspy voice. He wasn't asked to sit down, but Scott honed in on the sofa, part of the handsome blue and beige leather set in the spacious professionally decorated office.

"I'll be with you in a moment," said Eric Bowman without raising his eyes from his work.

Scott waited a good ten minutes then picked up a Wall Street Journal

Bittersweet House

among the financial magazines. He leafed through the paper, breathing deeply to assuage his nervousness. The old man kept him waiting. What the hell for? He wasn't late. Dad or not, Scott was irritated, but he wouldn't give way to his passion. He learned to submerge his anger and mollify his father--worth any sacrifice for his inheritance. He put the paper down and studied his father's face. Flesh fattened his square jaw, but his mouth still bore a determined line. A handsome man at sixty eight, with silver hair, Eric had just enough wrinkles to pay homage to his life experiences. The elder Bowman could still be a formidable business foe. Scott stared at the Persian carpet. The leaves in the pattern reminded him of the woods in northwest Connecticut where he and his dad went camping. His mind wandered back in time when he and his dad would fish and then cook their catch over an open fire. He recalled carefree days as a teenager when his dad bought the Hobie Cat and taught him the skills of sailing. Although they often butt heads, they respected each other. When had the closeness vanished?

Finally, Eric looked up from his papers.

Scott rose, strode across the room, and took the chair facing the oversized mahogany desk. "I've called you prior to a full meeting with the officers to get your views on the possible takeover of BuiltRite Boxes, and to go over the feasibility study."

Scott cleared his throat, "I don't have it with me, but I've been working on it. I'll have it ready for Thursday's meeting."

His father glared at him, "How can we even think about this acquisition when you haven't completed the study?"

"It's mostly done. I couldn't finish it because I felt sick last week," Scott avoided his father's stare. "Must have had a virus."

"The only bug you had was in your ass," Eric thundered. "This takeover is important to the growth of our company. If you put in more time, you'd have come prepared."

Scott leaned forward and stared at his father, "What do you mean 'if I put in more time'. I'm here most Saturdays. All that's left of the study is the risk factor. I'll have it done by Thursday."

"I expected the study completed today so you and I could find the weak spots. You know this is a crucial period. I need you here during the week and Saturdays. Scott opened his mouth to speak. His father held up a hand, "Spare me the lies. You weren't here Monday when I needed you. I called a meeting of all the department heads, including you, our financial officer. It was imperative that you be here."

Liz Barzda

Scott bit his lip. "I told you I was sick."

"I called your apartment early Monday morning."

"I went out for cough medicine the doctor called in."

Eric's voice rose. "Don't embarrass yourself by saying another word. You weren't sick enough to gamble at Mohegan Sun."

Scott's jaw dropped. "Where did you get such a story? I wasn't there."

The elder Bowman's neck and face took on a bright flush, the vein in his forehead visually throbbing.

"How can you be so stupid?" he barked. "One of your cuties called here to report seeing you there. I won't tolerate a liar. Not only are you cheating the company, you don't even have a loyal girlfriend."

Scott whimpered, "It's all a mistake. I can explain."

His father held up a hand, "Not another word." Dots of perspiration formed above Eric's mouth. Scott wondered why the old man was beginning to sweat. So unlike him.

"I suggest you spend this weekend completing the feasibility study if you wish to continue with the company. We'll go over it Sunday night."

"Don't worry, it'll be ready."

"Worry? Yes, I worry. About you. You've had a fine education. You even have the brains to match. You're in the catbird seat of this company and some day you'll run it, but you haven't lived up to your potential. With your financial and technical expertise, I expected you to guide us in a possible buyout that would strengthen Bowman Plastics."

"If you spent less time socializing and con... on... the...the..." his father stuttered between short breaths. Scott stared at him. Was the old man losing it?

Eric held his hand to his head, "I don't feel right.. feel light-headed." His coloring turned ashen. He struggled for air. Pain, registering across his face, distorted his features.

"Dad! What's wrong?"

His father clutched his arm and writhed in agony. Perspiration poured from his face. He gasped for breath. Dumbfounded, Scott leaped out of the chair. "Dad! Talk to me." No response. Scott caught him as Eric slumped forward. "Hang on," Scott screamed.

He laid him down gently and scurried to the desk. Papers and office paraphernalia flew as he groped through the drawers frantically searching for aspirins. Nothing! "Fuck it! Dad, can you hear me? Don't die on me." He grabbed the phone and dialed 911.

Bittersweet House

"Hello, I think my father's having a heart attack. We're at Bowman Plastics, 100 Amity Turnpike, Seacliff." Scott repeated the address. "Yes, operator you have it right. Hurry." Scott held his father in his arms. "Hang on Dad. Help is on the way. Don't die on me. Please don't die on me."

Chapter 27

Margaret waited nearly thirty minutes past their agreed meeting time. Along with being a liar, Raquel Lopez is apparently unreliable. Margaret planted a smile on her face as Raquel swung into the coffee shop at 4:30. Despite the steamy weather, the girl appeared cool as an autumn breeze, and sexy with a full-lip sensuous smile, smooth olive complexion, and long-lashed dark eyes. Her white v-neck cotton blouse and jeans clung to her curvaceous body. She gracefully slid into the booth facing Margaret.

"I'm glad you could make it," Margaret said with a forced smile. "I asked you to meet me here so we can get to know each other--in person. A friendly chat over coffee is a good first step, don't you think?"

"Yeah, sure. Sorry I couldn't meet you for lunch, but you know I've got to work. Nice that you called so often. Anyway, the phone calls were great, and I love talking about Greg."

Raquel focused on Margaret's silver-blonde-streaked hair and expensive linen suit. "I'll bet we have a lot in common." Her lips curled upward, but her eyes belied the smile.

Margaret ignored the remark and decided to tread slowly. "Would you like a Coke, or coffee? How about a sandwich?"

"No food, thanks." Raquel cupped her face in her hands and leaned forward. "Do we start with a chat? Chatting isn't my thing. On second thought, what the hell. What I'd really like is to start with a drink. Sure could use one, but this isn't the place. Is it? Coffee for me, then."

"Did you get held up at work?" Margaret asked as she waved the waitress over and ordered another coffee.

Raquel shook her head. "Not really, but God, what a day! Foremen checking on inventory, asking for tools, and what all." Raquel took a deep

Bittersweet House

breath, turned her head and lifted one barely perceptible eyebrow at the two tight-jeans on the muscular workers a few tables away. "I shouldn't complain about my job. Work is work. You have to go with the flow, right? You should know about that, being a successful businesswoman, right?"

Margaret ignored the question. Discussing her business was not on the agenda. "Looks like you don't want to talk about your business. So what do you want to talk about, Aunt Margaret?" Raquel giggled, "You don't mind if I call you Aunt Margaret? It's just that Greg and I are so close, you're practically my own relative."

Margaret studied Raquel. Unfortunately, character didn't match face and form. She believed the girl would go to any lengths to hang on to Greg. And his pending fortune. Her lies would wreck his future and have a devastating impact on his family.

The waitress ambled over with the coffee pot. "More coffee?"

With a sheepish look, Raquel announced, "Changed my mind. I'll have two jelly donuts with my coffee." She wagged her finger at the waitress. "Make sure they're fresh."

"I'll have another coffee." Margaret brushed her hand across her brow, although the cafe was relatively cool. The thought of Raquel being part of the family was distasteful. "You know Greg means the world to us. He's like the child we never had. His happiness concerns us. You do understand, don't you?"

"I sure do. You say that you love Greg, well so do I. We agree on that, so there's no problem." Raquel fingered her gold chain. "It'll all work out." The frowning waitress returned and plunked down the donuts.

Margaret took a sip of coffee. "What do you mean by, it'll all work out?"

"Greg and I have plans," Raquel replied while stealing glances at the fellows seated across from them. She turned her attention back to Margaret, laughed and held up a soggy donut. "Can't resist these things. What was I saying? Oh yes, I told you that day at the beach that Greg doesn't plan to go to college. Like I said, he doesn't need college. He can go on working at the plant. I think he can work his way all the way up to a foreman. He's smart, you know."

Margaret's mouth tightened. "We're all aware that he's smart, and that he planned to become an architect. He needs to get a college degree to realize his dream."

"His dream? His is the same as mine--to be together, now, not some day in the far, far, future. Especially now."

141

Liz Barzda

"What do you mean 'especially now'?"

Raquel tittered, "I'm pregnant."

Margaret frowned. "I don't believe it. You can't be."

"What do you mean I can't be? I am." Her lips stretched into a challenging smile.

Margaret stared at Raquel before answering. "Are you sure?"

"I'm sure."

She marveled at the girl's ability to play the innocent. Would she abandon the charade? Would she tell Greg she made a mistake about the pregnancy and ask for his understanding? Unlikely. The conversation didn't appear to be heading in that direction. Margaret harbored no guilt about exposing Raquel's perfidy. She watched her devour the second donut. "How far along are you?" Raquel wiped her hands on the paper napkin then flicked her long black hair over her shoulders. "I'm three months. Work doesn't bother me. Sometimes the guys come into the cage pretending they need supplies, but instead ask me for dates. I just laugh them off."

"That must be flattering for a young woman like you."

"Yeah, sure, but I keep telling them I've got a boyfriend. Greg's the only guy for me-- now and forever."

Margaret eyed her confrontationally, then softened her expression and reached for Raquel's hand. "You're so young. Won't it be difficult to give up partying, pretty clothes, and going out whenever and wherever you choose? You can't do that when you're bogged down with a baby. Think of sleepless nights, late feedings, and a crying infant. Raquel, being a young mother is difficult. You'll give up your youth and freedom for years."

"How bad can it be? Greg and my parents will help out."

"It needn't be difficult. There is a way out, you know."

Raquel pulled her hand away and shrieked. "I wouldn't think of such a horrible thing. My people don't do abortion."

"I think you know that's not what I meant." Margaret looked deeply into Raquel's eyes and lowered her voice. "Have you thought about giving up your baby for adoption?"

"Certainly not. We take care of our own." Uneasiness crept over Margaret. The girl certainly didn't express genuine joy in her pregnancy. *I think she's lying.* Nevertheless, in the most sincere tone Margaret could muster, she asked, "Can you two afford it? Having a baby is expensive-- hospital bills and all those things babies need. You'll also have the expenses of setting up housekeeping."

"Don't worry; I don't." She looked around for the waitress. "I'd like

Bittersweet House

another cup of coffee," and without missing a beat, continued, "I may put the baby in day care and go back to work. Greg will work construction full time with Arcara. Greg can fix up the basement. Maybe his father can help out with some money. What do you think?"

Margaret gritted her teeth and suppressed the desire to throttle the girl. "Do you honestly think this is what Greg really wants? You know he's enrolled in Yale and starts in September. I doubt he wishes to abandon his dream of becoming an architect."

"He already has," Raquel snickered. "I told him I was pregnant."

"You told Greg you're having a baby?"

"That's right."

"How does he feel about the baby?"

"He's happy about it. Just think, the Easter bunny will bring it. Isn't that adorable?"

"Rachel, did you do a home pregnancy test? Sometimes, those tests are mixed up or misread."

"There's no mistake. There's a baby on the way and I'm happy about it."

Margaret bristled but willed herself to remain calm. "So, your doctor confirmed your pregnancy? I hope he's a good doctor. By the way, what's his name?"

"That's right, the doc said I'm pregnant. Boy, you are full of questions today, but I don't mind answering them. I have nothing to hide. His name is Dr. Shinu Patel."

Margaret leaned forward. "Wrong. You are not pregnant and never will be pregnant by Greg. He'll learn the truth."

"What are you talking about?" Raquel rose and screeched, "You know nothing. I'm having your nephew's baby."

"Sit down, Raquel. You're after Greg for the money. Well, honey, there is no money until he turns thirty-five. It's all tied up in a trust. Are you going to stick around for seventeen years just for the money? Go catch yourself another man while you've still got your looks, because you'll never have Greg. So think about it. You went to see Dr. Patel but it was for a herpes test, not a pregnancy test."

Raquel resumed her seat reluctantly and her eyes narrowed. "How do you know? Whoever told you that is lying."

"Lying? I think you've cornered the market for that."

"Answer me. Who told you? You've been spying on me. There's gotta be a law against that."

143

Margaret looked searchingly into Raquel's eyes. "What you've done is morally wrong, Raquel. Don't you know that?"

Raquel shook her head. "You're pissing me off. I want to know where you got your information."

"It doesn't matter how I found out. Suffice it to say I have connections in the medical field. You're finished with Greg. He'll never trust you again."

"Forget the 'Suffice to say' stuff," Raquel mimicked. "I'll tell Greg I had a miscarriage. He'll believe me. He loves me, so stuff it."

"He won't believe you. I have proof you were never pregnant. There are ways in the medical community to get this information. Either you tell Greg today that you're not pregnant or I will."

"You're putting your nose where it doesn't belong. You can't blow me off, bitch."

"I'll say it just once more, Raquel. Tell him today."

Raquel sprang up, turned on her heels, took a few steps and swung around screaming, "Fuck you Auntie Margaret! And here's more news. Your darling nephew and I are getting married."

#

After driving up and down Seacliff Mall's crowded parking lot, Margaret finally found an empty slot. It was a distance away from the main entrance, but she was lucky to find anything at all. Shoppers were streaming in from the city's offices and the suburbs.

Emotionally drained, she decided to pick up salad, crab cakes and fruit from Ciro's Gourmet Shop. Take-out food would have to do for dinner. She seemed to have lost her appetite, but that was rarely the case with Jack. She locked the car and headed for the mall's entrance, but two people embracing in the car a row ahead caught her attention. Jesus, they were women. Margaret did a double-take when she realized she knew one of the women. It was Raquel! An older woman with cropped hair had her arm around Raquel, pulling her close and kissing her. Margaret stared then took a step back out of sight. Their conversation wasn't audible, but there was no mistaking the visual. The woman had both hands in Raquel's hair and repeatedly kissed her.

"I can't believe it! They're making out in public!" Margaret murmured to herself. Wait till Jack hears about this. And how will we tell Greg? Oh God, poor Greg.

Chapter 28

Neither Kevin's funeral, nor Eric Bowman's heart attack, deterred Katherine from La Petit Spa's morning inspection. She agonized over Scott's refusal to take her calls. Could she put him out of her mind? Perhaps she had no control over her broken heart, but control over her business was a given.

She examined the white orchids on the reception desk, satisfied herself as to their perfection then proceeded to La Petit Spa's sitting area to examine the table adorned with lavender double lisianthus and pink oriental lilies. Fresh coffee, miniature scones and Limoges china awaited her pampered clients. She then surveyed the hair salon, massage, and skin care treatment rooms. All neat and in apple-pie order. Back in her office, Katherine called up the appointment schedule on her computer. Definitely a full house, excellent for a weekday. In spite of the plethora of customers, she felt queasy. Thoughts of Scott and his father invaded her mind. Nausea overcame her.

She dashed to her private bathroom, just making it to the sink, and threw up her breakfast. She splashed handfuls of cold water on her face and rinsed her mouth. The mirror reflected an anemic, ill-looking woman.

No wonder you're sick. You caused a good man to have a heart attack. You're detestable. Scott will never forgive you. You've lost him and all your feminine tricks won't get him back. Katherine reached for the hairbrush on the counter and vigorously brushed her hair as if the motion would banish all evil thoughts. Almost 9 o'clock. Darlene would arrive soon. Had she learned of Eric's heart attack? How would she behave? Five minutes later the receptionist rushed into her office and threw a newspaper on her desk. "Have you seen this? It's horrible. What if the old man croaks? Why did you have me make that call?"

Liz Barzda

Katherine stared at the photo. The caption read Eric Bowman, president of Bowman Plastics and community business leader, hospitalized after a heart attack. "Darlene, I'm sorry," Katherine said as she drummed her fingers on the newspaper. "Believe me; I could cut out my tongue. I didn't know my prank would lead to this. But I can't undo it." Darlene snatched up the newspaper. "I thought it was a joke, like you wanted to get back at Scott for something silly he'd done." Her voice rose. "Suppose his Dad doesn't make it. He's probably on his death bed. I feel like I'm party to it. Have you any idea how this has stressed me out?"

"I know how you feel, but you have nothing to reproach yourself about. Believe me, he's going to recover. I checked with the hospital. They said he's doing well," she lied. "He'll probably be released tomorrow." Darlene bent down, put her hands on the desk and looked into Katherine's eyes.

"How long have you known about his heart attack?"

Katherine met her stare. "Like you, I read about it in yesterday's paper. Trust me, he'll be all right. Besides, we don't know our phone call caused the problem. Scott and his father never got along. I suspect it's a power struggle. I'll make it up to them. I know they'll forgive me."

Katherine knew no such thing but prayed she'd be forgiven. Besides, experienced employees were at a premium, and she wasn't about to lose this one. She reached for Darlene's hands. "Say you understand."

Darlene pulled back. "You guarantee me that he's all right? He won't die?"

"How can I guarantee anything in life? Look, this is difficult for both of us. To show you how sorry I am, I insist you take the day off. I'll have Mae take the front desk. Go home and rest, or go shopping. After a good night's sleep, you'll feel better tomorrow."

Darlene stalked out of the office. "I hope you're right," she flung over her shoulder.

"See you tomorrow morning."

Katherine rubbed her forehead. What a sham, trying to convince Darlene all would be well. The only truism was that she, the instigator, in a fit of jealousy, set in motion an action that caused his attack. Could she make amends? Would she ever feel like a decent human being again? Is there any point in calling the hospital? Probably not. All she'd learn is the obligatory, "He's resting comfortably."

It'd been three days since she acted on impulse. Perhaps if she put a name to it, called it what it was--treachery--she could sweep this incident from her mind, like it never happened. But no, she saw herself telling

Bittersweet House

Darlene to make that fatal call. The scene repeated itself over and over. If only there was a button for dissolve and fade away. She willed herself to settle down to business. At the computer, she reviewed Darlene's supply orders and the monthly expenses. The mortgage and interest costs jumped out at her. Available cash showed she could only cover the interest on her bank loan payment this coming month. It wasn't enough that she'd ruined her relationship with Scott and caused his father's heart attack; now she could kiss good bye the idea of a loan from old man Bowman.

Katherine worked through lunch. Between talking to suppliers and soothing customers' minor problems that loomed gigantic in their minds, time raced by. At three o'clock she gulped a cup of tea and munched a muffin. Afternoon progressed into evening. Thankfully, the last customer kept her hair and manicure appointment, but canceled the massage and was out by eight o'clock. Katherine sat at her desk and wondered what now? Food held no appeal. She'd go home, put on the boob tube, and follow her cleaning woman's advice to "drink your miseries away." If her jealousy hadn't goaded her into brainless action, she and Scott would have gone to dinner or taken in a movie or better yet, rented a sexy video and made love. She'd seen a T-shirt advertised: "Call your village. Their idiot is missing." Well, she should get one and wear it.

She shook her head and muttered, "Scott is out of your life. Face it." In all probability, the only man she truly loved had written her off. It torched her soul. Mournful thoughts bounced from Scott to Kevin. Images of Kevin's funeral took hold. How full the church was. How pale and out-of-it Sandra appeared. How unapproachable Scott seemed. The thought of railing against God put her to shame. Why couldn't she realize that life was still sweet? Katherine swallowed hard, told herself she'd survive, and thanked God for her friends. Their sympathy and insight helped to made Kevin's funeral bearable. But the secrets that surfaced the morning they bared their souls astonished her. Why did she have to be the first of the foursome to spill her guts? *Admit it, you were always a blabbermouth.* It's all out in the open now. Perhaps the Barren Babes can breathe easier, can help each other over life's disappointments. Linda's revelation of Christopher's infidelity was a shocker. Certainly, she knew couples who survived infidelity, but Linda and Christopher? Their marriage had seemed solid. So much for outward appearances. Never mind Margaret. Katherine knew she'd do most anything for her nephew Greg, but the steps she'd taken in proving his girlfriend wasn't pregnant surprised them all. And sweet, unassuming Zita showed she could challenge her ex to protect what

Liz Barzda

was rightfully hers, and would thumb her nose at the world if they couldn't recognize Peter Romano's worth.

Katherine rose, stretched her arms over her head, then ran her hands over her hips to her knees in an attempt to iron out the wrinkles in her sepia silk dress, or was it the wrinkles in her life? She opened the credenza, removed a crystal glass, and poured in sweet vermouth, whiskey, and a cherry. She smiled to herself and said aloud, "I deserve this."

After a hearty gulp, warmth spread throughout her body and lifted her spirits. Surely, the BB's proclamation of woes acted as a catharsis, a first step in righting wrongs, in rebuilding their lives. They needed to talk in depth on the direction their lives were taking, perhaps to plan the future. She'd first talk to Mother Superior Margaret, and then the others. After downing a couple more swallows, she punched in Margaret's home phone number. Following the perfunctory greeting, the conversation focused on Kevin's funeral. "Yesterday was one of the saddest days of my life," Katherine moaned. "The funeral was like reliving Kevin's death. It's enough to make you want to scrap everything and head for New Zealand."

"Kat, you've got to have faith in the future. And you've got to forgive yourself."

"Like Scott and his dad will forgive me?"

"In time, yes. You can't pull the plug on life. Trust me, things will get better."

"Will they get better for Linda?" Katherine asked, unable to hide the bitterness in her voice. "Looks like she's in a no-win situation. I don't know whether she still loves him, but I doubt it. It would be near impossible to live with a man who's pining for his mistress and son. I certainly couldn't do it. Linda doesn't deserve that from Christopher or anyone. No woman does."

Margaret agreed, "I get pissed off when I think what he's done to her. And the poor thing's lost her brother-in-law, and her sister seems to be in a fog. Sandra seemed detached, as if she had no idea where she was or what was going on."

"I wonder what will happen with Tiffany? Do you think Kevin's folks will stay awhile and take care of their granddaughter?"

"I hear they've planned to return to Pennsylvania. Linda's parents will probably stay and look after her in Sandra's home for a while until she's able to function."

Katherine thought about that for a moment, then let out a hollow laugh. "Our lives are running amuck, like the devil is trailing us. Maybe

Bittersweet House

it's time to shake him off the way the Shakers did. Now that's an idea!" Her tone turned serious. "Margaret, we've all been friends for more than a decade, called ourselves Barren Babes because that's what we are, but maybe it's time for a name change. Why don't we call ourselves the New Shakers? Isn't that a fitting name as we're not reproducing? Just like the old Shakers in New York and Pennsylvania, we'll just die off."

"Don't get morbid, Kat. We may not be reproducing, but there are young people in our lives, like Greg and Tiffany. And you never know what the future holds. "Shakers is hardly the name for us." Margaret couldn't suppress a laugh. "I was thinking of white orchids. Like the flower, we're difficult to grow, but when handled correctly, we deliver beauty. I know I'm being silly, but at times frivolity helps. Seriously though, the Barren Babes moniker suits us, don't you think?"

"I suppose so. On a more important note, it seems to me we're all floundering. I don't want to sound like a crybaby, but we need to talk out our problems."

"Honey, don't worry. You're not going to hell. I'll see to it. They don't call me Mother Superior because I'm beautiful," Margaret snickered. She expected a smart come-back from Katherine, but none came.

"Kat, are you all right? Do you hear me?"

The feeling of warmth the whiskey provided evaporated like dew in the Sahara. Katherine swallowed hard and shut her eyes tightly to ward off tears. In a tiny voice, she implored, "Margaret, I really need your help."

Chapter 29

It had been a week since Kevin's death. The Cape Cod house on Cherry Street was loveless. Gloom reigned.

Sandra wandered aimlessly about the house like a specter seemingly unaware of her child, sister, or parents. Having withdrawn from all human contact and everyday activities, she slept for hours, ate little, and talked even less. Tiffany cried in vain for her mother's attention.

The Beatties, concerned over their daughter's mental state and Tiffany's fears and confusion, convinced them to stay and do what they could.

Tiffany remained close to her grandparents. Over and over she pleaded, "Please don't leave me like my Daddy."

Linda called her parents daily to ask if they needed anything. She could stop by in the morning to help her mother grocery shop or to drive her niece to the playground. Friends and neighbors helped with hot dinners and ran errands.

It was a tough week at WSEA for their "Golden Girl." Breaking news of the Russian satellite station that exploded in space, and the massive student uprising in Egypt that aimed to install a fundamentalist government, kept Linda busy. Taking time off was out of the question. As an anchor, she had to deliver the news, write the special reports, and prepare for her weekly *Connecticut Chronicle* program. Her mind shuttled to that horrible night after the memorial service when Tiffany asked why her Daddy wasn't home. Time and again, Linda pictured the look on Tiffany's face when she sobbed, "Where's my Daddy?" Linda recalled how her mother stroked Tiffany's hair to soothe her. "Daddy was hurt in a very bad accident, but he doesn't hurt anymore, and he's in a better place."

"If he's in a better place, why can't I go there?"

Bittersweet House

"Someday, but not now," her grandmother replied while wiping the child's tears.

"Your Mother, Auntie Linda, your Grandpa and I want you here with us."

"Mommy doesn't talk to me anymore." Linda wrapped Tiffany in her arms. "Darling, Mommy isn't feeling well, but Grandpa, Grandma and I will always talk to you. I've got a great idea. How about coming to spend the weekend with me?" Linda thought it better not to mention Uncle Christopher. Who knows if he'd even be home?

"Can I? Can Mommy come, too?"

"If Mommy feels better, of course she can come."

Those scenes filled her mind as she approached her sister's home. How will Sandra and Tiffany be this morning? She held her breath and rang the bell. Her mother's face lit up at the sight of her. "You really didn't have to come. I know how busy you are." She kissed her daughter's cheek. "Bless you for being here."

"You've been doing double duty, Mother. I'm sure you could use some help."

"Are you all right? Have you been getting enough rest?" Emily asked as she led the way to the kitchen.

"I'm fine, Mother. Been working like crazy, but you know I love it."

Emily's brow furrowed as she searched her daughter's face. "You look tired. Have you eaten?"

"I had some yogurt. I don't have much time, but you can make me a quick cup of tea with some toast."

Linda watched her mother's movements as she put on the kettle, slipped bread into the toaster and placed two mugs on the table. Emily appeared distracted, and her shoulders drooped. "I know you're terribly worried about Sandra, Mother, but she'll be well again. Did you take her to the doctor yesterday?" Emily smiled as she served the toast and tea, but her eyes appeared listless.

"Dr. Deloff says its situational depression. He has no idea how long it will last. She's so tense; the doctor put her on an antidepressant. She looks right through the three of us. Tiffany, her friends, her appearance, mean nothing to her." "Surely there's something we can do to help."

"I thought your father and I would care for her in Camden. Dr. Deloff said she needs stimulation and to get back into a routine. He said it's essential, otherwise she'll collapse. He told me that we've got to be sure she takes her medication. We should prod her to talk to us. Urge her

Liz Barzda

to exercise, perhaps starting with a half-hour daily walk, make sure she gets proper rest--that doesn't mean sleeping all day. He said she must stay busy, not isolate herself. He suggests she try a gym. Emily's voice took on a pleading tone, "Urge her friends to visit and talk with her. Try to get her to join a support group."

Linda nodded, "I could drop over at dinner and talk with her. I'm certain Darlene would encourage the girls in their circle to come over. Eventually, they could try a new beauty routine on her or exercise with her."

Emily frowned at the mention of Darlene. "Isn't she the young woman who drove the car Kevin was following?"

"Yes." Linda chose not to elaborate.

Her mother sat quietly for a moment, then said in a slow, soft, voice, as if she were pulling a reluctant thought from her mind. "How is Darlene faring after the accident?"

"She's devastated about Kevin's death. She needs constant reassurance that the accident wasn't her fault. Darlene and her boyfriend were very fond of Kevin. The four often double-dated."

Emily's face took on a pensive expression. "I feel for her, and for Sandra. And for Kevin's parents. After the memorial service, Kevin's mother asked me if Tiffany can visit them in Pennsylvania soon. I said that Tiffany was too young to travel alone and Sandra wasn't up to a trip; but that she and her husband were welcome to see their grandchild anytime.

"I noticed that Maria wouldn't even look in Sandra's direction at the service, but she did speak to me briefly before they left. 'I hope Sandra has nothing to reproach herself for,' was all she said before leaving. That sounds incriminating, don't you think?

Linda said nothing. She sipped her tea and took another bite of toast. Perhaps her mother would talk of something else and not repeat the question. But Emily, wracked with pain by the tragic death of her son-in-law, continued to question. "Do they have any reason to blame Sandra for their son's death? And why was Kevin following them in his car? I assume he was following them?"

She realized her mother was intuitive, but Linda couldn't reveal Sandra's capricious ways and add to her mother's pain. "I really don't know, Mother."

"I often wondered why Maria dislikes Sandra."

"I don't know that her mother-in-law actually dislikes her. I think she doesn't understand that Sandra is a lively, passionate woman."

Bittersweet House

"Yes, that must be it," agreed Emily, then added, "I wish she were less passionate and more responsible." She sat quietly for a minute, leaned forward and met Linda's eyes, "Tell me, were Sandra and Kevin having problems?"

Here it comes, Linda thought while she tucked wisps of hair behind her ear and turned slightly away. "Why do you ask?"

"Something is wrong. Things don't add up." A pained expression crossed Emily's face, but quickly vanished, "I suppose there's no point in dwelling on the past. We must think of Sandra and Tiffany now."

"Look Mother, I can spend the weekend here. The sofa will do just fine. Perhaps I can get Sandra to talk to me, at least attempt to get her started on a routine. Maybe we could walk on the beach."

"That would be wonderful, dear. But what about Christopher?"

"He won't mind. He's on a business trip to London. I expect him home tomorrow." Without realizing it, Linda pursed her lips. *He damn well better not mind.*

Her mother gave her a questionable look. "Are things okay with you and Christopher?"

"Of course, Mother. It's just that we've both been so busy." *What's one more lie?* "I know it's difficult for you and Dad, but we've got to believe that Sandra will recover. Caring for the two of them must be wearing you down. The station owes me some comp time and things should simmer down there in a few days. I could spend a while with Sandra to give you and Dad a little relief."

"That would be nice, dear, but I plan to be here for a few weeks. Your father will go home this weekend to check on the house. Then we'll see how things are progressing." Emily chewed her lip. "What about that special investigative reporting job you're working on?"

"I hope my boss will allow me to postpone the story for a while."

Her Mother shook her head. "No. I don't want you to postpone anything on account of us. Your Father and I will manage."

"But we don't know how long it'll be before Sandra recovers sufficiently to care for Tiffany."

"It doesn't matter dear. Your Father and I will do it as long as we can, and when it gets too much for us, we'll hire competent help. We can afford it. You mustn't worry," Emily said and quickly changed the subject. "I put Tiffany to bed just before you came. I'm sorry you missed her."

"Me, too. I did promise she could spend the weekend with me, but that'll have to wait. I'll peek in on Sandra for a few minutes. "

Liz Barzda

"See if you can get her to come down."

Linda found Sandra curled up on her side with her hands resting on her cheek. She touched her face and gently pulled her to a sitting position. "How are you doing sleepyhead? It's time to get up."

Sandra made no sign of recognition, looked past her as if she were invisible. "First, we've got to make you presentable." Linda reached for a hairbrush and blusher from the dressing table. She ran the brush lightly through Sandra's long, chestnut hair, then applied color to her cheekbones. "There, that's better. Did you hear that Jackie's kid sister, Amy, won the Miss Seacliff Pageant?" Sandra remained expressionless. Linda went on, "Michele has learned tattooing and is opening a parlor geared to women. Isn't that amazing? Who would have thought she'd do such a thing? She's so conservative." Linda thought it better to stay clear of mentioning men or children. Maybe a joke would help.

"Can you sing opera?"

"Of course!"

"Do you sing Faust?"

"I sing Faust or slow--whatever you want."

No response, not even a flicker of recognition. A couple of weeks ago, Sandra would have moaned, "God, you're corny and you don't even live on a farm."

"Come on," Linda said as she led Sandra to the dressing table. "Look how pretty you are!"

Sandra stared blankly at the mirror.

Linda gently put her arms around her; bit her lip to suppress her tears.

Chapter 30

Zita spent Saturday reviewing the Forest Park project, coordinating newspaper ads and TV pitches with the contractor's schedule and the selling timetable, and checking with Joe Arcara. He reassured her that his crew would start digging within a month. His ability to deliver wasn't a problem, but days of unpredictable rain, and God forbid, a hurricane could throw off the schedule. She followed up on the full-color brochure touting Forest Park's custom-built luxury homes, pleased that the printing company agreed to a guaranteed delivery date. She jotted a note to herself to include a review of the latest advertising details with Margaret on Monday.

Zita glanced at her watch, 5:50. Peter said he'd pick her up at her office at 6 o'clock. She shut down her computer and made a stab at straightening up the paper piles on her desk, when she noticed the post-it reading "follow up" on a draft bank proposal.

"Hell, I forgot about this," she muttered, but decided it could wait till Monday. She dashed into the bathroom to freshen her makeup. Wouldn't a light tan have added to her overall appearance? With her Irish coloring, no way could she tan. Luckily, makeup covered her freckles. At the very least, nature could have made her taller like Linda, who commanded attention when she walked into a room. Zita sighed. Better to be satisfied with what she had. Peter said she was a dynamite package. She stared at her mirrored reflection. Luminous eyes that danced with joy stared back. Just the thought of him made her tingle with pleasure.

#

Liz Barzda

Pleased that Peter's reservation secured an outdoor corner table with a view of the Long Island Sound, Zita attempted to block out the din of other Summer Playhouse diners. She vowed to clear her head of all distractions, including business. Especially business. And concentrate on Peter. He planned an evening of dinner and the musical at the adjoining Playhouse, and she would not spoil the romantic feeling by talking shop. What a blessing to feel the fresh breeze that blew in after five days of energy-sucking humidity. The scent of the sea and the fragrant roses bordering the walled patio pleasured her senses. They ordered vodka tonics and agreed that talking business was *verboten*. She turned her gaze from the sea and smiled at him. He reached across the table, lifted her chin and looked into her eyes. His lips curled into a characteristic easy smile. "There isn't anything in nature that comes close to matching the looks of you. Have you any idea how much I love you."

"I have a feeling," she said stroking his cheek. "It's probably because I'm so damn sexy." She paused a moment. Her voice took on a serious tone. "Seriously, Peter, this isn't a one-sided affair. I truly care about you. You're compassionate and a good human being. When I'm with you I feel wonderful and protected, yet you don't smother me."

"I don't deserve those compliments. I'm just an average guy."

"Don't put yourself down. You're a real man, with your feet on the ground, a good heart, and the right amount of ego for success."

He looked embarrassed. "I can't believe a woman as beautiful, educated, and successful as you are could love me. To top all that, you can do anything. I've seen you in action. Beneath that pussycat look is a she-lion."

She gave a coy wave. "You're much too complimentary, but I do love it."

The waiter brought their drinks. Peter tasted his, was silent for a moment as if deep in thought. "Now for a question that doesn't deserve attention, but I'll ask it anyway. Has David been around?"

"No, thank God."

"I told you his threats were just to save face. Trust me. He won't bother you again."

Bittersweet House

"How can you be sure?"

"I'm sure."

He covered her hand with his. "You still look disturbed. What else is bothering you? Emptying your mind of Parker Advertising Agency would be like asking the IRS to cut out auditing citizens. Seriously, hon, you know Arcara & Daughter Construction Company's crew are up to the task of keeping to the building schedule, so why the preoccupied look?"

"It's my nature to sweat the deadlines. But I'll try to do better. Look," she raised her hands and blew. "Poof, all worries out to sea." She held his face in her hands and kissed his lips. "Now, I'll think and talk only of you, you gorgeous man."

She reluctantly released him. They both leaned into their seats, stared at each other as if to absorb the essence of one another. Finally, Zita said, "This view is like a seascape in the flesh, only more beautiful because it's real. Just like you, Peter. I want to hold this time, to freeze it in my memory. Yet, it dissipates so quickly, like summer turning into autumn before you're ready. But not you. You won't dissipate, will you?"

"Never."

"Sorry, I'm a little down, but last week was one of the worst in my life. Kevin's funeral tore everyone up. Then I learned Sandra is in a deep depression. Her parents are staying with her. Linda is doing everything she can to help."

As much as she loved Peter, she couldn't mention Linda's marital problems. She felt a loyalty to her best friend and the other BB's. It was too soon to reveal everything.

"It's Kat we're all worried about."

Peter noticed Zita had finished her drink. "Would you like a refill?"

"No, thanks." Zita checked her watch. "It's quarter of seven. We should order dinner if we want to make it to the play on time."

After ordering, Peter asked, "Why are you all worried about Kat? Does she still have that crazy idea about borrowing money from the mob?"

"Scott and his father were arguing right before Mr. Bowman had his heart attack. Kat was counting on that loan from Mr. Bowman, but Scott broke up with her, so she can kiss that low interest loan good bye."

"Kat should get real," he grimaced. "Doing business with the Mafia is a dangerous game. There's a better way."

No way would Zita reveal her friend's underhanded action; she'd rather Peter learn it from someone else. "What do you mean 'There's a better way?'"

Liz Barzda

"I mean I can get her that loan from my Uncle Joe."

"He'd advance her half a million dollars? Why would he do that?"

"Because I'll ask. He'd do almost anything for me--within reason, and a lien against Kat's property."

Zita grew thoughtful. "I hope he's not...I've heard rumors."

"No, he's not part of the Family. Those Mafia stories are old wives' tales. But if you're talking about Uncle Joe's old man," Peter chuckled, "that's another story. The old fellow's been known to smash a few knee caps in his days. Not to worry though. Joe's legit, but sometimes a little rambunctious. I think my uncle will probably charge her two points less than your friendly bank, and he'll still make a good profit. Naturally, he'd look over her books and work out a repayment schedule."

"You're a prince. You know that, don't you?"

"I'm doing it for you." Peter looked into her eyes and said softly, "I'll do anything for you. That loan is no big deal for Uncle Joe. He can afford it. Guarantee he wouldn't lose any money. Besides, his son Roland--you know Roland don't you? Did you know he dates Darlene Moore, the Spa's receptionist?"

"I heard she was seeing him."

Their conversation was interrupted with the arrival of their beef tenderloin platters. Peter cut his meat, sampled the lemon steamed potatoes, and muttered, "This is really good. Where was I?"

"You were talking about Darlene."

"Right. Darlene keeps her eyes open. She sees how the business is heading in the right direction since the renovation; and naturally, she tells Roland everything. So you see, sweetheart, Joe has good reason to consider the loan."

Zita beamed at her lover. She couldn't believe how magnanimous he was. It touched her deeply that he'd go out of his way to help a friend of hers, someone he hadn't even met.

They ate their meal with an eye toward the time. Peter looked at his watch. "Zita, don't rush," he said as the waiter appeared with the check. "The theater is just next door. We have a few minutes yet. Finish your coffee, I have something to say."

She sipped her coffee, then gave him her full attention.

"You know, I've been around a bit, never married but loved plenty of women-- make that made love, rather than loved. And I've told you about buying into the business. I have a schedule--of where I want to be

158

Bittersweet House

in five years, in ten years, and beyond. I'm reaching my goals. But there's more."

She looked at him with admiration. "Peter, I never realized how focused you are. She chuckled, "And I thought you were just a pretty face."

"I want more-- a full personal life."

"I don't know what that means."

"It means I want you. Marry me."

Chapter 31

The thought of facing his old man made Scott nervous. Nevertheless, he thanked God that his Dad was alive. Scott had no illusions about himself. Shirking his responsibility at the plant, then lying about it, undoubtedly brought on his father's heart attack. Scott knew he deserved the sleepless nights and the guilt that permeated his waking moments. Would his father recover completely? He must get through to him, explain his shoddy behavior, convince him that he has finally grown into a man who seeks forgiveness.

He rang the bell and waited to be admitted into the large Tudor house in Highland Park, the enclave of Seacliff's first families. When was the last time he visited his boyhood home? He'd meant to see the old man before this, but time had a way of sabotaging his good intentions. The 15-room home held pleasant memories of his youth, mostly centered around his mother. When his father dealt with him brusquely, she soothed with love. He recalled her attempts at playing down the severity of her diseased heart, obviously to keep him from worrying. Although she'd been dead ten years, he still missed her. He visualized her writing notes at her desk, or at the dinner table sitting patiently while his father vented his anger over the incompetence of a new executive.

In his occasional visits after his mother died, Scott would subconsciously run his hand over the top of her fireside chair in the den, as if to recapture her presence. The sturdy housekeeper opened the door and smiled. "It's good to see you, Scott. It's been quite a while."

"Too long, I'm afraid. Good to see you too, Helen. How's he doing?"

"He was depressed, but seems better now." As he followed her through the long foyer into the den, Scott was pleased to find his father dressed

Bittersweet House

and sitting in his favorite recliner. Scott walked toward him with an outstretched hand and a smile. The old man looked pale, and his mouth no longer bore that determined line. His wavy silvery hair had lost its luster and looked like combed cotton.

"Hi, Dad. You're looking pretty good." As much as he wanted to hug him, Scott hung back. Neither of them had demonstrated affection in years. Why would they now, especially after that dreadful fight?

His father shook hands, but his tone was business-like. "Hello, Scott." Not exactly an enthusiastic welcome.

Scott plowed ahead. "I was at the hospital every day when you were in intensive care, but they wouldn't let me in. They said no visitors."

"I wasn't up to visitors."

"Dad, are you really okay?"

"I'm coming along."

"Mind if I have a drink?"

"Help yourself."

Scott poured a shot of bourbon, downed it and faced his father.

"What does your doctor say? Are you on medication? Did he give you a special diet and exercise program?"

Eric ignored the questions and rose slowly. He stepped into the foyer and called for his housekeeper to bring tea. "It's good to see you walking." Eric made no comment.

Why didn't his father answer the questions? His indifference stung. Scott realized he hadn't the insight to know the old man's true feelings.

"Dad, please. I'm here to ask your forgiveness for what I've done. I hate that I caused your heart attack."

"Forgive you? Yes, I forgive you." The voice lacked warmth.

"Please say it like you mean it."

"I do mean it. But I see things differently now. What happened between us is forgotten."

"I know I've disappointed you, Dad. I realize you gave me every opportunity to rise to your level, to continue the business you built. I admit I played around when I should have been working, but that's all in the past."

For the first time in his life, Scott felt shame. Shame. How long had it been since he heard the word?

Eric's eyes bored into his son, but he said nothing.

Scott had bared his soul. The awkward moment passed when Helen

161

Liz Barzda

entered carrying a silver tray set for two, "I remember that set. Mom always brought it out for her club friends."

"Thanks, Helen. I'll handle it now," Eric said. She ignored him, set the tray on the coffee table and left.

"I wish that woman wouldn't treat me like an invalid. To make matters worse, I'm off booze for good." The business and community leader who considered a 12-hour day normal, if followed by a couple of bourbons, shook his head. "Never thought I'd say those words."

"There could be worse things in life."

Eric frowned. "Easy for you to say." In a more friendly tone asked, "How do you like your tea, son? "Uh, one sugar and lemon," Scott stammered. Eric handed him the tea and offered Helen's homemade low-fat cookies. "Damn doctors. Put me on a diet that would kill any red-blooded man. Can't even have a brownie."

Scott waved the cookies aside. "Dad, can we discuss what happened between us? I'm here to tell you how sorry I am about not doing my job. But it's different now. I've been in the office every day, full days. And I've completed the BuiltRite Boxes buyout study. I knew the board wouldn't take action without your approval, so everything's on hold."

Eric sipped his tea, put the cup down and studied his son. "BuiltRite will be a priority when I get back. Assuming no other company moves on them first."

"Dad, let me prove to you I can do the job." Scott leaned forward. "You know I'm up to it." Had his father lost complete confidence in him, or did he intend to teach him a lesson? Scott tried to read the old man's face; all he could decipher was aloofness. Whatever the reason for his indifference, it hurt. Apparently, now was not the time to press.

"Scott, I'm going to level with you. My heart attack was a shock. I didn't realize how sick I was. I don't intend to fall back into old habits. Life is precious, wonderful. I'm ready to lead a new life, to enjoy what's left of mine. I trust you'll also learn something from my experience.

"This attack taught me more of life. I became depressed and apprehensive as to whether I could still run the company. I'm fortunate to have a cardiologist who's also a friend. Roger Mellnick didn't mince words. He told me that depression usually sets in after an attack. He pointed out that exercise and learning more about my condition will bolster my self-esteem and restore my sense of independence. The attack was a wake up call."

"Sounds like you have the right doc, Dad. What kind of exercise regime?"

"A half-hour daily walk. But there's more involved in total recovery."

"What do you mean?"

"My doctor has helped me to understand that love and spirituality play key roles in recovery. He said I should do things that rekindle the spirit, like writing a letter to a friend I haven't heard from in years, start a flower or vegetable garden, take a child to the zoo, smile at someone I can't stand. I got the idea."

Scott stared at his father.

"This really is your old man talking. Let me tell you about one of my newly found interests." He took a deep breath. "When I began walking around the house, I spent some time in the kitchen watching Helen cook. I never had any notion that cooking could be so creative. She let me fool around in her domain. Before I knew it, I attempted a few dishes, substituting my own spices." Eric laughed. "And I'll be damned, I liked my own creations. I think I'll sign up for a cooking course."

Scott continued staring at his father. Is this the tough old guy I know? Regardless of what happened between them in the past, Scott was elated with his father's new attitude. He realized that the old man wasn't at all indifferent to him, and despite his fear of a damaged heart, opted to enjoy life to the fullest.

Scott bit into a cookie with gusto. How good it was to hear his Dad laugh again! "That's great, Dad."

"My new-found hobby will take up some of my time. In a couple of months I'll be back to work, but only part time." Eric looked at his watch and rose. "Time for my walk. Want to come along?"

"Sure." Scott let his father set the pace as they strolled, side- by-side into the woods bordering his property. Eric walked slowly, carefully avoiding low-hanging branches and exposed roots. "Scott, do you recall how proud I was when I shot that doe 5 years ago? Those hunting days are over. I don't ever want to kill another living thing."

They walked on in silence, each in their own thoughts. A blue jay scolded from above. Dry leaves crunched under their feet. Water trickled in the brook. Eric took a deep breath, stopped and turned to him. "Scott, I want to tell you how things really are with me. This is as good a place as any." He sat on a stump. "I mentioned how depression set in after my attack. My doctor told me that blaming others for one's health setback is a typical reaction of heart attack patients. I don't blame you or that woman

Liz Barzda

who called me and told me you were gambling. Revenge doesn't interest me. Life does."

Eric rose, held up his hand, and whispered, "Look there, through the swamp maples. Did you ever see anything more beautiful and peaceful than that doe and her fawn at the brook?" Scott smiled as he watched the deer, but his mind quickly shifted back to the woman who called his father to report the transgression. Who the hell was it? Could it have been Kat because she knew he fooled around a bit? She was certainly capable of such a devious act. He didn't want her doings to intrude on their afternoon. He'd deal with her later. Right now he was impressed with his father's renewed reverence for life. Before his heart attack, he would have seen the game merely as targets. Scott took a sidelong glance at his father, attempting to gauge his stamina. "We've been gone quite a while. Do you want to head back?"

"Yes. I've had enough walking for today." They meandered along in a companionable way, something Scott hadn't shared with his father in a long time.

Eric put his hand on his son's shoulder. "I have something else to say to you."

"What is it?" Scott asked, dreading bad news.

"Don't look so fearful. It's about your future, and mine, too. I expect you to carry on as vice president, to groom yourself to take over the presidency when I retire. In the meantime, Bill Simon will continue to act as comptroller and temporary CEO. I'll be relying on you to work under him until I return."

Scott beamed. "You've got it, Dad."

Eric put his arm around his son's shoulder. "Just one more thing, Dr. Mellnick said it's important to have people around that care about me and whom I care about. Love and forgiveness, that's what it's all about." They emerged from the woods and headed toward the house when Eric added, "Like that woman who had her employee call me to report your absence from work. I forgave her for being a snitch."

Scott winced. He couldn't believe what he was hearing. "You mean Kat? She called you and talked against me? When was that?"

"Before my heart attack; but that wasn't what I meant."

"What do you mean?"

"She came to see me yesterday."

Chapter 32

Margaret, Jack, and Greg's dad, Michael O'Neil, gathered in the Dolans' family room for hors d'oeuvres prior to sitting down to Sunday dinner. Margaret passed around miniature crab cakes and announced that dinner would be in half an hour. "These little things are terrific, Maggie," Michael said chomping on a crab cake.

"Did you invite me to dinner on this gloomy day because you miss my Irish wit, or is there something else in the wind?"

Margaret made a quick glance at Jack. "We haven't seen you in a long time. And yes, we missed your wit."

"Mike," Jack broke in, "you may not agree with what I'm saying, but I'll broach the subject close to our hearts. Margaret told you that we'd like to help finance Greg's Yale education."

Mike scowled. "I can take care of my son." His voice rose. "We don't need charity."

"Come on, Mike, don't be bullheaded. This isn't charity. You will agree that it's a tough financial row to hoe, even with Greg's partial scholarship? You said this year's tuition, room and board are paid for. How about the next three years?"

"Let me worry about that. Greg's education is my responsibility."

Margaret piped up. "Don't act like a thick-headed Irishman."

"I'm not being thick-headed. I'm talking like a father."

Margaret touched his arm. "You may think we're interfering in your business, but our concern is Greg's welfare. We know how expensive it is to send a kid to Yale. If we didn't love him so, we wouldn't make the offer."

"I can't take your money."

"You're not accepting it. Greg is," Jack interjected.

"Look, Mike, you know I promised Jennifer that I'd watch out for Greg as best I can." Margaret's eyes glistened with tears. "My sister died a painful death and you can assuage that miserable memory by honoring her wishes." She didn't like invoking her sister, knowing Mike had loved her passionately, but she was determined to keep her promise. She would not allow Mike to hamper her sister's plans for Greg because he was too damn proud.

"You know we love Greg dearly as if he were our son," Jack said. "We know you want what's best for him. Don't let pride and stubbornness stand in the way of his future. We can afford to finance most of his education. Let us do this for him in Jennifer's name," Margaret pleaded.

Mike sat stony-faced.

Jack faced his brother-in-law. "I don't know whether you're aware that Greg is the major beneficiary of our will."

Mike's eyes widened. Margaret continued, "Mike, we don't mean to lay a guilt trip on you, but surely you know how much we love that boy? Jack and I have always wanted children. It just didn't happen. We would never usurp your position as his father, but we do want to help. Let us do this for him."

Mike swept his hand across his forehead. "I don't want to go against Jennifer's wish, but you must know how difficult this is for me."

Margaret sat on the arm of his chair and took his hand. "We're family. Let's make this a joint effort. We'll pay his partial-tuition. You pay for room and board. What do you say?" Michael appeared removed from his surroundings with a faraway look in his eye. He was quiet for a few minutes. Finally, he said,

"You've made your point, Maggie, but then, you were always good at browbeating. I guess we can call it a family affair." Mike took in a deep breath, and managed, "Thank you, both."

Margaret bent down and kissed him. "Imagine, two Irishmen agreeing. This calls for a celebration."

Mike looked as if all the fight had been wrested from him, but Margaret knew it was a temporary deflation. It was time to change the subject and lighten the mood. She believed her brother-in-law would be revitalized after a good Sunday dinner and a few police stories. "Mike, how's the new drug-fighting program at Seacliff High? I've been reading about the rise of kids taking drugs at the junior high level. It's disturbing."

He shook his head. "It's not as good as we had hoped. The program is supposed to be a partnership between parents and principals. The object

Bittersweet House

is to get the parents to be vigilant and to talk to the kids about not taking drugs--and to be firm about it. We don't know if the parents are talking to the kids. Half of these parents don't show up for the meetings. There's a new program in the planning stage. Whether it succeeds or not..." He shrugged.

"How about you, Maggie? How's business? I've been reading the Seacliff Villas ads in "Seacliff Life". Very glitzy. That should make you another million." Margaret's face lit up. "I'm thrilled to say it's going well. We're getting inquiries, and Joe Arcara's promised to start digging in two or three weeks. The project looks like a winner."

"That's great." Mike looked at Jack. "And what's with you and Seacliff Hospital?"

"Things are finally moving. We got the approval of the Planning and Zoning Committee and the Ambulatory Agencies. Our two older buildings will be revamped into a cosmetic surgery center and a holistic medicine facility. But it's still a slow go with the architect and the construction crew."

Mike reached for another crab cake and took a swallow of beer. "Can't you lean on them? You're a community leader, President and Chief Administator of Seacliff Hospital. That should be worth something."

"You know better than that, Mike. But I can say that the renovation is a plus for the hospital," Jack responded with obvious pride.

Margaret jumped up at the sound of the doorbell. "That must be Greg. Perfect timing." She looked down at her brother-in-law and her expression turned serious. "Shall we keep our arrangement a secret?"

"Yes, I prefer it that way."

She left the room with a buoyant feeling and murmured a prayer, "Thank you, dear Lord. You always hear me when I need You." Returning with Greg, Margaret smiled. "Here's our boy." She attempted to take his hand but he pulled away. "Why so glum? Is something bothering you? Can't be so bad that you can't manage a smile. I trust it isn't earth-shaking." No response from her nephew. He just glared at her. "We'll have to do something to cheer you up. Would you like a beer before we go into dinner?"

He ignored her questions and faced the men. "Hi, Dad, Uncle Jack. I finally made it."

Mike rose to stand beside his son. "You could have ridden with me. I'd love your company."

"I had to be alone, to think about my problem."

Liz Barzda

Mike raised his eyebrows in mock disbelief. "What kind of major problem could you possibly have?" Before Greg could respond, his father gave vent to his feelings. "I consider myself lucky when you spend part of an evening with me, never mind a Sunday afternoon." Then as if to beat his son to the punch, uttered, "I can appreciate that you're working six days a week, and you're entitled to a social life, but an occasional evening at home might be a treat for dear 'ol Dad."

Greg waved aside the beer Jack offered and countered, "Come on, Dad, you're not that neglected."

"Not exactly neglected, but I am concerned. You're out every night with that girl. Come sit next to me and tell me her name?"

Greg sat and met his father's gaze. "You've heard me mention her often enough. Her name is Raquel Lopez. Why can't you remember it? Is it because she's Hispanic? Furthermore, I believe I'm old enough and responsible enough to know what I'm doing."

Mike frowned. "You know better than to accuse me of racism. And since when did I ever question your sense of responsibility? I didn't realize I was interfering in your life. You don't fault me for wanting to share a bit of your company, do you? Jack and Maggie, what do you think of that? Do you think I'm suffocating this guy?"

Greg bristled. "Do you have to bring everyone into my personal business?"

"What the hell are you talking about? Maggie and Jack aren't everyone; they're your aunt and uncle, for Christ's sake. We certainly can talk about family matters in front of them. We always have."

"This may seem like a little matter to you, but it's not. And how I choose to live is my affair."

Mike's ruddy complexion turned crimson. "I don't know what the hell you're talking about. I'm not criticizing your lifestyle, or your girlfriend. What's going on here?"

Greg jabbed his thumb at Jack and Margaret. "Ask *them*."

Margaret gasped and looked at her husband. Jack stared at Greg. "What's bugging you?"

Greg balled his fists and expelled a long sigh. "Since you're both reluctant to say anything, I'll fill in the blanks. Aunt Margaret, Raquel told me about her pregnancy. She said that you met with her and tried to persuade her to have an abortion. How dare you?"

He rose, yelling, "You want her to kill our baby. You're advocating murder-- you, a supposedly good Catholic. You tried to demean Raquel.

168

Bittersweet House

You called her a liar. She knows you disrespect her because she's Hispanic. Well, I love her. Do you hear? I love her. And I believe her."

Margaret faced Greg. "It's not like that. Raquel is lying to you. She isn't pregnant."

"Margaret, you knew about this situation and never said a word to me," Mike bellowed.

"I'm sorry, Mike. Maybe I should have told you, but I had to be sure of my facts. And I believe it's up to Greg to tell you, not me."

"Son, why didn't you confide in me that your girlfriend was pregnant? I'm your father. Surely, I have a right to know."

"You have no rights in this. It's our business, Raquel's and mine."

Margaret held up her hand. "Greg, please don't. You don't know the whole story."

"You mean the whole story you embellished with lies? Raquel told me you tried to get her to abort. Are you afraid there might be a dusky-skin baby in our family?" His eyes filled with tears. "Now you can all dance with joy; Raquel had a miscarriage."

"How dare you accuse us of racism? Margaret asked, unbelieving. "You owe us an apology.

"Son, listen to me," Mike pleaded. "Give us a chance. We just want to get at the truth."

"The truth?" Greg shouted. "What the hell do the three of you know about the truth? The only truth you'll accept is one that reflects your values."

Margaret interjected, "Greg, you've got to listen. Raquel was *never* pregnant. She went to the doctor for a herpes treatment, not a pregnancy test. I did mention putting the baby up for adoption because I wanted to get her reaction, to see if it would stir her to the truth."

Greg loomed over his aunt. "You're the liar. You're painting her a loser because she didn't complete high school and lives in the so-called wrong side of town. "You wanted Raquel to kill our baby. That's what this comes down to, doesn't it? How can you live with yourself?"

Margaret reached for his arm, but he jerked away. "Greg, please listen. You know Uncle Jack and I are not prejudiced. We take people as individuals. This has nothing to do with her background. It's about the kind of person she is, her character. Unfortunately, she's a liar and a schemer."

His look was withering. "You don't know what you're talking about. Raquel told me you would resort to anything to discredit her."

Liz Barzda

Margaret could no longer contain herself. "A psychologist friend of mine said Rachel has all the characteristics of a borderline personality disorder. She would not admit to a lie and would stick to her story even in the face of truth. People like her are chronic liars. They would do anything to avoid abandonment. Trust me, Greg. If you don't believe me, believe the experts who recognize her symptoms."

"That's bullshit. You think I believe those con artists? What do they know? They can't even agree among themselves." His voice grew louder. "You're all against us. Fuck it. Fuck you all."

He turned his back on them and ran down the long foyer. "Wait!" Margaret shouted, running after him. She reached for his shoulders. He shook her off.

"It's over, Aunt Margaret." He opened the door and never looked back.

"Love you," Margaret said in a teary voice as the door slammed.

Chapter 33

On Monday, Katherine called her close friends to meet at her condo after dinner. The desperation in her voice was obvious, even to her. But she didn't care. She needed them. In her mind's eye the scene of her gloating as Darlene telephoned Eric Bowman persisted. God would surely punish her malicious behavior. Although a lapsed Catholic, Katherine wondered whether confession would cleanse her soul. Perhaps the priest would have her do penance; then maybe her sins would be wiped clean. She missed Scott--yearned for him, missed his crooked smile, masculine smell, even his tacky jokes. His humor never failed to brighten her day. She'd tell him about her customers' peculiarities. He'd reveal the secret lives of notables he met through business. He'd laugh over her imitation of old money-bags, Mrs. Wright, who inquired in her best Miss Porter's School dulcet tone why permanents never went on sale in La Petite Spa.

Scott once chortled, "God, she could give Bill Gates a run for his money."

He told her about seeing the mayor, with a good-looking redhead, registering in an out-of-town motel. "That babe wasn't his wife, but it's none of my business. I made sure he didn't see me." She remembered thinking. *Of course you did; cheaters protect each other.* But she mustn't let her mind dwell on his peccadilloes. Look what it led to. She needed reconciliation and would do whatever it took to make it happen. Saturday had been tolerable. La Petit Spa's steady flow of customers kept her mind focused on business. Sunday was unbearable. Scott didn't call. Why in the world would he? How many times had she picked up the phone to call him and put it down, fearing he would slam it in her ear? But she would win him back--somehow. Though Scott's father had forgiven her, he let her

Liz Barzda

stew in her own hell and wouldn't advise her how to approach his son. Her friends would know what to do. They never disappointed. She checked her wine rack. No need for canapés. They would have had dinner by 8 o'clock. A few nibbles with drinks wouldn't hurt. Katherine filled pottery bowls with corn chips, cashews, nachos and salsa. Margaret, the first to arrive, pecked her hostess on the cheek and stared. "What happened to you? You look like hell."

"Good to see you, too Margaret." A few minutes later, Linda and Zita arrived. Katherine clasped her arms around one, then the other. "I'm so happy you came," she said.

Zita piped up, "Of course we're here. Your call sounded urgent. Whatever the problem, we can handle it."

"Thanks for the vote of confidence," Katherine said in a dejected tone. "Mine seems to have disappeared."

"Poor baby. You know you can count on us," Linda said.

They settled themselves expectantly and awaited Katherine's disclosure. With effort she put a smile in her voice to lighten the mood.

Margaret reached for her hand. "Kat, it hurts us to see you so down. You're the glamorous spa lady. Now what could be so devastating so as to bring on more suffering?"

"I'm not proud of myself. At Kevin's funeral we all owned up to our problems. I was the crybaby, the first to lay my soul bare. Well, I still have a slinky for a backbone." She couldn't control the tears that welled in her eyes. "Life sucks! I love Scott. I want him but I don't know what to do. Should I go to him on my knees and beg forgiveness?"

"Nothing is so unforgivable that it can't be corrected," Margaret said, encircling her arm around Katherine. "Own up to your mistake. Try to see Scott and apologize. Take him out to dinner. I know he cares for you. He just doesn't know how much. He can't be so heartless as to hold a grudge forever."

Katherine's looked hopeful. "Do you really think that would work?"

"It's a good shot. Take it," Zita said.

"No harm in trying," Linda added.

The phone rang. Katherine excused herself and took the call in the kitchen. She was surprised to hear Eric Bowman's deep voice. "Miss Horvath, I've given considerable thought to your visit the other day. I said that you were a foolish woman to have pulled the stunt you did. I forgave you for snitching on my son but said I couldn't help you make amends with Scott."

Bittersweet House

"I remember every word, Mr. Bowman, and I beg your forgiveness again for causing your heart attack."

"You weren't the cause. I neglected my health for business and let things get to me. That's over. I'm making a fresh start, and I suggest you do the same."

Katherine willed herself not to sniffle. "Thank you for that. Because of my stupid actions, I've lost Scott's love."

"We all make mistakes," Eric said. "One thing the heart attack has taught me is the value of life. It's a phrase we hear hundreds of times, but believe me, it's true. When you get to be my age, you realize how short life is. There's no time for accusations and revenge. I believe you're sincere in wanting to set things right with Scott."

"I'd do most anything to erase what I've done."

"This incident and my medical problem has had a surprising effect on Scott. He's begun living up to his responsibility to the firm, and to himself."

Katherine's heart hammered in her chest. "Thank you," was all she could whisper. *To herself she said I must also make sincere amends to Darlene--more than giving her time off*

"While in the hospital I took stock of my life. I see things differently now. Scott's turnaround has brought me more happiness than I can tell you."

"That's wonderful, Mr. Bowman."

"It should be wonderful for you, too, Katherine. Listen, this is what we can do to right it between you and my son..."

Beaming like a pre-teen in love, Katherine returned to her friends.

"I can't believe it! Mr. Bowman's convinced Scott to meet me at his home Saturday evening. He's a gem!" She chuckled, "I just thought of something-- he'd make an ideal father-in-law."

"Go girl," they exclaimed.

"Time for drinks," Katherine announced. "My special treat: a Robert Mondavi Chardonnay '98 or a Palo Cortado sherry. Pick your poison." They chose the sherry. "What do you say, Zita, do I pass the test as a wine aficionado?"

Zita swirled the glass, sniffed then tasted the sherry. "You're getting there. This is *delicious*." She gazed at her friends with affection. "It's wonderful to feel good again. Like old times. I don't mean to break the mood nor get maudlin, but we've known each other more than a decade. Remember how we gravitated to each other because we were childless?

Sometimes we laughed at the *Barren Babes* concept. Other times there was more hurt than humor."

"But love and ambition bonded us together," Katherine grimaced. "Sorry, I'm being sentimental and rattling on."

"Right on the mark, Kat," Margaret said. "Women are fortunate in one way men can't emulate or understand. Our friendships are intimate and long lasting. We revel in them. There's nothing more endearing than sitting down with a long-time friend and spilling your guts out while she listens intently, never criticizing you, just loving you."

"We're expert at that," Katherine interjected.

Margaret's eyes settled on Zita. "You're glowing all over. You look as if you'll burst if you couldn't tell. Out with it."

Zita giggled then tried to compose herself. "Life is beautiful. I'm almost afraid to talk about it. If I get too cocky, it might all disappear."

"Speak up," Margaret urged. My hearing is half a century old and I don't want to miss any good gossip."

"Happy to, with my fingers crossed. Peter has asked me to move in with him. I told him I'd think about it. After my miserable marriage, I wasn't sure I wanted to live with any man. I love Peter the way I thought I would never love a man again. But move in with him? Believe that he'll be faithful, will love unconditionally? Wash his shorts? Pick up his socks? Cook and clean? I think not. I told him that I just couldn't do it. He said that I had lost my belief in love because I was scared, frightened to trust again. He held me for a long time and, then asked me to marry him. How many couples take the death-do-us-part vow seriously--not many I'd wager. But Peter does. His pledge to love me forever did it."

Linda hoisted her glass. "A toast to you. Anyone who opts for marriage today is courageous in my book. You deserve all the best life has to offer. He's a fine man, Zita. You're good for each other."

Despite the ache in her own heart, Katherine wondered how Linda was faring with her problems. She searched her friend's face for the spark that lit up the television screen. Her assessment: a woman that appeared to have lost her zeal, almost passive in her composure. Still, compared to Linda's troubles, she preferred her own. The three embraced Zita.

"Time for another toast," Margaret announced. "Here's to Zita and Peter." The foursome clinked glasses. "We wish you happiness ad infinitum."

Zita glowed. "You've all been terrific friends. The downside to all this happiness is that I can't have children, but Peter knows that. He tried to

Bittersweet House

hide his disappointed when I told him, but he said he loved me without reservations. We're considering adoption--eventually."

"Dear God, I almost forgot. Good news for you, Kat," Zita continued excitedly. "Peter's Uncle Joe said he thinks you're good for a low interest loan, after he checks your books and tax returns of the last three years. He believes your business has even greater potential. Isn't that terrific?"

Katherine let out a sigh of relief. "Thanks a million, Zita. You're a lifesaver, or should I say a business saver?" Zita held up her hand, "I'm sorry to be monopolizing the conversation, but I have to tell you this. Peter said David was visited by a couple of hefty Samoans. They said nothing, just appeared at his door. He got the message. And the amusing part is, two days ago I spotted David in the bank with a withdrawal slip in his hands. If looks could kill, I'd be dead. I just smiled at him. David scurried from the bank like the rat he is. Well, that's it. Your turn, Margaret. What have the Dolan's been up to?"

"There's good and bad news Here's the good part. The real estate market is slightly softer, but--she broke out in a wide smile--" not in the Seacliff area. And my better half is steering Seacliff Hospital in the right direction. He convinced the hospital board to approve the renovation of two old buildings into a cosmetic surgery center and a holistic medicine facility. The difficulty is finding the money. But I have faith. Jack's a financial genius as well as a great administrator."

With a sad tone Margaret added, "Here's the bad part. I told you that Greg's girlfriend convinced him she was pregnant. Last Sunday he and his father came to dinner, and Greg said Rachel told him that I doubted her pregnancy. When I said she wasn't having a baby and I can prove it, he exploded. All hell broke loose. He screamed that Rachel had a miscarriage; that they had wanted the baby. He vowed never to see us again. "I made a big mistake not telling Greg's father that I knew about Rachel and her so-called pregnancy. He sure is pissed, telling me I had no right to keep him in the dark. He reminded me that Greg is his son, not mine. I have a lot of fences to mend."

"We know you, Margaret," Linda declared. "Guaranteed you'll work it out."

"I'll bet you can sweet talk Michael O'Neil into forgiving you," Zita said. "You meant to tell him but just couldn't approach the subject, right?"

Margaret waved her hand in dismissal. "He said I can't sweet-talk myself out of this mess. Not to worry though, I'll work on him. Some

Liz Barzda

schmoozing at dinner and a baseball double-header will convince him that I'm really contrite." She laughed then turned serious. "Greg is a different matter. He has to see that Rachel is a liar and conniver without humiliating him. Believe me; I'll give that a lot of thought."

Katherine noticed that Linda said little, just took in the conversation. "Say, Golden Girl, it's time we heard from you. What's going on with WSEA?"

"Some good news to report--my contract's been renewed for two years. Thank the Lord. And there may be another bright spot. I don't recall if I told you about a sensational story involving local politicians that could be coming my way? Could be that these characters are up to their butts in financial dirty tricks."

Linda's eyes shone with exhilaration. "The station gave me the go-ahead for an exclusive."

Katherine said, "It's wonderful to see you excited again."

"Way to go," Margaret added.

"I see a TV award coming your way," Zita prophesied.

"That should raise the station's rating," Margaret said as she nudged closer to Linda. "The *suits* will be grinning from ear to ear. Tell us who these sterling politicians are." Linda met her friends' eyes. "Sorry. No can do."

They groaned good-naturedly.

Chapter 34

"Is this Linda Cooper?"

"Yes, this is she. What can I do for you?"

Linda looked at her watch. It was 4:10 and she had two stories to write for her six o'clock news.

"I don't know if you have Caller ID, but it doesn't matter because I'm at a public phone. Listen carefully and you'll get the story of your career."

"Who is this?" Linda's antennae went up. It could be a crackpot. Maybe not. She listened intently to not miss a word.

"I'm a concerned citizen putting my future on the line to get rid of greedy bastards."

Linda snatched a pen. "If you're on the level, I'm all ears. What bastards are you talking about? What did they do?"

"No questions. Just listen."

She could hear the caller breathing heavily, obviously nervous about his revelation.

"Our illustrious mayor secretly spent close to a million dollars to purchase $2.6 million worth of life insurance for himself and five administrators. All of these policies carry a cash value. You can bet your bonus there's a lot more rotten in Denmark."

"How do you know this?"

"Don't ask details. Believe me, I've seen the proof."

"Give me a break. I can't run with this story without confirmation."

"You'll get it after you've done your part. Here's the drill: obtain Seacliff's budgetary reports from the mayor's office via the Freedom of Information Act Study it carefully." Linda rapidly wrote down the caller's information. "Wait a minute. What am I supposed to be looking for?"

177

Liz Barzda

"Isn't that the fun of it? Right now, all I can tell you is to look for discrepancies." Linda held her breath. She had to keep the caller talking to get the whole story.

"Are you jerking me around?"

"Listen, I wouldn't be wasting my time if I weren't sure of the facts."

"How is it you're privy to the mayor or the council's machinations?"

"I keep my ears open so I know what's going on. The public's taking a bath."

"So give me details," Linda said as she subconsciously wrapped a wisp of hair around her ear. "This is the first step of your investigating reporting. Listen carefully." She could hear his breathing accelerate. "What am I supposed to find?"

"I'm getting to that."

"Isn't this rather juvenile? What else do you have?"

This is enough for now-- enough to keep you busy, and inquiring."

Linda's feelings took a complete turnabout. This informer could be telling the truth. "You've got to give me more than that before I tramp all over searching for a maybe-story."

The caller laughed. "That's for you to find out. This deal is a two-way street. Do your homework on the first leg of this investigation. You show good faith and I'll give you more."

"How do I know there's more?" Linda shot back. "And how do I know you'll keep your end of the bargain?"

"Because your reporter's gut feelings tell you so."

"My gut hasn't made up its mind."

"Lady, when I start something, I carry it to its conclusion. Count on it."

"Why are you doing this? Are you one of those disgruntled city employees trying to get even with the mayor because he passed you over for a job you thought should be yours?"

"Don't you get it? These guys are using taxpayers' money, our money to cushion their lives. Somebody has to stop them. I'll call you in a couple of days. If you've completed the first leg of this investigation, we'll continue. That's it for now."

"Hold it. Why didn't you give this story to the papers?"

"You know damn well that more people watch TV news than read newspapers."

"You've got to give me more information if you want me to do a fair, credible story."

178

Bittersweet House

"You'll do the story. I'm certain of it. One other thing, don't waste your time trying to find out who I am." He hung up.

"Damn, damn, damn." She rose in a flurry, ignored the toppled chair, dashed to the office of news director Jake Cohen's, knocked on his door and rushed in. "He called," she blurted out. "You know, the guy whose story I'd kill to do?"

"What the hell are you talking about?"

"Do you remember I told you my agent overheard Councilman Zimmerman tell Councilman Chin that a Seacliff Sentinel reporter was nosing around asking all kinds of questions. My agent said Zimmerman was nervous as hell and kept asking Chin, 'What do you think he's looking for?'"

Jake leaned back into his leather high-back chair, "Can your informer prove this?"

"The guy's a snitch but he wants me to break the story. He's afraid the Sentinel reporter will unearth the facts and print all before he and I could get it out, robbing him of long-awaited revenge. He's given me some information and promises more damaging details in time."

"Why would he give you the story? Why doesn't he break it himself?"

"He knows more people watch TV news than read the papers. We know he's right," she said with pride. "Why doesn't he break the story himself? Self-preservation. He's scared shitless, but still hopes he can hold onto to his job."

Jake's deep-brown eyes glinted with approval. His journalist radar could smell news. He believed being confrontational with his staff kept them on their toes, but never to the point of losing an exclusive story. "Okay," he said. "If you think he's on the level, run with it."

Linda clenched fist shot up in the air, "Yes," she exclaimed. Her ear-to-ear grin remained on her face as she quietly closed the news director's door.

#

It was after midnight when Linda turned off the thruway onto Seacliff's back roads heading for home. She looked forward to a jacuzzi soak, mood music, and a drink, elements that would relax her and help put her day in perspective.

Although her boss was known as a hard sell, Linda was pleased he

Liz Barzda

acknowledged she could handle a special investigative program on City Hall shenanigans. Much too late for May sweeps month; nevertheless, the project excited her. It was the first good thing that happened to her since Christopher dropped his bomb.

The refreshingly cool night with a full moon illuminating the countryside matched her upbeat mood, a feeling Linda realized she hadn't felt in weeks. The north wind finally arrived and blew off the five days of humidity. As she neared home, Linda powered down the car windows, shut off the air conditioning, and breathed in the night air. She pulled into the garage and instead of entering through the laundry room, walked around the house, down the patio steps to the back lawn and the beach. The smell and sound of the sea soothed her, erasing career and marriage worries that littered her life. Surely, we were creatures that evolved from the ocean she thought. It must be so as we're drawn to water. A soak and drink could wait. She removed her shoes and sat on the sand. Her eyes roamed across the star-studded sky where no tall buildings and no flashing lights competed with the plethora of stars. The only man-made lights visible emanated from large, widely spaced houses. She had no idea how long she sat staring at Long Island Sound.

Shoes in hand, Linda trekked back to the house, brushing sand from her skirt, her mind refocused on work. How would she juggle Connecticut Chronicle interviews and the undercover political assignment and make it all come out right? She'd manage it because she must. Linda knew her career strengths. Of the interviews she coveted, she figured she snagged eighty percent of those she pursued. She laughed to herself. A piece of cake.

First, a check on her messages, then the creature comforts. There were two messages. "Linda, dear, it's Mother. I didn't want to call you at the office; I know how busy you are. But I had to tell you. Sandra is saying more than 'no' or 'yes'. She's actually verbalizing, you know, simple sentences. Seeing how she's improved, I plan to take her and Tiffany to Camden for a few weeks of recuperation. Can you come to dinner Saturday? If not, please call me. There's much I need to discuss with you. Bye for now."

Linda, thankful about her sister's progress, wondered what her mother could be thinking. She knew Tiffany would be starting school in a few weeks. She'd call tomorrow; dinner on Saturday would be fine.

Christopher's voice followed.

"Linda, I'll be away for another week on business in Wales. We'll talk

Bittersweet House

when I get back." No good-bye, no details of why and where in Wales he was headed. "Who the hell cares," she rose and punched the delete button. She'd love to delete him. He's lying. Her husband is spending time with his mistress and heir son. She had no doubt about it. Her head began to throb. They still hadn't resolved anything. Was there anything left to resolve? Christopher would have to make a move. Let the guilty party take the offensive.

Was there remaining even a spark of the love that once rose to bonfire heights? She wondered why she would even ask the question. How could he love her, sleep with his mistress, pine for his son, and still make sense of their lives? She pressed the heels of her hands into her eye sockets, and moaned. "God forgive me. I think I hate him."

Despite Christopher's agitating message, Linda slept deeply and rose refreshed. The shower added to her feeling of exuberance. She had banished her husband from her mind. She had neither the time nor the inclination to dwell on him. Work concerned her. So many details to iron out: the next interview for *Connecticut Chronicle*, ideas for possible future ones, requesting budgetary reports from the City of Seacliff under the Freedom of Information Act, and picturing how she'd comb those pages for hidden expenditures.

How long would it be before she could obtain the data to start the investigation? The sooner the better. What goodies would she find? Who's been living high off the hog with public money?

Chapter 35

Zita faced Margaret across a desk littered with the Forest Park and Seacliff Villa artist renderings. "I promised you the color brochures in a month, but since you're a good friend I pressured the printer. You'll have them next week."

"Thanks, Zita. I appreciate the extra effort. The sooner I get them the sooner I can go ahead with promotion. How far along is the TV commercial?"

"We're working on it now. The camera will reveal detailed drawings of the various luxury residences available to discriminating buyers. As you know, these houses have magnificent views of Long Island Sound with Italian marble foyers and bathrooms, vaulted ceilings, dressing rooms, and master bedrooms adjacent to sitting rooms with fireplaces. These are just a few of the features in the ten-room houses. I'm confident these homes will be snapped up despite the two-million price tag.

"You'll be able to review the film in two weeks. Believe me, Margaret you're going to love it." She cupped her chin in her hand and grinned at her client and long-time friend. "I never asked you how you managed to snap up the last parcel of Seacliff waterfront property. How in the world did you do it?"

"You know my parents are in the real estate business, selling mostly commercial. They have their ears to the ground and know what's happening around the area. They put me on to the waterfront property. They're involved in this whole enterprise. Jack and I couldn't swing it without them. It's a tremendous undertaking." Margaret's face lit up. "And a gold mine."

Bittersweet House

"I'm happy for you. Seacliff Villas is a sure thing. Now, how about a little pastry to go with the coffee?"

Margaret shook her head. "No thanks; I don't need any more hip padding. What I do need is a continuation of this good weather. If there are no rainstorms or hurricanes, Joe Arcara promised he'll begin digging Forest Park in a couple of weeks. Your development sketches that ran in the Seacliff Sentinel brought a lot of inquiries. I'm thinking of running the Seacliff Villas drawings in The New York Times."

"Smart move."

They reviewed the TV, newspapers, and glossy magazine advertising schedule. Zita promised that Parker Advertising would meet the deadline, enabling Margaret to give her contractor the go-ahead.

"So much for business; now let's get to the fun part," Margaret chuckled. "When's the wedding?"

"October 6," Zita replied with a dreamy expression. "I told Linda last night and asked her to be my maid of honor. Peter doesn't know the wedding details, but he says whatever I want is fine with him, so long as it's not a big production. I picture something simple, yet elegant, with just a few relatives and my dearest friends."

Margaret leaned forward in her chair and pressed in closer to Zita. "Where will it be? What'll you wear?

We'll probably be married in St. Paul's, followed by a reception at the Seacliff Yacht Club. I'll be wearing a Richard Tyler gown."

"Um. Sounds divine," Margaret purred.

"I reserved the church date first, and was lucky to get it," Zita continued, wrapped in an emotional high.

"If people are opting for living together rather than marriage these days, why does it take so long to get a church date? I can answer my own question," Margaret said with a sly expression, "Shacking up without a commitment still doesn't cut it. We all know what most women want -- that legal paper.

Zita rose. "I'll call Kat tonight and make sure she reserves October 6." Her face lit up. "Pretty exciting for a 42-year-old-broad, huh?"

"As the kids say, cool."

"Just one more thing," Zita added, "we're still on for the Choices Banquet, right?"

"Wouldn't miss it."

"I'll double check with Linda and Kat on the banquet. About the wedding, I don't know whether to broach the subject to Linda about

Liz Barzda

inviting Christopher. Who knows what their situation will be in October? And there's Scott, too. I haven't the foggiest notion what will happen to him and Kat."

#

At home, Margaret removed yesterday's left-over stew from the fridge. With a salad, French bread, and ice cream smothered with chocolate sauce, the quickie dinner would suffice. She had time enough to set the table and call her brother-in-law, Michael, before Jack arrived home around seven.

As expected, he hadn't phoned. Margaret, chagrined over the fiasco she created on Sunday, understood his anger. Should I have kept my mouth shut? If I didn't speak up, who would? Someone had to enlighten Greg about Raquel, no matter how painful.

She dialed her brother-in-law. "Hi, Michael. I hope you're no longer angry that I didn't tell you about meeting with Raquel."

"You bet I'm mad. You have a hell of a nerve keeping information like this from me."

"Of course, you're right. I met her a few times only to get at the truth. There didn't seem to be any other way. Now I realize that I should have consulted you. Please say you forgive me."

"Don't ever keep things from me that concern my son." There was no mistaking the anger in his voice. Neither spoke for a few moments. Finally, Michael said, "I forgive you because I'm supposed to be a good Christian."

Elated to receive Michael's forgiveness, Margaret plunged right in. It didn't cross her mind that her brother-in-law may not wish to talk about Greg's dilemma. "How's it going with you and Greg? I'm really worried about him. Has he talked about Raquel?"

"Greg is still madder than hell. He's seeing her again and refuses to hear anything derogatory about her. I've given up trying to reach him. He's so damn stubborn--yeah, I know, just like me." Michael's tone softened a bit, "But seriously, Maggie, any idea how to wake him up?" "I keep rehashing Sunday's disaster. It's tricky business, Michael, but you've got to take action if you don't want your son messing up his life with a lying sex kitten."

"What kind of action?"

"Like providing evidence that Raquel is cheating on him, with a woman."

Bittersweet House

"A woman?" Michael gasped. "I can't believe it! Raquel looks like a man's dream. Are you telling me she's bi-sexual?"

"Looks like it. And I can get proof."

"How?"

Margaret leaned against the counter, a feeling of emotional weariness surged through her. "Greg will never believe ill of her without substantial evidence. The proof will hurt him, but it can't be ignored. I was feeling rather low after Sunday's fiasco so I went shopping at the Seacliff Mall. Raquel and a woman were parked in the row ahead and to the left of me. I paused for a moment and watched them. My curiosity turned to shock when I saw the woman plant a lingering kiss on Raquel. They continued kissing for a while then finally broke apart. Shocked by what I saw, but not so disturbed that I didn't record the plate number."

"I think I know where you're heading. I'll get the name and address of the car owner from DMV and put a tail on her. I can't believe this mess. Eventually, one of my men will get a shot of her with her female lover in an amorous pose. Trust me, we'll get it."

Margaret sighed. "Unfortunately, this calls for revolting measures."

"No wonder your friends call you Mother Superior. Good idea, Maggie, even though it's not one of our finest hours." Margaret held the portable phone in one hand and with the other absentmindedly removed salad fixings from the fridge. She leaned on the counter, focused on her brother-in-law's words and said, "The difficult part is yet to come--getting Greg to see the truth and forgive us for action taken."

"There's no sense in beating ourselves up, though. He'll get over his anger--in time. I'll talk to you when there's something to report."

"Love you," Margaret said and clicked off.

Her fingers mechanically shredded lettuce into a bowl. She thought about Greg, Michael and her three friends. Feelings of guilt, sorrow, insecurity and elation flooded her senses. In her mind's eye, she saw Greg lambasting his father for plotting to prove Rachel a cheat, then she viewed Linda running away from Christopher, or was it toward him, and there was Kat with Eric Bowman waiting, waiting for Scott to arrive. It wasn't her nature to dwell on gloomy thoughts, Margaret reminded herself. Jack would come through the door any minute, and she'd give him a lingering kiss. Happy thoughts, that's what's needed. She'd dwell on Zita's wedding.

Chapter 36

Wendell Beattie swept Tiffany into his arms then kissed his wife and eldest daughter. He held Sandra longer, brushed his lips against her forehead, looked lovingly into her eyes then released her. He ushered the little entourage into his car for the hour ride from the Bangor, Maine airport to the family's comfortable colonial home on Camden's Chestnut Street.

Buoyed by her father's strength and being back on childhood turf, though only for a weekend, Linda retreated in time to youthful carefree days. The sight of schooners nestled in Camden's picturesque harbor, the flower gardens, and gracious houses of her home town renewed a sense of peace not felt for weeks. Surrounded by her folks, Sandra, and Tiffany, she planned to make the most of the weekend.

The sun had long dipped behind the house when Sandra and Tiffany went to bed.

Linda and her parents adjourned to the screened-in porch for a nightcap. A cool breeze, like a gentle kiss, blew softly through the porch.

"I had hoped Sandra would have been further along in her recovery. She still seems distracted," Wendell commented as he accepted a bottle of beer and a glass from Emily.

Sandra's come a long way, dear," Emily pointed out. "You notice how she'll answer your questions, granted with just a yes or no, but she is talking a bit. And in time she'll do more. At least she's eating now. Her doctor said that people vary in their expressions of grief, and if death of a loved one occurs without warning, shock may last a long time."

Linda sipped her vodka collins and said, "He told me that acute grief symptoms gradually lessen and within a couple of months the grieving person is able to function. We can't gloss over the fact that Sandra doesn't

Bittersweet House

exhibit much emotion in being home, but perhaps revisiting childhood haunts will rekindle her interest. I know her favorite spots. "I'm hopeful she'd open up on revisiting them. I thought we might take a picnic lunch to Lincolnville Beach tomorrow. If Sandra's up to it, would you and Dad care to join us?"

"No thanks, dear," Emily replied. "I think I'll stay in with Sandra."

"Mother, I'm sure it would be the first year you haven't volunteered for the Women's Club Craft Fair on the green. Do go and have a good time with your friends. I'll be with Sandra.

"That's so sweet of you. I would like to check out their plants and crafts.

"Dad, what are you doing tomorrow? Want to join us at the beach?"

"You know I don't like to sit on the beach and bake like a lobster," Wendell protested, "but I'll take my four beauties to the Lobster Pond for dinner. It's a hoot to watch Tiffany lick her sticky fingers."

"Great, Dad. Haven't been there for a while."

He shook his head in mock frustration. "What I don't do for you women!"

Linda wrinkled her nose. "Oh you poor-put upon male."

"Since I have an 8 o'clock tee time with the guys, I'll say good night."

"Linda, how about Sunday? Any plans?" Emily queried.

Linda rose, yawned, and stretched. "Gosh. I'm bushed, Mom. It's been a full day. About Sunday, if you think Sandra and Tiffany are up to it, we could bike or drive up to Mount Battie."

"I remember when you and your sister were tykes how you loved to climb the stone tower to see Acadia National Park and Mohegan Island."

The far-away look in Emily's eyes faded and her face registered concern. "Linda, I believe we need to talk about Tiffany. After discussing it with your father, we decided to keep Tiffany with us for a few weeks. I think she and Sandra will gradually interact more. Do things together."

Linda's eyes widened. "But mother, Tiffany starts school next week."

In a calm, paternal tone, Emily countered, "It's more important for the child to be with her mother than worrying about missing a few days of kindergarten. Sandra may not be functioning 100 percent, but I do believe Tiffany's presence will help her to bounce back. They need each other."

"But her little friends would already have settled in," Linda pressed. "Don't you think it would be unwise for Tiffany to miss weeks of school?"

Liz Barzda

"No, I don't, dear. It isn't like she'd fail her SAT's for missing a few days, or even a couple of weeks of kindergarten."

Linda wondered why her mother was being so foolish. The child needed a new environment, needed to be with younger people, kids who could relate to her.

"I see your point, Mother," Linda concurred and began to pace. "But I thought it would be a nice change if Tiffany spent some time with me. It would give Sandra breathing room and time to recover completely. I hadn't realized you'd planned for Tiffany to stay here that long. I really would like to have her with me," Linda asserted. She stopped pacing and took a drink. Under her breath she mumbled, "I need her with me."

"What's wrong, dear? You're as skittish as an alley cat."

"Nothing," Linda insisted as she wrapped a strand of hair around her ear, a nervous habit that wasn't lost on her mother. "But isn't caring for an active child too much for you physically?"

Emily ignored the reference to age. "If Tiffany can stay with you for a while, who would take care of her when you're working?"

"Mom, I didn't mean you couldn't handle Tiffany, but I could do it with Mrs. Brody. She's a widow and free from responsibilities. I know she'd move in if I needed her full time.

Emily turned away and focused on the backyard trees illuminated by moonlight. She lowered her eyes and clasped her drink. "Why are you so adamant about this? Is there something you're not telling me?" She raised her eyes and fixed them on her daughter. "My intuition and your actions tell me there's something more than Tiffany's welfare eating at you. Is it Christopher? Lately, you seldom mention his name. It's as if he doesn't exist."

Linda rubbed her forehead. *Why does Mother have to ask questions now? Is my behavior so obvious that the whole world wants to dig into my business?* "Oh, Mother, it's so tawdry," she moaned. "I want to forget about Christopher, forget the shambles he made of our marriage."

Emily's expression changed from curiosity to concern. She cleared her throat and in a hoarse voice asked, "What are you talking about?"

In an effort to spare her mother emotional pain, Linda tried to bury the problem deep within, but could no longer suppress it. Like bubbles in a glass, it surfaced and she couldn't contain it. "Christopher has a mistress and a baby nearly two years old," she blurted. "He never let on about his affair. I found out by accident when she called from Boston. The baby was ill. She wanted Chris there."

An expression of disbelief spread across Emily's face. "A mistress, a baby, I can't believe it." Her brow creased and her face became flushed from anger. I can't believe it of Christopher, that he could hurt you so. Linda gulped air to catch her breath.

"Christopher always said that children would hinder our careers." Tears glinted anger in her eyes. "He convinced me that we should put children on hold. This from a man who *secretly* visited his mistress and son and kept me in the dark." Sobs garbled her words. "It's unbearable."

They clung together. Linda buried her head on her mother's breast.

"I'm really sorry, darling. Christopher's done a terrible thing, but you mustn't let it break you. You can't fall apart. As Earnest Hemingway said, 'Courage is good under pressure.'" Her mother stroked her shoulder and added, "He'll get what he deserves. No matter what happens, remember that Dad and I love you."

"I know you and Dad love me, but I feel unworthy of love, as if I'm not entitled to be loved. "It must be so," Linda sobbed," otherwise Christopher couldn't lavish his emotions and sperm on another woman."

"That's not true. You're a loyal, generous, loving woman. And if your husband's lost his way in life, that's his problem. You've got to be strong for yourself." Linda broke free of her mother's arms.

"It's an anathema, a curse. He's made my life hell and completely destroyed my trust. He's made me afraid to trust anyone. Some days I believe I hate him enough to want to destroy him. Other days I wonder if there's any charity left in my soul. I'm not sure I know who I am anymore. She wept uncontrollably.

Chapter 37

Katherine ambled around Eric's study--better than sitting, crossing and uncrossing her legs and checking the time every few minutes. Finally she sat and began to fidget in her chair. "Are you all right?" Eric Bowman asked.

"Sorry, I guess I'm just nervous. Didn't you say Scott would be here at 8 o'clock?"

"Promptness is not one of my son's strong points. But you're probably aware of that. Would you like a drink while we wait?"

"Thanks. It might help."

Katherine couldn't refrain from twisting her fingers together in frustration. "He's so late. She dreaded to ask the question, but did so anyway. "You don't think he's forgotten, do you?"

Eric didn't answer. "What would you like to drink?"

A torturous thought crossed her mind. He's not answering me because he doubts Scott will show. "A Bloody Mary if you have it." She rose, pressed her hands over her buff linen skirt, strode over to the sofa table and picked up a silver-framed photo of Scott and his mother. "Your wife was a beautiful woman." She made no reference to the adorable towheaded child cuddled next to his mother.

"Yes, she was. She's been gone ten years. I still miss her." He handed Katherine her drink. "Unfortunately, mine is straight tomato juice," he added with a grimace. She inspected the seascapes and still-life watercolors dotting the walls.

"Jane was a watercolor enthusiast. I prefer oils," Eric commented.

"The paintings are lovely," Katherine said, then turned to watch the doorway.

Bittersweet House

"Let's sit down. Tell me about your business." *He's probably attempting to deflect my nervousness. How considerate.* "I'll be happy to. You know how it is when you truly love something, you never tire of talking about it. Luckily, there was room to expand La Petite Spa in the back where skin and massage rooms were added. My interior decor created a color scheme of silver, gold, and chocolate. The silver-framed Mexican mirrors and the chandelier from Austria added a rich glow. And the fountain in the courtyard... Oh, I'm sorry Eric, I'm rattling on. You can't be interested in all this."

"But I am. You don't realize how animated you are when you describe your business. It's a pleasure to see you so absorbed. Now wasn't the time to inquire whether Scott asked him to grant her a low interest loan. For a few minutes Scott left her mind as she and Eric laughed over the idiosyncrasies of the spa's grande dame customers. When the laughter abated, stillness filled the room. She looked at her watch again. Scott was an hour late. She felt herself sliding deeper into the chair, wishing it would envelop her. "He's not coming, is he?"

"Apparently not. I'm sorry, Katherine."

She loathed to make a fool of herself in the front of her lover's father, but could not suppress the tears that welled in her eyes.. He rose, wiped her tearing eyes with his handkerchief and pressed her to his chest. "I don't want you to suffer over my son."

Katherine took a deep breath. "Why would he say he would meet with me when he didn't mean it? Why does he have to lie?"

"I don't know. Perhaps he's trying to even the score-- not a manly thing to do."

Angry now, she said, "I'm starting to feel we'll never get back together."

"You never know what the future holds. Perhaps it's good we don't."

He smiled. "Like not predicting a heart attack."

She couldn't refrain from talking about her lover. "We've always had a rocky relationship. I've never been able to trust him. He'd bedded every good-looking woman with a pulse. Despite that, I still love him."

"Chemistry will always play a part in choosing a lover. Most of us know that and have been a party to it." A look of concern crossed Eric's face. "Perhaps you need some distraction. Would you like to go out for coffee, or a walk down the beach to clear your head? You'll feel better."

Eric smiled at Katherine's hesitation. "You're wondering if I'm up for it because of my heart attack? I am. Walking is part of my recovery regime."

Liz Barzda

"Mr. Bowman. I want to go to bed, cover myself, and never get up."

"I know how you feel."

"How would you know how I feel? You had a good marriage. I'm sure you and your wife had love and trust."

"Yes, we did. But prior to my marriage, I had a one-sided relationship I thought would finish me. Rejection is a terrible thing, but it doesn't kill you."

"Mr. Bowman, do you think Scott's written me off for good?"

Eric took her hand and eased her off the sofa. "He doesn't discuss his love life with me. Who knows? He may have a change of heart someday." He placed his hand on her back. "Shall we go? I think we know each other well enough to be on first-name basis. Call me Eric."

"All my friends call me Kat."

"I hope you count me as one of your friends."

#

The night seashore scene pulsated with life. Teenagers skated, couples walked their dogs, young women in minuscule swimsuits ogled muscled athletes, and vice versa. Eric parked his car and he and Katherine strolled along the winding sidewalk that paralleled Long Island Sound. Light emanating from the lanterns added a soft glow. They walked the piers that dotted the beach and relished the cool breeze that blow in from the water.

Eric said, "You look lovely with your hair dancing in the wind."

"Thank you." She turned her face and stared at the distant lighthouse. If she concentrated on the view, maybe Scott would recede from her thoughts.

The sound of Eric's voice brought her back. "What do you say we amble over to the Blue Dolphin for coffee and dessert?"

"Fine," she answered, trying for a smile in her voice.

Their table faced the glass wall with a choice view of the water.

Despite being emotionally drained, Katherine admitted, "This is nice. I didn't realize I was tired." She scanned the dining room and focused on couples with eyes only for each other. They brought a lump to her throat. "I think I'll have tea with lemon, and would you please ask the waiter to bring the dessert menu?" If she gorged herself with sweets, perhaps it would remove the bitterness in her mouth.

"I'll stick with decaffeinated coffee." Eric said, "No dessert for me.

Bittersweet House

My diet is restricted to light almost sugarless desserts that are tasteless. Cooking is my new-found hobby. I never realized the creativity involved. What's your favorite food? Maybe I can dish it up."

"I'm not a fussy eater, but I confess I love almost any kind of pasta."

Eric laughed. "My first attempt at pasta was a recreation of the flood in Fantasia. I didn't realize how quickly spaghetti and water could create a tidal wave. Water was everywhere: on the counter, the stove, the floor. Helen, my housekeeper, screamed. The poor woman slipped and landed on her butt trying to shut off the burner. Thankfully, only her dignity took a beating."

Katherine laughed. "I'm sorry Eric...it really...is funny...I can see her sitting in a puddle on the floor."

He joined in her laughter. "It's unforgivable to get your jollies at someone's misfortune. Don't tell Helen I told you. If she found out, she'd never forgive me." His raucous laughter blended with her giggles Time slipped by as they related humorous incidents.

"It's getting late," Katherine said. "Perhaps we should go."

On the drive back to his home to pick up her car, Eric stated with conviction, "I had a ball tonight--I hope you did, too."

"I did," she answered. "The weatherman promises a breezy Sunday, perfect for sailing." He appeared to hesitate and then said, "Can you think of a better way to spend a day? How about it? Game for a sail?"

Katherine thought for a nanosecond, "I'd love to."

#

Although it was late, Eric rang his son repeatedly. "Scott, I'm glad to have finally reached you. I'm calling you at your home rather than interrupt you at work on Monday. You owe Katherine and me an explanation. You made a date to meet her Friday night at my house. Remember that? She expected you to be here as did I." Eric took a deep breath. "You hurt her and embarrassed me. Your excuse better be good."

"Dad, you might say 'hello' before lacing into me. Sure, I'm guilty for not showing up. Horsewhip me if it makes you feel better, but I can't stand that woman. I felt pressured to show. You insisted I be there." Scott's voice rose. "Anyone as underhanded as she is has no place in my life. I don't intend to see her again. Ever."

"That's no excuse. When you make an appointment, whether business

Liz Barzda

or social, you should keep it (or at least a phone call to cancel). You owe Katherine and me an apology."

"I apologize to you, but I won't apologize to that woman. That's it, Dad. I have nothing further to say on the subject."

He hung up without a good-bye.

\#

Eric proclaimed Sunday, with its cloudless powder blue skies and a north-westerly wind, ideal for cruising. It was one of those rare, late summer days in New England that promised to develop into a clear, star-laden night. He and Katherine boarded the Seth Hawkins Schooner at 6 pm with anticipation of a memorable lobster dinner cruise. She craned her neck to view the top of the majestic two mast ship with furled red sails. Impressive, as were the helm, and the polished teak deck. A deck hand played a concertina--probably the equivalent to piping folks aboard ship, she imagined. The guests were a mixed bag of young singles with their lovers and middle-aged couples out to renew their romance. A handsome, blonde Apollo looked her over. His partner inspected her with pursed lips. Did he think she was the old gentleman's mistress? Their glances and whisperings meant zilch to her; all she wanted was a good time.

The auxiliary motor took hold, and the big ship glided out of the harbor and passed a number of buoys as it headed for deep waters. Out of the channel, the wind filled the unfurled red sails. "The sight of those sails puffing themselves out always gives me a thrill," Eric confessed.

"I've never been on a sailing ship before, but I see what you mean," Katherine said. "This is exciting." A bartender accommodated guests at a makeshift bar, and the concertina provided romantic background music. Eric stuck to tomato juice and brought Katherine a Bloody Mary. They watched the first mate expertly handle the helm, and peppered him with navigation questions.

The Seth Hawkins dipped and rolled; but Katherine, to her surprise, was neither nervous nor seasick. She was exhilarated. Eric put his arm around her as they hustled to the seats sheltered from the bow spray. The crew passed out picked lobster meat with fixings on paper plates. They watched the setting sun spew its rainbow colors on the horizon, while a musician regaled them with folk songs and sea chanties. Despite the sea's action, Katherine enjoyed her dinner, licking butter-soaked fingers with a gusto she hadn't felt in days.

Bittersweet House

As the ship sailed along the Connecticut coast, the sky turned to darkening shades of twilight blue. A half moon and stars appeared in the sky. Katherine breathed in the sea air. A sense of peace engulfed her. The therapeutic waters were magical. "Kat, you look relaxed, lovely in the moonlight. It's good to see you so content."

"I didn't realize I could unwind just by being on the water. Thank you, Eric. This was a grand idea."

He slipped his arm around her. "Have you ever considered a longer sea voyage --like a cruise to Alaska--separate cabins, of course. We'd see eagles, brown bears, caribou, and do all the touristy things?"

"Eric, are you aware that your face lights up when you talk about Alaska?"

His eyes peered into hers. "I had no idea," he teased. In the background, someone sang along with the concertina to the strains of *Take Me Home, Country Roads.* A soothing atmosphere pervaded the ship as it sailed into the harbor. "I'd like to see you again," Eric said.

Chapter 38

The canopied skylight of Seacliff's Shoreline Mall glowed with miniature lights formed to resemble shooting stars. Twinkling lights on stage patterned the celestial sphere of constellations, creating a heavenly aura.

Captains of industry, patrons of art, and those whose only claim to fame were their bank balances, gladly ponied up $500 to see, and be seen, at The Starlight Fashion Extravaganza cancer fundraiser.

Zita and her sales manager, Ted arrived early and check-listed last minute details with the mall's management people. Weeks ago, Zita prevailed upon Ron Richards to narrate the show. "I'm yours," he said, "if you promise no one will take my assigned seat next to Linda." "It's a done deal," Zita replied. "You're sitting at my table next to her" *He's beaming. Easy to read that face. I'd say, he's got the hots for our Linda. How could I have missed it?* True to his word, Ron worked with Zita on timing and delivery. The day of the show his rich voice described the parading outfits as music from hip-hop to classical played in the background.

High-priced models cat-walked down the runway in sport togs of autumn plaids married to checks and winter coats of various lengths and colors from iceberg to sinful scarlet.

No tacky brides and bridal party fashions for this show, Zita decided, but a display of gowns with matching furs. The most glamorous ones were worn by local radio and TV personalities, actors and visiting celebrities. The audience applauded an actress in a peach fox cape over a peach silk halter gown. They oohed as a radio personality removed a long red velvet coat hemmed in sable to show off a full-skirted matching gown. Ahs of admiration swept the cavernous hall as Linda sauntered down the runway. "The ice princess comes to life, in the form of WSEA's Golden Girl, Linda

Cooper." Ron announced. "Notice how the drape of her silver lamé gown hugs her curves and flows into a train like slithering mercury." His voice warmed as he noted that "the overhead stars churned her blonde hair into glistening gold." Zita watched and listened from the sidelines. *You can't miss the emotion in those words. He's really in love with Linda.* At the conclusion, the models appeared in designer gowns and furs to thundering applause. Rainbow hues of a laser light show shot across the atrium ceiling in a dazzling finale.

When the applause subsided, Zita, Linda and Ron joined Katherine, Margaret, Jack and Peter at their table. "The show's a blast, Zita," Peter said. He kissed her on both cheeks. "Congratulations, you've raised a heap of money for cancer. I'm so proud of you."

Ron grabbed Linda's hands and looked around the table. "Wasn't she wonderful?" His eyes seemed glued to her face. "You look like a goddess plucked out of the universe."

"Really, Ron, that's a bit much." She flashed him a wide smile. "But thanks for the compliment. You were a perfect master-of-ceremony." He seemed appreciative but said nothing, just kept looking at her. "What do you mean terrific?" Jack asked. "They wouldn't even let him show his face, kept him behind the curtain. Let him be heard but not seen." Jack slapped him on the back. "Just kidding. You did a topnotch job, old man."

Laughter mingled with champagne and compliments. A supper of caviar with blinis, Crepe suzette and strawberry whip followed.

Zita infused with the night's success, lifted her glass for a toast. "Here's to best friends; and a special thank you to Linda and Ron whose talents made this show a true extravaganza." As they clinked glasses, Zita attempted to read their faces. She wondered at Linda's seeming happiness. Did Christopher belong to the past? Throughout supper, Zita noticed that Katherine seemed quiet, hardly indicative of her personality. *She's trying to put on a good front, but she' obviously down because Scott isn't here and she's the only one without an escort.* "Kat, what do you think of the model's makeup? She asked in an attempt to introduce a subject akin to Katherine's business. "Just fine," came the reply in a flat voice.

Obviously her thoughts were elsewhere.

The party broke up reluctantly with Ron insisting on taking Linda home. "May I come up for a nightcap?" He seemed so bent on a positive reply she hadn't the heart to refuse him.

The lights came on as they approached Linda's driveway. She led Ron

Liz Barzda

into the den and flicked on music to dispel the silence, hoping to continue the show's upbeat mood. "Would you like a brandy, Ron?"

"Sure. It would top off the evening."

She joined him on the sofa and sighed, a reflex from apprehension mixed with excitement.

"It's been one hell of a day, but so energizing."

She poured their drinks and lifted her glass.

"Here's to us, may we continue to partner good causes."

They clinked glasses and smiled at each other.

His eyes shone with love as he said. "You were the best thing in the show." He took a swallow of brandy, moved closer to her and drew her near. "I have something to tell you, partner." He paused a few moments as if to collect himself. "I ache just thinking about it. And I'll miss you like crazy, but I can't pass up the opportunity."

Linda's heart rate quickened. She hated surprised these days, wary of unforeseen bad news.

"Atlanta has offered me an anchor position and I've accepted." He downed his drink as if he needed it to carry on. "It's a chance to get into a larger market. It has only one downside--you won't be beside me."

"God, Ron, I never thought that would happen, not that you don't deserve it. You're perfect for the job. You've worked hard. I can't picture us not anchoring together.

"Have you given any thought to sending your video to Atlanta? I think they'd snap you up."

"Actually Ron, I did that three years ago to test the waters. I did receive an offer, but Christopher didn't want to relocate. So I turned it down."

"Give it some thought again, would you?"

"Don't look so crestfallen. Who knows what the future may hold?"

"Are you offering me some hope?"

"I don't believe I'll ever leave Connecticut. Yet there are times when I want to run away and never look back."

"But you have everything going for you."

She slipped from his grasp, stood by the fireplace facing him. "No, Ron, I have nothing going for me. My life is on hold. It's as if the world is spinning and doing things while I've been dumped into outer space without oxygen."

His expression said I don't know what you mean.

"I'm sorry if I don't make sense. It's just that life seems so unfathomable since I learned that Christopher has a mistress and a son."

Bittersweet House

Ron's mouth gaped open. "What? Am I hearing you correctly?"

"Oh, yes. I've known it for months. My hatred has simmered into anger, now I'm just numb"`

I can't believe this. You two were the envy of every battling and mismatched couple."

"*Were,* is the key word. That's my past life and I just as soon forget it."

"I can hardly believe this. It's a hell of a boot in the stomach. Linda, I'm terribly sorry."

"I'll live." Her expression turned apologetic. "We had such a lovely evening; I should have the good sense to not spoil it." She offered him another brandy, poured herself a double and gulped it down.

He drew her to him and wrapped his arms around her. "Delving into your business is the farthest thing in my mind, but I've wondered why I hadn't seen him around lately. I'd like to beat him senseless. What a cowardly bastard! Do you have any idea what you're going to do?"

"No, I don't. You know the old cliché--take one day at a time. That's how I'm living these days.

"My only concern is your happiness. I know this is not the moment, but I *can* make you happy. Let me try. He took her face in his hands, tenderly kissed her lips and neck. His hands eagerly cupped her breasts, then tasted and explored her mouth.

Amazed at her response, she neither pushed him away, nor asked him to stop. I must be tipsy she thought, but she didn't care. The petting felt so good.

Ron took off his jacket and flung it on the floor. He removed a condom from his wallet and unzipped his pants.

Linda watched as he put it on. "Do you go everywhere so prepared?"

He chuckled, "I wasn't an Eagle Scout for nothing."

She couldn't restrain a giggle. "Thanks heaven for that."

He covered her body with his, then pushed up her gown and quickly removed her lace panties. Her cries of delight and the wet warmth between her legs excited him further. He rained fierce kisses on her then pulled back to gently to heighten her passion. "Don't stop. Please don't stop," she said breathlessly. Her inner voice shouted, *You're vulnerable. Don't be stupid.* Her heart shouted back, *I don't care about being vulnerable. I want to be loved again.* His mouth tasted every bit of her. She drew the gown over her head and wrapped her arm s around his neck. He disentangled her arms and held them out so he could gaze on her ivory loveliness. "I've

Liz Barzda

dreamed about this for years. You're more beautiful than I had imagined." He sucked on her nipples, than licked a path down her body and explored the warmth between her legs.

Linda writhed with delight and lifted her hips ready to receive him. Ron penetrated her with two probing fingers. She gasped with delight, hardly believing that she could revel in his lust. It didn't matter that a tiny voice tried to be heard over sexual desire. *You're vulnerable and you'll regret this.* Ron removed his fingers and thrust his penis into her again and again. She held on to him, wanting more and more. He slowed down to savor every spasm of desire and to bring Linda along. "More, more," she cried as he changed pace. He kept the tip of his penis in, tantalizing her. She tried to hold him down and in her. He entered her fiercely, then gently, then over and over again bringing her to ecstasy until they exploded together. They clung to each other, not wanting it to ever end. He collapsed in a heap and whispered. "I love you Linda. I've loved you since the first day I saw you. This is what I've been dying to do for years. And it's more than my dreams had conjured up."

She kissed him tenderly. "You're a wonderful lover, Ron." Linda's mind was devoid of everything but how good it felt to be loved again, to have him envelop her in his arms, to feel his breath and heart accelerate, to know she has the power to excite him. His ardor surprised her, a lover women dream about, or was it just that it had been months since she and Christopher made love? She had broken her marriage vows, but had no regrets. She had done what she accused Christopher of doing, still she enjoyed every moment of their lovemaking. She'd almost forgotten how wonderful lovemaking could be. She felt whole again.

Chapter 39

Tiffany smiled shyly as she placed a white iridescent box in Zita's hand.

"For me? What a nice surprise! Thank you, sweetheart." Zita bent and kissed the little girl's cheek. "I'm so happy your aunt brought you to the brunch."

Linda cradled her niece's shoulder. "She'll be with me for a while; sort of a vacation."

"Auntie Linda said we're going to have fun together," Tiffany added. Her eyes widened as she spotted a fluffy cat meandering through the living room. She ran after it, "What's your name, kitty?"

"I hope you really don't mind Tiffany being here," Linda said. "I'm her temporary Mom until Sandra is able to care for her."

"Love having her," Zita said. "I've adored her since she was a baby. Kids add life to any gathering." She placed Linda's gift on the sideboard next to Margaret's and Kat's. "You're just in time for champagne cocktails," Katherine announced as she plunked sugar lumps and bitters in four glasses.

"How elegant. This is such a lovely way to spend Sunday." Linda sniffed the air, "Something smells delicious."

"Bless the caterers," Margaret declared as she viewed the bounty deposited on the buffet. "It's past noon and I missed breakfast. Do we eat before you open your shower gifts?" Zita raked a hand through her wavy hair and laughed. "Women over the big 4-0 don't have showers, but thanks for the thought, darling." Despite the disclaimer, the thought pleased her. "Women who say they abhor showers are lying." Katherine smirked. "Anyone with the courage to enter the institution of marriage today deserves a windfall."

Liz Barzda

"Now that I have the loot, I have to feed you," Zita joked. "Help yourselves to the buffet." Tiffany appeared with the cat dangling precariously in her arms. "Can Kittie eat with me?" she asked as the cat struggled to break free. She deposited the animal on the broad ottoman and announced, "I'll eat here with Kittie."

The women sat at the dining table and complimented their hostess on its mauve and white color scheme, noting that her mauve silk pants outfit continued the color décor. Between all the admiration and mouthfuls of quiche and lobster, Zita begged her friends' attention. "Perhaps I've already mentioned the wedding, but did I give you all the details?" she asked playfully. She gave them a quick rundown. You'll forgive me for repeating myself--I never dreamed I could be so happy."

"Enough, already," Margaret said. "Seriously darling, you deserve the best."

"Thank you, Margaret. Thank you all for listening to me. One more thing, Peter's chosen his cousin Roland as his best man." Zita gave a tiny smile. "That's all on the nuptials. I promise. Help yourselves to fruit, desert and coffee."

Tiffany piped up, "Zita, when are you going to open the presents?"

"How about right now? And you can have all the ribbons."

Tiffany scooted next to her on the sofa. "From Margaret," Zita announced as she read the card and opened the satiny blue box. She held up two tickets to the Metropolitan's Opera House's fall production of *Carmen*. "How thoughtful, Margaret. You know how much I love opera, as does Peter. This is a real treat. Thank you so much."

Zita undid the wrapping on Katherine's glittering gold box. She held up the invitation to trawl for marlin aboard the Kingfish out of Montauk. "What an original idea. Guess I mentioned that Peter and I are into fishing. Can't wait to catch the big one. You're a sweetheart." Tiffany snatched the ribbon from Zita's hand and handed her the next box.

Zita admired the square shiny red box and gave Tiffany its matching ribbon. She opened the gift and stared at a watercolor painting of yellow roses and red poppies. The card read, "Yellow is for friendship, red is for love. You deserve both, Linda."

Zita rose and kissed her best friend's cheek. "Linda, an original by Brenton Foster. This is much too extravagant. But it's gorgeous. Look at the dewdrops on the flowers. I love it."

"It's just a token from me to remind you of your new wonderful life to come."

Bittersweet House

Zita shook her head in disbelief. "You've all been too generous." She felt Tiffany tugging at her pants.

"When are you going to open my present?"

"Right now." Zita carefully unwrapped the white box. She held up the silver grape scissors and grinned. "Something I actually don't have. Thank you, Tiffany."

"Auntie Linda said she'd bet anything you don't have grape scissors. Can you cut pictures out of a magazine with them?"

"Probably not," Zita said, "but you can snip some grape stems if you wish."

Tiffany skipped over to the buffet table as Zita refilled her guests coffee cups. Like a geyser bubbling and bubbling, Zita felt love flowing over her. More than anything, she tried to retain that feeling. This was not the time to think of love gone awry. Her mind refused to cooperate and kept reviewing sorrowful chapters in her friends' lives. Christopher definitely would not be at the wedding; she didn't know about Scott. Since Linda's revelation of her husband's mistress and son, Christopher's name seldom came up. And Kat hadn't said anything about seeing Scott, nor hearing from him.

Linda pushed aside her half-eaten apple baklava to announce, "Listen up. I have some good news to report."

The words brought Zita out of her daydream. What a pleasure to hear good news for a change.

"Sandra is with my mother in Maine, and gradually recovering her health. She's aware of those around her, talks a bit, and takes walks." Her face lit up. "And Tiffany will be with me until Sandra is well. She's a delight and..."

Margaret interrupted, "Who'll care for her while you're at work?"

"Mrs. Brody agreed to move in. She's widowed and loves kids. We've worked out a schedule: I'll be with Tiffany in the morning, have breakfast with her and get her off to kindergarten. Mrs. Brody will be with her in the afternoon. I'll have dinner with them, get Tiffany ready for bed, then return to the station."

"Sounds like you have it down pat," Katherine said, then mumbled, "What an exhausting schedule."

Three pairs of eyes fixed on Margaret as she ambled to the sideboard. "Oh, I guess it's my turn. You're wondering where I stand in the Rachel-Greg love saga. To begin with, I apologized to my brother-in-law, Mike, for not telling him I had proof that Rachel lied to Greg about being pregnant.

203

Liz Barzda

And that I saw her passionately kissing a woman in a car. Mike reluctantly forgave me."

Zita's mouth fell open. "You're kidding. You mean she's bi-sexual?"

Linda and Katherine just stared at Margaret, awaiting details.

"Mike, being a cop, can easily get evidence about Rachel's gay romance. I'm certain he's able to convince Greg of Rachel's plots and lies. But how do I impress on my nephew how sorry I am to have conspired behind his back? How do I regain his love and trust?" "It'll take time, but he'll come around," Zita said. He's still a teenager and not as mature as he thinks. I'm positive he loves you and Jack more than he admits."

Tiffany pursued the put-upon cat through the living room into the dining room. "Come back, Kittie. Why does she run away from me, Auntie Linda? Can we take her home?"

"I'm afraid not, dear." Linda patted her niece's head. "Zita would miss her. Speaking of home, I have to run. I have to write a story that's due tomorrow. "Thank you for a lovely time, Zita. Tiffany, say thank you to Zita."

The child's eyes focused on the cat hiding under the coffee table. She pouted but managed a "Thank you".

Zita bent down and took Tiffany's hands in hers. "You're welcome to come anytime to see Scheherazade. Did you know that she's a Persian cat, just like her name and the story?"

Tiffany shook her head and frowned. "What a funny name."

"Linda, wait a minute," Katherine said. "I haven't added my revelation to this confession. Hardly happy news, nevertheless I'll share it with you all. I think I've told you that Scott promised to meet me at his father's home. He didn't show. I thought I would die of embarrassment. Eric made no excuses for his son's action, nor any predictions whether Scott would forgive me. Eric was so kind, so understanding. He realized I was stressed out, and persuaded me to go for a drink."

Zita noted the first-name basis. "Last Sunday, Eric took me sailing on a dinner schooner. I never realized how wonderful an evening on the water could be. We had the best time. Eric is kind, like a father."

Margaret's eyebrows arched. "Well, that's a turn of events,' she muttered under her breath.

Linda withheld comment. *So much for missing Scott*, Zita mused.

Chapter 40

On Monday Margaret reviewed the completed Forest Park and Seacliff Villa brochures, along with the Seacliff Villa TV commercial. She placed a large ad in The New York Times real estate section then called Zita for an update on the TV commercial. Zita reported the commercial was on schedule and ready for viewing the following week.

Her ambitious real estate ventures kept her focused on business. Nevertheless, the outburst with Greg lingered in her mind. She tried to blot it out, but it persisted in tormenting her. Jack called and suggested dinner out and a movie. After her stressful week and working all day Saturday tying up the publicity loose ends of the two major projects, Margaret welcomed a pleasant night out. She'd give anything to erase the painful look of betrayal on Greg's face and the hurtful words that poured from his mouth.

On the way to Gourmet Maison, their favorite French restaurant, Jack brought her up to date on the revamping of Seacliff Hospital's two older buildings. He made no attempt to hide the excitement in his voice as he described the architect's plans of an atrium in the holistic medical facility, and bedrooms with dressing rooms in the cosmetic surgery building. "The drawings are completed. Now comes the difficult part, getting the architect and the building contractor to coordinate in moving the project along."

Margaret smiled and affectionately patted the back of his neck. "I know how frustrating it is when a project is in the embryonic stage and isn't moving as fast as one envisions. The board trusts your judgment. They know you're on top of the renovation. Because you keep a sharp eye, the buildings will be beautiful."

"Thanks, darling. You're an ego builder. I love it," Jack said squeezing

Liz Barzda

her thigh. They rode in companionable silence until Margaret lowered her head and rubbed her forehead. "What a time for a damn headache! Jack, stop at CVS. I need to get some aspirin. I want to enjoy the movie."

They hurried out of the car for the coolness of the pharmacy. Margaret homed in on the pain reliever aisle while Jack browsed the isles. She paid for her purchase, then her eyes scanned the store in search of her husband. She found him in the corner near the hair products talking animatedly with Greg. Her nephew looked agitated, moving his hands and shaking his head. Margaret just stared. Should she go over? Should she try to talk to him, try to convince him how sorry she was for the other night's nasty business? No matter what Greg would say, she was determined to make amends. "Hi, Greg. How are you?" She realized that he hadn't noticed her in the store as his face registered surprise. Then the expression turned to anger.

"I have nothing to say to you."

"That's not the way to greet your aunt," Jack said not with displeasure. Greg turned on him. "I had no intention of speaking to either one of you, but now that you have me cornered..."

Jack interrupted, "We're hardly holding you captive, Greg, but I do think it's time you acted like the adult you profess to be."

"I am an adult, but you two chose to treat me like a child." His face became flushed, "I can never forget how you, Aunt Margaret, conspired to demean, to almost destroy Raquel, Aunt Maggie."

Greg's intentional use of the sobriquet Maggie, which he knew his aunt deplored, wasn't lost on her. Despite the obvious hurt, Margaret was determined to reach him, to convince him they had only his best interest at heart. Before she could comment, Jack fired back, "If Raquel feels destroyed, it's of her own doing. I'm certain your Dad has enlightened you about Raquel's lies and plots."

Greg scowled, "She denied it and insisted you two are out to get her."

"You know that's not true," Jack said. "She cares nothing about your education, your future. Money and good times are all that interest her. Come on, Greg, own up to the fact that your aunt did what she deemed necessary because she loves you and wants to secure your future."

"Did you have to be so underhanded, so deceitful?" "Would you have reacted any differently than you did at my house? I'm sure your Dad has told you that Raquel was seen kissing a woman, quite passionately, too."

Greg snapped, "I don't believe it. It's another lie to keep us apart. It

Bittersweet House

won't work. Even if I believed you, which I don't, tell me how you two managed to get the evidence?"

"Greg, that's enough!" Jack said. "Whatever was done had your best interest at heart, done to protect you."

"Why couldn't you two have talked to me instead of plotting behind my back? I have nothing else to say. Good-bye."

Margaret reached for his arm. "Greg, please..."

He shook free.

"I love you," she said. He looked at her and dashed from the store.

"I can't believe this," Margaret cried. "How will we ever get him back? How can we get him to trust us again?"

"Forget it. He's still nursing his hurt. It'll be awhile before he's mature enough to see the whole picture." He took her arm to lead her out. "Only time will ease his pain--and ours."

"I hope this won't change your mind about giving him the money for Yale? It took a heap of convincing before Michael agreed to accept our gift. And now this."

"Don't worry, hon. Once Michael's given his word, he'll stick by it. Greg will never know we helped finance his education. Your brother-in-law is smart enough to keep his mouth shut about this. And he knows enough to not badger his son about forgiving us. He'll let time soothe Greg's hurt. We've got to do the same."

Chapter 41

Monday, usually a normal-paced day at La Petite Spa turned into a hectic one. Clients, other than the regulars called in for last-minute appointments. The traffic kept Katherine focused on business all day. On the drive home she reviewed the profitable day with gratification, but a boring evening loomed ahead. Although never one to lack for a date, Katherine generally preferred her own company to the men who buzzed around her. Salesmen who plied their wares in her salon, guys in the gym, and those in the local watering hole were eager to take her out. None could measure up to Scott. She'd try to forget him for the moment and concentrate on dinner.

At home in her industrial-chic furnished condo, Katherine relived the pleasures of Sunday's sail with Eric. However lovely the scenes, they couldn't block out the previous night. She saw herself sitting in his home waiting for Scott to appear. The fact that he didn't show, disappointing both of them, proved Scott didn't give a shit. *What* a *hard hearted friggin' SOB.*

Katherine inspected the fridge with little interest. Cold chicken, leftover spaghetti and fruit didn't tempt her. Anger had killed her appetite. She poured herself a tall glass of orange juice, sat at the kitchen table, and stared at the portable phone. Would Scott be in his apartment on a Monday night? Even *he* wouldn't be catting around on a Monday night. Why did her mind dwell on his infidelities--because he had cheated on her in the past and is probably getting it on with his secretary right now. When she spied them together, they appeared more personal than business-like. But that doesn't necessarily make him guilty of jumping her bones. *Don't be an idiot. You know it's so.* The devil in her screamed that they're going at it right now. Katherine lowered her head and rubbed her forehead as

Bittersweet House

if to clear her mind. Her emotions swung from labeling him a fornicator to absolving him of all guilt. She felt as if her capacity to love warred against the desire for revenge. Could she detect what was real and what she concocted in her imagination? *You're pursuing him* her conscience screamed. *You're right, but I don't give a fig.* She loved Scott, wanted him back and couldn't accept that he rejected her forever.

She craved his arms around her, his body on top and in her. *There's more to our relationship than just sex; we're in tune.* She recalled the things they shared, like movies, food, even politics. *Just because I yearn for him doesn't mean he'll ever be mine again* her inner voice taunted. *I'll get him back. Just watch me.* The only way to find out is to pick up the phone.

Katherine's breathe quickened. She wiped perspiration from her forehead, then reached for the phone and dialed Scott's number.

It rang four times, then a "Hello."

"Scott, it's Kat. I've got to talk to you. Please don't hang up. It's about Friday night. You promised to meet with your father and me. We waited for hours and you didn't show. You disappointed two people who love you."

"I don't intend to discuss my engagements with you," Scott said in a angry tone.

"Please don't hang up. I know I did wrong, but how many times do I have to beg you to forgive me? Don't you believe that we're all entitled to one mistake?

"Your jealously cost me dearly. My father lost faith in me as a man and as a worker. It'll take me a long time to build his trust. You expect me to close my eyes to your stupidity, to say all is forgotten?"

"I know I have some wicked characteristics, but I swear I'll change. Give me a chance to prove it. Remember what the Good Book teaches. Let he who is without sin cast the first stone. That Biblical wisdom is meant for all."

"Since when are you so steeped in the Bible?"

"That's mean. Can't you give me a little credit? We didn't study the Bible at catechism, but you'd be shocked to know that I've read most of it I've memorized that verse and it's always stayed with me. I know that I'm not without sin. Neither are *you.*"

"Trying to throw your guilt on me won't change my mind."

"You're stubborn, but I didn't think you were heartless. Do I have to go on my knees to make you understand?" No response. It seemed like minutes. Finally, she said, "Aren't you going to say anything? You just want me to go on suffering, don't you?" The tears began and her voice trembled. "How long, Scott? How long before I've completed my penance?"

"You want *me* to whitewash your vengeful streak. That's your problem. You work on it."

"How about *your* faults? Should we go into your infidelities? How many times have you cheated on me?" Her voice grew louder. "Are you still humping your secretary? You expected me to forgive you anything. And I did. I closed my eyes to your weaknesses."

"I've never committed to you.. It's none of your business if I see other women."

"True, you certainly wouldn't make a commitment, but you did say you loved me and I was the only woman for you. Please, give me another chance."

Katherine sensed his hesitation.

"I don't have a timetable for forgiveness." Then in a softer, less aggressive tone, he added, "I think we've talked enough for now." No good-bye, just a dial tone.

Katherine took a deep breath. Her head dropped, her arms went limp, her eyes closed. The conversation exhausted her, yet it hadn't gone too badly. Scott didn't forgive her, but neither did he cut her off completely. His "we've talked enough for now" gave her hope. She'd work on him slowly. Little by little she would get him back. All of a sudden she felt ravenous. She poked into the fridge and took out chicken, fruit and salad fixings. Sated with the comfort food, Katherine acknowledged that the devil that often prodded her retreated from her mind. With the right attitude and one day at a time concept, Scott would be hers. She smiled as if it were a done deal.

Chapter 42

No matter how many times Gregory O'Neil sat in Raquel Lopez's living room, he reacted negatively to fuchsia walls and tropical-colored birds. The color scheme made him feel as though he was enveloped in a jungle. *Concentrate on Raquel's winning qualities, not on superficial matters like her clothes and home décor.* He watched her with pleasure as she walked toward him.

"Hi handsome hunk." She placed her arms around his neck and gave him a lingering kiss.

"Hi," he said, then removed her arms and headed for the sofa. "Where are your folks?"

"At the movies, every Tuesday, like clockwork." She sat close to Greg and stroked his face. "We have the whole place to ourselves." She smiled and wet her lips. "What's so important that you had to see me right away? You sounded *so* serious."

Greg focused on the orange dress that hugged her breasts and hips. Kissing her hello wasn't enough; he wanted to run his hands over her body and enter her. But not now. He had to learn if there was any truth to his aunt's accusations. *Raquel couldn't be a cheat, liar and manipulator.*

"So what's the big discussion that couldn't wait?"

"It's no big deal, but I was wondering. Did you tell my aunt we were planning to get married and fix up your folks' basement?"

"I might have mentioned it. Why?"

"Don't you think that's a little premature?"

"What do you mean premature? Didn't you say you'd like to spend the rest of your life with me?"

Liz Barzda

"Yes, but I didn't mean getting married now. I meant in the future. We have a lot of living to do first."

"We talked about living together and you thought it was a terrific idea. So I went a step further, like making it legal. What's wrong with that?"

"Nothing is wrong with it, Raquel, but you misunderstood me. I meant getting married in the future. Right now I plan to concentrate on becoming an architect. For that I need a college degree. Surely, marriage can wait. Maybe in a few years..."

"How can you say I misunderstood you? You said, 'We'd be together always, and that I was the only one for you.' You even mentioned putting off college. I asked you how you like working construction and you said it was okay."

"Putting off college is temporary, a matter of money. I've been accepted at Yale, but I know it's a reach for my Dad to finance my education. My plan is to save for a couple of years and take out a student loan. Things may work out for us, Raquel. You've got to be patient. We're having a good time now aren't we?" He looked away but wanted to offer her something as an afterthought. "Do you want to move in together?"

She made a face. "You led me on, Greg. And you barely can bring up the subject of moving in together. It's like you're holding your nose when you mention it. Are you afraid of what Daddy and Aunt Margaret would say? Or is it that you can't see yourself living in a basement?"

"We have a good thing going. Let's not spoil it."

"So, I'm good enough to fuck, to even live with, but not good enough to marry. Is that it?"

"Raquel, don't be crude. You know you mean more to me than a good roll in the hay. It's just that the timing is wrong. Let's not quarrel. He reached for her, but she turned her back to him. "I'm sorry you read something into our conversation that I didn't intend."

"Sure, shack up with the Latina babe, but heaven forbid, don't marry her."

"I can't believe your talking this way."

"If you loved me, you'd do anything I ask, like marry me. No, you'd rather take orders from your relatives. My love is not something to be put on hold for the future."

The tiny crack of doubt that had crossed Greg's mind since his aunt's accusations developed into a chasm of reality. "I believed my aunt was concocting stories about you." He frowned at his stupidity. "Actually, my naiveté is almost comical. Can you believe my only objection to

212

Bittersweet House

getting married was that we're too young? My aunt said you were never pregnant."

Color drained from her face. "What are you saying?"

He rose and faced her. "Raquel, you're a liar!" He felt the blood rushing to his head. "You lied about your pregnancy, and there's the other big lie. Your other love-- you know, the woman." Despite the hurt, he laughed at the irony of it all. "I'm not gender prejudiced, but isn't it rather tiring and confusing to keep your love timetable straight?"

"I don't know what the hell you're talking about. I'm not a liar. Who ever told you these cock-and-bull stories? Who was it?" she screamed. "You believe your old aunt? How could you? She never liked me from the beginning." Rage distorted her lovely features as she ranted on. "She's a Gringo witch. She tried to break us up. Why don't you tell the bitch to piss off?"

"Stop it! Why are you saying these horrible things?"

"Because you believe her and not *me*. You owe me. You said you love me, so I expect that, and more. You got me pregnant. Now you have to take care of me. Do you understand? I thought you were a man. You're nothing but a little boy who trails after his daddy and his auntie. The miscarriage was painful. You're not going to write me off."

"What hospital did you go to when you started bleeding?"

"I don't have to answer such a stupid question"

"Why not answer if you have nothing to hide?"

"Seacliff Hospital," Raquel hissed.

"No, you didn't. My aunt knows many of the key people in the hospitals. They said you weren't listed."

"I don't believe you. How would she know these people?"

"Because her husband, my Uncle Jack, is president of Seacliff Hospital. When you have that kind of clout, information is available."

"Your precious Auntie Margaret is all screwed up." Raquel sucked in air. "She doesn't know her ass from her elbow."

"I've finally come to my senses and realize my aunt was telling the truth. If you lied about the baby, it's easy to believe you'd lie about your female lover. And you expect me to believe you love me? Maybe when hell freezes over! How sad that you get a high from lying and plotting. There's something twisted in your character if you must resort to blackmail tactics. I did love you, Raquel. I thought we had something good going. Obviously I was way off the mark."

"You're the liar. You said you'd love me forever."

Liz Barzda

"Forget it, Raquel. It's over."

"No, it isn't. You're going to pay." She grabbed his shirt sleeve.

"Let go."

She put her arms around his neck.

"I said let go."

"No."

She hung on as he released one arm, but then she raised the other hand and scraped his face with her blood-red nails.

Real blood began to drip. "Look what you've done! My aunt isn't crazy. You are." He held his hand over the damaged cheek. "You can go live in the basement by yourself. Have a happy life, Raquel."

Greg drove home with conflicting emotions. Had he really love this screaming, foul-mouthed woman who clawed his face? He did vow to love her forever. But she always appeared fun-loving, a sexy, free spirit, never revealing the frenzy part of her character. His scratched cheek was a testament to that. What a fool he was. He must get her out of his mind. He didn't want to think of the questions he asked Raquel and definitely didn't care to review her answers. He refused to let his mind dwell on his Aunt Margaret's accusations, yet his conscience kept pricking him. *Admit it, she was on the right track. Does that mean she has a right to delve into my business and* make *a mess of my life?* He shook his head and tried to focus on his job, his home, the weekend, anything but his former girlfriend.

He breathed a sigh of relief when he arrived home. Dad was out. Good thing. Greg wasn't in the mood to respond to questions about his scratched face. He cleaned the wound and applied a bandage.

The telephone rang. "It's probably that pig, Raquel," he said aloud. He picked up the handset, expecting a harangue from his now-ex-fiancée. He was brusque. "What do you want?"

"Greg, this is Aunt Margaret."

"Oh, it's you."

"Greg, don't hang up. Listen to me. I know you hate me for interfering in your life, but I did what I thought was right. It was my duty. I promised your dying mother that I would protect your future. I know you've heard this before, but I couldn't forsake my obligation. I'm sorry if I bollixed up your love life. I hope you'll find it in your heart to forgive me. She waited for a response, but there was none. Greg, please speak to me. I love you."

"I'm not up to talking now. Maybe another time."

He hung up, put his hands to his face, and cried.

Chapter 43

More than a month had passed since Christopher left for Wales on business. Linda had no idea when he'd pop up again. She didn't care. *Why couldn't he just fade away?* Having Tiffany and Mrs. Brody in the house with her supplied a sense of companionship, if not security-- strengths that her husband should have rendered. To feel Tiffany's arms around her and hear her laugh lightened Linda's heavy heart. She longed to have her niece permanently, but it was not to be. Her job was a temporary one. The time spent with Tiffany, and the discipline involved in caring for her, paled in comparison to the joy the child imparted. *How ironic life is*, Linda mused. The tragedy of losing her brother-in-law and her sister's depression brought the girl closer to her.

Linda found Tiffany more entertaining and challenging than she had imagined, but could she guide and discipline her properly? Unfamiliar with the psychology of parenting; she'd pilot by love and common sense. Breakfast with her niece started the day on an uplifting note. A little chatterbox, Tiffany asked questions about kindergarten, whether there were other children in the area, and why couldn't they have a dog? Linda and Mrs. Brody filled the child's time with fun and learning activities. Her aunt taught her to tell time and how to recognize coins and paper money. But around dinnertime, Tiffany withdrew emotionally from the women and asked for her mother. "I'm sorry darling. Your Mommy isn't with you because she's not well, but she's getting better every day. She thinks of you all the time. She misses you."

"Why can't I be with her?" Tiffany sniffed. "I miss my Mommy."

"I know sweetheart, and she wants to be with you. If she knows you're a good girl, she'll get better sooner. You want that, don't you?"

Liz Barzda

Tiffany wiped a tear with her finger. "I think so. How long will it take?"

Linda hugged her. "Your Mommy will be well before you know it. Then you'll be together. How about your bath now?"

"Can I see a video?"

"It's too late for that, but after your bath I'll read you a story."

As Linda soaped her, they sang "Itsy-bitsy spider." Tiffany laughed and said, "let's do it again." After the bath, Linda read Dr. Seuss's "Green Eggs and Ham, the child's favorite story. "Again," Tiffany insisted.

#

In her office the next day, Linda received a call from the informer. "I assume you received the Freedom of Information papers requested by station WSEA from City Hall?"

She assured the informer that she had and asked to meet him at seven that evening at the Seacliff library picture file area. Linda had one purpose in mind: to get at the truth, and to get the story, even if it meant bringing down Seacliff's Democratic mayor and his cronies. At seven P.M. she strode to the designated area and noticed a man sitting in the corner. The informer appeared to be a person of his word, at least regarding appointments. Linda sat and leveled her gaze at him. "I think it's time I knew your name."

"Jessie Wilkes."

"Let's start from the beginning," Linda said. "Why are you doing this?" "I've already told you. I don't intend to repeat myself. Isn't it enough for you to help clean up city hall? Think of the political expose that would skyrocket your TV career. You could go national."

"And what will you gain from this?"

"Justice. For being passed over as Comptroller, the position the mayor promised me. I was the stupid head accountant believing the job I coveted would be mine. 'You'll get that position. Hang in there,' the mayor said." Wilkes let out a derisive laugh, "He strung me along--too long. Now, about you. Let's be honest. Breaking the story means more to you than the city hall cleanup. Right?" He didn't wait for a response. "You have all the information you need. Just read between the lines."

Linda ignored the sarcasm. "Tell me how you know so much about the insurance situation. I assume it is fraudulent."

"I'm an accountant, privy to financial information."

216

Bittersweet House

Linda studied Wilkes--brown hair, brown eyes, brown-checked sport shirt, tan slacks. In the brownness of his persona he almost dissolved into the room's mahogany paneling. Hardly a standout in any municipal government department. No doubt he blended into the city hall office woodwork, as well, an overlooked bureaucrat without charisma waiting for the promotion he desired. Wilkes continued, "I examined all the insurance papers and know for certain the mayor and his boys are sticking the city with inflated life insurance policies that they can borrow on at low interest rates. The public doesn't have a clue on the worth of these large policies or the perks emanating from them."

"And why is this information not available to the public?"

"Because it's buried in department finances normally unrelated to insurance, and I'm the guy reviewing the insurance bills. You can find the proof in the nine-page budget transfer resolution adopted by the Council. That's just the tip of the iceberg. There's a blockbuster coming."

"Tell me."

"This story is juicer than even you had imagined. I've tipped off the FBI about the insurance. They're investigating the whole sorry mess. The life insurance gimmick is now part of the 24-count federal corruption indictment against the mayor charging that he orchestrated a conspiracy to take more than a half-million dollars in payoffs. Guaranteed that he'll be indicted on twenty-four felony charges, including racketeering, bribery, extortion, mail fraud and tax evasion.

Linda attempted to hide her excitement by asking passively, "Where do I come in?"

"I have copies of the nine-page, routine budget transfer resolution adopted by the city council. These papers detail the misappropriated funds to finance the insurance policies for the Mayor and his aides. This is just for starters. More damaging information will be coming."

"Good," Linda said. Her eyes focused on the briefcase in his lap. "May I have the papers?"

"Just a minute. I want your word that you won't reveal the source of this information. My name is never to be mentioned regarding this matter. Agreed?"

"You have my word." Linda held out her hand. "The papers, please."

He laid them on the table and chuckled. "I have a bonus for you. I didn't mention it before as I had to be certain you'd meet with me before handing over the *piéce de resistance*. This video will put you in the big time."

Liz Barzda

Although her stomach felt as if it was doing the Mexican Hat dance, she gave him an innocent smile. "What's it about?"

"It's been known for years that Ed Kaminsky, Seacliff's esteemed financial director, is a womanizer, and that he has a chippie on the side. His wife is fed up with his infidelities and plans to divorce him. What a shock when Valerie Kaminsky phoned me." Wilkes shook his head and laughed, "Hard to believe, but she said that her husband, the mayor, and some council members were at a municipal government conference in a tony Virginia resort boozing and groping pretty party workers. Apparently, they didn't notice that one of the boys--tipsy, but able to handle a camera--videotaped the group for the fun of it. Seems this jokester shoved the video into Kaminsky's luggage, thinking the chairman's old lady would find it hilarious."

"And his wife just handed you the tape?"

A satisfied look spread over Wilkes's face. "I told her that all hell will soon break loose about her husband, the mayor, and some council members regarding unauthorized insurance. Her husband's name and his girlfriend's will be front-page news and the top story on TV. That set her off. She called the tape 'a fuckin' souvenir' and gave it to me with her blessing," Wilkes said with obvious glee.

"Doesn't using subterfuge disturb you?"

"No. And it shouldn't disturb you if you're concerned with truth in government."

Maybe this guy feels used, but he's a user, too. It's the way of the world, Linda told herself. She gathered the damning sheets and video. "Our attorneys will review the information, the video, and contact the FBI before the station will run it."

"How long will that take?"

"Hard to tell, but I'll do everything to get the ball rolling."

Wilkes eyes narrowed. "You'll see that everything I've given you is valid."

"I hope so, for both our sakes."

Chapter 44

Katherine circled green grapes, apricots and pineapple around miniature bran muffins. She readied her silver tea set, purchased years ago as a gift to herself when she landed a job in an up-scale beauty salon. Not that she used it often, but this seemed the perfect time. Fresh yellow and peach roses scented the living room, chosen to coordinate with her peach silk pants outfit.

How thoughtful of Eric to take time off from work on a Wednesday afternoon to pay her a visit. She had no qualms about the spa functioning for a few hours without her direction. She looked forward to seeing Eric, not like a lover whose presence would pump up her heartbeat, but like a protector who admired her and wanted to ease her pain. Yet, if this were all it was, why had she fussed with flowers, silver, and why the concern about coordinating colors? She valued the dear man's friendship and told herself that their platonic relationship held no hiding desires. Eric had taken her out three times last week: for a coffee break during her working hours, for lunch in a town bistro, and yesterday for dinner at Seacliff's best Italian restaurant. He called her at work and insisted on seeing her that evening. Although worn out from La Petite Spa's usual Saturday business frenzy, Eric's reassuring, manner had a soothing effect. It promised to be a lovely evening of easy conversation savored over tea. Among Eric's many attributes, one stood out. He never bored her. They'd talk over the day; she'd relate her attempts to pacify irritating clients with their impossible demands. In her best boarding school inflection she'd imitate Mrs. Bradford (whom she referred to as Mrs. Broadbeam), demanding to know why she was kept waiting fifteen minutes. He'd laugh at her dramatization then told her about wading through Proust's seven volumes of *Remembrance of*

Liz Barzda

Things Past, plus the *Atlantic Monthly.* He asked if she found his interests dull, never touching on their dissimilar tastes or generational differences. She noticed that when he'd mention names or events she had no knowledge of, rather than explain, he'd drop the subject.

"No, you don't bore me with your synopsis of the classics and analysis of today's business climate. I haven't read many of the great books." Katherine gave out a self-mocking laugh. "Actually, I've read only a couple of them, but I do believe in expanding my literary horizons." She had no intention of admitting that her taste ran to People magazine and Danielle Steel novels.

One of his endearing characteristics was his way of looking directly at her. No matter how many people occupied the room, he focused on her. It was as if she were the only person there. Her thoughts were interrupted by the ringing phone.

"Hi, Margaret. Yes, I've got a minute. I'm expecting Eric in five."

The momentary silence wasn't lost on Katherine. (She knew Margaret, Linda and Zita didn't approve of her seeing Eric, even though they hadn't said a word. *I don't give a damn.*)

"I won't keep you long, Kat. I just wanted to know what you're wearing to Zita's wedding. I found a lovely pearl-gray, silk suit with shell to match. What do you think?"

"Sounds perfect to me. It'll bring out your eyes and blend beautifully with your hair."

"How about you, Kat? Find anything yet?"

"Not yet, but I think I'd like an ankle-length tea dress. Something chiffony. Maybe in cranberry. Sorry, Margaret just heard the bell. Got to run."

"Love you," Margaret said and clicked off.

Katherine opened the door to a smiling Eric and ushered him to the sofa. "It's really comforting to have you here. "How was your day?" Before he could reply she asked, "How do you like your tea? Forgive me, Eric, I should give you a moment to respond. It's just so comforting to have you here that I get ahead of myself. I do remember, you take lemon and one sugar with your tea, right? How about a low-fat muffin?"

"No thanks."

She watched approvingly as he sipped his tea. "Now, tell me about your day."

"He put down his cup. "It's not been a good day."

Suddenly she felt uneasy. His usual upbeat attitude was missing. What

Bittersweet House

could be wrong? She wanted the man who made her feel good, who said she was beautiful and talented. She wanted the optimist she knew. "What happened today?"

"I spent my day in deep thought--and walking. I wanted a clear head to make the right decision. To be fair to you."

"Eric, I don't understand. What do you mean 'fair to me'? This sounds serious."

"It is serious. I've given it a lot of thought, Kat, and concluded it's we're not right for each other. I say that because Scott told me you called him a couple of nights ago begging forgiveness and reconciliation."

"He told you that?" Katherine's eyes narrowed in anger. "How cowardly. He's just trying to get back at me." She raised her hand as if to stop Eric from responding. "I know I pulled a dirty trick on him." She let out a hollow laugh. "What goes around comes around."

Eric reached for her hands. "Listen to me. You're a lovely woman. You're smart and talented, but I'm not the companion for you. You still love my son. True, Scott shouldn't have gossiped about you calling him; nevertheless, you still want him. Realistically, I don't know if you two will ever reconnect; but I can't be a substitute for my son. You may think I'm cruel, Kat, but believe me, a substitute for the real thing never compensates."

Katherine's brown eyes flashed. "How can you do this? Aren't we good friends? Your friendship means more to me than you can know."

"Yes, we're friends now. But you know before long that friendship could develop into a sexual relationship. You think I don't want that? Of course, I do. What sane man wouldn't? I adore your personality, love to look at your pretty face, your body, lovely skin, your hair. Don't think I haven't fantasized about making love to you. I could visualize the glorious sex. But I refuse to look ridiculous. When I look in the mirror, I see a 70-year-old man straining to relive his youth." He let her hands go and looked away. "Confession is good for the soul, and here's mine: I feel revitalized when we're together, Kat, but regaining my youth through you is a temporary thing. I'd only be fooling myself. It's unfair to you."

"How noble of you."

Her sarcastic words hit the mark. "You're hurt. I understand that, but no matter how we rationalize it, it's a no-win situation. The difference in age may be negligible in the over-all scheme of things. What isn't negligible is your love for Scott. You'd always be thinking of him, thinking when and how you could get him back."

Liz Barzda

Stunned, Katherine countered, "We're friends who understand each other. Age shouldn't matter. I doubt that we would become lovers, but it's not a crime if a sexual relationship develops. Either way, I'm okay with it. I thought you were, too."

"You don't mean that, Kat. A sexual liaison with me would amount to lying to yourself. Furthermore, such a relationship can be harmful. Scott may feel I've gone behind his back to pursue you. If even a platonic friendship keeps my son away from you, you would eventually resent me. Don't ignore the fact that you still love Scott. You're always thinking of how to get him back. Isn't that right? Be honest with yourself. Scott's presence would hover over us. You must know it, too. And, on a lesser scale," Eric grinned as if he had to reveal a thought better left buried, "you don't know the people, the events, even the movies of my prime. You don't know the decades I fit into."

Katherine reached for his hand. "Is that important, Eric? Those are details in life, not as vital as appreciating and comforting each other."

Eric withdrew his hand. "In the grand scheme of things, these details are minor, but in the daily ritual of life, they're major. However, they're not what made me come to this decision. The thing is, you deserve to find love with someone of your own time, whether with my son or some other lucky young man. I don't know whether you and Scott have a shot at lasting love, but I hope you do. You still love him, don't you?"

Katherine glanced away.

"You don't have to answer. I see it in your face." He rose and walked to the door.

She followed him and asked in a soft voice, "Eric, are you sure? Are you really sure?"

"Yes. We used each other, and that's not how lasting relationships are built. It's true that I couldn't resist your good looks, so I used you to feel revitalized. And you, my dear, if you're honest with yourself, used me for revenge."

"That's not exactly true, Eric. I admire you. I enjoy your company."

"These are minor reasons. Your main objective was to get back at Scott through me. I'm not faulting you my dear, you're only human, but it wouldn't have worked. Guile has no place in love. Find love and treat it with reverence." He kissed her cheek. "I canceled the Alaskan cruise reservations."

Katherine watched the retreating figure. She closed the door, turned and leaned against it, staring into space.

Bittersweet House

She had no idea how long she stood there. Finally she ran into the kitchen with the platter as if demons were chasing her. She shoved muffins into the garbage disposal. "So much for the father." Tears trickled down her cheeks as she pushed grapes, apricots and pineapple into the drain. "So much for the son."

#

"Thanks for coming to the house, Scott," Eric said. "Sorry I called you so late."

"Ten o'clock isn't late for me, Dad. What's up?"

"I have a couple of things I wanted to discuss with you in person." Eric noted his son's weary expression. "Don't look so stricken."

"That sounds ominous. Is it about the feasibility study? I did tell you that I completed the study for the BuiltRite Boxes takeover. Looks like a guaranteed slam dunk.

"This doesn't relate to business, but in a way it does. It's about Katherine Horvath." Noting his son's scowl, Eric held up his hand. "Hear me out. I know there's been a problem between you two. And whether or not you reconcile is your business. But I want you to know that Kat and I have become friends."

Scott frowned. "What could you two possibly have in common?"

"Let's just say what we had in common was you. You and I've been all through her mistake in snitching on you, and I don't want to rehash that, but I do want to include you in my plan. Before we get down to details, would you like a drink?"

"Good idea. Make mine a whiskey, neat. Sounds like I'm going to need it."

Eric poured the whiskey and filled a tumbler with soda water and lime for himself. Scott took a couple of swallows, put his drink down and waited for his father to elaborate.

"Perhaps I should have told you that I took Kat out a few times," Eric said.

"Really, Dad. Am I supposed to be offended?"

"Don't play games with me, Scott. I'm being up front with you and expect the same. I took her out because she seemed so contrite, depressed really about what she had done. I felt sorry for her. We had a few laughs and that was all. Kat still loves you, although she hasn't the courage to admit it

Liz Barzda

to me. Why can't *you* be truthful? You still love her. In your heart you know she's more of a woman than all the others you played around with."

"And just what do you expect me to do, agree with you and fall into her arms?"

"If that's what it takes to keep you creditable. Tell me you don't love her."

Scott's turned his head and gazed at the wall of books.

"Of course, you do." Eric declared. "Good. We don't have to debate the subject any longer. I thought about this matter long and hard. The business community is rife with rumors that Kat's is in financial difficulties because of her expensive renovation. I've decided to give Kat a 20-year interest-free loan."

"You must be kidding. Why would you do that? Did she tell you that I promised to ask you for a low-interest loan? I'll bet she did."

"No. She never mentioned it. And why would you assume she did? Did you promise her you would speak to me about it?"

"Yes, I guess I did," Scott sheepishly admitted. "But why are you doing it?"

Eric sat back in thought. "To atone for my foolishness. And because the Bowman men treated her badly. You cheated on her. You were heartless in not forgiving her and not living up to your promise of asking me for a loan. Because I dated her without regard for the feelings of either one of you."

Scott sucked in a breath, "How big a loan?"

"A mil"

Scott wrinkled his forehead. "So much?"

"Yes. I have faith in her as a business woman. I hear she has a thriving clientele. I have no qualms of getting my money back eventually. Plus, I can afford it."

"It's your money."

"Scott, it would behoove you to be more magnanimous. By the way, why didn't you ask me for a loan for Kat?"

Scott bowed his head. "I meant to. I just didn't get around to it."

"I see. Since you couldn't manage that, I want you to do something for me."

Scott smiled. "Sure, Dad, anything."

"I want you to tell Kat of my intention of a loan. You can arrange the contract and payment schedule with my lawyer."

Scott looked astonished. "Me. Why?"

Bittersweet House

"Because, son I want you to feel what it's like to do something for someone and not expect anything in return."

Eric stood and led the way to the foyer. "I want you to explain my gift to Kat with an open heart. She must understand that there are no strings attached to this loan. And there shouldn't be any conditions to your relationship with her. The elder Bowman circled an arm around his son. "One more thing, don't wallow in the hurt that's been done you. Forgive and rebuild."

Chapter 45

The following week WSEA-TV's attorneys gave the go-ahead to Linda's exclusive investigative report. The report revealed that a twenty-four-count indictment was filed against Clarence Butterfield, alleging that the Seacliff mayor pocketed $425,000 in cash, gifts and services from developers and others in exchange for city approval on their projects and contracts. WSEA-TV filmed the mayor in a public appearance expressing his outrage at the indictment. An FBI probe snared a circle of Butterfield's confidants and associates.

On Thursday the station ran Linda's story piggyback with the drunken party video on the six and eleven o'clock news casts. She detailed the buried insurance policies, noting the policies were tucked within routing envelopes of year-end budget transfers and unrelated issues. Although Butterfield and another top official subsequently dropped out of the plan, the policies-and-approval process drew the attention of the FBI and IRS. The exposé received state-wide publicity and garnered the station's highest rating of the year. Phone calls and e-mails flooded the station. Most of the kudos were for Linda. A few citizens criticized the station for running a sleazy video of the city's top officials, but the majority e-mailed their enjoyment of the politician's party antics.

Management assured her that the mayor's trial, slated for next year, was part of her exclusive assignment. Because she broke the biggest political story of the year, her boss promised her a hefty bonus and extended her contract from two years to five years.

#

Bittersweet House

Despite the all-day rain, Linda felt renewed by her co-worker's compliments, most of whom insisted her scoop would earn a Golden Tube award. She thanked God for the fantastic week. But Christopher intruding her thoughts put a damper on everything.

She tried in vain to block him out. And as much as she hated him, a part of her longed for their past life. The sight of his BMW in the garage unnerved her. He'd been gone more than a month phoning her only once. Why did he have to be here now, just as things were going so well?

She deposited her keys on the foyer's Chinese chest, slipped off her shoes and hung her dripping raincoat in the laundry room. The thought of facing him filled her with despair as she climbed the stairs to their bedroom.

"You're home," Christopher said. He looked at her with no hint of warmth in his eyes. "It's time we had that talk you never seemed to be able to work into your schedule."

"I don't have time to work a talk into my schedule." Her voice rose. "You're the absent one. Why do you refer to it as your home? You're the stranger here."

"Because it *was* my home--a real home once. A sanctuary with a wife who truly cared about me. It's time to resolve this craziness." She looked away from him in disgust then noticed the two large suitcases on the floor.

"I see you haven't unpacked. Off on another business trip?" she asked trying for a note of sarcastic indifference in her voice.

"I haven't unpacked because I'm not staying. I'm leaving you, Linda. Thought about it for months. I've been like a mad man trying to decide what to do. And you haven't helped. I've asked you repeatedly to think about our lives, but you said nothing. You did *nothing*. Now I've solved the problem. Finally I have the courage to do it."

"Courage? How dare you even mention the word, you Judas! You have the courage of a mouse. You lived a lie. You let me go on thinking we had a fairy tale life. Your friends referred to us as the perfect couple, handsome and successful. Remember that, Christopher? When did you decide we weren't the perfect couple? When did you decide you wanted something else? You slept with me all the while you yearned for your real family. Resolve our difficulties? How civilized of you! How difficult was it when you were sleeping with your whore? How about when you were making a baby? And now you want me to resolve *our* problem. She began to laugh, a laugh that took on speed and volume.

Liz Barzda

"You're hysterical. I won't listen to an irrational woman."

"Listen, you selfish bastard! I was a good wife to you. I loved you. And I showed my love. I went along with your plans even if I didn't agree with them. You promised me we would have a family some day." Linda made a mocking face. "'Just be patient, my darling,' that's what you said. I bought into it, like an idiot, because you convinced me babies can wait, careers cannot."

"You went along with me willingly. You wanted a career and the attention and adulation from a TV audience. You still do."

"How dare you attempt to whitewash yourself? Why don't you mention how you screwed around and ran up to Boston every chance you had to be with your mistress and baby? I believed you when you said your consulting business required long absences. You forgot to tell me those trips were extended to visit what's her name, and your bastard son."

He caught her hands and held them tightly. "That's enough."

Outside thunder rolled around the darkened sky, followed by flashes of lightning.

Linda neither saw nor heard the furious forces. Blinded by rage, she cried, "While you were making love, did you both laugh at poor Linda, the little woman back home who didn't have a clue of what was going on?" Christopher turned away. "My lawyer will be in touch with you. You can sue for divorce. You'll have a settlement, and the house."

A feeling of desertion, mingled with hatred and revenge, surged through her. She detested the need to know, but couldn't stop herself from demanding, "Tell me what drove you from me? Tell me how you could lead such a life? I have a right to know."

He picked up the luggage and said, "We had a good marriage in the beginning, but your family always came first. Your parents and your sister. I got tired of your bailing out Sandra time after time. I tried to get you to realize that she would never grow up if you continued to rescue her. I was second place in the family dynamics. You're a good enabler, Linda, but a lousy wife." He turned his back and headed for the door.

"Don't you turn your back on me. All this verbiage is a lame excuse for infidelity. You wanted excitement, variety in your sex life? As far as being second place in my life, that's a lot of horse shit. You were never second place, and you know it. Just because Tiffany is with me for a short stay doesn't make me an enabler. Sandra lost her husband in a horrible accident. She's suffering from depression. She's weak and needs help. I can't desert my sister or my niece. Can't you see that? Where is your compassion?"

228

Bittersweet House

He dropped the suitcases and faced her. "How many times can one be compassionate and look the other way?" Christopher shot back. "You're sensitive to everyone's pain. You suffer when you can't take their pain as your own. Haven't you figured it out yet? You can't absorb everyone's emotional problems and nourish a marriage. You can't bear the thought that Sandra doesn't need your perpetual help. Did you ever think she might grow up if you weren't always there with a net?"

"You're using this enabler shit as a smokescreen to break up our marriage without guilt. The real reason is *her*, isn't it? Is she better in bed than I am? How about kinky sex? Was that what you craved? Whips and chains?" Linda flailed at him. "TELL ME."

Christopher snarled as he grabbed her wrists, "If you're so desperate to know, I'll tell you. I met Betti through business. I had no intention of getting involved."

"Please don't say 'I didn't look for it. It just happened.' If you mention that old chestnut, I'll croak from laughter right here."

"I'm telling you the truth when I say that I didn't pursue her. She came on to me. I admit to being flattered. Betti had time for me. I was number one in her life. It wasn't just a casual affair. She cared about how I felt, what I thought. She's kind and loving. We clicked together."

"Have you forgotten? I was all those things to you and did all that. Your use of the past tense is correct. There's more, isn't there?" Linda saw the answer in his eyes. She yanked a couple of tissues out of the box and wiped her eyes. "What's the grabber? What's making you walk out on a 17-year marriage?" And in a bitter note added, "Not that I care; I just want answers."

"All right. You want to hear it all? You may not believe it, Linda, but I wanted to spare you pain. The affair, as you insist on calling it, grew from admiration to love. Then when Sean came along, life opened up to me as I never could have imagined. He's my flesh and blood. I feel immortal through him. Betti and I have created a family. I have peace now and a feeling of completion I never felt before. That's something you wouldn't understand."

She slapped his face with as much force as she could muster. He swayed back in surprise. "That's for stealing from me the chance to find out, to be a mother and build a family." The tears that she thought were under control gushed forth. Get out. Now! And *never* come back."

Christopher shook his head then picked up his bags. "Linda, I'm sorry for you. Sorry for us that we couldn't make it. I never meant to hurt you."

Liz Barzda

And like a last volley, he added, "But I must do this. Betti and Sean are my life."

Chapter 46

A refreshing breeze blew away the day's humidity on the night of the Celebratory Banquet. A full moon and countless stars illuminated the heavens. Linda drank in the beauty of the night, but sadness washed over her. Never again would the Coopers revel in the beauty of nature, or of each other. The realization that she was now virtually a single woman, doomed to arrive and leave events alone, left her feeling detached. Tonight she'd debut as a loner at the banquet. Linda closed her eyes and muttered, "It's a preview of life as a soon-to-be divorced woman. Get used to it."

Eight days ago Christopher walked out on her. If she could, she'd skip the Banquet and stay home and wallow in her sorrow. But she couldn't disappoint her friends. Through sheer will Linda managed to get dressed, but forcing a smile was nearly impossible. The past week at home allowed her to grieve without the inquisition of co-workers. She had called her boss and told him she'd be out for a week due to stomach flu. She didn't answer the phone, but left an "I'll get back to you" message on her voice mail.

The week of isolation heightened her self-doubt. She couldn't believe that Christopher saw her only as an enabler, a shallow woman without common sense. She searched her mind and heart and had to admit she'd no inkling of Christopher's growing unhappiness. After repeatedly reliving their argument, she realized he never asked if she were happy. It was all about Christopher. No matter how often she lectured herself about bolstering her courage, she knew the kind of life that lay ahead. Like a mantra, she repeated, "Just for tonight, Linda, gather your courage and put on a good face."

She chose a yellow silk cocktail suit that would cast a sunny glow on her complexion and highlight her pastel blonde hair. No eye-catching jewelry. Just simple pearl earrings and necklace.

#

The Regency Grand Hotel drew four hundred of the city's beautiful people, mostly women, to hear noted author Mary Trapp Toddman. Crystal chandeliers and candlelight created a shimmering rainbow of colors that flattered the bejeweled women.

The Barren Babes were to meet at eight o'clock. It was eight-thirty when Linda handed her invitation to the hostess and spotted the assigned table.

"You look smashing," Zita said as she checked Linda out from head to toe. She patted the chair next to her. "Sorry we didn't have the good manners to wait for you."

Linda's eyes went from Zita, to Margaret, to Katherine. *What a good-looking threesome they are.* She never included herself to make it a good-looking foursome.

"Zita's been filling in the details of her upcoming wedding," Margaret said with obvious pleasure.

"I'm sorry I was laid up with a stomach flu," Linda said, "and couldn't help you decide on the flowers, menu and table decorations. There are some people you just can't depend on." She smiled. "Am I forgiven?"

Zita patted her best friend's hand. "Don't give it another thought, Linda. Everything is falling into place. I'll repeat the details."

Katherine and Margaret rolled their eyes.

"Okay, just the minimum report," Zita said. "I managed to snag a florist, who just opened a shop outside of Seacliff. He's anxious for business, and, despite the close date, guarantees the flowers for the church and the table centerpieces will be done on time. She's arranging pink and peach roses for the church, and floating others in old-fashioned fishbowls and votive candle cups to mark each place setting for the reception." Zita took a breath. "I just signed the Connecticut Symphony harpist to play during dinner."

"How romantic," Margaret said. "How about the menu?"

"The Yacht Club's chef is doing layered crepes with paprika chicken, a chocolate whipped cream wedding cake, of course, champagne."

"You're making my mouth water," Margaret said. "What about your dress? What's it like?"

Bittersweet House

Zita raised her chin as if her privacy were being invaded. "You'll have to wait and see. All you'll get out of me is that it'll be long, seeing our wedding is at 4 o'clock."

Linda passed on the consommés then addressed Zita. "I promise to be available for help and to coordinate my dress with yours."

Margaret said, "We all watched your terrific Butterfield exposé. That video is the death knell of the mayor's career."

"It gets better," Linda revealed. "I learned that the mayor and his buddies will be indicted soon. Seems the FBI and the IRS carried on a five-year investigation into Seacliff's municipal corruption. As much as I abhor his actions, I'm rather sorry for him. Butterfield started out to improve the city but got sidetracked by greed and ambition."

"The guy's an idiot and guilty as sin," Katherine scoffed. "But I'm unclear as to the status of sin these days. Is it still considered immoral?"

"Only if you're caught," Zita quipped. She focused on Linda. "You know we're just teasing. Virtually all the state media played up your story. You should be proud of yourself. You're a cinch for a Golden Tube Award. What do you all think? Am I right?"

"It's a triumph!" Margaret said. "I predict a network job coming your way, or at the least, one of the top ten markets." Katherine and Linda waggled their heads.

Zita turned to Margaret. "Dare I ask how things are with you and Greg?" Before Margaret could respond, the waiter laid platters of squab in white wine with wild rice and apples before them.

"This looks divine," Margaret said. Her expression turned from pleasurable anticipation to concern. "I don't mind your question. Jack and I ran into Greg at CVS. Jack spoke to him first. He's still angry and wants nothing to do with us. I did call him. He said he couldn't talk now, perhaps another time, but he didn't hang up." She looked away and said in a low voice, "I'm hopeful he'll forgive me."

Linda cut a bit of her meat and curried fruit, put her utensils down and said, "At Greg's age, lust is mistaken for love. He still has some growing up to do. You and Jack deserve better from him." Her friends stared at her as if she were a stranger. "I'm sorry," she said, circling wisps of hair around her ear. "I have no right to preach or give advice."

To deflect attention from Linda, Zita focused on Kat. "You're quiet this evening."

"Do you want to hear my sad story?"

Zita, Margaret, and Linda leaned in closer.

Liz Barzda

"Remember my telling you that Eric talked me into accompanying him on an Alaskan cruise? It seems he had a change of heart. He tried to convince me that I was entitled to more, that we were of different generations. He insisted that by taking up with him, I was closing myself off from younger men. Wasn't that noble? Would you believe my horoscope predicted a renewed romance looming on the horizon? Huh," she sputtered, "what the hell do the stars know? They should all end up in a black hole."

Katherine eyed her friends, trying to gauge their response. Since they said nothing, she took a deep breath and continued, "I asked Eric if my history with his son had anything to do with his decision. He said he had no idea whether Scott and I could reconnect. I kept probing. He admitted that Scott told him I'd called, begging to see him. That put the kibosh on the cruise and our friendship. Eric believes my actions confirmed that I still love his son. I'm not ashamed to admit that I'll work at getting Scott back. I considered Eric a friend and told him I'd accompany him on the trip only because I missed Scott dreadfully. I suppose, subconsciously, I tried to fill the void with his father. He asked me if I were being honest, perhaps hedging my bets? I don't know." Her eyes began to mist. She looked down at her plate. "Why do I have such conflicting emotions?"

Sounds of glasses clinking, plates being removed, laughter and talking from surrounding tables resonated throughout the room. At the *BB*'s table, silence prevailed. The three women looked at Katherine with pity in their eyes.

"Aren't you going to say anything? How about poor Kat? She's a loser in picking men." The mist in her eyes turned to tears. "I promised myself I wouldn't cry. Screw them both. I'll find someone else. Damn you, Scott. Wherever you are, I hope you're suffering as much as I am."

"Don't punish yourself, Kat," Linda said. You've been punished enough."

"Perhaps it's what I deserve."

Margaret jumped in. "What we deserve is another bottle of wine." She caught a waiter's eye, held up the wine bottle and mouthed 'the same'. "You've got guts, Kat. If Scott's out of your life for good, you'll find someone else, someone who'll appreciate your smarts and beauty. Hell, if you and Scott are meant to be together, you'll get him back."

"Good ol' Margaret, the eternal optimist. Where is it written that the world owes me anything?"

Bittersweet House

"Well, at least I didn't mention that old bromide 'life isn't fair,'" Margaret said with a throaty laugh.

"You just better not," Katherine threatened. They all chuckled.

Katherine wiped away tears with her hand, reached into her bag for a tissue then turned her attention to Linda. "Say, girlfriend, you look down-in-the mouth. Isn't it enough that Zita and Margaret have to cheer me up? I hate to see you joining the legion of losers. What's with you? Has Christopher done something else to further fuck up your life?"

Linda's eyes bore into Zita, Margaret and Katherine as if to gauge their reactions before stating, "Christopher left me."

The women stared at her.

Zita's hand shot up to her mouth. "It can't be."

"You're joking, aren't you? Katherine sputtered. "Men leave women like me, not like you, Linda."

"Not you two?" Margaret said with regret in her voice. "Not the perfect couple? It's enough to lose faith in mankind."

"It's true," Linda said. "The perfect couple is kaput, a thing of the past." Her voice quivered. "Perhaps it never was. I have little faith in mankind these days. Any word containing man in it should be suspect. That said and done, can you stand the details?" She didn't wait for them to respond, just forged ahead as if revealing all would lessen her pain. "Living with Christopher was impossible. It's been months since I found out about his mistress and baby. I had no way to fight them. It was as if I were paralyzed. When I finally got my head together, I reasoned the onus was on Christopher--let him find a way out of the nightmare. We had a horrible fight. He accused me of being an enabler, loving my own family more than him. I slapped him. I wanted to hurt him as he had hurt me."

Linda's eyes roamed the ballroom, as if she needed time to compose herself before continuing, "I guess in my heart I knew he had to leave. There was no other way. I loved him deeply once. My feeling for him is laced with hate and longing."

Zita's eyes filled with compassion, "Linda, I'm so sorry."

"Don't be. The torture is over."

Margaret said sympathetically "Linda, I can't believe it."

Linda swallowed. "Time will take care of everything. Isn't that how the saying goes?"

A look of distress crossed Katherine's face. "How could the bastard do that to you?"

"Thanks for your concern. I wasn't aware that for months I lived in a

Liz Barzda

loveless vacuum with a man who wanted out. I'm glad he's gone." Linda tried for a smile. "Don't look at me as if I were dying. I have Tiffany--if only temporarily. And my job is solid with my contract renewal. Life goes on. You needn't be quiet on my account; I can take comments." She tried to appear composed, but her eyes couldn't disguise the inner turmoil. The waiter returned with a second bottle of Chardonnay and quietly filled their glasses.

Zita fingered her glass and said, "I'm not one to constantly put on a brave face, but let's admit it, we've been through hell lately. And we're still grieving. But we needn't. It takes more than life's adversities to lay us low. The *BB's* are like a salve that soothes the hurt and obliterates the past." "We may be *Barren Babes*, but we're also goddesses of love and beauty," Katherine said, then added, "Some goddesses we are -- looking for love in all the wrong places."

"Sometimes life sucks," Zita said.

Margaret studied her friends' faces. "We've had some bad times, but we're resilient. Despite our childless state -- or should I say because of it -- we've bonded and developed lasting friendships. Just one more thing before I get off the soapbox. Don't ever give up on love and beauty. Life is drab without it. And let's not give up on men, either." She chuckled, "It's still heartening to have the warmth and trust of a good man next to you. Of course, if he's beautiful that's a plus."

"Is that for Linda's and my benefit?" Katherine asked.

"It's for all of us," Margaret replied. "The love we have for one another strengthens us. Still there's no harm in spreading a little to men as well."

"Sorry, Margaret." Linda paused a moment, then added, "It may be a long time before I can spread love among the masculine gender."

"I'm with you, Linda," Katherine interjected. She wrinkled her forehead and continued, "However, there may be some exceptions."

"Men may cheat on us, families may disappoint us, business partners may bamboozle us," Linda said, "but *we* endure."

The room quieted as the *Choices Magazine* executive manager strode to the podium and introduced Mary Trapp Toddman. Linda heard the welcoming sounds of applause but couldn't concentrate. So many revelations lately, so many upheavals. She looked to the podium as the special guest began to speak, "Life is filled with choices: the choice of raising a family, the choice of centering your life on a career, the choice of combining both. Remember the TV ad that emphasized 'you only go around once'? An old-time Hollywood comedian once said, 'If you do it

Bittersweet House

right, once is enough. On his death bed he rescinded the quote. 'I was wrong. One life isn't enough.' One life is all we get, so it behooves us to make right choices.

"Sometimes life doesn't play fair with us. It offers many temptations but little time to pack it all in. I've spoken to many women across the country who telling me that they're on *overload*. Business, children, and home responsibilities, are a mix akin to harvesting stomach ulcers. It all comes down to a question of priorities. The unrealistic vision of women as CEOs/happy homemakers/and Mother Earth rolled into one is no more. We can grab brass rings that hold desired elements of our life, but perhaps only one brass ring at a time. You A-type personalities may break through the glass ceiling in time; yet most women find balancing a career, family and home doable but in a shaky way--something or somebody suffers.

"It needn't be. If you're realistic, if you choose wisely, life can be pleasing, even exciting. It's like savoring one delectable desert at a time, rather than gagging on a bag full of candy..."

"Bull," Katherine whispered. "Can any one of us honestly say we had a choice in life? It leads us where it pleases." Suddenly a cell telephone ring emanated from Katherine's purse. "Damn it, I thought I shut the blasted thing off. Sorry, this may be an important business call." She reached into her purse, cupped the phone's mouthpiece and said a faint "Hello." Her eyes widened as she listened. "I'll be there." Her mouth stretched into a wide smile. Linda leaned in. "Good news?"

Katherine's face lit up like a teenager invited to her first prom. "It's more than good. It's perfect. Scott wants to see me tomorrow." Zita said in a muted voice, "Kat, here's your chance to grab hold of what *you* want--that brass ring."

Margaret winked. "Way to go, Kat." Katherine glowed. "I knew the stars would come through for me."

"Going around once isn't enough," Margaret moaned. "I have wrongs to right."

The speaker droned on..."although life can be hectic, and sometimes spins out of control, there are forces aiding us, offering more choices. Medicine is on the brink of extending the average life span to a century. Technology will lead us to the planet Mars and beyond. Life will extend to horizons only dreamt of in the past. Robots will perform the drudge work in every household. And all this will happen sooner than we thought possible. Choices are more abundant than we ever imagined." Toddman scanned the room, ready to impart her last nugget of wisdom. "So don't

Liz Barzda

be afraid to grab hold of what you want. Ladies and gentlemen, the choice is yours."

Linda heard the words but wondered if the speaker's observation on life was realistic. *Did Zita , Kate and Margaret have choices? Maybe. Did she have a choice in her marriage? Perhaps.* As the applause intensified, Margaret asked, "What did you think of the talk?"

"It's pie in the sky," Katherine offered.

"Fine," Margaret answered, "if we're still around to take advantage of all the choices. "Choices in life may be unpredictable, but our friendship is not." Zita focused on her friends. "Because of you, I've learned to trust again. She reached for the wine. "I propose a toast--here's to hope."

Margaret said, "We must believe that our desires will be fulfilled-- here's to faith. Katherine raised her glass. "The one ingredient in life that makes it all worthwhile--I give you love."

They looked at Linda.

She stared back at them. She had nothing to offer. If only she could rid herself of the cynicism that penetrated her soul. Christopher labeled her an enabler who craved adulation. His words gnawed at her. It was time to examine her heart. Was it the adulation of TV fans and not the work that kept her in the business? Did her repeated rescue of Sandra stunt her sense of responsibility? Linda's heart was laid bare to conceit and culpability. She *must* give Sandra breathing room on the way to responsibility. She promised God she *would*. She asked God to banish vanity from her heart. Was it just a few weeks ago that she sought solace in church? The priest's words raced through her mind. "*...ask God to give us the Grace to be able to forgive as he has forgiven us.*" Linda prayed silently, "*God, help me to do your will.*" Perhaps she did have something to offer. She clutched her drink then saluted, "To forgiveness." To herself she said, "*I forgive you Christopher and I forgive myself.*"

Chapter 47

Sitting in Continental's business class section, Linda waited for takeoff to Atlanta. Could last night's dream of battering by a hurricane be a precursor of the future? She prayed that not be the case. Still, scenes of a bittersweet summer with its heartbreak and unexpected love streamed through her mind. Christopher, his mistress and son were gone from her life. Her failed marriage, like a disease, finally found an antidote--her husband's departure. *An enabler,* he had called her. The accusation devastated her. As much as she wanted to erase his words, it pained her to acknowledge that he was right. But it also forced her to face her inadequacies-- wanting to solve everyone's problems. His words, *you can't right the world's ills,* seared like a hot iron on her brain. She'd work on letting go. Sandra and others would have to learn to navigate life's perilous roads without her.

The well-dressed middle-aged woman seated next to Linda opened a briefcase, removed papers and pen and focused on her work. Thankful that the woman would be occupied with business, Linda returned to the privacy of meditation. She reveled in her pregnancy and the prospect of being a mother. Her TV career seemed like something out of the past, inconsequential and belonging to another time.

She leaned back into her seat and closed her eyes. Recollections of sore nipples, ravenous appetite and tiredness that hinted at her condition filled her mind.

The e.p.t. window read *Pregnant.* Although shocked at the realization that she had a baby growing within her, her heart overflowed with happiness. She would *keep* this baby. No sense in probing how it happened. She knew damn well how it happened and had no regrets. How ironic that the only time she was with a man outside of marriage, his condom

Liz Barzda

had to be defective. Linda stifled her guffaw. *I thought that happened only in novels.*

What about the father? Ron, the man she counted on as a loyal friend, was much more than that now. For a decade they co-anchored a news program, and through the years admiration grew into a special kind of love. A love that would continue to grow in mutual respect, a love selfless enough to establish a family unit, so different from the way she had loved Christopher--a far more dependable way.

She tried to picture the moment when Ron would learn that she's carrying his child, couldn't wait to tell him, to see his face light up at the news He called and e-mailed her every other day, telling her how much he loved her and tempting her with Atlanta's TV and cultural opportunities. His love never wavered. After Christopher's adultery, Ron's devotion opened Linda's heart to a new kind of love infused through strength and loyalty.

There was no purpose in analyzing her newfound happiness, no sense in trying to reason the meaning of life--or how one should live one's life. That's all in the past. She would learn from her sorrowful marriage. She'll block out the fact that her husband left her to be with his mistress and son--this from a man who never wanted children. She spends one night with a man, a friend who demonstrates love and compassion and gets pregnant. She watched him put on the condom, still she couldn't object. She was vulnerable, weak, needed to be loved and wanted a man's arms around her. *My predicament doesn't matter. I'm happy.* She wanted to stay in that glow of anticipation. A baby. Her baby. After all the years of longing! Forty two wasn't too old. Women have babies today when they're into their late forties, some into their fifties.

Linda yearned to tell her mother about the baby; discretion urged her to hold off a bit. She and Ron had much to talk about, plans to carve out their future. Her parents didn't hesitate when asked to stay with Tiffany and Mrs. Brody. As Sandra was making marked progress toward recovery, she, Tiffany and their parents would remain in Sandra's Seacliff home until Linda's return. Her thoughts rested on the BB's. The realization that Zita's forthcoming marriage to Peter, a man who truly loved her and helped her find her way back from bitterness to bliss, filled Linda with joy. She had no doubt that Margaret, their Mother Superior, would get Greg back into the family fold. Eventually he would learn how much his aunt and uncle cherish him. If the BB's were to bet whether Katherine would get Scott

Bittersweet House

back, her money would be on Katherine--wild at times, but also with the determination required to get back the love of her life.

As the seat belt sign and the captain's voice came on, Linda retreated further into her own world. She finally acknowledged to herself that Christopher's revelation of a secret family emotionally immobilized her, but that was the past. She realized that she was capable of taking action, no matter what. She visualized her future, a life with Ron and their baby. Her head was in the clouds, as for Ron, she knew his feet would be firmly planted on the ground. He'd do whatever it took to build a good life for the three of them. But she couldn't refrain from daydreaming. She pictured the baby crawling, first day at school, playing ball with Ron. *Wow, back up* she cautioned herself. There's a lot of preliminary details to attend to, like TV opportunities for her and locating a home in a desirable neighborhood. Her dream machine continued to imagine upcoming events.

As the plane climbed higher and higher above the clouds, Linda's preview of their future glowed like the rosy hue beginning to peek through the sky. Her baby, their baby, hers and Ron's, would be grounded in stability with a mother and father living together to raise and love their child--and to love each other.

END

In memory of Justin, lover, friend, teacher.